QUINN COLERIDGE

Heart of Gold

Published by Brompton Road Literary, LLC

ISBN: 978-0-998887-39-5 Print.
ISBN: 978-0-998887-38-8 Ebook.
Cover Art by: James T. Egan of Bookfly Design
Brompton Road Literary, LLC Logo by: Green Cloak Design
Interior book design by: Bob Houston eBook Formatting

Contact the author for contests, giveaways, and book release news at her website: authorquinncoleridge.com.

Brompton Road Literary
Where art and commerce meet.

Dedication

As always, this book is dedicated to my mother Elaine, my guiding light and guardian angel.

Love is the only gold.

—Alfred, Lord Tennyson

Prologue

Daisy

Pear trees blossomed on each side of the street, swaying to the gentle rhythm of the wind. Behind them, red brick row houses with black shutters faced one another like mirror images. Gleaming brass kick plates and antique knobs decorated each door. A girl walked along the street slowly as if her feet wished to go somewhere else. Her shoulders hunched against the weight of an overstuffed book bag with the name Daisy embroidered on the side. She ignored the pretty homes and headed toward the only one that wasn't. Nettles had overtaken the garden, the windows were smudged with soot, and bits of trash littered the front steps. The eyesore told everyone who passed by a different story. All of them cautionary tales.

Daisy took a deep breath as she finally drew up to the house. She unlocked the door with her key and the rusty hinges objected with a high-pitched whine. Her heart jumped at the sound. Daisy paused like an animal of prey, trying to determine whether it was safe to enter. The refrigerator in the kitchen emitted a soft hum and radiator pipes clanked and hissed. A clock above the fireplace mantel ticked softly. Just harmless, every day noises. No fresh cigarette smoke that she could detect, no television blaring or voices shouting. Not even a whiff of aftershave or stale beer.

Still poised for flight, Daisy stepped over the threshold and automatically froze in place when the floorboards creaked under her feet. Ten seconds passed, twenty, thirty, but nothing happened, so she exhaled quietly and closed the door.

Everything must be okay. She'd have heard by now if it wasn't.

Daisy dumped her school bag on the kitchen table. A violent rumbling began in her stomach as she took off her scratchy uniform jacket. Loosening the striped blue tie at her throat, Daisy wished she were twenty-five instead of twelve. Then she'd have a job and money. Food. Nice clothes.

The refrigerator held nothing but an apple, a carton of Indian takeout from the week before, the heel of a loaf of bread, and an opened bottle of wine. Her stomach rumbled louder, so she grabbed the apple. It felt a little soft, but she rubbed it on her sleeve until it looked shiny and took a bite. Sweet, a bit stale, yet Daisy wasn't about to complain.

She bit into the apple again and glanced across the hall into the living room, nearly choking on the fruit. Her mother slept on the sofa, disheveled, snoring softly, but still beautiful enough to break hearts. Daisy's heart in particular. Over and over again. *Why did she pass out this time? Alcohol? Drugs? A mixture of both?*

Daisy knew she should leave. Go to the park or the shops for a few hours. But she couldn't do it. Not when her mother looked so vulnerable.

What if he gets angry? How will she protect herself?

Daisy took a step closer, then another. "Ma?" she whispered. "Ma?"

Wake up. Please, wake up.

Daisy sensed movement rather than saw it. Lunging for the door, she dropped the apple and it bounced on the rug as a large hand gripped her shoulder.

Alec.

"You're late," he said. "Why? What have you been up to?"

The low, angry voice made her shudder. She stomped on his bare foot with the heel of her loafer, and in his intoxicated state, Alec lost his balance, cursing loudly as he fell. Daisy ran into the hallway and through the kitchen. She scrambled outside and kept running until sweat trickled into her eyes and the street names blurred.

Go faster. Faster. He'll be so mad.

Humid air clung to her hot face. She knew people could read her shame as if it were branded on her forehead. How could they not when Daisy felt so conspicuous? A drop of rain hit the sidewalk. Then another. Another. It fell softly at first but grew into an almost violent frenzy, bouncing up several inches after striking the cement.

Daisy squinted at a three-story building of graceful, Georgian architecture and felt lucky for the first time in months. She crossed the street and went inside. It smelled good, like potpourri, wet wool, and old leather. Keeping her head down, doing her best to blend in, she toured the library with an eye toward the exit and listened for Alec's voice. If he found her, could she get away fast enough? Would anyone help if she screamed?

Daisy entered a reading room on the second floor and walked through the aisles, her fingers touching each book she passed. They beckoned to her as sirens would a sailor.

One caught her eye, her breath. Daddy had taken a copy

just like it when he packed his bags and left. The red leather cover and gold writing had glowed against the clothing piled in his suitcase.

"Tennyson was the only true poet who ever lived," he sometimes said after drinking too much. "His words make music."

In fact, had Daisy been a boy, she would have been named Tennyson. Or if not that then after some dude called Keats. She took the book off the shelf and sat down at a table. Turning the pages at random, Daisy stopped at a poem called "Maud." Time passed, people moved about the room, but these impressions were vague. Her full attention was solely on the book.

Always I long to creep
Into some still cavern deep,
There to weep, and weep, and weep
My whole soul out to thee.

She snapped the book shut and slid it down the table. Daddy could keep gloomy old Tennyson. A middle-aged man sitting in the next chair looked up, frowned, and then went back to writing in his notebook.

Emotion bubbled to the surface, but Daisy willed it away. Those few lines of poetry left her feeling raw and exposed, as though Tennyson knew the darkest parts of her heart. Like he had seen Daisy crying alone in her room, too afraid to sleep or even breathe. She glanced at a pile of books near her elbow. The one on top was a pretty shade of grayish blue. The color soothed some of that raw, exposed feeling.

Daisy read the title of the book. *Jane Eyre*. Her lips lifted into a crooked smile as she picked it up. "I remember this one. Teacher read it to us at school."

The man sitting nearby grumbled about children making

noise in adult sections of the library. "And where are the parents?" he muttered. "No sense of responsibility these days."

You have no idea, sir. None at all.

A male voice crackled through a hidden speaker and announced that the library was closing. Daisy slunk down in her chair. She didn't want to go home. But another fifteen minutes passed and the polite voice echoed through the speaker once more. Move along, he might as well have said. We're shut until tomorrow.

It was then that the idea formed. Through the reading room doorway, Daisy saw an open closet. Rolls of toilet paper filled its shelves, mops and brooms lined up along the wall.

Daisy considered the big, unlit space and the aching in her stomach subsided. The closet was a beacon of hope, as welcome as a lifeline to a lost soul. Someone could hide inside it without being noticed. Just slip across the empty hall and kneel behind those huge boxes. Easy-peasy.

Maybe if I hid in there, I could stay over this one night. Ma's so out of it, she won't notice.

Daisy stood up, still holding the copy of *Jane Eyre*, and walked casually toward the door. She paused near a notice board and pretended to study an advertisement for a book club until the last bunch of stragglers left the reading room. The final one to go was the grumpy man who sat at her table. He nodded and then strolled down the hall. Daisy waited until he took the stairs to the main floor. *Right. The coast is finally clear. Now pretend you're 007.*

Quick yet careful, Daisy stepped into the maintenance closet and climbed behind a wide stack of boxes. The smell of bleach and cleaning products was so strong she almost sneezed. Hunkering down, Daisy made herself as small as possible. The book she held felt warm against her palm. Almost like it was alive.

Something metallic rattled down the hallway and entered through the closet door. Peeping between the boxes, Daisy saw that it was a cleaning trolley. An apron-clad woman with purple hair stood beside it, headphones over her ears. Evidently a cleaner of sorts. The woman stretched, rubbed her back a few times, and shut the door hard. Everything went black. It was the darkest dark Daisy had ever known. Growing disoriented, she started to panic when keys scraped inside the lock and the cleaner walked away. Daisy took deep breaths and counted silently. She nearly fell asleep huddled in the corner.

The library had been quiet for some time when Daisy roused herself and tried the door knob. Gratitude flooded her heart when the lock popped and released its hold. She opened the door, silence beating against her ears. It had seemed like such a friendly place before, but now there were too many shadows.

As she hurried back to the reading room, the sound of her shoes striking the floor echoed loudly and made her uneasy. Daisy sat by the window, fearing that someone might still be in the building. Maybe they'd heard her footsteps and would come to investigate. *How do I explain being here after hours? And what about Alec?*

She imagined him down on the sidewalk looking up at this very window. He would break a lock and climb the stairs to the second floor. But there were no sounds. Only Daisy's fast breathing and the pounding inside her chest. She shifted to a more comfortable position on the couch. The back of her legs felt gross and sweaty from the fake leather.

Fingertips edged with white, Daisy clutched the copy of

Jane Eyre. Don't cry. Only babies do that. You're safe until tomorrow.

She wiped the moisture from her eyes and opened the book. With the light from the streetlamp outside shining through the glass, the page was easy to read. Words like these never failed her. They replaced reality with something better.

Daisy wondered if other people felt the same. She took a pen out of her bag, turned to the last page, and thought for a while before writing in small, curvy script:

Dear Reader,

If you love books as I do,

we shall be great friends.

Daisy XOXO

A half smile on her face, she studied the message and felt almost guilty, knowing that Jane Eyre would never approve. Daisy hugged the book and wished with all her heart. "Starlight, star bright. Please, oh please."

Imagine having a friend like her . . .

Life wouldn't be so scary then. It couldn't be with Jane to confide in. Daisy closed her eyes—fatigued after being afraid for so long—and pictured the governess in her mind, whispering the woman's name like a prayer.

Seconds passed and Daisy felt as if she were drifting off into sleep, then a gentle voice replied, "Yes? You called?"

Daisy nearly jumped out of her skin. A small woman wearing an old-fashioned bonnet and cloak sat on the opposite sofa. Daisy rubbed the grit from her tired eyes and took a second look.

The woman was still there.

In fact, she wore a rather determined look on her face as she pulled off her gloves. "Well, young lady. I can see I have my work cut out for me this time."

"Are you a g-ghost?" Daisy whispered. "Am I dreaming?"

"A ghost? Don't be silly, child. I'm Jane Eyre."

Rising to her feet, Daisy judged the distance to the door. She might make it if she ran fast. Jane pointed at the couch. "Do sit down. It's rather rude of you to think of leaving when I've traveled all this way."

Daisy sat. "But you can't be real."

Jane raised a dark, arched brow and made a tutting sound. "Close your mouth, please. It isn't attractive or polite. Who says I can't be real?"

"Every sane person in the world."

With her pale skin and fine gray eyes, Jane was the spitting image of Daisy's mother, before Alec came into their lives. "That's it then," Daisy muttered. "I've lost my mind. I'm not very surprised, actually."

Jane shook her head. "You're perfectly sane. Just very alone and afraid."

Shivering, Daisy rubbed her arms and decided that a make-believe sort of companion was better than being alone, even if the outside world would consider it madness.

She touched the first word of the first chapter in *Jane Eyre* and lifted her eyes to the woman seated so primly across from her. "Would you promise me something?"

"If I can."

"Don't leave," Daisy whispered. Pleaded.

"I won't," Jane said in Ma's voice. "I'll stay for as long as you need me."

Chapter 1

Portland, Oregon

L ife was good twenty-four hours ago.

Was being the key word. Past tense.

Simon Phillips knew this in his gut. Just as he knew everything since then had gone to hell somehow.

Where am I? What happened? His muscles felt stiff where they rested on a hard, cold surface of some kind. Blinking rapidly, Simon opened his eyes against the blinding light overhead and inhaled a cinnamon sugar scent, thinking suddenly of the snickerdoodle cookies his grandmother had baked years ago. He detected something else as well.

Is that tequila?

The floor gleamed white beneath him. Simon recognized the Carrara marble and realized with sudden horror that he was in the executive bathroom at his law firm. While his brain urgently told him to move, his motor skills struggled to obey. The room spun when Simon finally pulled himself to his knees. He exhaled slowly and noticed the snickerdoodle-impersonating air freshener attached to the wall. More surprising still, the essence of Jose Cuervo clung to him like cheap cologne.

Leaning his head against a nearby sink, Simon tried to

remember. *What's with the booze? And why am I on the floor in my Tom Ford suit?*

Then, through the mental fog, the memories came flooding back in gruesome Technicolor. *It can't be true.*

Except that it was.

"Shoot me now," Simon muttered. "I'm as good as dead anyway."

Leonard Cronin walked through the door at that moment. "Would that I could oblige you but there are laws against that type of thing."

The senior attorney was about as senior as you could get without being a corpse. Occasionally, when he wasn't billing hours to a client, Leonard had a refined, Southern gentleman way about him—until he began contract negotiations and became the Four Horsemen of the Apocalypse rolled into one.

Simon stood up, but his body swayed. Every sound, however small, echoed between the marble floors and walls, striking his brain like a mallet. He felt ill, thirsty, and in need of a shower.

"You've been in here sleeping all day." Leonard removed his glasses and slid them into his breast pocket. "The bigwigs are getting tired of using the public lavatory."

Is he kidding? "Are you kidding?"

"Does it look like it? Some of the partners were worried you had alcohol poisoning and wanted to call nine-one-one, but I thought an ambulance parked outside the firm would be bad publicity."

"Thanks, Leonard. Your concern is heartwarming."

"Oh, I had that new guy, First-Year-Neblyn, check on you from time to time."

Simon rubbed his face with his hands, wishing himself

anywhere else. "I'm so sorry. My lapse in judgment was monumental."

Leonard gave a wry nod. "You interrupted a roomful of lawyers in the middle of an important deposition."

"Hardly a roomful," Simon objected. "A dozen at most."

"A dozen angry attorneys who now hate your guts."

"That's an exaggeration."

"No, it isn't." The old man made a choking sound as he snorted and laughed at the same time. "You climbed on the conference table and started quoting Shakespeare and the Old Testament. I never realized you were so well read."

Simon felt his face go scarlet as he remembered calling the other lawyers out. The ones who cheated on their wives, taxes, billing charges, and so forth. Or worse. These truths were common knowledge, but nobody dared to say them aloud.

Given enough tequila, Simon apparently did dare. "I went to the hotel bar after meeting with my clients. I never intended to have more than one drink."

Leonard's amusement disappeared. "Why? Things didn't go well with Jim and Ed?"

"It was a bloodbath. Bickering, tantrums, name-calling . . ."

The old man motioned with his hand for Simon to cut to the chase. "Did they come to an agreement and sign the contract or not? A lot of money was at stake for the firm."

"Yes. In the end, they both signed."

Leonard watched Simon in the mirror. "So why the tequila?"

"You've obviously never met Jim or Ed. If you had, alcohol consumption would make sense."

"Well, go for one of those Shirley Temple deals in the future, Simon."

He winced at the volume of his mentor's voice. "Please, stop talking so loud."

Leonard soaked a hand towel under the faucet, squeezed out the excess water, and gave the towel to Simon. "Put that on your face. It hurts just looking at you."

Simon held the compress over his eyes, grateful for a moment of silence. It didn't last long, though. Leonard's voice adopted a fatherly tone when he said, "You're a bright, ambitious young man. There's an edge to your personality, a killer instinct, that's crucial for the career you've chosen."

"Um . . . thank you?" Simon murmured from behind the towel.

"You're welcome. We can't make money in this business without being competitive and tough."

"You, and dear old dad, taught me well." Simon sensed a "but" coming in the next sentence.

"*But* I've seen a definite change over the last year. I've watched you become increasingly agitated and disgruntled."

Tossing the hand towel into the sink, Simon turned to face Leonard. "If I have too much *edge* it's because business is booming. Sixteen-hour days bring results, don't they? And I haven't heard any complaints when the cash rolls in."

"You never will," Leonard said, eyes shrewd. "As a corporate lawyer, your job isn't philanthropic. It's mercenary. You ensure that your client comes out on top of any given deal. If they win, we win big. You're one of the firm's most valuable assets. But we also know that with insomnia, high blood pressure, and an ulcer, you're falling apart at thirty-three."

"I'm fine—"

"Hardly." Leonard stepped close enough for Simon to notice the tiny paisley pattern of his bow tie. "Given your current, overtaxed state, we are taking proactive measures. We can't just stand by and watch you implode. Therefore, your fellow partners have made a unanimous decision. We are requiring you to take a leave of absence—a couple months or so."

"You can't be serious."

"As the grave, son. Two months to decompress and attend therapy or stress management classes, whichever you prefer. And if you try to weasel out of it, we'd like documented proof of treatment."

Swearing softly, Simon pushed away from the sink. "This is ridiculous, and a little offensive. Next thing I know, you'll be asking me to pee in a cup."

"No, we won't," Leonard replied. "Everyone at the firm knows you were under the influence."

"I had a few drinks. Big deal. Name one partner, other than yourself, who hasn't done the same at some point. There's no need for all the drama. A weekend off, and I'll be fine."

Leonard did not look unkindly as he placed his hand on Simon's shoulder. "I came to the hospital the day you were born. I've known you your whole life and something's not right. I'm worried."

Desperation made Simon lightheaded. "What about my clients?"

"You've been working hand in hand with Wright, Blake, and Hughes, three of our brightest. They'll manage things for you." Leonard walked to the door and opened it. "Your secretary's bringing over a new set of clothes."

"What's the point?" Simon growled.

Anger flashed across the old man's face. "The point is to put on a good show for those barracudas out there who watched you make a fool of yourself yesterday. Have a little pride as you walk through the firm, Simon. Believe me, you don't want your colleagues to see you looking like a hobo living under a bridge. That professional image you've cultivated for so long can still be salvaged."

After Leonard left, Simon stood in the center of the bathroom, too stunned to move, and then forced himself back to the sink. He rinsed his mouth for a solid minute, but his breath still smelled foul.

There was a discreet tap on the door before Linda, Simon's secretary, entered the bathroom. She'd brought him a bespoke suit he'd picked up on a rare vacation to Milan.

"I hope I got the right one, sir," she said, cheeks flushed. "You have so many clothes in your closet."

Simon slipped the suit out of its garment bag. "Thank you, Linda. Sorry for any inconvenience."

"No problem." She offered him a tin of Altoids. "I thought you might need some mints, too."

"Great."

"Let me know if you need anything else."

"Thanks. I will." Simon didn't move until Linda had shut the bathroom door.

Unlike everyone else at the firm, she wouldn't judge him for slipping up. It was more Linda's style to jump in and fix things instead, like he was one of her four teenage boys.

Feeling slightly better, he used the facilities, changed his clothes, and carefully hung his rumpled jacket and trousers in the garment bag. The poor Tom Ford would never be the same. Simon considered defying Leonard and refusing to take the two months off. He could raise hell and dig in his heels, but Simon wasn't sure it would work. Leonard was relentless, if opposed, and he could make day to day existence at the firm miserable. And Simon admitted that he had said some pretty unforgivable things to the lawyers at the deposition. Maybe he should go along with Leonard's demands, just until the dust settles. A week or two at most. His clients wouldn't suffer in that amount of time. He'd keep in touch with them and ensure they were happy.

With this decision made, Simon walked out into the bustling hallway. People looked at him with interest, eyes searching his face as they walked past. He could practically hear the rumor mill buzzing.

His office was as sleek and immaculately organized as always. A memo sat in the middle of the rosewood desk. The note informed Simon of a conference call scheduled for the next morning with Wright, Blake, and Hughes. The very call where he would turn over his workload to the other attorneys. He tore up the memo, tossed it into the trashcan, and dialed Leonard's extension.

"I'm sorry. Mr. Cronin isn't accepting calls," Leonard's secretary said.

"May I leave him a message?"

She coughed. "Mr. Cronin told me to tell you he isn't accepting messages either."

Simon rolled his eyes. "Please inform Mr. Cronin that Mr. Phillips won't give up so easily and will contact him soon."

Linda entered the office. Her chin-length auburn bob looked shiny and neat. "I thought you might like some ibuprofen."

"I would. What time is it?"

"Five o'clock."

Linda handed him the pills and a bottle of water.

He took them and smiled. "You're a lifesaver."

She sprang into secretary mode when the phone at her desk rang and hurried to answer it. Simon looked out the office window with its view of the choppy, gray Willamette and thought about his situation. Even though the idea of leaving the firm for more than a day was painful, like losing an appendage, Simon reminded himself that he could outwit Leonard by playing his little game. He'd do whatever it took to get back into the senior attorney's good graces.

Simon had just swallowed the ibuprofen when Linda returned with a cardboard box. "Would you like help gathering your personal belongings?"

His conscience nagged at him as they sorted through the stuff in his desk. "I hope you can forgive me, Linda. For everything that happened yesterday."

She chuckled indulgently. "Oh, don't apologize, sir. It was fun. You can really dance."

He almost dropped the box. How did she know? Simon hadn't busted a move since partying in college with his fraternity. "What are you talking about?"

Linda stopped sorting and looked up. "You challenged everyone to a dance off in the hall, remember? The Robot with Melanie from Human Resources? The Running Man with Clint? The Moonwalk?"

Outwardly, Simon kept his composure, but inside he began to panic. *Oh, for hell's sake. I will never touch another drop of liquor until the day I die.*

"It was hilarious," Linda said, sounding disappointed that he'd forgotten.

Now Simon was the one blushing. "My behavior was totally inappropriate. I'm so sorry."

She patted his shoulder. "No one minded, especially Melanie. She keeps asking me for your private number."

Simon had no idea who this Melanie was. He didn't interact with Human Resources as a rule. It was a waste of time and earned him nothing. "Don't give it to her."

Nodding at Simon's request, Linda put his favorite stapler into the box. "I won't, sir. Though I know she'll keep trying."

They finished the project in silence, until Linda closed the last drawer and touched his arm. Her brows were puckered with concern.

"It's all going to work out," she said, sounding motherly. "Most people would love to have some time off."

Most people might, but Simon knew he wasn't one of them.

Chapter 2

Northwest Portland
Early morning of the same day . . .

K ate Spencer stumbled down the hall of her tiny apartment and banged her toe on the bathroom door. She grimaced at her painful toe, turned on the shower, and waited for the water to warm up. Leaning back against the sink, she dozed on her feet like a horse—a long-limbed palomino with heavily lashed eyes and a wild, golden mane. Her ability to sleep almost anywhere had been a lifesaver in medical school, but it didn't do much to ease Kate's fatigue at the moment. Instead, she just felt irritable and cold.

Hurry up, crappy water heater. I've got things to do.

Thirty minutes later, smelling of lavender and oatmeal soap, Kate sipped a cup of hibiscus tea and studied the calendar on the kitchen wall. She pulled the outdated, brightly colored Post-it notes off of March—or the month when winter rain became early spring rain—and tossed them into the garbage can, then flipped April's glossy page into place.

A whole week off. Yippee.

Having taken some paid vacation days at the hospital, she planned to spend them at her second job, the part-time one she really loved.

Kate's good cheer diminished as she picked up her Walther PPK/S. As always, it looked sleek and lethal. Perfectly maintained. And it should be since she cleaned it religiously after frequent visits to the firing range.

"Walther, you sexy beast," she whispered, checking that the gun's magazine was loaded. "What would I do without you?"

You'd be dead, a voice whispered in Kate's mind.

Her ring reflected light as she turned the gun and made sure the safety lever was engaged, then slipped it into the concealed holster on the back of her hip, just past the four o'clock position. With the gun now in place, Kate rubbed the thin platinum wedding band against her lips, savoring the brief contact with the cool metal. A line of skin peeked out from under the ring, a flash of pale white on her otherwise tan fingers.

While eating a toasted bagel, she played a message on her cell phone that had been saved and resaved many times. It hurt to hear it, but she couldn't stop listening.

"Hey, babe. Hope you're still sleeping. It's cold outside, but the sunrise was pretty. Lots of orange and pink. Miss you. Be careful today. Call me later."

His voice was rough as gravel, because he'd never been able to kick a fifteen-year smoking habit despite all the patches, prescriptions, and going cold turkey. A faint drawl showed his Mississippi roots. The kind that sounded natural saying "all y'all" "girl" and "hell, yeah." He spoke softly, as though he might awaken her just by leaving the message.

Mike had always been sweet like that. Considerate. Protective. Pain washed over Kate, as fresh and new as the first time she felt it.

A widow at twenty-eight.

Kate had never wanted to join that club, but it had found

her nevertheless. A sudden memory of flashing red and blue lights, the taste of blood, and her own screaming filled her mind. She collapsed in a chair and leaned forward, trying not to hyperventilate. *Calm down. Think of him, not that night.*

After sitting quietly for several minutes, the tightness in her chest loosened and the burning in her throat and lungs grew less intense. Kate rose from the chair stiffly. It felt as if she carried a physical burden, like an invisible weight encased her body. What would Mike say if he could see the way she lived? Would he be proud? Worried?

Kate's eyes filled with tears, and she wiped them away with the back of her knuckles. "I miss you so damn much." His rumbling laughter, his touch, the way he made her feel safe.

It was so easy to be bitter. Angry. Lonely. No matter how much she missed Mike, he was gone, and now all she had to hold was a gun.

Make that . . . *guns.* Kate was three-timing her first Walther with a larger PPQ, a Colt, and a Beretta. Those bad boys were locked up in the safe under her bed. None of them kept her warm at night. Merely breathing and alive.

She turned off the lights in the kitchen, tucked a motorcycle helmet under her arm, and locked the back door.

Kate headed to the carport, passing a series of neatly trimmed hedges. The air was cool and smelled of damp, growing things. This primordial atmosphere was one of her favorite parts of living in the Pacific Northwest. In addition to the overcast skies, the infinite shades of green.

Her neighborhood seemed peaceful as she scanned the street. Nothing too suspicious but Kate still felt a nudge of alarm. She imagined a tall man with brown shoulder-length hair and a killer smile standing across the road and then banished him from her mind. She wouldn't let that monster take another moment of her life. And if he tried to do it, Kate always had the Walther to set him straight.

Determined to put aside all negative thoughts on her first day of vacation, Kate whistled some Aerosmith while making her way toward a Triumph Bonneville. The motorcycle was sporty yet elegant. She put on her helmet, sat on the black leather seat, and thrilled to the purr of the engine as it came to life. Sure, driving a car to work would be easier. But it felt like a personal victory each time she rode her bike. Like kicking fear right in the face.

Kate put in one earbud and turned on the tunes. The bike revved with power as she pulled out onto the street. Heavy metal thundered in the left side of her head, but the playlist switched from metal to reggae to rap by the time Kate pulled up in front of a rambling, Depression-era structure with beautiful brickwork and massive archways.

Despite years of neglect, the old building still exuded gentility and charm and when it was saved from the wrecking ball and purchased for pennies on the dollar, Kate had murmured a prayer of thanks. That prayer was the first of many as she watched the former school transform into a community center with free health care available to needy families, among other things.

A drop of rain splashed against the sleeve of Kate's sweatshirt and watery sunlight filtered through the clouds, warming the pine needles in the gutter. The needles should have seemed out of place in such a busy part of town, but Portland was a city of contradictions. Moss-covered hundred-year-old trees stubbornly grew in their rocky patches of soil, ignored by the surrounding urban sprawl. Gazing up at the sky, Kate took off her helmet and replaced it with a Cubs baseball cap. They could win another World Series after all. Stranger things had been known to happen, right?

She walked across the cracked blacktop to find empty beer cans littering the sidewalk. As the smell of stale barley floated around Kate, she bent down to gather the trash. Then she stopped, shaking her head. *What am I doing? Larry and Earl drank the Coors. Let them take care of the mess.*

A small lot sat adjacent to the community center. The house that once occupied the space had burned down, leaving little behind except for a cement foundation and a few bushes. Larry and Earl considered it prime real estate for squatting. Their heavily patched tents were hidden among the overgrown laurel.

"Hey, guys," Kate called. "Will you pick up these beer cans, please? We can't have them littering the sidewalks."

Larry's hand emerged from the nearest tent and motioned for Kate to leave. "Not so loud. It's too damn early."

He sounded gruff and annoyed, but that was just his way. The fact that Larry spoke to her at all indicated they were friends.

"Too early for breakfast?" Kate asked. "I could microwave you some oatmeal with raisins."

The other tent rustled and Earl climbed out. "Oatmeal's okay, I guess, but no raisins. Raisins suck. Why are you blaming us for littering, anyway?"

Larry didn't join them, but he yelled out an answer. "Because we're homeless!"

Kate sighed. "That had nothing to do with it."

"Come on, blondie." Earl shoved his hands into the pockets of his camo pants. "Everybody picks on the homeless guys."

She studied him, checking for signs of disease or

malnutrition. Olive complexion, mid-sixties, slim build, clear amber eyes. His graying hair was pulled back into a man bun, held in place by a piece of red yarn. Although Larry was about the same age, he was much taller, usually angrier at the world, and kept his head shaved like he was still in the military.

When the police drove the transients out of their squatter's camp every few months or so, they always returned. Neither of them listened when Kate recommended shelters or counseling for mental health issues like PTSD after fighting in the first Gulf War. They sought her out for free medical care, however. Mostly ingrown toenails, spider bites, and ear infections.

It made Kate's heart sad that she couldn't help in a more meaningful way. She squinted at Earl's wrinkled, wind-burned face. "I saw you guys with a six-pack of Coors last night. You popped one open before I even left my parking space."

Earl scowled, creating even more wrinkles around his near-toothless mouth. "Yeah, well, we were keeping an eye on the community center. Don't want a bunch of juvies putting graffiti on the walls."

"I appreciate that," Kate said. "But we need the sidewalks clear when the little kids come for their exams and immunizations."

"All right," Earl finally agreed. "We'll pick up for the kids."

"I still say she's overreacting," Larry called from his tent. "We're Americans. We can drink if we want to. It says so in the Constitution."

"No!" Earl yelled back. "Beer is a privilege, not a right."

Kate held up her hand, nearly out of patience. The two men could argue for hours about nothing. "It's an alcoholic beverage. You have until the clinic opens to make those cans disappear."

Earl nodded, and she said thank you before stepping over said cans and walking toward the community center. Larry and Earl were probably flipping her the bird now that her back was turned.

"Don't forget the oatmeal," Larry reminded Kate. "No raisins."

Damn. She had forgotten her offer to make them breakfast. "All right. Give me ten minutes."

Kate ran up the front steps and crossed the wide flagstone veranda. After punching her security code into the keypad by the door, she smiled up at the lovely old building. "Here we go again, Your Majesty. Another day in paradise."

Chapter 3

S imon was just about to leave his office when Carter Wright entered the room. A Stanford graduate, Carter always pushed the envelope where fashion was concerned, with his spiky highlighted hair and California-cool organic linen suits. He had a big presence on social media and local newspapers interviewed him like he was a rock star.

"The king is dead," Carter announced, removing his sunglasses. "Hail to the new king."

Simon didn't gratify the announcement by looking up. He kept scrolling through the texts on his phone. "How very Shakespearean. *Macbeth* or *Richard III*?"

"Neither. Leonard told me you were taking a break." Carter put his briefcase down and shrugged off his jacket. "Which makes me the undisputed king of this firm."

King of egos, maybe, but not of Simon's turf. "You're premature, as always. I don't need a replacement."

"Office scuttlebutt says you're being furloughed by Leonard ASAP." Carter sat down in Simon's custom leather chair and put a hand to his ear. "Hear that?"

Simon looked at his watch. "Care to be more specific? I

don't have all night."

"The applause," Carter said in a manner that implied Simon was a dunce. "People will cheer when I win the *Annus Mirabilis* from you."

Simon's usual dislike for the man before him leveled up to loathing. "The *Annus Mirabilis* is staying in my living room. Where it's been for the last three years."

A veritable doppelganger for the Stanley Cup, the huge silver trophy was awarded at the end of the year to the attorney who brought the most money into the firm. Only the elite were invited to participate, at the cost of two thousand dollars each. The sizable pool of cash was collected quietly and given to the winner tax free, along with bragging rights, a vintage bottle of Dom, extra paralegals, limos, the nicest conference rooms, and a variety of other enviable perks. All in addition to the honor of hosting the *Annus Mirabilis* until the next competition.

The whole thing had started six years ago on the whim of the all-time top moneymaker in the history of the firm. With West Phillips, Simon's older brother.

Carter whistled. "Really? Three years? Time for a change, then. I plan to out earn you by September."

"Keep dreaming, Wright."

Simon sounded confident, but inside he was tallying up his numbers. With the forced leave of absence infringing upon his ability to collect revenue, it was possible that Carter could have higher totals in the long run.

Cursing silently, Simon picked up his pitiful cardboard box of belongings. "I'll keep in constant contact. You'll think I'm your shadow."

His nemesis had the gall to look sympathetic. "Take care of yourself, man. You look like hell."

Since killing Carter would get Simon arrested, he left the office and took an elevator to the parking level of the building. Leonard had suggested that Simon start therapy while on leave. Hard pass. That rabbit hole was one he never intended to traverse. Simon googled stress management courses and scores of locations presented themselves. One small advertisement caught his eye.

A community center on NW Everett? Around 18th Avenue?

Simon didn't have any clients or friends in that area. No one would recognize him or gossip at his expense or try to ruin his career. Simon dialed the number as he got into his car. According to the lady on the phone, a series of classes on stress management were beginning at seven that very night.

Surprised by his good fortune, Simon drove his silver Mercedes-AMG GT C Roadster down Park Avenue. Wind blew against his face and he put on a pair of aviator sunglasses. He told himself to stay calm. Stay cool. Linda might be right, after all. Things could turn out okay.

Then Simon's phone blared Beethoven's Fifth—the ringtone for Jack Phillips. His father.

Simon swore effusively but answered with an easygoing voice. "Hey, Dad."

"*Explain.*"

That single word was a conduit for so many other words: words like *failure*, *disappointment*, and *shame*.

Simon's eye jerked suddenly, as though it sensed a stressful situation and needed to tic. "I screwed up. I had a few drinks and got a little out of hand. The other partners suggested I take a few days off."

His father exhaled dramatically. "I heard it was more than a few days. How long is your leave supposed to last?"

"It's temporary, Dad. I'm fixing it."

"Of course. Why should I be worried?" The old man's voice dripped with sarcasm. "Do you know how I found out about your latest escapade?"

"Actually . . ." Simon rubbed his eye as it ticked again.

"Let me tell you, shall I? I was playing golf with Judge Harper. You remember the judge? Your sister is married to his son."

"Obviously I know Nick Harper." Simon glared at the upcoming traffic light as it turned from yellow to red.

His father's voice droned on. "Have you any *idea* what it was like for me to receive that call with the judge standing next to me hearing Leonard's every word? Do you, Simon?"

"Dad—" His gut tightened as Jack ignored him and went on talking. *Stay cool, stay calm. Everything's okay . . .*

"And what could I say to him?" Jack bellowed.

"Well, you—"

"That one of my illustrious boys, my legacy to the firm, which I, *myself*, founded, had alienated and offended everyone at work before passing out cold in the bathroom. Nick knew exactly which son I was talking about, by the way, and it sure as hell wasn't West."

Simon winced. It wasn't the first time he'd come up short when compared with his brother. That little gem was his father's favorite insult and no matter how much Simon had accomplished in his life, it was never enough. He'd never be the good son. "Look, Dad. I'm sorry. I—"

"I don't really care that you're sorry," Jack replied bitterly. "Did I raise you to be this stupid? Are they allowing idiots to graduate from Harvard these days?"

That last comment was it. Simon was done. He took the

phone from his ear, the words "embarrassment" and "jackass" audible from a distance. Holding the cell up to a vent, Simon turned on the air-conditioner full blast. The forceful current made his phone's sensitive receiver crackle.

Pretending that there was static, Simon shouted, "What, Dad? I can't hear you. Must have a bad connection."

Jack's voice turned strident. "Don't you *dare* hang up on me! I know what you're doing!"

"I'll call you later. Tell Mom I love her." He closed the phone and slid it into his jacket pocket.

As Simon sped by hotels and restaurants, he used every blue word he could think of and even invented some new ones, cursing himself, the day, and the bartender who had served him drinks the night before. So much for staying calm and cool. He didn't believe Linda now at all. Nothing about his situation was even remotely okay.

He almost missed the community center on NW Everett and cranked his steering wheel in order to make the turn. The parking lot was nearly full. Simon pushed down his sunglasses to study the building. It was enormous and sat back from the sidewalk, all gray brick and ugly archways. A small pyramid of beer cans decorated the front lawn.

His temper spiked again at being forced to come here and take this class. What a waste of valuable time. Simon remained in his Mercedes until a quarter to seven. He locked the car and walked toward the community center. The beveled windows winked at him as they reflected the setting sun. English ivy grew wild across one side, and pink and purple azaleas filled the stone urns at the top of the front steps, looking so bright and upbeat they hurt Simon's brain. A round bistro table with matching chairs occupied half of the veranda, as if they were waiting for someone to play an impromptu game of checkers or have a glass of lemonade.

In spite of his bad attitude, Simon recognized that an effort had been made to help visitors feel welcome. He took a deep breath and stepped inside. The air smelled of fresh paint, floor wax, and coffee. A handmade sign sat on a tripod in the foyer giving directions to room 101 for *The Basics of Child Care*.

A lobby stretched beyond the foyer, where three women waited on a wooden bench. Two were very pregnant while the other one had a blanket over her shoulder, nursing an infant. A mural covered the opposite wall, and a child of perhaps ten was holding a toddler up so he could see a bumblebee. She made a *buzz-buzz* sound and the child gurgled.

Along with the bee, the scene featured a cross-eyed butterfly and a winking Guernsey cow amid a profusion of daffodils, bluebells, and daisies. Simon nodded to the three women, completely out of his comfort zone in the family-oriented space. He tried to look casual as he walked over to the posted list of classes being held that night. His group met in the auditorium.

Simon wandered from the lobby into a long hallway. He turned a corner and headed toward the group of people gathering up ahead. Simon didn't get far before he heard a female voice. It was soft, a shade lower in pitch than usual, with an attractive, almost melodic quality.

The voice seemed to be coming from the office to his left. "Don't bad-mouth Spike," it said. "We've been together for years and he likes me."

Simon looked in through the office doorway and saw a boy leaning inside an ancient copier. The woman next to him had a round, smiling face and short dark hair. Somewhere in her mid-thirties, she wore black scrubs covered with dancing jungle animals and a pair of orange Crocs.

The teenage kid had a Cubs cap on backward and his sweatshirt was torn and dirty.

"Spike is possessed," the brunette in the Crocs said, slapping the kid's shoulder. "Pea soup's gonna fly out of him at any moment."

Simon was puzzled. The voice that had drawn him to the office didn't belong to her, yet there it was again, sounding indulgent. "No flying soup, Beth. Replace the toner cartridge and Spike's good to go."

The woman called Beth shook her head. "I don't need to when I have you around."

Happy, lilting laughter filled the room. "Sad but true," the voice replied after the boy closed the copier's side panel.

While Simon was wondering how that voice could be attached to a teenage kid, he saw the baseball cap come off. A messy ponytail tumbled down, trying to contain a profusion of dark blonde curls.

Wow. Not a boy. "Hello," Simon said to attract the blonde's attention.

But it was Beth who turned toward him. Her mouth formed a startled O shape. Simon was accustomed to looks of admiration. Women always responded to him like that. His eyes shifted to the right as the one with the wild mane and skater clothes lifted her face. His thought pattern shut down when they made eye contact. He forgot everything. Anxiety. His job. How to *breathe*.

She stood in the sad, run-down office, exuding vitality and strength. Her face reminded Simon of a fine painting, one filled with sunlight and smooth, pleasing lines. And pale gold everywhere, on skin, lashes, and hair.

Mermaid eyes, Simon thought. *Sea-green.*

Beth coughed loudly. "I don't think we've seen you around here before, have we?"

"No. No, you haven't. I'm Simon," he replied, tearing his attention away from the other woman.

"Well, hello. My name's Beth." She gestured toward the golden goddess. "And this is Dr. Kate Spencer."

Kate finally moved from her position by Spike the copier and took a step toward Simon. "Why are you here?"

He definitely felt a chill in her tone. *Is she frowning at me? And what's with the attitude?* Simon decided to give her another chance and extended his hand. "Nice to meet you, Dr. Spencer."

Looking as if his hand was infected with any number of contagions, Kate folded her arms. "We've met before. Quite a few times."

Met before? She had to be mistaken. He would have remembered her. "Forgive me but when was this?"

Beth gave Kate a gentle elbow to the ribs. "Why are you being so rude?"

"It's okay," Simon replied. "She's fine."

He glanced at Beth and then returned his attention to Kate. If the doctor was ice before, now she burned. Her eyes nearly glowed with a fiery greenish-blue light, like a medieval heretic facing her corrupt accusers. Kate had a temper and it was fully directed at Simon. For some perverse reason this made him want to smile.

Instead, he pointed out the obvious. "I get the feeling you don't like me much, doctor."

"That's a safe assumption."

Beth began to apologize but Simon ignored her. He knew

how to handle angry women. Usually they were girlfriends, who moaned about his schedule or lack of commitment, not strangers. "Why is that, exactly?"

Mermaid eyes glittering, Kate said, "This is the fifth time our paths have crossed. Each meeting worse than the one before, I might add. And you still don't remember me."

Call him a jackass, a playboy, or a bastard, but casting aspersions against Simon's mind was an insult of the highest order. He bristled at the mere notion of his forgetting anyone he'd met once, let alone five times.

"Gosh," Beth murmured, looking from one of them to the other. "Robert is going to be so bugged he missed this." The clock on the wall chimed and she touched Kate's arm. "I need to get those new mothers into class. Maybe you could show Simon where his group is meeting?"

"Fine," Kate replied, though she didn't look at him. "Follow me."

Simon was itching to finish their discussion, but Kate hustled from the room without a backward glance. He caught up with her halfway down the hall. The enormous building echoed with voices and moving feet. One wing was cordoned off with cables and Do Not Enter signs. Entire sections of the crown moldings and decorative wood panels were broken or missing.

Deciding to try a different tactic, Simon nodded at the old-fashioned finishes. "If I had to guess, I'd say this place was built in the twenties or thirties."

Kate kept her eyes straight ahead. "Thirty-one. It started off as a boarding school and later became a store, then an apartment building."

"And you've given it new purpose as a community center

and clinic?"

"That's right."

Simon looked down another hallway, with its cracked drywall and boarded-up windows. "Are you going to remodel the whole thing?"

"A little at a time. I'm cleaning and doing some repairs today."

Kate's paint-splattered clothes were proof of it. There was so much to do. The work must be overwhelming. "Don't you have a maintenance staff?"

She shrugged, cool as ever. "You're looking at the maintenance staff, Simon."

The devil's advocate in him arose. Kate as a maintenance worker didn't make sense. "And you spent all those years in medical school to do this?"

She stopped, hands on hips. He noticed the silver band on her third finger. Damn it. Married. This bothered Simon more than he wanted to admit. The sparks between them were far more interesting than any exchange he'd had with a woman in a long time.

Huffing out some air, Kate seemed offended on behalf of every janitor and repairmen in the world. "You're right, I didn't go to medical school to work in a run-down community center. I'm a pediatrician. If I pitch in when other stuff needs to be done, who cares? Being a part of this place is the best job I've ever had. Any other questions?"

"Many, as a matter of fact," Simon replied as they started walking once more. He still wasn't convinced by her impassioned little speech. "Does it pay well?"

The way she ground her teeth shouldn't have been appealing but somehow it worked for Simon. As he reminded himself that she was married, he almost missed her answer. They were still on the move and Kate was one fast walker.

"Is money the only standard by which you measure success?" she asked. "This is Nonprofitville. Little paychecks, lots of volunteer work. I'd give it five out of five stars on Linkedin."

Simon couldn't see the appeal of Nonprofitville, but he decided to play along. "That's a commendable attitude. And rare, I might add."

Kate's cheeks flushed deep pink. "Do you hear yourself? Do you know how patronizing you sound?"

"Not my intention," Simon replied, shaking his head. "I'm just trying to understand why you do what you do."

"It might be outside your scope of experience. My coworkers and patients are like family. Is Phillips, Cronin and Goddard anything like that?"

Interesting, Simon thought. *She's heard of the firm.* "How do you know where I work?"

"As I said before, we've met. Five times if you include today."

He felt like shouting, When? Where? But Simon remained silent while Kate led him to a set of double doors. They both reached out to grab the same handle and their fingers overlapped. Heat rippled up his arm. A simple touch and the space between them sizzled. Kate withdrew her fingers quickly and stepped back.

Ten seconds of loaded silence followed, so Simon motioned her through the doorway. "Please. I'd like to think I'm a gentleman."

"I'm sure you would," Kate muttered before entering the auditorium. She paused at the top of the aisle, looked back at him over her shoulder. "You came on a good night. The instructor gives lots of useful information, and the people in your group are nice."

He gazed over the assortment of humans seated before him. The auditorium had around forty people in it but a few stood out: the passive aggressive couple complaining just loud enough to be heard by their classmates, the Gollum lookalike listening to a podcast in the back row, the woman buffing fingernails that could kill with one swipe . . .

What had Kate said, that this was the "good" group? Good at what? Being annoying and weird? Having questionable hygiene?

Simon clutched his car keys. Maybe Leonard would reconsider if he went out to the Mercedes and phoned him, groveling. Maybe the partners would let him off with a stiff fine. A hefty fee was better than this.

Stepping backward, Simon realized Kate was watching him, wearing the enigmatic expression of a sphinx who somehow knew the answers to questions he didn't want to ask. Did she expect him to leave? To fail? He couldn't back out with her there, challenging everything he'd ever believed about himself.

Simon checked over the seating situation and chose a near-deserted section at the back. "Thanks so much for the escort, doctor."

Sphinx Kate nodded wisely, as if Simon had just passed the first test. "Let me introduce you to your teacher. Pete's an angel." She tilted her head toward a man with white hair. "Don't tell him I said so. I'll deny it."

Pete was handing out packets of reading material to his students. He brightened when he saw them.

"Just in time! I could use some help setting up the microphone, Kate. When I plug it in, it does that high-pitched, whiny thing."

She laughed briefly, and Simon's breath caught. The angles of her already amazing face, the bone structure and full lips, lifted into something perfect. He wanted to go on seeing her look that way, no matter what it took to keep her happy. Even when he knew she despised him, even when he wasn't all that sure he liked her, either.

Kate put her hand on Pete's arm and squeezed it affectionately. It irked Simon that she was so pleasant with other people.

"You know what to do," Kate told Pete. "Turn the volume down and don't get too close to the mic when you speak—"

"Technology isn't for old people, Buttercup." Pete gazed at her over the rim of his tortoiseshell bifocals.

"Okay, I'll check it. But I'm only doing this for your brownies. The whole office loved them. Beth said she wanted to marry you after she ate one."

He raised his bushy eyebrows in surprise. "How about I just give her the recipe instead?"

Kate grinned. "That might work, too. Let me introduce you to Simon. He's here for your class tonight."

"In that case, I'd better make it a good one." Pete handed Simon the packet. "Come on in. We're glad to have you. Make yourself at home."

As Kate went to work on the sound system, Simon took the seat he'd previously selected. Last row, across the aisle from Gollum. He flipped through the papers Pete had given him.

Nutrition, exercise, plenty of sleep. Blah, blah, blah . . . meditation, breathing exercises, etcetera, etcetera . . .

He lowered the syllabus to see Kate make her way up the aisle, stopping to visit when someone held out a hand, hugging a little old lady, waving if her name was called. She could have been a holy relic brought to life, the way these people responded to her.

Holy Relic Kate finally reached Simon's row. "Settled in?"

"As much as I ever will be."

"Good." Her attention immediately moved on to Gollum. Apparently, his real name was Chad.

They talked about his favorite podcasts and the graphic novel he was writing. Soon Chad was looking happy and relaxed. More like Smeagol than Gollum.

Simon watched Kate work her magic on the kid. What was it about her that effected people? It wasn't just physical beauty, though she had that in abundance. Couldn't be her ratty clothes. There was charm when Kate turned it on and magnetism in spades but that wasn't it either. Perhaps it was the warmth of her voice, the fact that she made eye contact with them, remembered things about their lives. She had something else, too. Something that said she understood somehow about hard things, about what people needed to get past them. About suffering.

Simon couldn't label this version of Kate. Yet he knew if it could be bottled and sold to the lonely, broken people of the world, he'd make a fortune.

Chapter 4

The next hour felt like ten years. Class members raised their hands a lot and Pete had a story for every question. The whole thing made Simon's ulcer hurt.

Now that class had ended, dozens of people were all leaving at once, so Simon waited in his seat until everyone had exited the auditorium. Passing through the empty lobby a few minutes later, he thought of the Thai food in his refrigerator at home. Simon's stomach rumbled. All he'd eaten that day were mints, coffee, and a protein bar Linda had found in his desk drawer. Satay chicken and peanut sauce would hit the spot quite nicely. Simon was only a few feet from the door when he heard the unmistakable sound of a drill. Was the handyman/doctor still at work? He looked at his watch. 8:15 p.m.

Don't turn around. Keep walking. You're not the Good Samaritan type. Besides, Kate hates you. And she's married.

Simon eyed the door, thinking again of the satay chicken. Dinner could wait, he supposed, even though his hungry stomach protested. The idea of a woman working alone at night in a big empty building bothered him. She'd have to walk to her car in the dark. Of course, Simon knew this was an assumption. Maybe Kate wasn't alone. Her husband might be there.

Now he had to go check and see what this guy was like.

What drew Kate to him? Looks, money, a brilliant mind? Simon already despised the man. He turned around and walked down the hall on the left. Light spilled out from the last room, and as he approached, Simon saw Kate putting her drill away. The brilliant, rich, good-looking husband was nowhere to be seen.

A door leaned against the nearest wall. Simon cleared his throat. "Can I help you with that?"

Kate put a hand over her heart, like Simon had surprised her.

"Sorry," he said, chagrined. "Didn't mean to scare you."

She shook her head. "Don't worry about it. You don't need to stay. I'm almost done."

Ignoring her, Simon took off his jacket, picked up the door, and moved it into place. "You'll finish quicker this way."

"How did class go?" she asked, slipping a door pin into the joint.

He shrugged. "Pete tells a good story."

"Yeah, he can really work a crowd." Kate took another pin out of her pocket. "Kind of like a grumpy Dr. Phil."

Simon moved out of her way. "But with visual aids and a full head of hair."

Her U2 sweatshirt pulled up a little in the back when she reached into her toolbox. Simon noticed the holster on her hip right away. The black textured grip of the gun inside it seemed wrong against her pale gold skin. It took a lot to shock him these days but this discovery did. Annie Oakley Kate? He never would have guessed this woman to be the gun type. She straightened up and set the toolbox on the exam table.

"Okay, Simon, that's it. Thanks."

"Anytime." Still curious about the gun, Simon wondered how to bring up the subject. Should he be blunt? Tactful? Ask to see her concealed carry license? Or better yet, just ignore the gun altogether?

Opting for the latter, he looked around the small room. White cabinets, white exam table, blue chair in the corner. Rows of numbers and alphabet letters adorned the walls. "Did you paint those?"

"Yes. And the mural in the lobby." She opened and shut the new door a couple of times and stifled a big yawn. "All right. Let's go."

Kate's manner was cool, though there was no hostility like before. Simon's appearance at her clinic must have been a shock, but she seemed resigned to his presence now.

He picked up her tool box. "You're sure this is the best job you ever had? I'm beginning to wonder about your resume."

Her lips twitched. "You'd fit in well around here. Sarcasm is our first language."

"So I gather."

Once they reached the office, she showed Simon where to stow the tool box in the closet. He watched Kate tidy up her work space for a few seconds. Tired Maintenance-Staff-Kate seemed fairly approachable. "When did I first meet you?" Simon asked, loosening his tie. "You said today was the fifth time?"

In the middle of writing a note, Kate stopped and said, "Yes. The first contact happened years ago."

"How many years?" Simon asked. "Two? Five?"

"Ten." She finished writing and stuck the note on a calendar. "You were in college. A couple of your friends were wearing T-shirts with fraternity logos."

Simon thought of himself in college—the parties, the wild rebellion against authority, the assumption he knew everything worth knowing. "Was it here or in Boston? Did I give you trouble?"

"You didn't give me anything, Simon." Kate sat by a prehistoric computer. Her slim fingers pushed the buttons to shut it down. "That's what made me mad."

He wrinkled his brow. "Excuse me?"

"You really want to know? Because it's kind of embarrassing for us both."

"Yes. Spill it. I have to find out what I did."

She began to fidget in her chair. "It was here in Portland. I was busking, trying to earn a little extra money. Scholarships covered tuition and housing, but I didn't have much cash leftover."

Busking? Simon was tempted to ask Kate to repeat herself, just to watch her squirm. "Am I correct in assuming that you played music for coins?"

Kate nodded. "Violin. I had my case open for donations and you guys passed by as I was tuning my instrument."

Crossing his arms, Simon tried to picture the scene. "And?"

"And two of your friends took out some bills. A ten and a twenty."

"What did I say? I was an ass in college."

Her face adopted a carefully blank expression, as if she wanted to shout in agreement but was resisting. "You gave me some advice, and I quote, 'Get a real job and stop wasting time on street corners.' Your frat buddies laughed and put the money back in their wallets."

She unlocked a drawer in her desk and withdrew a backpack and a black motorcycle helmet. Simon was shocked again. Kate rode a bike?

"My musicianship wasn't all that great," she went on, "and

your comment usually wouldn't have bothered me, but thirty bucks seemed like a lot back then."

"I'm sorry." Simon meant it. Drinking released some of his inhibitions. Good manners, for instance. And the filter that kept him from saying whatever popped into his mind.

Kate stood and slipped on her backpack. "It didn't help that your whole crew was plastered."

No, that definitely wouldn't have helped. "How did you know who I was?"

"I recognized your face from pictures in the newspaper. You and your family were in the society pages a lot."

"That's right," he said, rolling his eyes. "I hated when my parents dragged me to events with photographers."

Kate smirked. "Poor little rich boy. Had to smile on cue."

All the fatigue he'd felt earlier faded away. It was strange how their lives had connected so long ago. "Okay, I offended you while you were tuning your violin. What happened the second time we met?"

She pushed the off button on Spike the copier. He rumbled and then went silent. "Am I being cross-examined?"

Simon gave an innocent shrug. "Would I do that to you?"

"Absolutely."

They stared at each other, as if the first one to blink would lose face. Kate gave up when her eyes began to water. "Shoot," she said, blinking rapidly. "You win. Number two. Before entering medical school, I worked for the cleaning agency that your parents used. Only for a few weeks during the summer. I was scrubbing their bathtub and you came in to ask if your mom was home."

Kate had cleaned for his parents? "We spoke in the master bathroom?"

"Briefly. I don't remember much about their home, except that it was huge and already spotlessly clean. And the bathroom was a sea of white marble."

"It still is. My mother loves a good spa."

Simon knew that he must have been in a hurry that day, or preoccupied with something, not to have paid attention or really looked at her. Still, a lot of people had worked around that house over the years but none of them stood out in his mind. "Did we talk much, after I asked about my mom?"

"Sort of." Kate twisted her wedding band. She'd done it twice in the last ten minutes, but Simon wasn't sure if this signified anything. Was it a habit? Did she need to hurry home to her husband?

Although Kate didn't seem to be in a rush any longer. In fact, Simon got the feeling that she enjoyed reminiscing over the times he'd screwed up with her in the past. He kind of liked flirting lowkey with an impossible to get woman.

Kate flexed her ring hand. "I felt filthy from cleaning bathrooms all day, my hair drooped across my eyes, and my blue polyester uniform was two sizes too big. You were dressed like a cover of *GQ*. I didn't know where your mother was, so I said something sassy about not being her parole officer."

"Good one. What did I say to that?"

"Nothing. A girl was waiting for you downstairs. She came up to the bathroom—beautiful, perfect body, expensive clothes—and asked why you were wasting time talking to a maid when you were already late for brunch. You apologized and left."

"I apologized to you?" Simon asked, hoping he had. Ashamed, if he hadn't.

"No," Kate immediately replied. "To her."

"Oh . . . that's terrible."

"I hated you both." Her face remained expressionless but there was a small hint of humor in her monotone delivery.

Sly Kate. Her humor was a stealth punch to the esophagus. Simon wondered what would have happened if he had been less of a jerk that day and really looked at her, really paid attention to the hardworking woman in a uniform two sizes too big.

"Forgive me," Simon began. "I'm really—"

"Moving on," she interrupted before he could apologize. "The third time we connected was a train wreck. It is the pivotal one of the five that defines our differences. The event that still to this day makes me want to plan your funeral."

Totally unprepared for this deadpan assault, Simon felt like laughing, and not quietly, either. A big Santa belly laugh. But that wasn't his aesthetic. "My funeral, Kate?"

"Do you want an open casket or closed?"

"Ha, Ha. Neither."

"It has to be one or the other," Kate murmured. "You called the cops on my protest group."

I called the cops? Me? Simon relaxed a little. She was joking, using more of that understated humor. "You had me going there for a moment. Well done."

Kate held up her fingers like a boy scout. "Robert and I once worked at a clinic in southeast Portland. In the Lloyd District." She stopped and watched him expectantly.

She wasn't joking . . . "Still not ringing any bells, I'm afraid."

"One of your clients bought our building and decided to tear it down, to make way for a high-rise parking lot. I led a protest that attracted some media attention. Then you showed up in a limo to give a statement to the press. Some glib public relations crap, but the lady reporter ate up every word."

Simon sucked in his breath. Mortification nearly made him drop his Italian suit jacket. He did remember Kate this time. She was scary as hell that day, chanting with the crowd and stirring them up. "You're the angry woman with the sign? The one who tried to punch me? The police took you away."

She smiled sweetly. "They let me go an hour later."

"That soon?" Simon asked, still reeling.

The dimple in her cheek showed. "It was my first brush with the law, and I never actually punched you. I just wanted to."

Simon wondered what the hell had happened to his perfect memory. He never would have associated the livid protester with this beautiful doctor, but they were the same person.

When he remained silent, Kate turned off the overhead lights and motioned him out the door. They walked into the lobby and she checked that the bathrooms were empty.

Simon tried to put their clash at the protest in perspective. Maybe in the future, he might even laugh about it. Maybe Kate would too, though probably not. She returned to the lobby and he asked, "Was there near-violence when we met the fourth time? Did the National Guard intervene?"

Kate paused by the drinking fountain and the color seemed to leach from her face. "No, actually. You were nice. Helpful."

"Nice?" he repeated. That word had rarely been used to describe him. "When did that happen?"

"About three years ago," Kate said softly. "I was walking in Old Town on the worst day of my life. We passed each other and you noticed that I had been crying. You asked if I was okay, got my address, and hailed a cab for me. I didn't have my purse, so you paid the fare."

Nothing about what she said seemed familiar, but it felt true. Before Simon could question Kate further, a Rolling Stones song played from her cell phone. She answered the call and walked away as she greeted the guy named Robert.

Having nothing better to do, Simon glanced around at the ugly tan walls, the cracked ceiling, and inefficient windows. A display case stood in the corner. It was too modern to be original to the building and boasted a number of engraved plaques. Inner City Humanitarian Award for five years running. Excellence in Nonprofit Management. Recipient of the Associated Pediatric Care Endowment. Simon couldn't help being impressed. Despite its humble trappings, Kate's organization, the Hayden-Grace Clinic, had the respect of the medical field.

A thought crossed Simon's mind as he looked down at the stained wooden floorboards beneath his feet.

At the same moment, Kate must have finished her conversation. She walked across the lobby. "You're still here? I thought you'd gone."

"Still here," he said. "I just had an idea and I wanted to talk to you about it."

"Okay, but I only have a few minutes."

"I'll make it quick. As you know, I'm a partner at Phillips, Cronin and Goddard." He walked with her toward the foyer, their footsteps the only sound in the empty building. "Our firm makes charitable donations to worthy organizations."

The mention of a donation seemed to get her attention. "This place is about as worthy as you can get, Simon."

"I can see that. I wondered if I could speak to the other partners about your clinic. I think they'd be interested in contributing." He hesitated for a moment over his next words. "I have some free time presently, some days off from the firm, if you will. I'd like to help out around here."

"You?" Kate appeared shocked at first, then skeptical.

"Yes, me. Believe it or not, I used to be fairly skilled with a hammer. My grandfather was a craftsman. He built furniture and cabinets for a living, and I spent summers working with him as a kid."

Her face scrunched up. With doubt? Cynicism? Simon couldn't tell. "And you enjoyed that?" Kate finally said.

"I loved it." He held the door open so she could pass. "When Granddad died, I inherited all his tools. It'd be nice to have an excuse to take them out and use them again."

She stepped outside and scanned the shadows of the parking lot. "You still remember what he taught you?"

"Yes." The night air was cool, so he put his suit jacket back on. "Besides, Pete gave our class the assignment of developing a hobby. It's supposed to decrease stress levels. You'd actually be doing me a favor by letting me help."

Simon noticed the motorcycle parked near a big tree. Nice. Kate had good taste in bikes. When he glanced back at her, she was squinting up at him. Not a good sign.

"Your hobby development would be our gain," she replied after a moment. "We always have things that need to be fixed. I don't mean to sound ungrateful, but . . ."

Her tone seemed to indicate that he couldn't be relied upon and probably would give up at the first opportunity. "But what, Kate?"

She waved her hand, encompassing the community center and its grounds. "You're sure you want to involve *yourself* in all this? Our patients come to us from all over. Sometimes it gets messy and chaotic around here."

Getting Kate to accept his assistance was like negotiating a high stakes contract. "I think I can handle messy."

"The jobs we need help with aren't fun." After tucking her helmet under one arm, Kate punched a security code into an alarm system keypad. It flashed lights and beeped, indicating that the community center was locked. She turned back to him. "Would you mow lawns or replace windows? Retile a bathroom or help fix the roof? Good labor can be expensive, and I appreciate your offer. But you should know what you're getting into."

Simon regretted his good intentions. Her attitude was insulting. "Thank you," he said, tone bland. "I've been duly warned about the pitfalls of working here. Call me a daredevil, but I think I'll chance it."

Her smile shone in the dim light. "Funny, I didn't have you pegged as a daredevil."

"You'd be surprised."

"I hope you know what you're doing," she said with apparent reluctance. "I'll talk to the director of the clinic in the morning. I'm sure Robert will be thrilled."

A flicker of triumph shot through Simon. "Let me know what he says, and I'll contact the law office. I can start work as soon as you need me. Here's my card."

"Impressive."

"Thanks," Simon replied with an equally droll voice. "I have a box of three hundred in my car."

She pointed at the luxury chronograph on his wrist. "When you come to work here, you might want to leave that at home."

"Got it," Simon muttered. "No watches."

"Watches are fine. If they don't require a large insurance policy."

They walked across the parking lot and Simon checked out

the Triumph. It was parked close to the community center while his Mercedes was as far away as it could get and still be in the lot. Then he saw a figure standing in the shadows by the bike.

"Doctor?" the man called softly.

Kate turned toward the voice. "Oh, hello. How are you, Axel?"

"I need something," he said. "For my knee."

"You're in pain tonight?" She moved closer without entering the shadows.

But Axel left the darkness and came to her. "Yeah. I'm always hurting. I want some hydro."

Kate's face looked terribly sad when she shook her head. "You know I can't get that for you. I'm your son's doctor. I treat kids."

"I just thought . . ." Axel's voice drifted off. "Maybe you could write me a prescription."

"Have you been home lately?" Kate sounded soothing and calm. Simon could see she was in control, despite Axel's unexpected appearance. "How's Jenny?"

"She kicked me out. I'm down at the shelter now."

Thin and haggard, Axel looked as though his muscle and sinew had sunk in on themselves. Yet he towered over Kate by a good three inches. Simon moved closer and stood behind her. He figured he could take the other man in a fight if it came to that.

"Give me something, Kate," Axel said, lowering his voice. He glared at Simon like he wanted him to leave.

Simon glared back. He wasn't going anywhere.

Kate fished a 3x5 card from her purse and wrote on it. "This phone number belongs to a friend of mine. He's a doctor at the free clinic in Chinatown. He can determine your best course of treatment."

Axel flicked the card with a dirty finger. "I've been there. My knee isn't any better."

"Have you done your physical therapy?"

"It doesn't work."

Kate looked as though she had expected his response. "You have to be consistent—"

"Didn't you hear me?" Axel suddenly yelled. "I said it doesn't work."

"Okay, I understand."

He began to pace, his hands fisted. "No, you don't. Nobody does."

She wrote on the card again. "Some people do, Axel. This second number is for an addiction rehabilitation center. I think they have an opening available. All you need to do is call."

"I'm a junkie now?" the tall man asked. "You've been to my house, spent holidays with my family. How can you treat me this way?"

Simon's body tightened, ready to jump in if the argument turned violent. He followed every movement Axel made.

Kate lifted her hands, palms up. "All I'm saying is that you have a serious medical condition. Rehab is your best option."

"A medical condition, huh?" Axel's laugh was low and harsh. "Wow, thanks, Kate. I didn't know." He rocked side to side. "What am I going to do, use the phone at the shelter to make that call? It's out of order."

"You can borrow my cell."

Axel stepped back, muttering a dirty word. "Forget it."

He limped across the parking lot to the street and disappeared into the darkness.

Simon waited several seconds before speaking. "Is that

man a drug addict?" Kate headed for her bike and he followed her. "You shouldn't be here alone at night."

She put on her helmet and climbed onto the Triumph. "I usually leave with Pete, and Axel hardly ever comes by."

"What if I hadn't been around?"

"You were."

"I guess that's lucky then." Simon felt the voltage of her gaze.

She rolled her shoulders and said, "I don't want to discuss this situation. There's no way you'd ever understand."

"Try me."

A brief, hard smile crossed her lips. "Why? Do you care about him, Simon? Has your social conscience suddenly been awakened?" Kate backed her bike up so it was in line with the exit. "Axel isn't just an addict. I remember when he was a loving father and husband, as well as a good friend."

Simon could understand sentimentality but not when it put her life at risk. "Maybe he was at one time, but he doesn't seem that way now. He looks dangerous."

"Welcome to the real world." As soon as the words came out of her mouth, she grimaced. "I shouldn't have said that."

Then Kate got a look at the Mercedes. "It has an alarm system, right?"

Simon glanced briefly at his car, wondering about the implications of her question. "And GPS. Should I be worried?"

"This is usually a good neighborhood, but crime is increasing all over the city." Kate revved her engine. "Larry and Earl, those homeless guys living over there, will probably keep an eye on it if you give them ten bucks. See you later." She eased the bike out onto Everett, and sped off like a demon.

As Simon drove home, he considered the ragtag

community center and then his thoughts moved on to his lawyer friends. He knew they'd be astonished by his volunteerism at a nonprofit medical center. They wouldn't know it was just part of his agenda. The whole gig was merely a stepping-stone to impressing Leonard and the other partners.

He'd return to the firm a brand-new man, one admired for his reformed image. Or at least that was how it had to appear. Then Simon would get his office back and Carter Wright could go straight to hell.

Chapter 5

Daisy

Another night hiding at the library, another night of being afraid. Her heart pounded so fast she was scared it might burst. The maintenance closet was too hot and stuffy. *What if I die here and no one finds me until tomorrow?*

Daisy knew she wasn't really dying. This was just a stupid panic attack. Not even her first one. Not even her tenth, for that matter. She tried to distract herself by focusing on something positive, but the only thing she could come up with was the fact that the library was now empty. The final closing announcement had come across the intercom thirty minutes ago and the security guard was finished with his rounds at last. He had locked the front door and pulled it shut with a loud clang. She'd wait a while longer just to be on the safe side.

Crouched behind the boxes of toilet paper, Daisy concentrated on holding still. Huckleberry Finn, her newest imaginary friend, elbowed her in the ribs.

"Don't be afeard. He ain't gonna ketch us."

She was too scared to say anything aloud, so she nodded. Huck pushed his straw hat back and winked. "You ciphered it out real nice. Folks leave at closing, and the guard locks up after rounds."

"I know," Daisy whispered softly. "But I almost got caught last time. What if something goes wrong?"

"No cause for a flapdoodle. One time, Pap was drunk and of a mind to thrash me. 'Huck,' says I, 'you need an escape. A body can only take so much.'"

"It worked," Daisy murmured, smiling. "You got away."

He slapped the patched knee of his overalls. "Blamed if I'd stay under Pap's thumb! I set there a spell figuring, and a pretty bit of figuring it was, by jing. I lit out from Pap and hain't been back since. I reckon I know what's what."

Daisy nodded. "I expect you're right, Huckleberry Finn."

"Now don't go sounding like Aunt Sally. Just plain old Huck'll do. What time does that fancy watch-bob of yours say?"

She looked at her broach. It told time and looked like a cat's face. "It's after six."

A wide grin split his face. "Then you done it. Let's clip into the hall and have a gander."

Daisy climbed out from behind the boxes, careful not to knock anything down. She slipped her book bag over her arm and quietly opened the closet door. Nothing in the hallway but dark, empty space. The library was small, as libraries went, and Daisy could see most of the main floor from the top of the stairs. It was locked up and quiet. Not a soul in sight.

"Well, looky here," Huck drawled. "I knowed it would work."

She exhaled slowly and began to relax. "Thanks. I couldn't have done it without you."

"Aw, sure you could, but I had a fine time all the same. If you need me, you know where I'll be."

Huck gave her a conspiratorial salute before sauntering into the shadows. He was gone—in the blink of an eye—like a rabbit from a magician's hat. Her imaginary friends tended to vanish when she was no longer afraid.

Daisy entered the women's bathroom and switched on the light, feeling the cool, utilitarian atmosphere of the place. After taking off her rumpled school uniform, she turned on the hot water at the sink. She collected a palmful of the pearly liquid soap from the dispenser on the wall. Daisy washed her hair and body while leaning over the basin. She used the rough brown paper towels to dry herself afterward.

Braiding her wet hair was tricky, but Daisy managed two simple plaits. They hung past her shoulders like swinging ropes of gold. She opened her book bag and pulled out a clean uniform. It was a little baggy. The sweater had a hole in one elbow and the hem of her skirt was frayed. Would she get demerits at school for being sloppy?

Please don't let the lady in the office call home.

Daisy hadn't been there in two days, though Ma hardly noticed the passing of time. But it was safer if the school didn't make contact.

She dressed quickly and gathered her things together, making certain that the bathroom was spotless. The cleaners were coming the following day to do the library carpets. She couldn't be here then. Her insides began to churn as she tried to think of another place to go. Maybe the laundromat. It was open all night and had a good lock on the bathroom door.

Over the last few months, Daisy had found a number of places to hide, but the library was still the best. She couldn't stay there every night, only when the young day maid worked. The younger maid never paid attention to anything except the music she listened to on her headphones. She left the supply closet open all day until 5:00 p.m. on the dot, when she would put her key into the lock to secure the door without even checking inside first. It was easy to hide in the closet when the young maid was around.

No one noticed Daisy much anyway. She had a talent for being invisible.

However, the days when the old lady worked were a different story. The older maid locked the closet door just to step a few feet away.

Daisy stared into the mirror and saw a pale, skinny adolescent looking back. Plain, perhaps, but tidy. At school tomorrow, no one would ever guess she hadn't been home. Daisy left the bathroom and briefly thought about calling her mother to make an excuse for her absence.

Why go to all the effort, anyway? Ma never heard the telephone—she never heard anything. Not when she was with him.

Daisy entered the reading room, walking through the rows of tables and chairs to the couch by the window. Her heart thrilled as she put her pack down. What would she read tonight? A travel narrative? A glossy art book filled with beautiful pictures? A mystery? Surrounded by books, her choices were endless.

Daisy did have friends. They just weren't of the human variety. Some had leather skin and gold writing, others were paperbacks that fanned her face when she ruffled their pages. The shelves almost hummed as she carefully searched through them. How could ideas and thoughts and dreams ever remain still? Their energy vibrated through her.

Poetry seemed like just the thing. Some days it was the only way to soothe her mind. Daisy chose two volumes and brought them back to the sofa. She lay down, positioning herself so the borrowed light from the streetlamp outside fell across her shoulder. Daybreak would wake her long before the librarians arrived and then she would return to her hiding place in the closet until the building was unlocked. Once the side door was open, she would slip out quietly and take a bus to school.

Daisy decided to save the noble words of Walt Whitman for later and opened the Tennyson first. She now understood why her father loved him. He touched upon the darker parts of life and let you know you weren't alone. This particular volume was worn in the bindings from so much use.

After buttoning her jumper, she turned to "Morte D'Arthur," read the poem aloud, and looked up at the night sky. Daisy thought of the fallen king's words to Bedivere.

If thou shouldst never see my face again,

Pray for my soul.

More things are wrought by prayer than this world dreams of.

Closing her eyes, Daisy prayed for herself and her mother. And other lost souls.

Chapter 6

Northwest Portland

"**D**ude, it's a godsend. Call that man back before he changes his mind."

Kate sat at the counter in her kitchen, eating breakfast and listening to Robert on speakerphone. "So," she replied, smiling. "I guess that's an official yes from the director of the clinic?"

"You better believe it's a yes. How did you manage to hook this guy?"

Pouring herself a glass of chocolate milk, Kate said, "I don't know. I'm a little baffled on that point myself. He helped me hang a door and then twenty minutes later offered to speak with his law firm about making a donation."

Robert laughed. "What were you wearing when you hung the door?"

"I was fully clothed." Kate rolled her eyes and sighed. "You know, you're the big, obnoxious brother figure I never knew I wanted yet somehow got."

"Babe, you couldn't handle being my sister."

"How's that?" She took a gulp of the milk, happy just to be having this conversation.

Happy that it was also a sunny Saturday in April. This,

alone, was a miracle in Portland. Rain showers were typical until mid-June.

"Katie," Robert said. "If we shared the same gene pool, you'd have the red hair I got from my mother. Plus a complexion so white it incinerates after exposure to the sun."

She found herself grinning again and reached across the counter for a package of mini donuts. "I like redheads."

"Only because you're not one," Robert replied and took a bite of something crunchy. He was eating breakfast too. "What's this vibe I'm getting?"

"What are you talking about?" she asked, dusting powdered sugar from her fingers. "What vibe? I'm a vibe-free zone."

"Hmmm. Nope. I'm picking up some definite energy from you."

"Pfft," Kate said quickly. "As if." Once Robert began asking questions, he never stopped. She had to nip this subject in the bud. "You're imagining the vibes or the energy or whatever it is."

He paused, but she could tell his brain was working overtime. Formulating a strategy to wring information out of her. "I don't think so, Katie. Spill your guts to Uncle Robert like a good girl."

"I hate it when you call me Katie!"

As Robert crunched, she began doodling to keep her hands busy. Busy hands could not grab another mini donut. Kate looked down at her mindless scribbles. They were all of the letter *S*: large ones, small ones, some even underlined.

"You still there?"

"Huh?" Her elbow jerked and she almost knocked the cell phone off the counter. "Oops. Sorry, Robert."

If laughter could sound ironic, his did. "You were about to tell me why you're so jumpy."

"It isn't a big deal." Kate put her pen down. "Meeting Simon again was a surprise, that's all."

"Good surprise or bad surprise?"

Giving in to temptation, Kate shoved another donut into her mouth. Robert started to hum the *Jeopardy* theme song in the background. "Time's up, contestant. Answer, please."

"This isn't a trivia game."

"Quit stalling, Power Pack."

"Sheez, Robert. You're so nosy." She grabbed the last donut. "First the surprise was bad, then it became annoying, followed by sort of good, while also uncomfortable and guilt-producing. Confused yet?"

"Calm down." Robert took an especially loud bite. "You can't blame me for hoping you two hit it off. Mike's been gone three years, babe."

Kate's gut twisted into a knot. Being reminded of her loss never failed to make her feel sick and cold and sad all at once. "You don't need to tell me how long it's been."

Robert groaned apologetically. "You're right. I'm sorry, kid."

Kate crumpled the empty plastic package and tossed it into the garbage can. "As you already know, Simon and I met a number of times before." The words gummed together with the sticky powdered sugar coating her lips. "He's a gorgeous, rich lawyer who would probably sell his grandmother's kidney if the price were right."

"Ah." Robert's voice sounded all-wise. As if no other information needed to be shared. Then he asked, "What color are his eyes?"

"Light blue," Kate blurted out.

"And his hair?"

"Dark, thick, beautiful . . ." She leaned her head on the counter. "Shut up, Robert."

"I didn't say anything."

"You thought it!"

Robert exhaled like a surfacing dolphin. "Dude, you're right. But I had to ask. In all the years I've known you, you've never once commented on somebody's looks."

"Yes, I have," she protested.

"It doesn't count if it's an old person or a little kid, Kate."

She frowned at the doodle paper. "Generally speaking, all I *see* are kids and old people. You know this, yet you still bust my chops."

Robert snickered into the phone like a vaudevillian bad guy. "Hey, it's my job as your best friend, and I take that responsibility very seriously." Since Kate heard footsteps, she assumed he was walking around his house now while talking. "Call the lawyer and get that donation, Power Pack."

Cursing under her breath, Kate sat up and rubbed powdered sugar out of her hair. "You got it, boss."

————— • —————

Simon looked out the window of his study while drinking a double shot espresso. He had just ended a very businesslike call with Kate Spencer. She was still irritated by him. Less than yesterday, maybe, but the underlying vexation remained. Or maybe it was a habit after ten years of disliking someone. Simon thought he had worn her down a little, that maybe the grudge was fading, but her chilly tone just now indicated otherwise. Was she planning his funeral at this very moment? Closed casket this time or open?

Regardless of Kate's apparent disapproval, she did suggest that he drop by the Hayden-Grace Clinic at the community center the following Monday. But why wait? Simon wore an evil smile as he thought about surprising her today instead. If she and Robert could work over the weekend at the community center, so could he.

His cell chimed and for a moment Simon thought it was Kate calling him back, only to discover his nemesis Carter Wright on the line. They talked briefly about the recent sale of MSquared Software to Jacobsen Technologies and then Carter turned smug.

"So, Simon, the *Annus Mirabilis* is as good as mine. I've got an upcoming deal that will send me over the top. You can say goodbye to your winning streak."

"Trash-talking again, Stanford? You're so predictable."

"Just stating the facts, Harvard-boy."

Simon hung up with a bored sigh. Ennui took some effort since he really wanted to tell Carter where to stick his over-the-top deal. He thought for a moment, corporate lawyer senses tingling. Wright had sounded especially smug after they discussed Ed Moyer, one half of MSquared. The technology titan had been a client for nearly five years. A needy, emotionally draining client who forked out a lot of money to torture Simon over legal matters. Most of the time, the money compensated for the torture, and Simon wasn't about to let Carter steal him. He called his very bad, but pays good, client.

The line rang once and then there was the sound of wind and water crashing against something solid. Ed was sailing again. He took his boat out each day, rain or shine, insisting that the water was his muse.

"Simon," Ed shouted against the wind. "Can you hear me?"

"Very well, thanks. I'm calling to check in. Did you receive those documents I faxed to your home office?"

"Yes, and I spoke with Carter just an hour ago." Ed must have stepped inside the cabin because the outdoor noises grew softer. "He's helping me now."

Simon covered his cell and silently mouthed a few swear words before removing his hand. "Helping you with what, Ed?"

"Wright told me you were taking time off. How could you do that, Simon? You know it's not good for me to be at loose ends right now. I just sold my company and buried my favorite nephew in the same week."

The death of Ed's nephew had been sad, though not unexpected since Randall had struggled with COPD for so long. Simon attended the man's wake on Sunday and the funeral the following day—Ed's sister Louise crying on his shoulder at each event—and still managed to keep the sale of MSquared on schedule, finalizing the deal on Thursday.

"I know, Ed. I'm so sorry. I can't imagine how hard this must be for you and Louise—"

"No, you can't." His voice sounded angry. It always did when Ed began the torturing. "I'll work with Carter until your return. If I'm happy with him, I'll make a permanent switch. I want more service and consideration for what I pay." He blew his nose loudly.

Simon winced at the disgusting sound. "I'm just as committed and involved as I've ever been. What can I do for you?"

A grunting noise carried across their connection. Simon looked up at the ceiling in his study and hoped that his client wasn't using the bathroom. In the past, he had endured lengthy conversations with Ed on the toilet.

"As I told Carter, I'm looking for a place to build a school in Portland. The best technical college in the country. Something modern and cutting edge. I want to dedicate it to Randall. That way his legacy and name will live on."

"Sounds like a wonderful tribute, Ed. He taught at a tech school, didn't he?"

Ed grunted again. "Yes. He loved his job."

Simon picked up a pencil and note pad. "Carter's looking around for you, hoping to find a property for Randall's school?"

"Don't take that tone with me. What do you expect?" Ed yelled into the phone. "He was there! Where were you? Not in the office, not doing your job. No, you're out when I need you the most, spending the money you earned because of me."

Using his calm voice, the one that usually pacified angry clients, Simon assured Ed that his needs came first. "We've worked together a long time. I'm dedicated to helping you find the perfect place for your vision on this project, Ed. Randall deserves nothing less. I am here for you, no matter what it takes."

Whenever a client wanted property, Simon found it for him, even though he didn't actually have a real estate license. After the desired location was settled upon, a small cut of the deal went to one of the younger lawyers at the firm who did specialize in realty. They wrote up the paperwork for Simon, and the deed was done.

"I can handle this for you, Ed. We don't need Carter."

Ed blew his nose again. "I'd feel bad if I cut him out now. Why don't you both look? The first one to find me a place gets a bonus on top of the regular fees."

Simon snapped the pencil in half. He made himself sound

thrilled over the opportunity. "Text me your specs. I'm on fire, Ed. Randall's place is out there. I can feel it."

Ed whined for a while longer, calling Simon names and then weeping about his nephew. Ed was an indiscriminate weeper. If he was happy, he cried. Sad? Bored? Unfulfilled? More tears. Simon served as his scapegoat during these emotional outbursts. Eventually, Ed wore himself out and hung up.

Simon went in search of a drink, as he had after the sale of MSquared. Even though it was fairly early in the morning, he went to the liquor cabinet and poured out some Jack. Not enough to get drunk but he'd feel a buzz.

The whiskey burned down his throat like liquid fire. Simon had never enjoyed the taste of alcohol, just the aftereffects. Relaxation, momentary happiness, confidence—it was all there in the bottle. His body slowly began to unwind. *Keep calm*, he thought, *keep cool. Don't let Carter Wright take your client.*

Simon had an advantage over his competition in that he had plenty of people who owed him favors. Wright only moved to Oregon a year ago and was still hustling to make powerful friends. Simon called some of his contacts who knew the Portland real estate market, people who bought and sold property daily, and they agreed to research some leads and send him the listings. Inventory was limited, and a few of the properties sounded good, but none of them were perfect. He'd check them out later and forward the information to Ed.

Simon brushed his teeth to cover the scent of alcohol, then ate a mint on the way out the door. He still wanted to get going with his service at the community center. Leonard would applaud his initiative and the faster he started the sooner he could be done with the ridiculous leave of absence. Simon would have to be circumspect when it came to working with Ed. Leonard had to think he was decompressing, not competing against Carter.

While driving to the community center, he mulled over the information Ed had texted to him. The space had to be large and although Ed was willing to buy an existing structure in need of some renovation, tearing it down and starting over with a new build would be preferable. Simon decided that an hour or two was all he could spare helping Kate. The rest of his day would be devoted to Ed Moyer.

Simon almost missed the turn again on NW Everett as his mind whirled, but he swung into the lot at the last second and parked the Mercedes. Kate's bike and a green Subaru sat side by side near the big tree. About to compartmentalize his situation with Ed Moyer and Carter Wright to a back section of his brain, Simon stared at the community center. He pulled up Ed's specs for the tech school on his phone and reread the information several times.

I cannot be this lucky. It's not possible.

Simon didn't move, dazed by serendipitous good fortune. Damned if the lot size and location of the old place wouldn't work. Without doubt, Ed would tear it down and build something sleek and modern. His mind raced with the possibilities. What was the best approach to use with this Robert person Beth and Kate had talked about? It would require some finesse. Especially if Kate had influence over him. She was definitely attached to the crumbling heap.

The smell of cut grass floated through the open window of his car. It reminded Simon of childhood summers and Little League games. He got out of the Mercedes slowly and hooked his sunglasses in the collar of his T-shirt. Kate was pushing the sputtering, protesting mower in the opposite direction. Now there was a nice view.

Turning at the end of a neat row, she saw him and let the machine die. Her face resembled a pretty thundercloud. Simon reached into his car for a chilled bottle of Evian. He waved it at her, thinking that she somehow made the flecks of grass sticking to her pant legs and shirt look cute.

"What are you doing here, Simon? You're supposed to start on Monday."

"I thought you might want something cold to drink," he said, walking toward her. "You're a little flushed."

"I was flushed an hour ago. This is the ruddy stage."

Kate wore her hair tucked up under the Cubs cap again. Simon opened the water bottle and held it out like a peace offering. He smiled at the conflicted look on her face. Kate wanted the water but could she bring herself to accept it from him? The conflict lasted for about five seconds and then she took a swig.

He folded his arms as Kate drank more. "What's with this weather? Must be some freakish anomaly. I mean, April sunshine? Ridiculous."

She wiped her mouth. "If it makes you feel better, I hear there's a storm front moving in from the coast."

Simon looked up at the sky. "Nothing like a good storm to get things back to normal." He gestured toward the side yard, where a man was spreading bark chips. "Is that Robert? Can I introduce myself?"

"Sure. I'll go with you."

They started walking toward Robert when a man yelled Kate's name. A skinny guy in camo pants stood outside the tents in the vacant lot, waving at her. "Hey! You got oatmeal again today? I changed my mind about the raisins. They weren't bad."

Her ruddy cheeks grew even more red as she waved back to the camo guy. "All right, Earl, but I need to do something first."

Another man sat in a camp chair, reading. "Take it easy, Doc. It's not like we're going anywhere."

Simon thought of Kate's advice about his Mercedes from the night before. "Are those the guys? The ones who will watch my car for ten bucks?"

She squinted back at him. "Better make it fifteen if you want them to keep their beer cans away from your tires. Let's go see Robert."

Kate took off, as usual, and Simon hustled to catch up. "What's on the schedule today?"

"Removing that, for one." She nodded at the bright orange You Suck! painted on the side of the community center. "We need to clean off the wall and do yard work."

"And tomorrow?" Simon enjoyed the irritated expression she wore every time he spoke. "Wait. Don't tell me. You're sleeping in, eating pancakes, and going to the mall."

"No, though I do love pancakes." Kate picked up a piece of trash. "We're probably going to tile some bathrooms." She cocked her head and shot him an appraising look. "Still sure you want to do this?"

Simon put his sunglasses back on. "Do you always show so little faith in your volunteers, Kate? Are you hoping I'll fail? Believe me, I can work as long as you can."

"You might hold your own against regular, everyday doctors, but Robert and me? I don't think so."

"Really? And why is that?"

Kate gestured at their surroundings like the answer was

obvious. "We donate most of our free time—vacations, holidays, weekends—to work here and have second or third jobs in order to do it."

A deep chuckle erupted from a few feet away, punctuating their conversation. "Can't argue with her on that one. Though it would be interesting to hear you try."

Simon's first impression of the medium height, slightly built man was Academic Hippie. He wore an orange and blue tie-dyed shirt with baggy brown shorts and Birkenstocks. Red hair cut short. Black square glasses.

Extending his hand, the Hippie stepped forward. "Robert Hayden-Grace."

"Nice to meet you. Simon Phillips." They shook and the doctor had a surprisingly strong grip. "Good to be here today. What can I do?"

Robert gestured toward a huge pile of bark chips. "How do you feel about mulch?"

"As a rule, I'd say I'm in favor of it," Simon replied, picking up a shovel.

"Good thing, brother. We got a lot to go around."

"Hey, Power Pack," Robert asked Kate with a smile. "You gonna finish mowing the lawn or just stand there ogling us?"

She backed toward the mower. "Not ogling, Robert. Witnessing a historical event as our lawyer friend gets himself dirty."

Simon nodded in the direction of the homeless men. "You've got more important things to do. Earl's oatmeal isn't going to make itself."

"Just what we need," Kate muttered before going inside. "A lawyer who thinks he's funny."

Robert put Simon to work right away, loading and

unloading a wheelbarrow with smelly mulch. As he worked, Simon observed Kate carrying the bowls of oatmeal over to Larry and Earl. They tried to take the food, but she stepped back, glancing at some scattered beer cans. The vagrants grumbled and gathered the cans. When they were finished, Kate smiled and handed them their oatmeal. Simon pretended to be absorbed in his work when Kate walked back toward the lawn mower and started it up. But he was aware of everything she did.

He and Robert painted, weeded, pruned trees, and moved rocks. "My back is killing me," the doctor finally muttered. "I'm too young to feel this old."

The disgruntled expression on Robert's face clearly showed that he wasn't too happy working at the community center that weekend. Simon had changed his mind about leaving after just an hour or two of service. He wanted to observe Robert and Kate. Learn what their plans were for the clinic and the crumbling building that housed it, whether Robert had ever considered selling or had offers from buyers.

While the doctors still worked, Simon went on a short break and took a series of photos of the community center and surrounding property. He sent them to Ed, who responded with a positive text. Randall had lived in Northwest Portland when he was younger and loved the area. Simon knew when he'd hooked a client. Ed was hooked.

As the afternoon wore on, Kate and Robert joked with each other, but there were also occasions when they disagreed about how much they needed to spend on fertilizer or if new sprinkler heads were a waste of money. Simon wondered if the two doctors ever argued about more serious matters, like the hours involved with the upkeep of the place or the cost of future renovations.

Kate ignored Simon for the most part. In fact, she only seemed to meet his eye at the exact moment he thought about leaving for the day. But Simon wasn't about to give her that satisfaction, even if it did mean getting a sunburn. And an aching back. And blisters because he had refused to take the damn gloves she'd offered him. The woman was driving him insane.

Chapter 7

Kate turned off the power washer with a sigh. You Suck! only looked brighter and more noticeable after being sprayed down. If the graffiti had been cool or artistic, she would have left it alone, but this was an orange disaster.

"Oh well," she said. "Can't win them all."

Simon muttered something to himself as he inspected his blistered hands. Then the rich, pretty lawyer looked up and Kate lifted her chin. *Are you going to quit now? Take your Mercedes and drive away?*

Hell no, his squint said. Simon went right back to painting wood trim and shutters with a level of perfectionism that made Kate roll her eyes.

Ease up, Perry Mason. The world isn't going to end if you drift outside the lines.

She didn't feel too bad about his blisters, though. He'd been offered gloves and had refused them. Next time—if there was one—Kate was sure he wouldn't make the same mistake. As Robert often said, every education cost something.

Since the wall needed to dry before she could paint over the graffiti, Kate started another project. One that nobody liked doing. The extension ladder wobbled a bit as she climbed to the top and began cleaning the rain gutters. All kinds of stuff ended up in there: dead birds and mice, leaves, mud, and for some strange reason, a size four Disney princess flip-flop.

Sunlight beat down on Kate's shoulders, warming her muscles as she worked, but it felt almost therapeutic. Laboring for a good cause made her feel alive. On the other hand, sweating throughout the morning had permanently adhered the cotton material of her T-shirt to the skin on her back. She inhaled an earthy scent and couldn't decide whether the smell came from her or the compost in the gutter.

Pushing back her Cubs cap, Kate climbed down the ladder. She grabbed the water bottle Simon had given her earlier and took a gulp. The Evian was warm, as if it had just come out of the microwave. Even though Kate was thirsty, she couldn't drink it. Instead, she poured the last of the bottle over her arms to dislodge the dirt and bits of debris.

The sun seemed to grow even hotter as Kate walked inside to get some change out of her backpack. Putting five quarters into the antiquated vending machine, she pressed A-4 and heard the rattle and thump of her Gatorade sliding into the tray below. The guy who stocked the drinks hardly ever came by, and it was big news for the staff when he did. After buying two more Gatorades, she went in search of Robert and Simon.

Passing Simon's perfectly painted shutters, she found him with Robert, planting a tree. Kate could hear their low voices talking back and forth. As she drew near, Robert laughed and punched Simon in the arm like they had been buddies forever.

Kate did a double take. Buddies? No two men could be more unalike.

Robert was completely oblivious to her presence as he determined which side of the tree to face toward the community center. Simon had an odd look in his eye, like a man on the edge. Or one who couldn't be bothered to give a damn anymore. Had they broken him on his first day?

He acknowledged her attempt at cleaning the graffiti. "It's spotless, Kate. You could have a fallback in sanitation if the medical thing doesn't work out."

Robert frowned. "Don't even think about a fallback. I need you bad at the clinic, Power Pack."

"Power Pack?" Simon asked. "Where did that come from?"

"She keeps us all going," Robert said, talking around Kate. "Like a supercharged battery."

"Hello. I can hear you." She handed a Gatorade to each of them and inspected their work. "How's it going?"

"Robert's a tyrant." Simon gave her a smart-ass grin. "But I'm sure you already know that."

Kate crossed her arms, smiling back the same way. "He has his moments."

As Robert walked around the tree, Simon drank the Gatorade. He looked at the flavor name and then toasted Kate. "Fierce Grape. My favorite."

She twisted her wedding ring. Being the object of his undivided attention made her twitchy. "What if I had brought you a Citrus Cooler instead?"

He winked. "Even better."

What was that? Is he flirting with me? Am I liking it? Kate feared that she did indeed like it. Too much. To deflect Simon's interest, she pointed at Robert's Douglas fir. "What's taking so long?"

"Technical difficulties." Simon leaned against his shovel, clearly tired. "Some call this a tree, but I'm not convinced. It seems to have a will of its own. I'm pretty sure I heard it say it didn't want to get planted."

"Well?" Kate called to Robert. "How does it look?"

"Like it was donated, sweetie," he answered, pushing some branches aside. "I think I want to turn it to the left. There's a big hole in the front."

"That's my cue." Simon dropped the shovel and handed the Gatorade back to Kate. He turned the big, ungainly tree just as he'd been told.

But Robert yelled for him to stop. "Bro, the left side is even worse. Swivel it around the other way."

"You make that sound so easy," Simon murmured, moving the monster into place.

Over the next quarter hour, he manhandled the tree according to their commands, finally setting it down with a thud.

Kate fanned herself with the Cubs cap. "Douglas is ugly, any way you look at him."

Simon nodded. "The landfill called. They don't want Douglas back."

She began to feel sorry for the evergreen. "We could cover it with lights at Christmas and hide the bare spots. The kids would enjoy that."

"Dude, we can't afford that many lights," Robert said, laughing.

"No, but you could set it on fire for the Fourth of July," Simon suggested as he resumed his place at the tree.

In the end, the planting required all three of them to get the job done. Once the tree was in the ground, they stood back to admire their handiwork.

"Wow. It's big and green," Kate said, because there was really nothing else to say.

"Exactly what I was thinking, give or take a few words." Simon tugged on the bill of her Cubs cap and picked up his shovel.

She exhaled as he walked away. Simon wasn't what she'd expected. He was funnier, for one thing. Entertaining. Kate frowned. She didn't want to like Simon.

———— • ————

The sun slipped down the sky and hid behind the west hills. Clouds of gold, pink, and yellow glowed in the hazy light. Natural beauty was lost on Simon. All he cared about was eating something hot and going to bed. He brushed a twig off of his T-shirt and waved as Robert drove away in his Subaru. Simon doubted he had ever felt more disgusting in his life, covered as he was with dirt and dried perspiration. Kate came in a close second to him in degrees of filth. Nevertheless, the dirt on her cheeks made her teeth look extra white.

How does she manage to pull off sexy and grubby at the same time?

While Kate locked up, he sat on the front steps and said, "I don't know about you, but I'm starving. Want to get pizza? We could use the hood of my car for a table. No self-respecting restaurant would allow us through its doors. We're a health code violation."

Simon wasn't sure what he and Kate would talk about or if they could keep from bickering for an entire meal.

She set the alarm. "Hood for a table, huh?"

He twisted around and looked up at her. "Would your husband mind? You getting pizza with me?" Simon would mind, if Kate were married to him and some other guy wanted to take her out to eat.

Gazing at the sky, she seemed to think over his question. "No. Mike wouldn't be threatened by it."

Larry and Earl shouted her name. They had been yelling things at Kate and Robert all afternoon. "Who's the new guy, Doc?" Earl asked. "He doesn't look like he belongs here."

Kate assured him that Simon was just another volunteer. "Trust me. There's nothing to worry about."

"You sure?" Larry asked. "'Cause we can come over there if you need us."

"No," she replied. "I've got things under control."

Earl scowled at Simon one last time. "Okay, Doc. We've got your back."

"Thanks, guys. And I want you to help him too. Keep track of his car, make sure it stays safe when he's here."

"Twenty bucks," Larry said. "The going rate."

"Wait," Simon called back. "I thought it was fifteen."

"Not for you." Larry went inside his tent.

Feeling ripped off, Simon followed Kate toward her bike. "About that pizza. What will it be? Supreme? Pepperoni?"

She shook her head. "As tempting as that sounds, I can't join you."

"Why not?"

Kate put on her helmet and climbed onto the Triumph. "I'm babysitting for some friends tonight."

Her response threw him a curveball, and he lifted an eyebrow in surprise. "Of your own free will?"

"Yes."

"Well, you have fun with that," he said and spun the Mercedes key ring on his finger.

"I will." There was another flash of white teeth before she reached into her backpack and took out some trash bags. She gave him two. "For the pretty leather seats in your car."

Simon looked down at himself. "I never thought I'd get this dirty."

"I did." Kate backed up the bike. "Thanks for all your help today."

"No problem."

Giving him a little salute, she said, "See you when I see you."

After Kate left, Simon unfolded the black plastic bags, putting them over the buff leather. He sat down in the Mercedes and worried that the sheer synthetic bag wouldn't be enough protection against the amount of grime on his clothes. It occurred to Simon that although he had thought about the law firm during the last eight hours, there had been moments when he'd forgotten about his job altogether. Moments when he hadn't even thought about Ed Moyer and his tech school. This realization panicked him. What was he without his practice? Without his enormous salary from clients like Ed?

As soon as Simon got home, he would get cleaned up and then begin devising a plan to get Robert to sell the community center. He didn't seem to have the same attachment to it that Kate did. Simon thought he'd be willing to sell, given the right incentive. Kate would probably hate Simon for his involvement in the deal, but he could handle that. She had wanted to annihilate him with her fists a few years ago.

Thankfully, Kate had been carted off by the police before the civil protest grew more uncivil. All that enmity because Simon arranged the property sale that led to her clinic building being torn down. He figured if history repeated itself, they would both survive and move on.

Simon glanced down at his muddy jeans. The ones with the

artfully distressed seams and pockets, which had cost two hundred bucks and were never intended for actual labor. They were trashed. His arms and legs ached, but more than anything, he was hungry.

He pulled up to a pizza parlor drive-through window and ordered an extra-large pepperoni with mushrooms, olives, green peppers, and onions. The risk of mouth injury due to bubbling-hot cheese and toppings didn't stop Simon from eating a piece on the way home. He'd never consumed anything in the Mercedes before, but that fifteen-dollar pie was probably the best thing he had ever tasted.

Chapter 8

The smile Kate wore as she waved goodbye to Simon and rode out of the parking lot lasted half a city block. The whole babysitting thing was a lie. She could have had pizza with him, even though the idea seemed disloyal to Mike. That in and of itself made Kate say no.

Besides, if she had gone, they might have really talked. Which meant Kate would have had to tell Simon about herself. The last thing she needed was pity. Because everyone pitied a widow, especially the young ones.

It was better for all concerned if she and the lawyer kept things strictly about the renovations at the community center. He had been helpful. His work was done well. And if he also brought in donations from his legal contacts, then she could keep things professional.

As if he'd look twice at a stupid cow like you, a voice whispered at the back of her mind. Julian's voice.

"Shut up," Kate said aloud.

An image of a handsome man with long brown hair appeared in her memory. So tall and well dressed, a wolf-like smile creasing his face.

Sweat formed at the base of her neck. She imagined what Mike would tell her if he were here. *Hold on, Kate. Don't let him mess with your head. You're too strong for that.*

She exhaled slowly. The cruel voice wasn't really Julian's, of course. It was just a flashback. After all these years, he could still scare the hell out of her.

Kate took another deep breath and concentrated on driving the Triumph.

Don't think about him. Relax. Everything is fine.

As far as Simon went, she didn't need to worry. He wouldn't stay long. People like him never did.

Feeling better, she turned up the music in her earbuds and sped down the street.

———— • ————

The following afternoon Simon knelt on a recently tiled floor, mixing brown grout in a bucket. It was his tenth circle of hell: boring, thirsty work that took a toll on the spine, shins, and kneecaps. Somewhere beyond the bathroom, Robert was playing AC/DC on a boombox and the music carried down the hall.

Kate had yet to utter a negative word. Had spoken very little in fact. At the moment she was wiping away excess grout with a wet sponge. Her satisfaction with the work was evident and it bugged him.

Simon tossed a cloth in her direction. "Hey, Kate?"

"What?" she answered without looking up.

He crawled a little closer on his knee pads. "I'm hanging on by a very thin thread here."

"You can tough it out, big guy."

Surrounded by beige squares, Simon didn't think he wanted to. "Look at this floor. It's hideous."

Kate shrugged. "We did get the tiles for next to nothing."

"Whatever you paid was too much." Simon pushed his bucket aside. "To be honest, the whole place should be gutted. You could move somewhere better. Newer."

He felt a little like the devil on her shoulder, coaxing her to see the community center as a burden rather than an asset.

"No, thanks." Kate kept her focus on the grout but her breathing grew more rapid. Her posture turned stiff.

Was he tempting her to move? Did she not see that the renovations were a lost cause? "Why do you do this?" Simon asked gently. "Why keep working so hard?"

Kate put down her sponge and looked at him. Her blue-green mermaid eyes were honest. Enough to make him flinch. "Because I love this place," she finally whispered. "It's my masterpiece. My Sistine Chapel."

"The girls' bathroom?" Simon asked, incredulous.

She laughed silently, shaking her head. "Of course not. I meant the community center as a whole."

Simon bit his tongue. They had been getting along fairly well for several hours, and he didn't want to ruin it. He surveyed the cheap tile, the out-of-date countertops, the metal cubicles just waiting for the toilets to be reinstalled and he believed her. As a lawyer, Simon had learned to read people. It was crucial in his line of work.

After spending most of the day with Very Quiet Kate, he was getting a sense of who she really was. She used words as a shield, but her facial expressions said a great deal more, especially when she didn't think he was looking. They showed tenderness. Dedication. Hope. As if this money pit was the most important contribution she could make to the world.

Kate wasn't the tough cookie he first imagined her to be. She was a Double Stuf Oreo: hard on the outside, soft and sweet within.

Light shone through the glass block window at her back, haloing her golden head and shoulders, and Simon felt a tiny divot forming in the cynical veneer he wore like a second skin. His devil-on-her-shoulder act dropped like a stone.

He hadn't realized that Kate was still watching him. "Hello?" she asked, waving her fingers. "Have you lost hold of that thread?"

With his thoughts interrupted, Simon was a little slow on the uptake. "What did you say? Lost hold of what?"

Standing up, Kate put her hands on her hips. This was her go-to stance when she dealt with Simon. "Maybe I'm the one who's lost it." She reached down toward a bucket of water. "Did you think I would put up with you insulting this place? Hating on our beige tile? I can't be held accountable for what I'm about to do. I've waited ten long years for this."

There was the Sly Kate humor he liked. Her eyes twinkled with mischief. "I don't get it," Simon murmured. "You've waited for what?"

He had barely asked the last question when a sloppy wet sponge hit him square on the side of his head. He froze in place, dripping cold water, stunned by her actions. No one had ever dared to do such a thing to him.

Simon sputtered like a waterlogged cat. "W-why? H-how?"

Cackling, Kate scrambled backward and grabbed another sponge. "You brought it on yourself, Phillips. Your attitude needs adjusting."

He wiped off his face on his T-shirt. "And grout water is supposed to help me adjust? Let's be reasonable, Kate."

The dimple in her cheek showed. "Should we? I don't think so. This is for telling me to get a real job when I was busking!"

She hit him with another sponge. It struck his chest and bounced on the floor.

"This is for not apologizing after your girlfriend said I was a waste of time." Kate threw another missile but Simon dodged it.

Maybe she was right and some things were beyond his scope. He didn't know what was happening. Spontaneity? Fun for fun's sake? A decade's worth of suppressed rage?

He dipped his sponge into the brown water. Whatever this was, Simon was in. It was the craziest thing he'd done since college. But raising hell was like riding a bike, you never entirely forgot how.

"You shouldn't start something you can't finish, doctor."

"Who says I can't?" She tried to hide behind a sink, but he aimed and threw his weapon, hitting her back.

Now Simon was the one cackling. He felt free. Light. And without taking one drink of alcohol. Then Kate returned fire.

Five minutes later, Robert peeked inside the bathroom. Both Simon and Kate were soaking wet. She was squatting on the countertop with the tap running and a sponge in her hand. Simon was holding a bucket up, about to pour the whole thing over her. They paused when Robert cleared his throat.

"Can't leave you two kids alone for a minute, can I?" he said, shaking his head. "And Beth says I suffer from Peter Pan syndrome."

Simon and Kate nodded at each other, like it had been planned ahead of time, and attacked Robert simultaneously. He covered his head, sliding to the floor amid puddles of water, buckets, and sponges.

"Come on, dudes. I surrender. I'm a pacifist."

Monday dawned with clear, blue skies. The storm front ended up passing Portland to settle on Seattle instead and Kate enjoyed the pleasant morning air by walking to her favorite bakery for a croissant and a cup of tea. The clinic was closed on Mondays, so she could take her time for this little indulgence. Kate sat at a small table by the window, munching the croissant, and considered the things she, Robert, and Simon had accomplished that weekend. They'd packed a lot of projects into the last two days and she felt a twinge of sympathy as she remembered Simon limping to his car after tiling for hours.

Kate smiled as she thought of their water fight. She had never intended to start it but something inside her snapped. Where had all that silliness come from? It wasn't like her to goof around. Was it just that she was tired? Did the tension she felt around Simon bring her to the breaking point? Poor Robert, getting caught in the crossfire. His Birkenstocks made a squelching sound for hours afterward.

Kate bought some pastries for Simon and Robert, thanked the bakery owner, and walked home. She wasn't expected at the community center for another hour but it felt wrong to waste time indoors. Kate decided to clean a garden shed that sat behind the old Victorian where she rented a basement apartment. Her landlord had asked for volunteers to organize it but so far no one had. The shed was the Bermuda Triangle on dry land.

When Kate looked for something in its usual place, it wasn't there. At the same time, unexpected things seemed to materialize within the haphazard collection of junk, storage boxes, and gardening supplies.

A half-empty bag of cat food? Who did that belong to? And a box of bicycle parts? Some ski pants?

The shed was mostly hidden from the house, tucked at the back of the garden beside a red maple. Kate opened the rusty door and noticed a pile of cigarette butts on the cement floor. They were still warm, the air faintly blue with smoke. Who had left them there? A teenager experimenting with cigarettes? Someone trying to hide their habit? The discovery made the croissant in Kate's stomach turn to lead.

Only one teenager lived in the three-story Victorian, and he ran on the varsity track team at Lincoln High, trained hard, and prided himself on eating a strict keto diet. She couldn't picture him sneaking a smoke. An older gentleman on the second floor favored a pipe on occasion, though he and his wife were on a cruise, so it couldn't have been him. Then there was the single mother with twin girls who rented the rooms above Kate. Did she step out to light up? But why in the shed of all places?

Kate swept up the cigarette butts and tidied the shelves. She moved a recycling tote out from under a workbench where it overflowed with papers and cardboard and plastic. Everything mixed together. Thankful for her canvas gloves, Kate gathered the newspapers that had fallen to the floor. She leaned forward, noticing a hidden pile of mouse droppings.

"Ewww!" She shuddered, holding the newspapers at arm's length. "Scratch the whole Bermuda Triangle theory. This is a condo for rodents."

Reaching for more papers, she noticed something familiar about the man looking out at her from the society page. It was Simon, smiling as if he shared a juicy secret with the photographer. He wore a tuxedo, but his bow tie and top button were undone. Women of varying ages crowded around him, all of them beautifully dressed and attractive. Kate skimmed through the article about a glamorous New Year's Eve party in the Pearl District. The ladies were laughing at the camera, lifting their champagne glasses in a toast. Simon had a bottle of Veuve Clicquot in one hand.

Kate settled against the workbench. When Simon appeared at the clinic a few days ago, she'd immediately recognized him. Although he was a bit thinner now, his cheekbones more pronounced than before. Faint lines bracketed each side of his mouth and there were dark circles under his blue eyes. His face seemed colder, wearier, than it did in the New Year's photograph. Hungry for something.

Not for food, or a person. Not even for wealth. Kate couldn't quite put her finger on it, but she'd seen that same expression before. Her mother had always felt empty. Searching for the next thing to bring satisfaction and purpose to an otherwise empty life.

She tossed the newspaper into the recycling bin and pulled out her cell phone. Mike's voice filled the gardening shed. "Hey, babe . . ." Kate knew the message by heart, her lips forming each word as he said them.

Robert climbed up to the roof on the extension ladder. He gathered the split, damaged shingles and flung them, like Frisbees, to the ground below. "I love the smell of hot tar in the morning."

Kate hoisted a stack of new shingles onto her shoulder and carried them up to Robert before Simon could take them from her.

"Thanks, but I've got it," she said with a brief smile.

Today she was Polite Kate.

Simon tucked the hammer handle into his belt loop, got a

box of nails, picked up some shingles, and followed her up the ladder. From the ridge of the roof, the houses in the surrounding lots looked better groomed than they did at street level, and the tall shade trees seemed to reach out to Simon, as though they were offering him a soft, leafy hand.

Kate pulled a tube of sunblock out of her pocket and tossed it to Robert. "Time to reapply. You're looking a little red."

"Ouch, Mommy. My testosterone just took a hit."

She laughed. "Your testosterone can survive a little zinc oxide. You did say you incinerated in direct sunlight."

"My ancestors were cave dwellers." Robert rubbed a generous handful of SPF 90 all over his neck, face, and arms before throwing the tube back to her. "All right, dudes, I'm greased up and smell of coconuts. Hand me a shingle."

Simon relaxed as he listened to them. He realized that he enjoyed noncompetitive projects. Liked being part of a supportive team that didn't smile to your face and then try to stab you in the back an hour later.

By four, the roofing was finished. Robert was the first to climb down, followed by Kate. Simon had just started his descent when a young boy appeared at the bottom of the ladder. He had a brown, heart-shaped face with dark eyes and dyed-blue hair. The boy stepped back as Simon cleared the last few rungs.

"Hey, Marcus," Kate said, bumping the kid's knuckles with her own.

He grinned up at her. "My mom said I had to get out of the house for a while so she could sleep. I thought me and Tony would walk over and see if anybody was here."

"Is her job at the convenience store working out?"

"She hates pulling nights," Marcus replied, shrugging.

"But it pays more."

"More is good," Kate said and turned to the other child. "How's your baby sister feeling, T?"

His freckled face brightened. "That new gas medicine helped. She doesn't scream so much."

Kate took his basketball, spun it on one finger. "Bet that's an improvement."

"Yeah," Tony agreed. "I thought she was going to explode."

"Hear that . . ." Marcus muttered.

Taking some quarters out of her pocket, Kate grimaced at the sun. "You boys want soda? The guy filled the drink machine."

"Really?" Tony's eyebrows lifted two inches closer to his hairline. "He never fills the machine."

Another new side to Kate. Maternal. Good with kids. He'd assumed she would be as a pediatrician but it was interesting to see firsthand.

"So, you're Marcus?" Simon asked with a smile. "Cool name."

"Yeah." The kid gave him the once-over. "Who are you?"

"Simon's helping us out." Kate handed the money to the boys. "You want that drink or what?"

"No, ma'am. We can get a soda later."

"Why not now, Marcus?" she asked, leaning down so they were on the same level.

He gazed steadily at her with wide almond-shaped eyes. "Because you're going to play a game with me and Tony."

Simon could see that Marcus knew Kate would say yes. But she made a good show of hesitating. She didn't give in right away. "First to ten wins? I'm too tired for anything else."

Marcus shook his head. "Come on, Dr. Kate. You got to give us something. Full court with the winner at twenty-one."

She held up a silencing hand. "Half court and twelve."

Simon wondered if the boys had ever considered studying law in the future. In mediation, they could make a killing.

"Fifteen and we get the ball first!" Tony said triumphantly, dribbling like a pro.

"Done." Kate shook his hand. "You guys know how to make a deal."

Robert began stretching out. His joints popped and snapped. "Why do you always want Kate to play and not me, Marcus?" he asked, sounding offended.

"'Cause you hurt yourself every time, man."

They walked a few blocks to a park with an open court and hoops without nets. Robert put his boombox down on the cement and chose a Led Zeppelin song. Simon and Kate stood toe to toe at the free throw line. He smiled, enjoying their proximity. Athletic Kate was kind of cool.

What was she, 5'7", 5'8"?

"Five foot nine and three-quarters," she answered, like a mind reader.

"Why the statistics?"

"Just felt like I was being sized up." She twirled the ball on her finger. Simon wanted to ask her how she did it but he resisted the urge. Her mermaid eyes took on a steely expression.

"Wait," he asked, smiling again. "Have I made you mad?"

"Why would I be mad?"

He shrugged. "That's what I'd like to know."

She motioned to Marcus and switched places with him. The kid had the speed of a hungry cheetah. He dribbled up the court and passed the ball to Tony, and then Tony sent it back to Kate for a perfect three-pointer. They used a different strategy each time, but the result was usually a basket. Robert and Simon were bigger and sometimes had the advantage in blocking, but Kate defended her side of the court as if her honor were at stake. In the end, Simon managed to score ten points and Robert only fell twice. But it wasn't enough to win.

Back at the community center, Marcus and Tony relived their victory while they drank cold, water-beaded cans of pop. "Awesome game!" Kate called after the boys as they turned the corner to walk home.

"I don't know why I do this to myself," Robert complained. "You are *mean,* Power Pack. You're a mean, mean woman."

"C'mon. Don't hate the winner, hate the losing." Kate patted his shoulder. "You want an aspirin?"

"Yes. I want two. Two large ones, please." He limped up the front steps and opened the door. "They need to create a new sport, one that does not involve running, jumping, good aim, or any kind of momentum. No gravity, either."

Kate chortled. "I think that's called chess."

"See?" Robert said, pointing at her. "You're mean."

Robert went inside to get the pills and Simon stretched out in the solar-heated grass. Despite some fatigue, he felt good. Strange, but still good. Almost like an alternate-universe Simon. One who played basketball on Monday afternoons and took naps in the sun.

He watched Kate from under his half-closed eyelids. "Does this happen a lot?"

She sat down a couple feet away. "Almost every week."

"So, what's the story with Robert?"

Kate looked over at Simon. He could tell she was guessing at his motives for asking about her friend. "Why do you want to know?"

"Just curious."

Shrugging, Kate seemed to come to the conclusion that it was okay to answer. "He turned thirty-eight last month. Calls everyone dude—young or old, male or female—"

"I've noticed. Why does he do that?"

Her laughter sounded like a soft huff of air. "As a teenager, Robert tried to be a hippie, but it didn't work out. His grades were too good. He never found his niche in the whole subculture movement."

Simon sat up a little. "And?"

"Robert earned a scholarship to Johns Hopkins. He's worked in Africa, India, and Romania. You should ask him to tell you his stories."

"Does he have a family?"

Tossing a leaf at Simon, she said, "Lawyers ask a lot of questions."

"Guilty as charged," he murmured, batting the leaf away.

"He has parents and a grandmother." Kate tilted her face toward the sun. "His rich Aunt Lily passed away without a husband or kids. Robert was her only beneficiary. He bought the community center with his inheritance. Depending on the day, he's either happy about the decision or regretful."

A flicker of self-interest motivated Simon's next question. "Regretful enough to sell? I know someone who might be interested in buying. He's willing to pay above market value."

The relaxed, sleepy quality about Kate disappeared. "Bite your tongue. Robert can't sell. The people around here need the clinic and classes held at the community center."

Damn. He should have been more tactful. It didn't do Simon any good to antagonize Kate at this stage. Smiling, he said, "Point taken. You don't want Robert to sell. Aside from you two and Beth, who else works at Hayden-Grace?" Simon pulled himself upright and rested his forearms on his knees.

Her body grew more tense, instantly on guard. "Full of curiosity today, aren't you? Why?"

"I like to know the people I work with."

Kate watched him for a moment and then seemed to accept his answer. "There aren't that many people to know since our staff is so small." She loosened the laces on her purple Chuck Taylor high tops. "Tanya is a nurse. She's from North Carolina, loves karaoke. Nina's a social worker with a wild sense of humor."

"How wild?"

"You wouldn't want to share her jokes around your mother or your minister."

Simon understood. Dirty humor was popular among his kind of lawyers. "Off-color, then?"

"Extremely."

"Well, don't quit now. Tell me about your other coworkers."

Her face brightened. "Charlene's the therapist. Her youngest is starting-college this fall, so she and her husband are looking forward to traveling now that the nest is empty. We have some instructors for the evening classes, like your teacher Pete. Beth, you already met."

"The nurse in jungle scrubs," Simon agreed.

"She's a single mom." Softness seemed to suffuse Kate's being, making her appear younger and slightly wistful. "To Cameron and Josh, really sweet boys. Beth and Robert started dating last fall."

Simon noticed a gold chain hanging out of her shirt. It must have swung free during the basketball game. Attached to the chain, a St. Christopher's medal and a platinum man's ring nestled against the curves of Kate's body. The ring was the exact match for her wedding band. He inhaled slowly, grasping a hidden truth. Simon had believed there was a husband at home and she'd allowed the misconception to go on.

He leaned a little closer and Kate turned to look at him, their faces only inches apart. Simon remained quiet, admiring the healthy color of her skin and the gold flecks in her blue-green eyes.

Kate was transfixed. Spellbound. Her pulse raced, and she felt a little dizzy. Simon's voice was low and gentle. Not something she expected from him.

"I got off on the wrong foot with you, Kate. Many times. I'm sorry. Can we call a truce?"

He extended his hand and Kate looked at the strong, solid shape of his fingers. His face seemed sincere. He meant what he said.

A little bewildered, Kate agreed and they shook on it. "Truce."

After a moment of silence, Simon took up their conversation from before. "I've heard about everyone at the clinic but you."

She took the easy way out. "I'm not very interesting."

Simon moved his long frame to the side, giving her plenty of space. "Tell me something about yourself. How did you and your husband meet?"

Did he know about Mike? Was he feeling sorry for her? "Um. Let's see. I was walking in the North Park Blocks just before dark and a mugger told me to give him my purse. There wasn't much inside, so I handed it over. Next thing I know, this man comes out of nowhere and tackles the mugger. Michael Spencer to the rescue."

"In the nick of time. He must be a great guy."

"He was." Kate swallowed, suddenly nauseous. She took a sip of Gatorade, giving herself time to think. "He was . . . a cop. Women had been mugged in that area before. Mike was passing by in his patrol car and pulled over to help. The rest is history."

She studied a single buttercup. It was the one spot of yellow growing in an expanse of green. Kate twisted her band around and around until Simon reached out and laid his hand across hers. She didn't pull away. It was so nice to be touched. Simple human contact, nothing demanding.

The whole obnoxious lawyer persona was gone. "That chain you wear," he said, pointing toward her necklace. "It has a Saint Christopher's medal. And a man's ring. Plain platinum, like yours."

Kate moved her hand from under his. She had tried to keep the chain hidden inside her shirt. Simon must have seen it and made his own deductions.

His voice was surprisingly kind. And insightful. "You still feel married, don't you? So you wear your ring."

If people were rude or callous, Kate wasn't fazed in the least. She could defeat a bully with words or throw a punch if the situation called for it. But unexpected compassion was her undoing. She wasn't about to break down in front of Simon, however.

"I do feel married. Love doesn't go away just because someone dies."

Chapter 9

The door of the community center creaked open. "You guys want something to eat?" Robert's sudden appearance, the cheerful tone of his voice, shattered any sense of intimacy between Simon and Kate.

As he waved the doctor over, relief tugged at Simon. The relief stemmed from fear. That moment with Kate had been magic and it scared him. He'd gone out of his way to avoid real feelings with women. And how deeply involved could he actually become with Kate? Could he still hurt her by convincing Robert to sell?

Robert diverted Simon's attention again as he walked toward them, carrying a brown paper sack. "Got you deli sandwiches, kids. Chips, too."

Simon caught a flying can of Coke. "Thanks, Robert. I owe you."

"Don't worry about it. You'll be buying me meals one of these days. Katie, here's your turkey on rye."

"Thanks," she replied quietly, taking the sandwich.

"Got a lot done today, didn't we?" Robert sat down beside Kate and smiled. "I'm going to finish some paperwork, but then I'm gone. What are you doing tonight?" He tapped the side of her shoe with his own.

She opened a small bag of potato chips. "Just going to visit my dad. It's his birthday."

"Let me guess. Pie instead of cake."

"I'm way too predictable," Kate said and bit into a chip.

Robert grinned. "You? Never."

She unwrapped her sandwich but didn't take a bite. "Strawberry pie is one of the few things Dad's willing to talk about."

"Be glad he isn't longwinded. At least this way you'll have an early night after working so hard. Rest up for that potluck at your church tomorrow."

Watching them converse so easily, Simon felt like an outsider once more. He turned to Kate. "You go to church?" This was unexpected, even from a woman who constantly threw him off balance. Not one person Simon knew went to church potlucks.

"Yeah, Kate's a real puritan," Robert cut in. "Don't offer her a cigarette, drugs, or a beer. She won't touch the stuff."

An impressive side-eye from Kate. "Thanks, Robert, for being my spokesman."

"Don't be mad. Religion isn't for me, but who am I to judge if you enjoy living by a set of archaic rules?"

Simon remained quiet. He wasn't about to enter this philosophical minefield but watching them butt heads was fun.

She put her uneaten sandwich down. "Patronize all you want, Robert. Really, don't spare my feelings."

He pointed at her with a kosher pickle. "Dude, you can hold your own against anything I say, rule-sheep or not."

Rule-sheep? Simon started to laugh but quickly turned it into a cough. He had called a truce with Kate, and he didn't think she would appreciate further teasing since Robert was already mocking her enough for two people.

She slipped her food back into the bag. "The universe is governed by rules—or *laws*—if you will. People have named said laws after the scientists who discovered them. Pascal's law, Bradford's law, Birch's law . . ."

"Yeah, yeah. I got it." Robert moved his hand in a continuous circle. "Newton's laws of motion, laws of universal gravitation. You're just talking down to me now."

"*I'm* talking down?" Kate interrupted. "How ironic. Actually, my point is that if the universe can stoop to obey a rule or two, why can't you?"

Ding, ding, ding. Simon had to give that point to Religious Kate. He turned toward Robert, like a spectator at a tennis match. How would Mr. Johns Hopkins respond? Not with much, as it happened.

Robert chewed thoughtfully. "Whatever, Power Pack. I don't want anyone forcing me to act a certain way. Not even God."

"God doesn't use force. He allows you to choose." Kate exhaled and said nothing more. She ran her fingers through the grass until a ladybug climbed onto her thumb.

Simon watched Robert and Kate's body language— annoyed glances, stiff posture, legs moving out of touching range—and realized that a fissure could easily develop in their friendship.

He tamped down his emotions regarding Kate. She made him want more of the magic he'd felt earlier but maybe that was a weakness. An obstacle to prevent Simon from helping Ed Moyer get what he wanted. West used to say that relationships were transitory, while careers lasted a lifetime. West was usually right. Simon watched Kate drink her Gatorade, realizing once more how different they were. He didn't want to change his life and she deserved a hell of a lot better than him.

Simon's logical lawyer side suggested that he help the rift between Kate and Robert along, if necessary, to further a deal with Ed to buy the community center. Having driven by the old place the night before, Ed was now obsessed with it. Nothing else would do. The location was perfect, and the sheer size of the lot plus the limited means of the current owner were also ideal. Guilt filled Simon until he felt sort of unclean. Even with all the deals he'd finagled, all the adversaries he'd crushed over the years, guilt had never entered into the equation before. Why now? It wasn't the time to grow a conscience.

Carter Wright hadn't found anything on the market to catch Ed's eye, and playing Kate against Robert was the obvious answer. They'd upgrade to a nicer property in the suburbs for the clinic, and Ed would build his memorial to Randall. So, why was Simon hesitating, feeling sick at the thought?

If he could make this happen, the *Annus Mirabilis* trophy and title were guaranteed to remain with him for another year. His father would be appeased, West's legacy would remain intact. And destroying Carter's plans was an even sweeter bonus than the one Ed had promised.

Robert cast a rueful grin at Simon. He must think the tension over the subject of religion versus atheism had caused him to be this quiet. Not Simon's own twisted thoughts.

"I'm sorry, man. Didn't mean to freak you out."

"No. No, it's fine," Simon replied. He wasn't an atheist but he wasn't religious either. Not since the nuns at his private Catholic school had drilled catechisms into him, day after day. Mass, confession, altar boy: it all happened so long ago.

"I'll get on that paperwork." Robert stood up and stretched

before shaking Simon's hand. "You helped out a lot, dude. Thanks."

He stooped over and lightly kissed the top of Kate's head, saying, "Love you, babe. See you tomorrow.

"Bye, Robert," Kate murmured, watching her friend walk away. Face blushing, she turned back to Simon. "I'm sorry too. We have fundamental differences. He believes that God either doesn't exist or is entirely to blame for the world's suffering. He likes to bait me, and I'm dumb enough to fall for it. I apologize if we made you feel uncomfortable."

She was apologizing to him? The one who wanted to sell her Sistine Chapel? Simon felt his soul sink a little closer to hell.

"Don't worry about it, Kate. I wrangle with people for a living."

She picked up the trash from their meal. Simon followed her to the dumpster with the last of the garbage. He shot a wadded-up ball of paper into the dented metal box. "Where was *that* when I needed it earlier?"

Kate laughed. "Thanks again for the free labor. I hate to admit it, but lawyers might give doctors competition in the work department after all."

He wiped grass off his pant leg. "The secret is to appear useless in the beginning and then surpass everyone's expectations later on."

"That's the secret?"

"Works every time." As they walked to the parking lot, Simon noticed Kate fidgeting with her ring again. Did she regret telling him she was a widow? Was that why she seemed withdrawn?

After climbing onto her bike, Kate started the motor, letting it idle. "I better get home. It's almost six, and Dad's waiting for his party."

"Enjoy the pie."

"Thanks, Simon. See you later."

Before he could get into his Mercedes and follow Kate's Triumph out of the parking lot, a vintage Mustang drove in.

The redhead at the wheel lowered her window and smiled. "Well, well. I ought to come in on Mondays more often. What's your name?"

Simon introduced himself.

"You're volunteering? *Here?* This just keeps getting better and better." She removed her black oversized sunglasses. "I'm Nina Close."

He shook her hand. "The social worker with the wild sense of humor."

"My fame precedes me. Who told you, Robert or Kate?"

"Kate."

Nina grinned. "Then you heard the nice things. If it had been Robert, your opinion might have gone the other way."

"That's doubtful." Simon looked over the Mustang. "You probably get this a lot, but you have one sweet car."

"Ask me nice, and you can drive it sometime."

Nina parked the Mustang and walked toward the community center. Simon had to appreciate the fact that she knew how to move. Exuding confidence in her white tank top and black miniskirt, Nina reached the front door and smiled at him over her shoulder. She demonstrated that sixth sense some women have in knowing that men can't help but watch them.

Once she was inside the building, Simon turned to unlock his Mercedes, thinking over Nina's offer to test drive her Mustang. Why not accept? It would certainly sidetrack his thoughts from a lady doctor with mermaid eyes who was out of his league.

———— • ————

Kate unlocked her front door and stepped inside the little apartment. The celebration with her dad had left her feeling slightly depressed. Their family get-togethers didn't feel like family at all. He liked the book she had given him, and they ate some delicious pie. Yet after thirty minutes of nearly one-sided conversation, there was no reason for Kate to stay longer.

Her shoes made a thud on the floor when she kicked them off. She dropped her coat and purse on the kitchen table and made a cup of herbal tea. As she sipped it from a Kiss Me, I'm Irish mug, Kate realized that being alone was often easier than being with people.

She changed into a pair of flannel pajama bottoms and a Portland Timbers jersey. Then got into bed and put in her earbuds, choosing a playlist Mike had made for her. He loved rock, some country, but classical too. She turned the music up until the swelling notes overpowered every other sensation.

It took her a while to realize she was asleep. In her dream, Kate opened her eyes, reached out to turn off the lamp on the nightstand, and saw her dead mother sitting at the end of the bed.

Tess was wearing the fleecy robe Kate had given her one Christmas, and her brown hair was clean and glossy. She had always been such a beauty, soft and dainty with a wide mouth made for smiling. Black Irish, Kate's father had called her. His silvery-eyed Celt.

Her mother's cheeks were flushed, and she radiated warmth and affection. It was painful to experience that love, but

Kate felt it as fresh and strong as if she were still the young, awestruck girl she used to be. There was the haunting scent of Shalimar . . . It was impossible to think of Tess without her perfume coming to mind. The tall gold bottle with the blue-fanned stopper always sat on her dressing table next to a strand of pearls.

"I've missed you, my sweet, and look how grown up you are." Tess beamed. "You've made me so proud."

Kate touched her own cheek, amazed that she hadn't known she was weeping, amazed there were tears left to be shed.

"You were the best thing I ever did." Some of the light left her mother's face. "Sorry, angel. Didn't say that enough when I was alive, did I? I'll say it now, if you'll listen. Thank you for taking care of me, love. You tried so hard to help." She studied Kate, looking sad. "There's an ocean of unspoken sorrys and should-haves between us, isn't there?"

The lovely eyes grew dark with emotion. "That's what gives me pain—the things I did wrong by you during my life. I can't bear the thought of that."

Kate hid her face, wishing herself away while wanting to remain. She felt her mother's fingers gently stroke her hair and heard the whisper of an Irish lullaby.

"Shh, shh now, pet. You can't hold on to the anger and hurt forever. And you still feel responsible for me. Is that right? You needn't, Katie love. It's not your job anymore. I'm at peace now, and I want you to be happy."

In all Kate's childhood, she had never seen Tess like this. Serene, calm. Her mother's face was so dear and so unfamiliar. Silent tears coursed down Kate's face, and panic entered her heart. Time was running out.

Don't go. Don't leave me.

Kate reached out, and Tess squeezed her hand, smiling brightly.

"Be happy," she said, seconds before Kate woke up.

It had been years since she'd dreamed of her mother. All her progress, all the protective barriers she'd built between herself and her childhood, suddenly crumbled, leaving Kate newly wounded.

Truth will always win out. Isn't that what they say?

The truth was it didn't matter that Tess had broken her heart a thousand times. Kate would always love her desperately— always miss her profoundly, even though she had lived years longer without her mother than she'd ever spent with her.

Truth won but it hurt. Despite the tragedy and trauma, despite having met and married Mike Spencer, no one had ever loved Kate as much as the woman who nearly destroyed her.

Chapter 10

Rain pounded against the windshield as Simon drove through the Portland suburb of Dunthorpe. The jarring, slashing sound of water and wipers did nothing to ease his mind. It wasn't that he was apprehensive about going home. No more than usual anyway. Simon hadn't been over to see his parents since Christmas. Or maybe New Year's though the exact date didn't matter. Even if he had been the paragon of a dutiful son in the preceding months, it wouldn't change things now.

His slipup at work eclipsed all else, good or bad.

Simon remembered being afraid of his father in the past. Most of his early childhood, in fact. On his tenth birthday, he'd been sent to detention for talking during a test at school. Jack had come home from the office (something he rarely did during daylight hours) and asked Simon to join him in the study.

About as friendly as a firing squad, his father asked, "What's this I hear about you cheating during a test, Simon?"

"No, sir."

"Are you calling me a liar?"

"N-no, sir." Simon's mouth went dry and his lips stuck to his teeth. "I m-meant that I didn't cheat. On the t-test."

"Stop stammering this minute! I pay the administration of

your school handsomely. I should think they're capable of hiring teachers skilled enough to detect whether a ten-year-old cheats or not."

Simon had fisted his hands, feeling small and stupid. "I-I did talk to Alex, sir. He's the b-boy who sits across the aisle from me."

Jack checked his watch. "Why?"

"The kids at school pick on Alex."

"So?"

Simon wanted his father to understand, but the silence in the room made him even more nervous. "They took the p-pencils Alex brought from home and broke them."

"Why didn't the boy raise his hand and tell the teacher he needed one?"

"She was in a hurry and didn't see him raise his hand. I said he could have one of mine."

His father leaned down and looked him in the eye. "It's a relief to me that you aren't a cheater."

"Yes, sir."

Jack put a hand on Simon's shoulder. "But I want you to learn something from this. Education is the key to your future. You have to concentrate on that from now on and not let anyone distract you from your job. Alex's business is his own."

Simon felt confused. "Sir?"

"Being nice to an unfortunate boy won't win you anything in the long run, but outperforming the other children in your grade will. In order for you to be a credit to this family, you must excel."

Simon did what Jack said, hoping that his father would grow to like him. He had turned his shoulder and ignored Alex when his friend needed help. He'd worked harder than the other kids at school, his grades surpassing them all, even his older brother. West, the son his father never scolded. The popular kid, well-liked by both students and teachers, who made everything look easy.

It had been a short phase in Simon's life, those days when he had blindly followed Jack and tried so hard to please him. A few years of obeying without question at Catholic school and at home, yet never receiving the praise and attention he yearned for, tarnished the image Simon had of his father. At thirteen, he stopped obeying . . .

The rain beat even harder on his windshield, breaking through his memories. Simon drove to the crest of a hill and saw the roofline of a stone mansion through the gloom. It could have doubled as a golfing clubhouse or a reception center for an elaborate wedding. The grounds were beautifully maintained but lacked warmth or any indication that a real family lived there.

The teenage Simon couldn't get out of his parents' house quick enough, the lonely, enormous rooms stifling as a prison. He chose friends specifically to annoy Jack and became the family hellion. Simon rebelled whenever he could: staying out late, going to parties, playing soccer more than studying, yet he still graduated with a perfect grade point average at the top of his class.

The hellion part of his personality was only slightly less apparent now that he was an adult.

Simon pulled the Mercedes alongside a speaker box by the front gate and pushed the red button. "Hey Mom and Dad, it's me."

No answer. He waited a moment before punching the security code into the keypad. The gates buzzed and then slowly opened. Simon followed the long, tree-lined drive toward the house. He tapped the steering wheel with the palms of his hands. Hopefully he and Jack wouldn't have one of their infamous shouting matches today.

His brother West didn't shout. He never made stupid mistakes that embarrassed the family. No, West brought reflected glory to their parents through his charmed life in Dubai. Simon wasn't jealous. He loved his brother, but it was sometimes hard to identify with someone that perfect.

Simon parked near the enormous detached garage and followed the breezeway to the back door of the main house, using his key to enter. He found his parents eating breakfast in the dining room. A fire popped softly in the hearth.

Jack tossed his napkin down on the table. "Why haven't you called? Let me guess . . . *phone problems.* Since Friday, I believe?"

Simon kissed his mother on the cheek. "I didn't mean to worry you."

"It's okay, honey," she said, squeezing his hand. "We're just concerned."

"Concerned?" Jack interrupted the exchange. "Your mother has been beside herself! You might have considered her feelings at the very least."

Just like that, Simon felt like the stupid ten-year-old in his father's study. "I'm sorry, Mom."

The skin on Jack's face grew flushed. "Sorry doesn't alter a thing in my book. You drink too much, we all know that. But why would you do it and then go back to the office? You've finally achieved equity partnership at the firm. Don't you want your colleagues' respect?"

Simon chose not to match his father in volume. It would

only make his mother upset. He took off his coat and hung it over a chair. "I don't know why I went back, Dad. I can't explain the things I said at that deposition. Insane clients, job stress, burnout, who knows?"

"Suck it up, son. You want to be the best? Pay the damn dues." His father walked over to the fireplace. He turned his back toward Simon and watched the flames. "You were always coddled too much in my opinion."

Simon sat down at the table. "The 'dues,' as you call them, never end."

"What you've done at the firm is a spit in the ocean if you intend to have a career like mine. Or your brother's."

Simon crossed his ankles, counting to ten in his head. *Keep calm. Stay cool.* "News flash. I'm not you or West, Dad."

"Weston doesn't have problems like this. He knows what's expected and does it."

That was the real problem. Simon wasn't West. Every argument they had spiraled down to this fact. "It would be nice to have a father who doesn't compare me to my siblings. But you don't care what I think or feel. You never have."

"Sweetheart, of course we do," his mother interjected.

"Don't interrupt his pity party, Cecily. He's enjoying himself."

Simon rose to his feet and said, "This whole argument is unnecessary. I'll be back at the firm in a couple of weeks. They need me, or at least the money I make for them."

Jack left the room without speaking another word. For a moment, Simon watched the doorway before turning to his mother. "Sorry to ruin your breakfast, mom. I know you don't like it when we fight."

"It wasn't the worst one I've seen." She got up from the

table and went to Simon.

In her late fifties, Cecily Phillips was still a beautiful woman with thick, dark hair and bone structure that only got better with age. Simon looked like his mother while West resembled Jack.

"I love you, Mom. I'll get things worked out, don't worry."

"I know you will, and your dad does, too." Cecily put her arm around Simon. Her eyes seemed more troubled than before. "Will going back to the firm make you happy in the long run?"

"I've never wanted to do anything else." Simon gave her a hug. He didn't like to cause Cecily stress. "Don't worry."

They walked through a sunroom filled with white, overstuffed furniture and a conservatory where miniature orange and lemon trees grew. The flagstone floors formed a herringbone pattern, lit from a series of skylights above. Simon hadn't thought of these rooms as opulent before, but they looked that way to him now. Almost shockingly so.

Cecily squeezed his shoulder. "Honey, if this is all about the job, then forget it. Lawyers change firms. They do it all the time. Worse comes to worst you can go somewhere else, and your dad will get over it eventually."

Simon recognized the comfortable warmth that had sustained him so often as a child. Through the periods of chaos in his life, Cecily had always been the calm in the storm. "Don't worry, Mom. I'm fine. I like where I work. It's in my DNA."

<hr />

It was a relief to return to his own house, the showdown with his father finally over and done. Simon opened the French doors that led from his study to a large formal garden and walked outside. He sat on a teak bench and looked at the view of the green and gold valley below.

A new bottle of scotch sat with various other containers of alcohol in the cabinet back in his study. It called to him, offering relief from family issues and all the other demons in his head. Simon had drunk himself to sleep the night before. A total of six times over the last month, in fact. Jack had said that he drank too much and everyone knew it.

To hell with his father and his judgments.

Simon didn't answer the call of the damned scotch, even though his hands shook and his head ached. He closed the French doors and decided to go for a hike in the Hoyt Arboretum. An uncharacteristic choice, but it was something to do when he had nothing to do but drink himself into another stupor.

One of the major selling points of his West Hills home had been its proximity to Washington Park, but he had never really taken advantage of that fact. The vast parklands looked primeval and wild. Birds sang and a light breeze stirred the branches of the fir trees high above as he followed an incline to the trailhead.

An hour into his expedition, a brief, intense rain shower fell, and although he heard the soft beat of raindrops hitting needles and branches, he remained relatively dry under a giant redwood. The occasional drop of water permeated his shelter and tapped his arm, like a light, friendly touch. Waiting for the cloudburst to pass, Simon had time to think. His surroundings inspired a sense of awe, even wonder, though he lived close by and could have visited at any time over the years.

Strange, how in this peaceful place he didn't carry around the nagging desire for more that usually drove him. What some called ambition, felt like a sickness. It was an ache inside his bones. But not here. Simon walked the trail back toward his car slowly, in spite of the weather, savoring his new appreciation of solitude.

A man stumbled onto the path from an adjoining trail. His eyes were bloodshot, and his shorts were dirty. He didn't look like some of the homeless who frequented the wildest parts of the arboretum, just intoxicated and confused.

"Can you tell me how to get to Fairview Boulevard?" the man asked, gesturing with a half-empty bottle of Bud. "I got separated from my friends."

Simon pointed in the right direction. "Over that way."

"Thanks."

As the stranger passed him, Simon was tempted to reach for his beer. It smelled stale, flat, but he wanted it anyway. Such an urge seemed so desperate that Simon felt ashamed. Ashamed and thirsty.

Chapter 11

The bubbling surf rippled around Kate's knees. It gently pulled the hem of her batik sarong back toward the Indian Ocean as the tide receded once more. Hot sunshine made her muscles loose and relaxed, and her mind hummed along without a care, or even a single cohesive thought. The island pulsed with life, the colors shockingly vibrant, as if they dared you not to notice them. Kate smiled and sipped icy mango nectar as Stevie Wonder sang a love song in her ear.

Unwelcome sounds intruded upon her daydream. Honking cars, Spike making copies, a baby crying. Beth's laughter.

"Where did you go today?" she asked, tapping Kate's earbud. "Ooh, the Seychelles Islands. Kind of far away for a lunch break. I can't even make it to the diner and back."

Refusing to open her eyes, Kate willed herself back to paradise. If she ignored the voice, maybe Beth would go away. At least for the next seven minutes.

"Is Robinson Crusoe there with you?" Beth asked.

Kate gave up and surrendered to her friend's persistence. "No," she muttered, pulling out her earbuds and pushing the stop button on her tropical playlist. "I was looking for sea turtles, actually."

"I'd have gone with the hunky explorer instead."

Kate finished her can of fruit juice. "You're a mood killer, you know that? I still had time on my break."

Laughing, Beth took a bite of a cookie. The ones Kate had hidden behind a bunch of folders. "Look! I found your Mint Milanos."

"I'll have to think of a better place next time."

"Use some ingenuity," Beth replied. "I'm part bloodhound when it comes to Pepperidge Farms."

Kate visited the restroom to brush her teeth. She rinsed the juice can out before dropping it into a recycling bin next to Robert's desk. As usual, her lunch hour consisted of two diverse elements: a quick, uninspired sandwich and a vicarious, cerebral vacation courtesy of Google. So far this month, she'd visited Hawaii, Ibiza, and Crete.

Checking over her scheduled appointments, Kate saw that she was booked solid, one patient after another. Ear infections, croup, flu, etc. She glanced over a medical chart and heard little Ella whining softly in the exam room. Kate put an encouraging smile on her face and opened the door.

"Hi," the young mother said. "Sorry I had to call you so late the other night, waking you up and everything. I was just so worried about Ella's fever."

Kate rubbed some gel sanitizer over her hands. "Don't give it another thought, Marie. That's what I'm here for."

"You're always so nice about it, but I feel guilty disturbing you. I never dreamed you'd come to my house to check on her."

"It wasn't a problem." Kate smiled, warming the chest piece of her stethoscope before resting it on the baby's skin. "I didn't want you to wake the rest of your kids to go to the ER, and they're too young for you to leave them alone."

Marie shook her head. "It's still too much to ask. Doctors don't make house calls anymore."

"Some do." Kate listened to Ella's heartbeat and then checked her eyes. "I want to help, Marie. It's only been a few months since you lost Paul, and I know the first year is the hardest. You call when you need me, and I'll be there."

"Thanks. That means a lot," Marie said, swallowing rapidly.

Touching Ella's round cheek, Kate said, "You sound better than you did, sweetheart, but let's look at those ears. We don't want Ella hurting."

Hours later, after her final appointment, Kate threw a pair of disposable gloves into the garbage can and washed her hands. A familiar male voice bantered with Robert in the office.

Well, well . . . the lawyer was back.

She'd assumed he was a three-day community-service type but it had been nearly two weeks and Simon showed no sign of stopping. As she drew closer to the office, Kate heard him describing a wooden shelving system, until Robert interrupted him, sounding as excited as a kid opening his birthday presents.

"Dude, you're awesome! It's going to be so cool to have all that storage space available. We're finally going to get ourselves organized around here."

Kate couldn't help gagging a little. She had kept the clinic organized for years on her own, and they had done just fine without any fancy shelving. But a few words from Simon and Robert was over the moon. Looking around the office, Kate saw that the entire Hayden-Grace staff had assembled: Beth, Tanya, Charlene, and Nina.

"Get in here, Power Pack," Robert called. "Simon's building cabinets for us."

"That would be really helpful," Nina purred softly, her tiny diamond nose ring glittering. "Do I get a one-on-one consultation for my office? I may have some special needs."

Simon took a pencil from behind his ear and wrote something down in a notebook. "Tell me what you want, and I'll get to work on it."

Nina's eyes gleamed like Simon was a bonbon and she had a sweet tooth. His jaw was covered with dark stubble. It made him seem disreputable somehow, as did his tousled hair and the old jeans and black T-shirt that molded themselves to his body.

Charlene raised her hand, and Simon nodded in her direction.

"I've always wanted a bigger space. Could we knock out the north wall in my office? I'd have twice the room, and I think my patients would appreciate that."

"Let me check it out and see if it's structurally feasible." Simon wrote in his notebook again.

"Y'all sing karaoke?" Tanya asked.

Kate turned toward the nurse. Tanya never talked to new people. Patients, maybe. Because it was unavoidable. Unfamiliar guys of her age group? Never.

"I don't think I've ever tried it," Simon replied.

Tanya shrugged. "You can come with us sometime if you want."

"Thanks."

Kate was about to break up the lovefest when Robert asked Simon when he could start building.

"Day after tomorrow? I need to go to the lumberyard and the hardware store to see what materials they have available, and we'll have to get the design elements worked out."

"You're a stud. Keep me informed." Robert zipped up his

hemp hoodie and adjusted the straps of his yellow man-clogs. His messenger bag went on next and he looked ready to go.

"Sorry." Simon moved aside so Kate could get to her desk. "I didn't see you standing there."

"It's okay. Don't let me interrupt."

"You can sit in my chair," Robert said to Simon. "I'm taking Beth over to pick up her boys."

Beth sighed. "Yeah, the van's in the shop again. My mechanic and I have to stop meeting like this. People will talk." She lifted her heavily loaded purse. "You'd think I could get some kind of workout from hauling this thing around. I'll probably end up looking like Quasimodo."

Kate sat down. It felt good to get off her feet. "You could take some of the stuff out or change arms from time to time."

"I need everything in here! I have to plan for any disaster with my kids, and I can't switch sides. I've used my left shoulder since I was fourteen."

"I'm just saying." Kate grinned. "There are options."

"Dude, are we going?" Robert asked Beth, tapping his watch.

"We are. See you guys at seven. Do you want me to bring that warm spinach dip, Kate?"

"Absolutely. It's the birthday girl's favorite."

Robert hustled to the front doors and held one open for Beth. She grinned as she passed him. "Can I drive?"

"Not in this life," he replied, following her toward the parking lot.

Simon closed his notebook. "Are we sure they're not already married?"

"Nope," Nina answered. "You've heard the expression twice shy? Well, multiply that times twenty and it might fit those two. They have some serious issues about the M-word."

"Oh, it'll all work out in the end," Charlene said, ever the romantic. "Robert and Beth are destined to be together. They just don't know it yet." She pulled out the top drawer of Kate's desk. "Any chocolate in here by chance?"

"Sure." Kate swiveled her chair to the side. "Help yourself."

Charlene smiled like the Cheshire cat. "I'll have the one with the coconut."

Nina was next. "Uh-huh. There you are," she said, picking out a peanut butter cup and tossing a caramel candy bar to Tanya. "Thanks, Katie-face."

Kate hated that nickname with the blistering heat of a thousand suns, but Nina used it anyway.

"No problem," she muttered. "Does that take care of you ladies for today?"

"I think it does," Nina answered, following Charlene and Tanya out of the office. She paused at the door to gaze in Simon's direction. "You're coming to the party, right?"

His face went blank. "What party?"

"It's my birthday!" Tanya shouted from the lobby. "You're invited."

Kate sat back, thinking that Simon must have performed a voodoo rite on the people around her. Charlene was happy, Tanya was talking, and stranger yet, Nina was being fairly nice.

It had to be voodoo—or some mind-altering virus.

Nina whispered a breathy goodbye to Simon before leaving.

He seemed oblivious to her departure and leaned closer to Kate's chair. "What's this 'Katie' thing? Do people really call you that?"

She frowned down at the papers in her hand. "Don't even think about calling me Katie. No one will ever find your body if you do."

Simon tapped the pencil on his knee. "It might be worth it, though. To see your eyes flash and your face turn a rainbow of colors, like a mood ring from the seventies. Angry smoke escaping from your ears."

"Open casket or closed, Simon. It's up to you."

He laughed, continuing to tap the pencil. Even though they were alone in the office, Kate couldn't bring herself to meet his eye. It wasn't fair that he looked so good without trying. Those jeans weren't fair. His shoulders weren't fair. That smile especially was not fair.

Disgusted with herself, Kate decided to check on her schedule for the next day. She liked to know in advance who she was seeing. Simon leaned back in Robert's chair, and it creaked loudly. He sat up again, springs squeaking. "Why doesn't Robert replace this thing?"

Kate couldn't respond. His voice wasn't fair, either.

"How long has he had it?" Simon persisted. "Did the chair come with the building?"

"I have no idea," Kate said, finally looking up.

Simon was eye candy all right. She moved her focus to Spike. The copier never made her blush.

Getting up from the squeaking chair, Simon asked, "Would you rather not talk?"

That was it exactly. Not talking would be great. They had shared an incredible moment, when Simon had seen her necklace and guessed about Mike's death. Since then, things had been awkward and Kate didn't know why.

She closed her schedule and lied like a rug. "I'm just

worried about the party for Tanya. You know, hostess jitters."

"Completely understand," he replied, smooth as silk. "I can take a raincheck and give you one less guest to worry about."

She paused, wondering if he was manipulating her or being polite. Sometimes it was hard to tell. Kate chose to err on the side of good manners. There would be plenty of people at the party. Enough that Kate wouldn't have to talk to him at all.

"Please join us, Simon."

"Are you sure? I don't want to impose."

"No imposition at all." Kate wrote down her address and handed him the piece of paper. "It's easy to find."

* * *

Simon arrived at her home at seven fifteen and cursed the necessity of having to park in the busy Nob Hill location. He had circled her street for ten minutes trying to find an open spot. The best he could come up with was three blocks away. Simon juggled the takeout bags in his arms as he opened the gate that led into her front yard.

He felt ravenous, which was a damn sight better than the nausea he'd been experiencing since giving up alcohol. His so-called sobriety was really more of a break than a permanent change, just to see if he could go without for a while. Would he have a drink tonight at the party if it was offered? Everybody served booze, right?

Simon glanced down at the paper in his hand and checked the address. This was it, all right. He followed the path around the big Victorian and took a set of brick steps to the basement apartment. Small, clear lights hung around Kate's doorway, and clusters of brightly colored balloons glowed on each side. He rang the bell and Kate opened the door.

"Wow!" she said, motioning toward the assortment of bags and boxes. "What do you have there, Simon?"

He lifted the arm with the red and white containers first. "I remembered seeing a collection of fortunes on Tanya's desk. I figured she must like Chinese." Then he showed her the pizza boxes. "She also collects menus from Italian restaurants."

"Very observant. Come in."

She led him into her kitchen, and Simon talked as he unloaded the bags. "I eat out a lot. I'm known at the firm as a takeout savant."

Kate opened the Chinese food. "This smells amazing! I was worried everyone would be bored tonight. I tend to cook the same things over and over."

Simon inhaled the aroma of ginger and garlic. "Chicken and pork stir fry, steamed dumplings, fried rice." He threw the empty bags into Kate's trash can and paused to look at her. "The pizza is pepperoni and sausage with extra cheese. I hope that's okay. I thought you could keep the leftovers for later if I brought too much."

She handed him a serving platter. "Leftovers are doubtful. You underestimate our ability to eat. Tanya will love all of it."

It took several platters to accommodate all the food. They set them on the dining table alongside the other potluck contributions. There were bottles of soda and sparkling water, but no alcohol. None. Not even wine.

In an odd way, it made Simon relax. He wasn't going off the wagon tonight, then. Yet his body wanted to get smashed. Perhaps the intensity of that urge was what scared him enough to stay sober.

He looked around Kate's home. The kitchen was a narrow galley style that connected to a small dining room. He guessed the space had probably served as a pantry at one time, before the home was divided into apartments. All the other guests had arrived before him and were already seated. Several boisterous discussions were going on at once.

Simon greeted Tanya, Robert, and Beth. They talked with him for a while and then went to get food. A line had formed around the dining table, so Simon waited in the living room. The walls were painted gray and the crown molding was crisp white. A fire crackled cheerfully in a red brick fireplace, and Dvorak played in the background.

An oil painting caught his eye. It hung in a small alcove, and he could only see one corner of it. He stepped through the arched doorway into the nearly hidden space.

Alone with the artwork, Simon studied it closely. The landscape portrayed the wild, uncultivated English countryside, veiled in shadowy, subdued light. It was a beautiful, atmospheric rendering, but it lacked any hint of sentimentality, emitting instead a stark, explicit realism. Like something done by the Hudson River School artists but without so much romance.

I've been to lots of museums, but I've never seen this before.

The scrawled signature at the bottom of the canvas was too convoluted to read.

Simon turned to see if the room had any other treasures to offer. His breath caught when he saw the portrait behind him. Blue-green eyes gazed into his, innocent and trusting. Kate must have been around six or seven when she sat for it. She wore a charcoal-gray dress with a black velvet collar and matching sash. Her right hand held a teddy bear, each fingernail a perfect oval. Kate's hair was long, with loose curls over her shoulders, the flaxen color gleaming against the dark backdrop.

Stepping back, he analyzed the composition. It was a remarkable piece of work. Every element of the picture faded away, receding into nothingness, except for the child. The creamy skin, soft pink lips, and vivid eyes seemed so real he expected her to move. Almost like a tribute to the Dutch painters of the seventeenth century, this one reminded him of Vermeer.

The artist was inspired, love and affection in every stroke. Simon leaned close to see if he recognized the signature. It was the same unintelligible script as before. He suddenly felt self-conscious and turned around to find Kate standing in the archway, a plate of brownies in her hands.

Simon cleared his throat. "I hope it's okay that I came in here."

"Sure." She glanced back toward the dining room. "Your food's a big hit. You should get your share before it's gone."

Simon didn't want to eat. He was fascinated by the paintings. "These are remarkable, Kate. I don't think I've seen their equal in a private home, except for the gallery at my parents' house. They're really into art." Watching her face, Simon saw he'd hit a nerve. "Did you know the painter?"

Kate seemed to look everywhere but at the painting. "It was my mother. I guess you could say she was into art, too." She hesitated before taking a step into the alcove. "Tess was gifted, and I'm proud of her work, but it's not always easy for me to be around. I keep it in here, for days when I feel like remembering."

"I'm sorry," Simon replied, moving toward the doorway. "I didn't mean to open old wounds."

She grew preoccupied with the plate in her hands. "Some

wounds don't heal, no matter how old they are." Her voice was neutral, betraying nothing. "And please don't feel bad about complimenting Tess. She was remarkably talented and deserves recognition."

"Your dad lives in Portland, right?"

"Yes. He's a professor at Reed."

Kate offered him a brownie and he took the one on top. "Is it okay to talk about parents, or is it taboo, like politics and religion?"

A smile lit her face. "As a topic of conversation parents are usually acceptable. We wouldn't be here without them, after all."

Simon laughed. "No, we wouldn't. And we can't trade them in. There's no warranty."

They left through the archway together. Her shoulder brushed his. "I'm sure they feel the same way about us sometimes."

"Not in your case, Kate. Mine, however, desperately want an upgrade." He took a bite of the brownie and flavor exploded over his taste buds. "Damn. These are good."

"Pete's recipe. He adds a little coffee to the batter, to bring out the chocolate flavor."

"It works." Simon noticed the single gold heart that swung from Kate's bracelet. It was a simple piece of jewelry, and he could see that the surface of the charm was dented and scratched.

"What happened to your heart?"

Kate looked perplexed. "Pardon?"

"The heart on your bracelet. It looks damaged."

She rubbed a finger across the charm. "It has been over the years."

"I know of a good jewelry repair shop. My mother uses them. I could get the number for you."

"No," she replied, shaking her head. "I like it this way."

Her answer was classic Kate. She always seemed to have a different view of the world. But really, was there a woman alive who preferred beat up bling?

"You want it to look that way? Can you tell me why?"

Pretending to karate-chop him, Kate said, "I could, Simon, but then I'd have to kill you."

Amused skepticism must have shown on his face. "You know what this means, Kate? I have to hear the story behind that charm."

She gave the plate of brownies to Beth and brushed crumbs off her hands. "It's a long, involved tale. So tedious that it's only shared in short installments to spare the listener undue hardship."

"Like Scheherazade."

"Are you saying I'll face execution if I bore you?"

He grinned. He'd forgotten how fun it was to talk with her. They hadn't spoken a lot lately. "I don't think I'll be bored, Kate."

"Trust me. You would." The gong in her grandfather clock chimed. "Oh, listen to that. Saved by the bell!"

"Come on. I want the story, Spencer."

"I don't know you well enough." She turned toward the dining room, mumbling about the food running low.

Simon followed her down the hall to the kitchen. "So if we get to know each other better, you'll tell me about it."

"Perhaps."

"I'll hold you to that."

"Simon!" Nina entered the kitchen, her face glowing with

laughter. "Where have you been? Come sit by me."

* * *

Robert hugged Kate at the door. "You did it, Power Pack. Great party."

It had been surprisingly great. She wasn't sure why and decided not to examine the light, happy feeling in her heart too closely.

Kate gave Robert the balloons to take home for Beth's kids. "The company made the night a success."

"I think the hostess had something to do with it, too."

"Love you, Kate," Beth called from outside, dangling a set of keys. "Hurry, Robert, or I'll start the Subaru without you."

"No, you won't. The Subie is sacred, woman."

Kate laughed as Robert dashed after Beth. "He can run if he has to," she murmured and closed the door.

Turning, Kate saw Simon dump a stack of used paper plates into the garbage can in the kitchen.

"Stop that! You're a guest."

He washed his hands at the sink. "I want to help. Thanks for letting me crash the party."

She had originally planned not to talk with him tonight and hoped to lose herself among the other guests. But it hadn't worked out that way. The lawyer looked domesticated and cute as he straightened the dishtowel that hung on her oven door.

"You had a valid invitation, Simon. There was no crashing involved."

"Regardless of how I ended up here, I'm glad I came." He tilted his head toward the living room. "You've got quite a collection of books. Do you mind if I take a closer look?"

"Go right ahead."

Kate loaded the dishwasher with platters and utensils while Simon snooped. He was watching the goldfish swim around her fish tank when she joined him. Kate pointed to an orange and white one.

"That's Atticus."

His mouth only twitched a little but his eyes smiled. "You have a fish named Atticus?"

"Yep. Don Quixote's over there dreaming by his windmill." She sprinkled a few flakes of food on the surface of the water. "The little guy hiding under the sea grass is Lord Byron. He's mad, bad, and always jumping out of the tank."

"Atticus, Don Quixote, and Lord Byron . . ."

Kate turned on the tiny light. "Hemingway died yesterday and I had to flush him."

"Sad. The bell tolled. I'm a big fan of Mr. Hemingway." Simon squatted down near a stack of records and flipped through them.

She liked that he was familiar with literature. "You come from a family of readers, don't you?"

"Not so much my dad," he replied, taking out an Eagles album. "But my mom loves books."

Kate thought of her own mother and it felt like a cold shadow over an otherwise sunny day. "Mine only cared for one."

He stood up. "Really? Which was her favorite?"

"*The Great Gatsby.*"

Nina walked in without ringing the bell and Kate hoped that her disappointment at seeing her coworker didn't show. Nina was best tolerated in small doses and those had been filled earlier in the evening.

"Hey, guys. Nice party, Katie-face." She smiled at Simon.

"I took Tanya home. You ready to go?"

"Go?" He looked puzzled.

Nina rolled her eyes. "You said you'd take me out for coffee. We're going to talk about fixing my office. Any of this sounding familiar?"

Simon slipped his hands into his pockets. "Yeah. But isn't it a little late tonight?"

"My favorite coffeehouse is open until one." Nina raised an eyebrow. "You don't have a curfew, do you, Simon?"

He smiled. "Haven't had one of those in years."

She linked her arm with his. "Then let's go."

"Okay." Simon turned to Kate. "Come with us. I don't think I've ever been to an actual coffeehouse."

"No," Kate said, crossing her arms. "Thanks for the invitation, but I'm too tired."

It was only half a lie. Kate was worn out after a long day. But mostly she didn't feel comfortable being a third wheel when it was so obvious that Nina wanted Simon all to herself.

"No more stalling, handsome." Nina pulled him across the living room.

He looked back, resisting the pressure on his arm. "Thanks again, Kate. I really enjoyed the evening."

Simon winked at her, a private signal of appreciation. Kate winked back just as smoothly. I like you, he seemed to say. Like you too, she silently answered.

━━━ • ━━━

They walked the three blocks to the Mercedes. As Nina inspected all the bells and whistles the machine had to offer, Simon thought of the photograph he'd seen at Kate's house. She looked so happy, posing with her husband at a lake, a forest of evergreens in the background. Mike had fair hair, a tough build, and brown eyes that looked like they wouldn't miss much. His arm was around Kate's waist and she was laughing.

Simon had distanced himself from her for nearly two weeks. Until today, when they were sitting in the office at the community center and she blushed while looking at Spike instead of him. He lapsed then on the whole distancing idea.

His competition with Carter Wright was on hold. Ed Moyer was having marital problems, which he unloaded in minute detail during a phone call. Including the most intimate problems in their love life. Simon preferred the way things used to be, when Ed merely used the toilet in the background.

Nothing was going to happen on the tech school project for at least another two weeks. Not until after the Moyers received intensive marriage counseling at a luxury resort in the southwest. Meanwhile, Robert had given Simon a list of remodeling projects that extended into the horizon and he felt ridiculous working his butt off building shelves that would likely be demolished if Ed bought the property. It was a hell of a situation, being caught between two different men with conflicting goals. Since Leonard was still not taking Simon's calls, he had little to occupy him other than playing handyman in Nonprofitville.

He put his career problems away, in that dark corner at the back of his mind. Nina was still admiring the Mercedes. They drove to the coffeehouse and Simon ordered a Kona blend. Nina was beautiful and confident, but he still couldn't seem to generate any interest in what she was saying. The place was crowded and noisy. So different from the peace of Kate's house. Those few hours with her had been an escape from all the things that caused him stress. Thinking of Kate made him remember the picture of her with Mike.

How did he die?

Nina liked to talk, and Simon was sure he could get her to tell him the whole story, but he didn't ask. His moral compass might be skewed, but even he knew that something as important as the loss of a spouse deserved better than idle gossip.

The key to learning the truth would be gaining Kate's trust. Enough that she would want to open up her heart.

Chapter 12

Daisy

She sat under a desk with her legs stretched out, her too-big secondhand shoes twitching rhythmically in the darkness. The only light in the small cubicle radiated from the red ON switch of the stereo built into the wall above.

Dim as her vantage point was, Daisy could still see the gum, stale gum at that. It was stuck to the wood near her head, long since chewed and hidden by its original owner. And the brown particleboard from the seventies?

Did fake wood furniture ever fool anyone?

Under that desk, in the library listening room, her mind and spirit soared far, far away. A large pair of headphones covered her ears, and she was filled to overflowing with the strains of Tchaikovsky. Daisy pictured an enchanted winter forest with glittering snowflakes weaving delicate patterns through the air. The snowflakes transformed into ballerinas, their sure, swift feet fluttering like hummingbird wings across the frozen wilderness.

She imagined the light tap-tapping of the dancers' pointe shoes on the ice. It wasn't the first time she had obsessed over Balanchine's Nutcracker. The production had haunted her mind for weeks. In fact, it had changed her forever.

Daisy had watched it on a DVD in the media booth. Wonderstruck, she played the disc over and over. Deep inside, she had known it wasn't a dream since living people performed the parts in the ballet.

Until that moment, it was as if she had been denied color her entire life—and then suddenly she was free to experience it. Daisy realized she had been wrong in her belief that life was dark and harsh, that wonderful things only existed in the realm of books. By watching the ballet, she had seen with her very own eyes that there was more. Not everyone lived her ugly existence.

This gave Daisy a reason to hope. It meant she could change things. Her new understanding shattered the boundaries that had hemmed her in. She was consumed by the desire to learn and experience, and the night hours were too short for Daisy to do all she wished. Time flew by until her eyelids grew too heavy for her to concentrate, and only then would she put her studies away, stumbling to the couch by the window to steal a few hours of sleep.

Her shoulders were sore from leaning against the desk, so she removed the headphones and stretched. She climbed out from her hiding place, took a parcel from her school bag, and switched on a flashlight. After unwrapping the parcel, she found herself holding a book. The burgundy leather shone under the title's gold lettering.

"*Les Misérables*," Daisy cried out with joy. "Jean Valjean, Fantine, Inspector Javert . . ."

"Bit posh, ain't it?" Eponine Thenardier asked, strolling into the little room. Her dark eyes gleamed. "A prize such as that could fetch a tidy sum."

Daisy smiled at the French waif who snuck out of her

imagination now and then. "Maybe so, but I'd as soon sell the stars as part with a single page. My father lives in America and he sent it to me. It's my birthday. I'm thirteen."

"At least your papa remembered," Eponine pointed out.

Daisy sobered, losing some of her pleasure in the gift. "Only because he feels guilty about forgetting me the rest of the year."

Eponine sighed. "I was not always like this, you know."

"Yes." Daisy understood. Life could change in an instant.

"My parents once cared for me."

"Mine too."

"Peas in a pod, aren't we?" Eponine looked at the headphones sitting on the desk. Poked one with her finger.

Daisy hugged her birthday book. "Most children don't realize they have anything to lose."

"You do understand . . ."

"It's nice to have you around, Eponine." Tears welled in Daisy's eyes. "I'm quite lonely sometimes."

Dark curls bobbed merrily as Eponine cocked her head. "Like I said, two peas in a pod."

Daisy smiled and reached into her bag for the roll she had saved from her school lunch. It was enough to stop the rumbling in her stomach. As Daisy chewed, she imagined having a feast of roast chicken, potatoes, and carrots. A crumb from the roll fell to the floor.

Daisy couldn't leave a mess. No matter what.

Invisible pins and needles pricked her feet when she reached out to pick up the crumb. Daisy shook her legs, hokey-pokey fashion. She put the headphones away in their cubbyhole and slid the Tchaikovsky recording into the return slot before taking her usual place on the couch in the reading room.

Snuggling into herself, Daisy opened *Les Misérables.* It whispered a welcome as she turned the stiff pages, the shiny trim dazzling her eyes.

Chapter 13

Southwest Portland

A flick of the light switch, and Simon could see everything in the basement storage room. Memories he had not thought of in years came flooding back. Brushing dust from the scarred worktable, he felt the past pull at his heart. The table was sturdy, having sustained the vision, sweat, and elbow grease of several generations of carpenters. It reminded him of the only hero he had ever known personally.

Thoughts of his grandfather were always bittersweet. Simon didn't like to focus on why it hurt or how he'd let him down. Joseph Phillips had been a simple man. Woodwork was his passion, carpentry his trade.

A large man in life—more comfortable outdoors than working inside—he had looked so still, so much smaller, at the funeral home. Simon had stood at the front of the chapel by the casket while the rest of his family wept together in the pews. His own tears were too private and raw to be shed in public. Restraining himself took a great deal of effort, but Simon held it together. He counted the nicks in his grandfather's square capable hands. Each scar told a story brought about by years of making beautiful, useful things from pieces of wood. Usually, wood that no one else wanted.

As a boy, when Simon stayed with Joseph in Seaside, he had felt like one of those scraps of pine or oak that his grandfather transformed. He had never worked so hard as he did then, apprenticing to a master carpenter over several summers. Simon knew that Joseph had loved him and tried to teach him what he could about the important things in life. When he died, Joseph left his shop, and its contents, to one person.

Not West, not Jack, but to Simon, his former apprentice.

He had fallen out of touch with Joseph during those last years before his death. He wasn't there to say goodbye at the end, but that wasn't what haunted Simon.

The last time he had looked into the depths of his grandfather's eyes, the same Phillips blue he and his father had inherited. Simon had felt *less*—less of a man, less of a person—because all of his wheeling and dealing hadn't achieved as much as he had hoped. A simple man like Joseph wasn't fooled by outward appearances. He knew if something was worth the time and effort and when it wasn't. Would his granddad consider him a success now? The house, the car, the bank account? Or would he be disappointed?

Simon thought he knew the answer. It hurt.

Joseph's treasures were precisely organized throughout the storage room. The carving sets and mallets. The collection of knobs, pulls, and hinges from the early 1800s. Simon opened the black and orange cases that held the power tools: the drills, saws, and pneumatic nail guns. He took a chisel from a gray metal toolbox. The weight of the chisel felt good in his hand, as though it had been made for him to hold.

Simon lifted a block plane from its hiding place at the bottom of a cardboard box. "Woodworking tests your mettle and your muscle," Joseph often told him. Shaking his head at the memory, Simon knew his mettle and muscle hadn't been tested in years.

He had been awkward with the plane as a boy, but with practice, he'd learned to use the tool. Simon also learned to love the man who had instructed him with such patience and kindness. Remembering Joseph made his eyes burn and his heart feel too large for the area it occupied.

It made him want the oblivion at the bottom of a bottle. Would he always fight those desires? Was it something he'd have to live with for the rest of his life? Simon opened more boxes and hated himself for being weak.

***

It grew humid in the early afternoon, like a rainstorm threatened to fall at any moment. Simon closed the kitchen window and sat down on a stool at the island. He had spent hours sorting through the woodworking tools and just finished carrying the ones he would need that day out to the garage. His hands shook a little as he read the newspaper. Low-grade nausea had settled in his gut. Not enough so he would actually vomit, just a queasy feeling that made Simon wish he could empty his stomach.

The front door opened and the alarm system pinged that "I'm deactivated" sound. His housekeeper came into the kitchen with an armful of groceries. She jumped a little when she saw Simon and dropped a sack of pears. Her face looked horrified as the fruit bounced all over the floor. Simon took the bags from her and put them on the counter. After they picked up the pears, he asked if there were any other groceries in her car.

"No, Mr. Phillips. I got it all in one trip."

"Good," Simon replied, smiling. "How are you?"

"Fine. Everything is fine."

They put the provisions away, and Simon had his first real conversation with his housekeeper. He could not remember ever making the effort before. Mrs. Lee had worked for him for six years, and he was only now thinking of her as a person. Once Simon got her talking, she could not be stopped. She was a grandmother of three who lived with her daughter in Beaverton. A newly sworn in American citizen. A maker of pear tarts and a gardening enthusiast.

Mrs. Lee tidied up the kitchen and prepared the recycling to go out to the garage. Wine and beer bottles jangled against each other in the bin. Simon turned to the next page in the newspaper. What must she think? Probably that he was a drunk. An overwhelming need to get away struck him. Where could he go? The mall? A restaurant?

Simon needed to burn off whatever was eating him up inside, so he took his old Nikes out of the closet and put on a crimson pair of Harvard sweats and a T-shirt. A quick run sounded like hell on earth—everything did right then. He'd exercised off and on through the years, but no serious training since his college soccer days. His cardiovascular endurance most likely needed improvement.

How difficult could it be? Once an athlete, always an athlete, right?

The run started smoothly as he coasted down the hill and leveled off at an easy pace. By the thirty-minute mark, Simon began to think he was an idiot. A masochistic idiot who kicked his own ass. He shifted his shoulders to relieve the stitch in his side. His knee and foot ached from old sports-related injuries.

"Damn," Simon muttered, catching sight of the huge hill separating him from his house.

If he collapsed on the side of the road, who could he call to come get him? Certainly not any of his lawyer friends. They were billing hours, working for clients. Kate? Robert? Nina surely would drive over, but Mrs. Lee was a better bet. He couldn't make that call, however. His cell phone was still sitting on the kitchen table.

Simon distracted his brain from the throbbing signals being sent to it from his blistered heels and aching lungs. He concentrated on the work he planned to do at the clinic and nearly wept tears of gratitude when the end of his driveway came into view.

After being nauseated all morning, Simon finally threw up. All over the ivy growing alongside his mailbox. He wiped his mouth and lay down on the cement pad next to the garage. His lungs labored to get enough oxygen.

Was he having a heart attack? A stroke? Both at the same time?

A squirrel scolded him from a giant pine. "Shut the hell up," he yelled back. "Who asked your opinion?"

The squirrel sounded a bit like Carter Wright. Only more intelligent. Ten minutes passed and Simon came to the conclusion that he wasn't actually going to die. With his heart rate almost back to normal, he staggered inside and headed to the shower. He tossed his crappy running shoes into the garbage can in his bathroom.

It would be a cold day in hell before Simon put the damn things on again.

He eyed the Nikes while brushing his teeth the next morning. The shoes smelled bad. The insides showed bloodstains from his blisters. They belonged in a hazardous waste container.

Simon left the bathroom and congratulated himself on casting the whole idea of running aside. Then he ate a croissant with jam, plus some bacon and eggs. The contents of the newspaper barely registered, but a vitamin advertisement did. The male model had silver hair and swung a tennis racket. He wasn't young, but everything about the guy looked strong and happy. A lot stronger and happier than Simon.

There was some cursing involved when he pulled the Nikes out of the garbage and put them on. The following thirty-minute run hurt just as bad, if not worse, as the day before. His muscles knew what to expect this time, so they began screaming after the first few steps. When Simon finally approached the last hill, he stopped and heaved eggs, bacon, and croissant with jam into a rhododendron bush.

This had to be the end. Death by puking up a lung. Simon hoped that Kate would go with the closed casket after all. Nobody needed a viewing today.

But he wasn't that lucky. His body didn't give out. It hauled itself up the last incline with a dogged determination and Simon collapsed on the driveway. He loved the cool paving bricks so much. They understood his pain like no other. The Carter Wright squirrel taunted him just like yesterday. Gasping for air, Simon flipped off the squirrel/lawyer, plotting its death by electrocution, drowning, wolf attack . . .

Yet miraculously Simon arose, tossed the old pair of shoes into the garbage again, showered, dressed, and drove to the community center.

The delivery truck had arrived from the lumberyard on schedule, and Simon helped unload the supplies. When this was done, he went to the west wing of the building and propped a back door open with an aluminum trashcan. Then he set up a portable table saw on the lawn in order to keep most of the noise and mess outside.

The cloakroom was a walk-in affair with a rectangular island in the center. It had large windows that provided plenty of light and tall ceilings. The bones were good but most of the beadboard and crown molding were broken or missing. By six thirty that night, he had removed the old wood, cleaned the space, and started measuring and cutting new trim.

Simon heard a crowd of people passing the cloakroom. He looked into the hall briefly, recognizing a few faces here and there. Gollum, the lady with the scary pointed fingernails, and the passive-aggressive couple. Simon knew that Pete taught the Stress Management class several times a week and didn't care which one his students attended. It wasn't Simon's usual night, but he decided to drop in and get it over with.

Once his equipment was put away, he borrowed a set of keys from Tanya and quickly locked up the cloakroom. Simon skidded through the auditorium doors just as Pete was closing them. The older man looked him up and down, taking in the dusty jeans and work shirt.

"What a difference a couple of weeks make," Pete said with a wry smile.

"At least on the outside." Simon almost smiled back, but he was too tired.

"Did you remember to bring the syllabus I gave you?"

"I'm afraid I left it at home."

Pete gave him a neatly stapled stack of papers. "Here. This is the last one I have. Did you do your homework?"

"Yes. Exercise. Better diet. Hobby."

The older man looked surprised. "In that case, you earned yourself an A-plus-plus."

Simon sat in the back as Pete picked up the microphone and welcomed the class. The sound system made a loud, whiny noise, drowning out a few of his words. The group in the auditorium tittered, and Simon looked down at the syllabus. Subject of the week? Faith.

Whoa, whoa, whoa. What?

Simon squirmed in his seat. He would leave if the class was centered on theology. But Pete just shared a few medical studies, statistics, and so on. His main point being, people lived longer and had less stress if they believed in something. For their new assignment, Pete asked them to eat one superfood at each meal and to sit quietly for ten minutes while performing deep cleansing breaths. He also wanted the class to find something to believe in. Whether it was God, public service, Greenpeace, or something else, they were free to choose. Pete wouldn't follow up. It was a private experiment.

"Think about it. You can have faith in your grandkids or your spouse. In the garden you planted in your backyard. You can even have faith that the sun's going to rise tomorrow morning. You can do it," Pete said, smiling for the audience. "I believe in you."

Bemused, Simon followed the crowd like a lemming as they exited the auditorium and headed for the front doors. "You must be working too hard," Beth said as he walked past her.

Her voice brought him to his senses. "No. Just preoccupied. Why are you here so late?"

"I'm waiting to lock up."

"Can't Pete do it so you can go home?"

Beth held a fountain drink in her hand. The soda and ice sloshed around inside the cup as she swung it toward him. "What is this thing called home, Simon? I think I've heard of it somewhere but I can't be sure."

Simon liked Beth. She reminded him of his favorite sister Liza. "Long day?"

"It's all right. I don't mind staying. Pete has a hard time with the security system. Technology isn't his friend."

Pete laughed on his way out. "Putting a crazy old man like me in charge is just asking for trouble."

"Yeah, crazy like a fox maybe," Beth replied, taking a sip of her drink.

She set the alarm and Simon walked with her to the infamous minivan that had cost so much to repair. "Are you working tomorrow?"

"I'm here at ten. I think Robert and Kate are coming in before me. Later, gator."

"Later."

Simon waved goodbye as Beth drove away and got into the Mercedes. He didn't turn the radio on during the drive home. Nothing in his fridge looked good for dinner, which was fine since sleep was the only thing Simon wanted. Stripping off his shirt, he headed for the stairs. The trip up to the master bedroom reminded his muscles that running and physical labor took a painful toll. As Jack said, a price had to be paid. Removing his shoes and jeans hurt. Walking to the bed hurt. Simon's body hit the mattress with a thud and he was out for the count.

Chapter 14

A fire truck sat in front of the community center when he arrived the next morning. He walked across the lobby to the office. Empty. The acrid smell of wet, charred wood permeated the air, and a few firemen stood talking at the end of the hall.

This couldn't be good.

As he passed the first exam room, Simon saw Kate sitting on the little white table inside. Robert held her hand over a plastic bowl, rinsing it with a bottled solution. A line of white, puffy blisters crossed her palm and fingers.

"What happened?" Simon asked.

Robert turned around and Kate looked up.

"Hey, Simon," Robert said. "We had a small fire. It's lucky Kate arrived when she did, or things might have been a lot worse."

"Doesn't seem so lucky," Simon replied, looking closer at her palm. "Are you going to be okay?"

Robert must have hit an especially sore spot because she winced. "Yeah. I acted without thinking. The stuff in the trashcan by the back door was burning, and I tried to move it outside."

Simon leaned his hip against the exam table. "Ouch. It's an

aluminum can."

"I know. I panicked. I should have remembered the extinguisher."

A fireman stepped in and cleared his throat. "It's one hundred percent out, Robert. Looks like the fire in the trashcan smoldered for hours because the wood shavings were damp. We think it had just started on the wall when your fearless doctor here arrived."

"Brainless doctor, more like," Kate muttered.

"No one is saying that, ma'am. I would advise you to leave the dangerous stuff to the trained professionals next time."

"Believe me, I will. Although I hope there isn't a next time."

"You and me both," the fireman said. "It appears that a window was left open in that room by the west doors. Some kids probably climbed in wanting to make mischief or a homeless person needed a place to sleep. You really should invest in a better alarm system. The one you have is ancient and only detects if the doors are locked. It doesn't monitor windows." He stepped back a pace, like he was needed somewhere else. "Check things over and report any theft, Robert."

"Will do, Jed." Robert shook his hand.

"We're heading out now. Take care, Kate." Jed grinned and reached into the pocket of his coat. "The boys on the truck wanted me to give you this."

He handed her a junior firefighter sticker. Kate stuck it on her shirt. "Thanks. I'll be explaining this to the kids all day."

"We could use you as a volunteer down at the station."

Robert laughed. "Babe, you could wear the cool suit and the helmet."

"No thanks," Kate said. "Tell your 'boys' that their job is too hard for me."

A thought had occurred to Simon as they were talking. He'd opened a window yesterday when the afternoon sun had slanted into the cloakroom, making working conditions uncomfortable. Even though Simon remembered locking the cloakroom door before going to class, he'd forgotten to close the window.

Simon castigated himself for being careless and said, "I did it. I left the window open."

"What?" Robert asked, stopping mid-sentence. "What did you say?"

"I left it open. I was in a hurry and forgot." He shook his head in disbelief. "I'll cover all the repairs."

Robert looked dismayed. "We have insurance. You don't have to pay."

Simon felt sick. Kate got hurt because of him. "Your hand—"

"Is my fault, not yours. I was stupid." The brusque reply came with a shrug. "Intruders are sometimes a problem after hours. Even when the windows are closed and the alarm is set."

Robert taped a light dressing over Kate's palm. "You need some meds?"

"I'll take ibuprofen later."

"Okay. Well, drink a bottle of water and rest for a minute. I'm going to tour the place and make sure it's all right. And just so you know, Power Pack, this is just a building. Totally replaceable. You, however, are not."

Kate wiped her mouth after taking a drink. "Thanks, Robert. Love you too."

Simon stepped out into the hall with him. What little

conscience he possessed refused to be let off the hook so easily. "I can't believe I forgot. I'm so sorry."

Robert patted his shoulder. "Relax, man. It's going to be okay."

But Simon couldn't relax. The "keep cool, keep calm" mantra he usually used wasn't working. He went back to the exam room and gave Kate his arm as she slid off the table. "How can I help you? I need to do something to fix this."

She cracked a smile. "I'll be fine once my hand stops pulsing."

Normally, if there was a problem, Simon threw a little money at it and the problem went away. He didn't like to feel regret or obligation.

Simon also didn't like knowing Kate was in physical pain. "You need ibuprofen?"

"Really, I'm fine. I've got aspirin in my purse."

"But you wanted the other one."

"We ran out last night. Beth is bringing more in when she comes to work." Kate moved her fingers gingerly. "See, Simon? All good. Stop stressing."

He walked with her to the office, already planning which store to hit up for the ibuprofen. "I'll be back in a few minutes."

Once Kate had hustled through the entire community center, her tense muscles began to calm down. Everything checked out and all the equipment was accounted for. The only discernable damage was limited to the immediate area where the fire took place. Standing in the lobby, she was looking over the incident report when a stranger walked through the front doors. He wore designer golf clothes and sunglasses.

"Simon Phillips?" the stranger asked.

His voice set Kate's teeth on edge. It sounded rich and entitled. "I'm afraid he isn't here."

"When will he be back?"

She glanced at the clock on the wall. "Soon, I would think. Simon told me he wouldn't be gone long."

"Then I'll wait." The golfer scrutinized her over his sunglasses. His eyes rested on her junior firefighter sticker. "Are you the woman I talked to when I called his house?"

Kate felt her cheeks burn. Simon had a woman living with him? Why did the thought make her feel so let down? Sad, even. It really wasn't any of her business.

"Umm. No, sir. It wasn't me."

"A few months ago, late one Sunday night?"

Hugging a clipboard to her chest, Kate said firmly, "I'm a doctor here. Simon's a volunteer. We aren't socially involved."

"I see."

He walked the lobby a few times before Simon arrived.

"Dad?"

His father scanned their surroundings, lips pursed. "I had to witness this fiasco for myself."

Simon handed several large bottles of Advil to Kate. "The pharmacy on the corner isn't open yet, so I had to go to the grocery store."

"Thanks." She balanced the bottles on the clipboard and surreptitiously compared the two men. They didn't particularly look alike, except for the blue eyes. And the essence of privilege and money. Education, good taste.

Perhaps Simon had grown on Kate, improved a little since working at the community center. He didn't seem nearly as haughty and uptight as the guy in the golf shirt. Simon did seem ticked off, though. He wasn't happy at all to see Daddy.

"This is my father, Jack. Dad? Meet Dr. Kate Spencer."

"Are you sure you aren't the girl?" Jack asked. Then his face took on a knowing expression. "No, you're not. I think her name was Hillary or Heidi—"

"*Dad*," Simon interrupted. "Let's go across the hall. We can talk over there."

Kate hurried into the office, grateful to escape. She sat at her desk and unwrapped the safety seal on the Advil. After popping a few pills into her mouth, Kate realized her plastic water bottle was empty and went to get a drink at the fountain. She took a few sips of water as Simon and Jack argued just around the corner.

"Why don't you get off my back?" Simon sounded furious.

"I don't want you to ruin your life!"

"Leonard is fine with the situation. I'm doing exactly what he wants me to do."

Jack cursed and the sound echoed down the hall. "This should never have happened. You'll lose everything."

Simon walked away from his father and then came back. His voice was soft enough that Kate had to strain to hear him but his tone cut like a blade. "I'm working at this dump temporarily. If I could change the situation, I would, but I can't. Until I'm done here, don't come by again."

"Is your eye twitching?"

"Shut up, Dad."

Kate dashed back to the office before Jack and Simon found her eavesdropping. She looked over the vacation request forms on her desk and began working on the next month's schedule. It was hard to concentrate. Something cold and heavy had settled into the center of her chest.

Rapid footsteps crossed the lobby and a door slammed. Kate assumed it was Simon's father leaving the building. A blob of ink dribbled from her pen onto the schedule. She opened a drawer and took out some Wite-Out, dabbing it along the mark she had made.

As Kate rewrote the schedule, Simon entered the office.

"Is Robert around?" he asked. His face was hard as stone. Bitter. Remote. Like he hadn't been concerned about her just a half hour ago, enough to check two stores for the Advil.

Kate swallowed. Simon could be a little scary while in this mood. "He's meeting with an insurance agent. I think they're outside."

"Can I leave him a note?"

"Sure. Use that message pad over there."

Simon sat down in Robert's squeaky chair and began to write. Seeing him this upset did something to Kate. In the past, during those first five times they met, she wouldn't have cared but that had changed. Enough for her to speak up and feel sympathetic despite the fact that he had insulted the community center and called her masterpiece a dump.

"Simon? Why don't you give yourself a break?"

"What?" He looked up, frowning.

"Go for a walk or something. Call a friend."

Simon seemed to think about this idea and then rejected it. "I like to finish things once I start them."

She gave him a half smile. "Sometimes it isn't necessary. I heard you arguing with your Dad."

Simon dropped the pen. "My father drives me freaking insane. I lose it when I'm around him." He ran his hand through his hair and rose from the desk. "I'm sorry. Would you tell Robert I'll talk to him later?"

"I will," Kate agreed as Simon left the office.

The front door opened and closed. The strange feeling in the center of her chest grew even colder and heavier than before.

Chapter 15

Simon wanted fresh air. On the heels of his father's visit, the smoky smell that permeated the building was more than he could take. He sat down in one of the chairs on the porch and closed his eyes, opening them again at the sound of a child's voice.

The boy was probably six. He was skinny and had brown hair and matching eyes. Wearing a T-shirt with the letters L-E-O on the front, he talked noisily about airplanes as he walked down the sidewalk with his mother. She pushed a pudgy toddler in a stroller and appeared to be making her way to the community center. The three of them passed Simon and went inside. A few minutes later, the airplane expert returned. He leaned into the door, using his entire body weight to shove it open, and kicked the doorstopper into place.

"It's really stinky in there," the kid said, fanning the air with his hand.

"It really is," Simon agreed.

"I hate that smell. I feel like barfing."

"Me too. Is your name Leo?" Simon asked, pointing at his shirt.

The boy's eyes grew wide. "How did you know?"

"L-E-O."

Leo traced the letters. "I forget sometimes that it says my name. My dad told me Leo is like Lego minus the G. Do you like Legos?"

Simon couldn't help smiling. Leo was missing a front tooth, and he had an endearing lisp. "Yeah, they're cool. You can build almost anything with a set of Legos."

Leo nodded. "I know! My dad's really good at building."

"Are you here for an appointment?"

"No. Mom has to fill out some papers for Dr. Kate on account of we moved." The boy frowned and whispered, "We lost our house."

Simon had forgotten how honest children were. It made him sad that this little kid knew his home was gone and that the loss was something to be whispered about. Ashamed of. "I'm so sorry, Leo."

His thin shoulders slumped. "I loved that house. It had a big tree in the backyard with a tire swing."

Something warm welled up inside Simon. That was what mattered to him? A tree with a tire swing? It didn't take much to make Leo happy. "Do you like where you live now?"

"No." He shook his head. "My mom's scared all the time, and we have to stay in the apartment 'cause a lady was stabbed on the roof last year."

Simon's mouth opened but he had no idea what to say.

"It's my job to take care of Flynn." Leo stood up straight, looking proud. "He's barely two."

"Flynn's lucky to have you as a brother."

"He doesn't remember Dad, but I do."

This boy's life made Simon want to weep. His own problems seemed so petty and small by comparison. "Are you going to school?"

"Yeah, but I missed the bus. We're taking Flynn to daycare."

Simon heard a woman's voice in the lobby. "Leo? Leo?" she called.

The kid ran inside and brought Flynn back with him, pulling the two-year-old along by the arm. The toddler held a toy six-shooter against his chest. "Here's my brother," Leo announced. "He's got my old cowboy gun. It's kind of heavy, but he's strong."

"Your brother's cute."

Smiling briefly at Simon, Flynn and Leo's mother pushed the stroller through the doorway. The toddler climbed in, revolver and all. Kate followed them to the steps, waving. They walked a few feet, and Leo looked back at Simon. "Bye!"

He watched the little group until they were out of sight.

Kate watched them too. "Do you remember Axel?" she asked. "The guy you met your first night here? That's his family. Jenny, Leo, and Flynn."

As Kate passed Simon on her way inside, he touched her arm and she stopped. "The addict from the parking lot? The one who wanted you to give him drugs?"

"The same." Kate stood there, saying nothing more, and then she left him on the porch.

Simon leaned forward and processed what he'd just learned. What a crappy world it was, that innocent children had to pay for their messed-up parents' mistakes. Could anything really help those kids? Did people even care enough to try?

Then he noticed the cheerful petunias, the patchwork pillows on the porch chairs, and imagined how the community center might appear to Leo. It must be a constant in his changing world. A place he could depend on, where Kate, Robert, and

Beth would always take care of him and Flynn. Simon began to see Hayden-Grace with new eyes. Maybe all those kids Kate cared for were Leos and Flynns.

He felt like a heartless, money-grubbing villain with his plans to help Ed buy the property. What if the people in this area needed the community center here rather than at a better building in the suburbs? Would they fall through the cracks without it?

A woman laughed nearby, the sound low and sultry.

"I don't think a penny would cover your thoughts. They seem a bit too deep." Nina smiled down at him. "I said hello to you three times. No response."

"I didn't hear you."

"Obviously." She scooted past him and sat in the other chair. "Why isn't Simon happy?"

How could he explain? Did she even care? "Well, let's see. I left a window open by mistake, someone got in, and started a fire. Kate burned her hand while trying to put it out. Then my father dropped by to suck all the peace and hope out of my life. After that, I realized that the world is a terrible place and I'm the worst sort of villain."

The sultry laugh again. "Not a good day, then." Nina smiled wickedly "Hey, it's only nine-thirty. Things could still get worse."

"You're not helping, Nina."

She ran her fingers along the back of his neck. "Why don't you meet me after work tonight? I can make you forget all this."

Simon knew she probably could, but he declined.

"All right." Nina kissed him on the cheek. "Another time."

Cleaning the floors and walls in the lobby and hall took the rest of Simon's day. He pulled off the fire-damaged drywall and used a wet/dry vac to clear away the debris. Simon didn't hurry home after the work was done. His clothes were dusty and reeked of smoke, so he brushed himself off before entering a deli and ordered a sub. He sat at a table by the jukebox. A novelty in his life, to be sure. The music was loud, and the people plugging it with quarters seemed to be enjoying themselves. After wolfing down the sub, Simon tossed the wrapper into a garbage can and drove home.

A hot pounding shower eased the knots in his back and shoulders. He put on an old pair of shorts and slipped his feet into some moccasins. The walls of the house felt tight. Simon couldn't seem to unwind. None of the books on the shelves appealed to him or the satellite music channels that played over the stereo wired throughout his home. The study was usually his refuge with its fireplace, leather club chairs, and charcoal-burgundy color scheme. A masculine room, but at the same time polished and civilized. He sat behind the imposing desk and thought about the work he had done at the community center. Anything to avoid the cabinet across the room with the whiskey and gin in it.

Simon couldn't say that he felt better without the booze. Not yet at any rate. The jitters and shaking hands had diminished as well as the nausea. All that was left of his withdrawal symptoms was a constant headache. It squeezed like a vise around his temples, and pain relievers only dulled the sensation.

Rubbing his head, Simon checked his voice mail. He smiled as he listened to Greg Jacobsen's message. Chatty, buddy to buddy stuff, concern for Simon's well-being. Their personalities were polar opposites but that never seemed to matter. Greg was the kindest person Simon knew. Devoted to his wife and kids, he was still nerdy and loveable regardless of his financial success in the tech world. They had been friends long before Greg purchased MSquared Software from Ed Moyer and Jim Mayes. Simon called Greg back and left a return message.

The next recorded voice wasn't nearly so nice. Ed boomed from Simon's cell phone, slamming into his aching head. "I'm in Arizona and it's hotter than hell. Not sure if the counseling is doing any good with the wife. She still won't touch me—"

Simon felt like plugging his ears or throwing his phone into some bleach.

Ed sniffled but then became more businesslike. "Work on that property owner for me. His name's Robert, right? I want him in my pocket when it's time to deal. I want him to be so done with the place that he can't sell it fast enough. Or maybe I'll call Carter. He's in L.A. this week, isn't he?"

Damn Ed. And damn Carter Wright. Simon hated them both.

Turning in his chair, he found himself facing his own reflection in the window. The dark night, combined with the brightly lit room, made the glass a perfect mirror. Simon stared at himself and thought of his grandfather Joseph. Of Jack. Of West.

It made him want a drink so badly that he left the study and got the damnable Nikes out of the garbage can upstairs. Even though he had just showered, even though he was tired and had already run that morning, Simon put the shoes on.

He set a punishing pace as he ran through the darkness. His muscles began to burn and Simon thought of a pair of blue-green mermaid eyes. A beautiful face. A woman with a good heart.

Why don't you give yourself a break?

Kate had asked him that question earlier. What did she mean? To stop pushing so hard? To quit comparing himself to others? To find out what made him happy? It had been a generous gesture considering what she overheard when he argued with his father.

In his whole life, Simon had never wanted to impress a woman before. They usually hung around for a while and then went somewhere else, without leaving much of an impact. Until he stumbled across Kate for the fifth time. She made him think and feel and question himself.

Simon wasn't sure if he liked this new development or resented it.

Chapter 16

One month later . . .

His life followed a simple routine. Simon woke up, put on a newish pair of running shoes, and drank some water. After that, he ran for six miles. The daily exercise had been a tough adjustment, but his endurance had increased. He drank more water, ate better, and went to sleep earlier.

No alcohol of any kind in forty-five days.

His sobriety had not gone unnoticed by Leonard and the other partners. They had donated a modest amount to the clinic with the promise of a larger donation the following year. Simon had been invited back to the firm on two occasions to give his recommendations concerning a few clients he knew well. Although he currently participated on a limited basis, it was rumored he would be returning soon to his regular schedule.

The two cloakrooms at the community center were finished. They matched the design of the building and looked both brand-new and decades old. The fire damage was also completely repaired. Simon had installed insulation, replaced drywall, painted endlessly, hung light fixtures, and tiled again.

While working at home on a clear afternoon in May, Simon swept the garage floor of wood shavings and contemplated his streak of good fortune.

His plan to maneuver Robert into selling the community center was totally unnecessary. All Simon had to do was tell him the truth. The cash needed to update the money pit *was* astronomical. The shingles they had used to patch the roof would not be enough to withstand the next winter. The entire thing leaked and needed to be replaced, and that alone would cost thousands of dollars. Add on the antiquated plumbing, the electrical wiring that wasn't up to code, and—ka-ching!—it totaled thousands upon thousands more.

Robert had blanched a pastier shade of white when he learned what was required to update the boiler. Double ka-ching. Not one lie had been told. Simon didn't even need to mention that there were better places up for sale. Robert decided on his own to look at real estate online.

It was hard to watch the strain this was putting on Kate. The center was still her Sistine Chapel while the director mostly saw dollar signs. Simon's conscience should feel clear but somehow it didn't. Perhaps because every evil plan he made concerning the community center seemed to be coming true. Only now he wasn't sure if he wanted to win. Having slaved over the old place for weeks, Simon no longer liked the idea of it being sold or torn down.

He had put zero effort into the *Annus Mirabilis* competition but it was leaning his way. Carter Wright was stuck in California overseeing a nightmare of a hostile takeover. The acquisition of the target company had started to founder because some of the shareholders were dragging their feet. All Carter's wining, dining, and promises hadn't come to fruition.

At the same time, Ed Moyer and his starter wife were getting a divorce. The marriage counseling at the luxury resort hadn't worked. Ed still wanted to buy the community center, but he wasn't in such a hurry since his 1990s prenup appeared to have loopholes the size of Montana.

May sunshine poured into the garage and Simon stopped sweeping to run his hand over one of the cabinets he'd made for the clinic. The burled walnut was stunning and smooth and had been reclaimed from a condemned home in Eastmoreland. That he had found the walnut stacked in a corner of a derelict basement was nothing short of astonishing.

And if Robert did sell the community center, Simon could always remove the cabinets before it was torn down and install them at the next place. Robert had chosen the shape—tall arched panels with stacked molding on top. Everyone else voted unanimously on a medium brown stain with a catalyzed lacquer for the finish.

Simon wore a tool belt slung low around his hips, his old work clothes layered with wood dust and sweat after sanding down the walnut. He picked up his broom and went back to sweeping. Only yesterday, Robert had teased him about his hair. Simon didn't brush it back neatly like before and had let it grow over his collar.

Kate seemed to like his new image. They had become friends and spent hours together every day. He knew Tough Kate. Stubborn Kate. Funny Kate . . . The labels weren't adequate anymore, though she was all of those. She was also a lunchtime book reader who pretended to take vacations on Google. A lover of vintage sweaters and Doc Martens. A woman of science who believed that faith could heal. A sap for commercials with animals and movies with happy endings. A doctor who made house calls in the middle of the night but refused to wear a traditional white coat . . .

Beth had scolded Kate for not having enough style, saying that a killer body was being wasted under her thrift store specials.

She of the drawstring knee-shorts and cargo pants had replied, "I want the families I work with to feel comfortable around me. Casual is better."

No jewelry, bare earlobes, a touch of makeup. Just her, clean and real. How could any guy look at someone else?

I can't seem to, anyway . . .

Simon picked up the pile of debris and threw it in a trashcan. He finished cleaning the garage and checked the time on his phone. Robert had arranged for everyone to attend a soccer match at Providence Park. Simon had played as a midfielder all through high school and for two years at Harvard. He'd always been a Timbers fan.

There was just enough time to shower, get dressed, and eat a fast bowl of cereal. Simon accomplished all this while listening to music on his sound system. Aerosmith, Led Zeppelin, CCR. His recent obsession with classic rock was all Robert's fault. Finally ready, he got into the Mercedes and arrived at the venue with twenty minutes to spare.

The atmosphere of the city was festive in the twilight, as if the glittering buildings and bridges had waited all day for that very moment. The tantalizing aroma of burgers and pizza from the concessions stands hung in the air. Simon heard Robert and Beth approaching before he saw them.

"It goes against all my principles to ride in a minivan," Robert said emphatically. "They're boring. Ugly. Conservative."

Beth grinned. "You know I have kids, Robert. We just drove them over to Stan's house. I need a minivan."

"Having met Stan, I now see why you're divorced. He's the male equivalent of a minivan."

"Come on." Beth flashed another smile at Robert. "Take the kid-mobile out for a spin. It'll ruin you for any other ride."

"No, it won't," Robert said. "It'll ruin my self-esteem."

Nina and Tanya voted against Beth in the van/no-van debate. Kate hung back, walking a little slower than the rest, listening but not commenting. She wore dark jeans, a Timbers jersey with a black cardigan, and sneakers. Seeing him before anyone else, Kate smiled at Simon. The mysterious half-smile that killed him every time.

Beth let out a little whoop. "There he is!"

Robert handed Simon a ticket to the game. "No executive suite for you, dude. General admission all the way."

"He'll be fine," Nina said, rubbing Simon's back.

He stepped out of her reach. She had a habit of touching him, like it was her right. Simon admitted to flirting mildly with Nina at the beginning, but that was as far as it went. No dates since going for coffee the one time. He'd told her a few weeks ago that he wanted to keep things platonic between them. She acted as if the conversation had never happened and continued to push boundaries. Simon didn't want to be rude, but he was afraid it might be necessary one day.

"Follow me, everybody!" Robert said. "Let's do this."

After entering Providence Park, they found Charlene and her husband Tom standing near the concessions area, eating burgers. Kate looked at their food wistfully.

"Can I get you something?" Simon asked above the general noise of the crowds around them.

"No. I'll eat later."

Kate found their aisle and saved the seat next to her for

Simon. They watched people enter the stadium as the match time approached. The Timbers Army was out in full force, wearing team jerseys, hats, and hoodies. Most carried flags with giant axes on them and green towels.

When it came time for the national anthem, the spectators and athletes sang it acapella, and so loudly that Simon felt like soundwaves were hitting his body. Kate grabbed his hand when the first goal was made with a dramatic scissor kick. Diehard fans stayed on their feet throughout the match, yelling and clapping.

Simon and Kate stood when it became too difficult to see the playing field. What else was there to do but let go and cheer with everybody else? He protected her when some college guys got too rowdy. She asked him to explain various defense formations. A wager of five bucks might have been made between them predicting the final score.

After the Timbers victory, people continued to celebrate, showing no immediate plans to leave the stadium. The whole experience was exhilarating. Simon had forgotten the thrill of watching this sport live. He had loved playing it. Lived for the training, the camaraderie of the team, the invincible feeling of kicking the ball and watching it sail past the goalie. But a concussion, a meniscus tear, and a foot fracture had put an end to that phase of his life. He watched the team captain sign a jersey for a little boy and experienced some of the kid's excitement.

He felt Kate stir beside him. "Where did you go just now, Simon? You seemed happy."

He looked down at her. "I'm just glad I came tonight. It's been great."

Simon turned when Nina tapped his shoulder. "Tanya and

I are going dancing. You want to come with?"

He looked at Kate, but she shook her head. "I'm kind of rhythm-proof."

"Me, too," Simon lied. "You don't want to get me anywhere near a dance floor."

"I'll just bet." Nina looked skeptical, but she followed Tanya toward the exit.

"Tell us all about it on Monday!" Beth called after their retreating figures.

"Remember when we used to dance the night away?" Tom asked Charlene.

She stood up, purse in hand. "Let's go home, sweetie, before you get any ideas that might result in hospitalization."

Beth turned to Robert and Kate. "Since the boys are with their dad would you mind if I stopped at the grocery store before taking you home?"

"Okay by me," Robert said. "I'm totally out of chicken pot pies and Mountain Dew."

Kate stifled a small yawn. Her eyes looked tired and a little bloodshot.

"I can drive you," Simon offered. "If you don't want to go shopping."

"Thanks," she murmured. "That would be good. It's been a long day."

Kate was quiet once they were alone in his car. She folded her arms, and the charm on her bracelet reflected the muted interior lights, revealing the rich luster of twenty-four-karat gold.

Simon glanced over and immediately turned on the heater. "You're cold. I just saw your hands shake."

Kate leaned toward an air vent. Her hair blew back off her

shoulders. "Thanks. The warm air feels good." She looked embarrassed when her stomach growled.

"Are you hungry?"

"Starving. I missed dinner."

Checking his rearview mirror, Simon changed lanes. "Let's get something to eat. I lost our bet on the soccer match, so I'll get the tab."

"You owe me five dollars. Not dinner."

"What sounds good? How about Dan and Louis Oyster Bar?"

Kate rallied at his suggestion, a light in her eye. "I haven't been there in years."

"We're fixing that right now."

Simon maneuvered the Mercedes through Old Town until they reached a parking lot near Ankeny Street. Simon hurried to open Kate's door. She got out of the warm car and shivered.

He draped his jacket around her shoulders. The sleeves were too long, so he rolled them up a few inches. "Better?"

"Yes. Thanks, Simon."

Kate was a force to be reckoned with in most circumstances, but right then she seemed fragile enough to shatter with the next gust of wind. "The cobblestones can be slippery around here," he said. "Hold on to me."

"I don't need any help. I'll manage."

She took two steps before her heel slid out from under her. Simon caught her around the waist as she fell backward.

"Oops," Kate said, laughing. "I guess I need you after all."

"Exactly what I've been saying."

He put her hand in the crook of his elbow. They entered the restaurant and inhaled the buttery, brothy smell of perfectly prepared seafood. A hostess seated them in a corner booth. The waiter arrived shortly after to take their order. Prawn cocktails and bowls of cioppino with warm, crusty rolls.

Kate dropped her spoon and Simon motioned to the waiter for another one. "Thanks," she said. "But you don't need to take care of me."

Kate's face went scarlet and she touched his hand. "Sorry. I've just got this hang-up about people doing nice things for me. That sounds weird, doesn't it?"

"No," Simon replied. "It sounds like you're accustomed to serving others. You don't ask for much personally and you don't open up. Except with Robert and Beth."

She took a bite of the cioppino. "This discussion all started because of a spoon?"

Simon drank some Coke. "No, that was an allegory. It led to deeper things, such as you being a lone wolf. Next I plan to use a salad fork to philosophize about the purpose of life."

Kate laughed. "Please don't. I worked a double shift at the hospital and my brain cells are not functioning right now."

"All right, we'll stay with spoons. But what's wrong with letting someone do things for you?"

"Independence is safer," Kate said, sobering. "Relying on others just leads to disappointment."

Simon leaned back against the soft padding of the booth. "And they say I'm cynical."

"You are. So much."

"But that's me. I can pull it off. It's part of my charm."

The dimple appeared in her cheek. "Charming cynicism?"

"I work with what I'm given." Simon paused, unsure if he had the courage to ask his next question. Then he just did it. "Would you take a risk if real happiness was a possibility?"

Kate ate more of her soup, a thoughtful expression in her

eyes. "Depends on the stakes." She folded a napkin absently and then crumpled it between her fingers. "I don't want to be hurt. Ever again. It's too hard."

That was a big admission for a very private person to make. Simon didn't want to scare Kate away, so he held her gaze for a beat and changed topics. "Do you feel better after eating?"

"Lots better."

He nudged the dessert menu toward her. "They have great sundaes here. You want to try one? We can split it if you're full."

"I think you know me too well."

Simon felt like he was beginning to know Kate. He winked. Winking was their secret language now. "I know that if you had triplets you'd name them Ice Cream, Hot Fudge, and Sprinkles."

She snorted softly. "Don't forget Pizza and Chinese."

They ordered two sundaes when the waiter returned. Simon watched him fill their water glasses before leaving. "So we've made progress tonight."

About to take a drink, Kate held the straw a few inches from her lips. "Really?"

"Would you say over the last month and a half that we've become friends?"

"Yes." Kate squinted at him but her dimple appeared again. Simon loved that dimple. "Why do I feel like you're setting me up, Lawyer Man?"

He tapped the heart charm on her bracelet. "Remember Tanya's party? You promised to tell me about that charm after we became friends."

"Oh no!" she said, catching on. "No, no, no. Not that again. You're like a pit bull."

"Come on, Spencer. You can't hold out on me now. I want

the full story about why you won't repair it."

The waiter brought their sundaes and Kate took a swipe of the whipped cream. "You should really let this go. It's dull enough to lay grown men under the table in a coma."

"I can handle dull." Then Simon's thoughts grew distracted as she had her first real bite of the sundae. He tore his gaze away from her mouth, drank some Coke, and said, "Hit me. Let's see what you got."

The mysterious half-smile from earlier in the evening returned. Like always, it killed him. He wondered if Kate knew this.

"Even for a lawyer, you're pushy, Simon."

"Yeah, yeah, so I'm told. Get on with it."

"You won't stop, will you?"

"I'm no quitter, Kate." Simon waved his hand, making it clear that the floor was hers.

She ate a huge bite of ice cream. "Brain freeze. I can't talk right now."

Simon wasn't fooled. "Don't think so. Try again."

"All right," Kate sighed with disgust. "You win." Her voice became monotone, as if she were reading the phone book. "Once upon a time, a boy named Matthew met a girl named Tess. My parents. Dad was a Rhodes scholar at Oxford—Mom an aspiring artist from Dublin visiting her uncle in England. They met and sparks flew. As they say, opposites attract. Unfortunately, they were a bit too opposite for it to last. They divorced when I was eight. I lived with my mother until she died and came to America afterward to be with my father. The bracelet is a sentimental keepsake. The. End."

Simon studied her, chin on fist. "So why don't you fix it?"

"Maybe someday I will." She cocked her head, expectantly.

"Bored yet?"

"Not even close. There are some pretty big holes in that story."

"Do you do this to your clients? I feel bad for them."

"No digressing, Doc." Simon held her gaze and waited. It worked in the courtroom, why not here? "How did your parents meet?"

She groaned, evidently giving up the fight. "Matthew went to my great-uncle's pub. Apparently back in the day all the young people did. Tess was the pub darling. She drew men like moths to a flame."

"Do you look like her?"

"I take after my dad. She had the kind of figure men look at in calendars."

Simon nodded. "What attracted Tess to him?"

Kate finished her sundae. "From what I gather, Matthew was sweet and awkward. He held back, whereas the others didn't. I guess she thought he was different. I know she admired his intelligence. People always assumed Tess didn't have much because of the way she looked."

"She didn't like attention?"

"Oh, she liked it all right. An old-fashioned party girl was Tess, but with a serious side as well." Kate swirled the straw around in her ice water obviously thinking of the past. "She loved painting and desperately wanted credibility in that regard. Lots of talent, but her gallery shows were always failures."

"Why?" Simon asked. He'd seen the woman's work. It was brilliant.

"The critics said that Tess was a good mimic of other painters but lacked her own vision." Kate took a deep breath and folded her arms. "What did they expect? My mother didn't have a clue as to who she was. How could she paint like she did?"

Simon watched Kate's expression change from anger to regret. "Was your father supportive of her career?"

She absently caressed the heart charm on the bracelet. "I think he was just amazed she had more to offer than her beauty. He was swept away. The ironic part is that the very things which fascinated them about each other in the beginning caused the split."

"How so?"

"Matthew was quiet, bookish, and steady. Tess loved that at first but hated it later. He didn't talk or laugh enough for her, and she felt lonely and overlooked."

"And your dad?" Simon fought against the urge to take Kate's hand. If he did, she might bolt for the door and not finish the story.

She folded and unfolded her napkin again. "Dad adored my mother's emotional nature initially, but it was exhausting to deal with. He grew distant and she developed a drinking problem. It ended up being her downfall."

Kate lifted her eyes to his. "The bracelet reminds me of my parents. A perfect shiny heart wouldn't fit them. That's all there is to tell." She asked the waiter for the check and opened her wallet. "As Pagliacci would say, '*La commedia é finita.*'"

He did reach for her hand now. A soft, light touch of appreciation. "Thank you."

"You're welcome," Kate said with a wry tone. "I can see you have more fortitude than most men. Usually, they're passed out snoring by now."

The restaurant seemed quiet and he looked around. It must have closed at some point during their conversation, and the staff was waiting for them to leave. He insisted on paying, but Kate whipped out her credit card and shoved it into the waiter's hand.

The firm set of her jaw told Simon it was better not to argue. "Next time I pay."

"You've got a deal. And you still owe me five dollars from our bet."

The waiter checked the line where Kate had written in a generous tip. "Enjoy your evening," he said, smiling. "Come again."

Chapter 17

Simon followed her out of the restaurant and offered his arm again.

"I've never shut down a place before," she said as they walked to the car. "I hope we didn't make them work overtime."

He opened her door. "I think your tip made the waiter feel better about it." He entered his side of the vehicle and started the motor, immediately turning on the heater.

"The food was amazing," Kate murmured, sinking into the soft leather. "I loved the cioppino."

Simon pulled the Mercedes into late-night traffic. An electric zing surged through his chest as he drove Kate home. He had pictured her there in his car before, but the reality exceeded fantasy.

"Dinner was awesome, Kate. Thank you."

"My pleasure." She looked around her. "The interior of this thing is nicer than my furniture at home. What are all these buttons for anyway?"

Simon briefly explained the functions of the fully loaded automobile. Then he connected her cell playlist with the Bluetooth on his stereo. "Let's see what you've got here."

Heavy metal filled the car. "Is this what you listen to when you're influencing and shaping young minds at the clinic?" But Kate was paying absolutely no attention to him as she fiddled with the bass and treble controls.

"Where has this stereo been all my life?" She beamed like a child.

"You like it?"

"Are you kidding? It's righteous."

"Righteous?"

"Yeah," she replied, changing from Metallica to Bruno Mars and bouncing a little to the beat.

Simon turned down the tunes until he could speak without shouting. "You have a lead finger with the volume button. Are you warm enough?"

"I'm hot. On fire, in fact." Kate adjusted the seat warmer from high to low and made a joke in a Monty Python voice about toasted buns.

Silly/Sleepy Kate had arrived. Simon liked her already. "Are you okay? You said you worked a double shift?"

"Sleep deprivation can make me a little goofy."

"More like tipsy, except that I know you don't drink."

"Nope," she said, yawning. "But I do slur words when I'm tired."

Simon parked the car and walked with Kate to her door. "Careful, Spencer. You almost missed the last step back there."

"'Almost' only counts in horseshoes and hand grenades."

Fumbling with her keys, Kate dropped them on the welcome mat. He picked them up, opened the door, and laid them on her palm. "Yours, I believe."

"Thanks. Want to come in for a while?"

On any other day, when she wasn't so sleepy, he would have jumped at the chance. "No. It's late." He surveyed her face, softly touching her cheek. "Everything look okay in your apartment?"

Kate glanced through the doorway. "I guess. Except for the wallpaper in the dining room. I don't like it very much."

"You get funny when you're sleepy."

She looked up at him, her body language relaxed. Simon tried to shake the thoughts running through his mind. "I'd better go."

After giving her a peck on the forehead, he turned toward the stairs. "What was that?" Kate asked, grabbing him by the hem of his T-shirt.

Simon paused. "It's me being noble. You can't know how out of character it is. Really, you can't."

Reckless Kate gave his shirt a gentle pull. "Who asked you to be noble?"

Inwardly, Simon cursed his new sense of honor. Why did it have to show up now? "Look, you haven't slept in almost thirty hours. You're exhausted."

Kate lifted her chin in that way of hers. "Oh, please. What's the real reason?"

"I don't want to do something you'll regret."

"Maybe I want to be kissed."

To hell with his honor. Simon moved in close. Kate wasn't acting like her usual tough, independent self. Instead, he saw a lonely woman who wanted company. Comfort. How long had it been since she'd been held or kissed? Would any man's touch be enough, or did Kate feel something for him?

He lowered his mouth to hers, gently showing her that she was desirable. Beautiful. Seductive. It was sweet and intense, and she whimpered softly. Kate slid her arms around him, melting up against his body. Simon moved his hands down her back, savoring the smell of her floral perfume, her warmth. Somehow, he had known it would be like this if they touched.

Then, against all his instincts, he pulled away. Simon caught sight of her wedding ring and felt a stab of jealousy for a dead man. Kate didn't seem sleepy anymore. She looked scared. "I'm sorry. I shouldn't have—"

Wide-eyed, she touched her kiss-swollen lips. "Stop. Don't apologize. Let's . . . let's just forget it happened."

Simon was freaked out too. "Right. Okay. If that's what you want."

Which was ridiculous. Who could forget a kiss that moved the earth?

Kate hesitated, as though she were waiting for him to take it back. To convince her that she was wrong. Then she went inside and closed the door. Simon could hear the deadbolt slide into place. He returned to his car in a dreamlike state and started the engine. The roadster purred softly, but Simon didn't put it into gear. He looked out of the window, registering little of the empty street.

Whatever idiotic fear had struck him earlier after kissing Kate had been destroyed by the disappoint of not doing it a second time. Why the hell did they have to forget? What was stopping him from walking back to Kate's apartment and taking her into his arms again? She'd waited before going inside, watching him with a question in her eyes. Her face had looked disappointed when he remained quiet.

Simon rested his head on the window. If he could think of a good reason to hold back, he'd drive away. That simple. Just put it into gear and add some gas.

There was Kate's history with an alcoholic mother. He sensed how deeply that addiction had affected her. As yet, Kate didn't know about Simon's drinking problem. It seemed to be under control, but who knew how long he'd stay the course? Would she really want to get involved with a drunk? No woman in her right mind would take such a risk.

And Kate would despise him again if she learned about Ed's interest in buying the community center. She'd think it was a repeat of the other time, years ago, when she and Robert had been forced out of their building because of Simon. When the police had taken her away at the protest.

Simon looked back at the Victorian home where Kate lived and made a decision that would be easier for them both. He revved the engine a few times, put his car into gear, and drove away.

———————— • ————————

Kate shut her front door and locked it. Stunned, she leaned against the wood paneling in the entryway until her knees stopped shaking. Her lips felt kissed even with Simon gone.

She pushed off the wall and did what she always did when stressed. Cleaned something. Tired as she was, Kate loaded the few dishes in her sink, scrubbed the counters, and sorted through the refrigerator, tossing anything past its due date into the garbage.

"Damn it," she muttered.

Caring for Simon had never been part of her plan. Kate had tried to stay away. The last month had been difficult, but she'd made a genuine effort to keep things light. Yet the friend-zone didn't seem to work with Simon. He was too good at making her wish they were more than friends.

She pulled out a stool at the counter and sat down. The ring Mike had given her, the one she hadn't taken off since their wedding day, felt cold against her skin. Even as she looked at it, Kate knew Mike would want her to be happy. Love another good man and move past the grief.

She listened to the old message on her cell phone, but it didn't offer the usual comfort. After wandering around the living room, Kate put on a record that she and Mike had slow danced to many times. The soulful melodies hit her hard and made her feel all kinds of emotions.

Was she forgetting her husband's face, the look in his eyes, those mannerisms that were his alone? Moving on would be like losing him again.

At least as a widow, her pain was a known commodity. Was Simon worthy of her trust? Kate wasn't sure, but she did know he could hurt her. *Better the misery you know than the one you don't* . . .

She kicked off her shoes and got a drink of water. The glass seemed solid and real in her hand, giving her the illusion of self-control. But Kate almost swore that she smelled Mike's cologne, sensed his presence there in the kitchen.

Don't use me as an excuse to hide, he seemed to say. *Being alone doesn't prove that you loved me. I know—we both know—you did. Take off the ring.*

Almost like she was watching someone else go through the motions, Kate tried to pull off the platinum band. It didn't budge over her knuckle. The realization of what she was doing made her sick. In three years, Kate had never even considered taking off the ring. It was inscribed with one word.

Forever.

That was what Kate had always intended. But now her view of a life of widowhood was shaken, and it was terrifying. She would be insane to take a chance on Simon. Crazy to surrender her heart to someone new.

Regardless of this, Kate did have feelings for him, even if she hid them behind friendship when they met at the community center. She went into her bedroom and sat for a long time in the darkness. The wedding band felt tight as she pushed it back from her knuckle. *Forever, forever, forever* . . .

What had Tess advised long ago? Her mother wasn't the best of examples, but her insights sometimes held true.

"It's all pain, darling," Tess had said. "Love is pain."

Chapter 18

Two weeks had passed since Simon kissed Kate. During that time, they had danced around each other in a wary routine: acting aloof, speaking little, smiling even less, and rarely being alone together.

Simon waited outside the bank of elevators in the tall glass box that housed his law firm. Casually clad in good jeans, a blue button-down shirt, and a leather moto jacket, he rode the elevator to the twentieth floor and hand-delivered a file to his secretary Linda. It was filled with testimonials and success stories from the Hayden-Grace Clinic and the Northwest Community Center. He had put the file together since the partners liked seeing their donation dollars at work among the citizens. Even if those dollars didn't come close to actually financing the myriad of problems Robert had to deal with.

After hearing that Simon had dropped by, Leonard pounced. "How are you feeling? You look fit! Healthy."

"Thanks," Simon replied, shaking his hand. "I run now. Hell of a thing. It just sort of happened one day, and I've kept at it."

"You what?"

"Run. You know, put on shoes, go outdoors, and don't come back before circling a few trails."

"Really?" Leonard puzzled over this information. "How did those stress management lectures go?"

"I sent you documentation last month."

"You did? I don't seem to recall."

Simon began to worry until he saw the smirk on Leonard's face. He put his hand on the old man's shoulder. "Funny. Ha. Ha. You already know I sent it."

They went into Leonard's inner sanctum and talked for half an hour. Nothing really about firm business, just catching up. Simon emerged from the high-rise office building and breathed in the wonderful cocktail of city smells. Two parts automobile exhaust mixed with ethnic cuisine and a dash of tar from the ever-present road construction. A red streetcar zipped by on its way to the riverfront, and taxis idled at the curb as a street busker played Rimsky-Korsakov on his violin. Simon listened for a moment and wondered why the guy wasn't performing in a concert hall. Thinking of how he had treated Kate when she tried busking in college to earn a few dollars, he withdrew all the cash in his wallet—four twenty-dollar bills—and dropped them into the open violin case.

———————— • ————————

The following night was as good a choice as any for taking down the wall in Charlene's office. Classes in the community center were usually over by eight, so Simon expected the building to be empty.

The alarm system had been disarmed, and the lights were off. Simon's heart rate picked up speed as he crossed the lobby. He had never seen anyone act carelessly with security before. Except for him, when he forgot to shut the window in the cloakroom.

Look how well that turned out. Vandals started a fire.

Glancing into the office, he stopped dead. There, sitting at her desk in the dark, was Kate. She was bent over, head resting on her folded arms. Simon felt cold. Why was she here in the dark? Was she hurt? He walked toward her slowly.

"Kate? It's Simon." He saw by the small movement of her shoulders that she had heard him. "Can I turn on the light?"

Kate nodded and he flipped the switch. She sat up. "I didn't expect anyone this late."

Simon reached her desk and stopped. "It was a last-minute decision. I need to get started on Charlene's office."

As though his words bounced off her unheard, Kate stared straight ahead, saying nothing.

He gave her time. A minute passed, then he took her cold hand in his. "What happened? You worked at the hospital today, didn't you?"

Coming to herself, Kate looked at him for the first time since he had arrived. "It's been a hard day. I lost a patient."

Simon let the quiet drag on, allowing her the opportunity to say more.

Kate straightened some papers, aligning each one perfectly. "Just two years old. I've known her family for years, treated all the other kids. Held that baby the day she was born." Dry-eyed, she finished arranging the papers and stared at her trembling hands. "I couldn't save her. Nothing could."

"I'm sorry." Simon wanted to pull Kate onto his lap and rock her until she stopped shaking. "I'm so sorry. Can I do something for you?"

She shook her head and studied the bulletin board on the wall. Simon had no idea how she felt. He had never been involved in anybody's life that deeply or given much thought to death. At least not since his grandfather passed away.

"I'd like some time by myself, if that's all right."

———————— • ————————

By ten thirty, Charlene's office was a mess.

It had taken every bit of restraint Simon had to keep from checking on Kate but she joined him after a while, still dry-eyed and pale.

"I do need something after all."

He put down his sledgehammer. "Name it."

"Could I help knock down that wall? I think I'd feel better if I had a target to hit."

He gave Kate a few simple instructions and stood back. She put all she had into each swing, her arms visibly straining with the effort. Grief like hers was painful to watch. Simon went to his car, got a few things out of the trunk, and took extra time on the way back. He cleared his throat at the door, letting her know he was there.

"I have a mask for you, so you don't breathe in the dust."

She had removed the cotton top she wore to work, leaving her in a black camisole and smudged jeans. He could see where she had wiped her hand on her thigh. Sweat glistened on her collarbone and tears left wet tracks through the fine drywall dust on her cheeks.

With more tenderness than he knew he had, Simon pulled Kate to him—his arm around her shoulders, his body against hers. He wiped the powder from the curve of her cheekbone and tucked her head under his chin.

———————— • ————————

His warmth seeped into Kate, gradually thawing the cold inside. Simon felt so solid and alive. Drawing on his heat and strength, she took deep breaths and listened to the steady thud of his heartbeat.

He got her a roll of toilet paper. They sat down on the floor and Kate tore off a few squares and blew her nose. She leaned her head against his shoulder, hiccupping a few times. "If I thought about the way I look right now, I'm sure I'd be mortified."

Simon turned his head, running his gaze over her splotchy face. "Don't worry about it. I'd still suck face with you."

Her mouth dropped open in shock. "I haven't heard that terrible expression in years."

"I meant it more as comic relief than an actual pickup line." His bluer-than-blue eyes cut to hers. "Of course, if you're game, the offer's still good."

Tears clung to Kate's bottom lashes as she tried to smile. "You're impossible."

"I'm not. I'm just a guy."

"A good guy." She wiped her nose again. "Thanks for lending me your hammer."

"You're welcome."

They talked until nearly one o'clock but Kate didn't want to stop. Simon's voice, the way he listened, made her feel less fragile. The loss of her sweet, two-year-old patient still hurt but Kate no longer felt as if she couldn't breathe. Or that the dark side of her mind would block out all hope and swallow her up.

Simon touched Kate's arm gently. "How did you lose Mike?"

A chill ran over her skin. She had expected this question at some point but it still came as a shock. "No one at the clinic told you? Not even Nina, the world's biggest gossip?"

"No," Simon replied. "I never asked."

His arm rested against hers, warm and strong. She opened her mouth, unsure if any words would come out, but they did. "The accident wasn't anyone's fault . . ."

Her breath caught briefly. It still didn't seem real, even now. "The other driver had a heart attack and plowed into the intersection as we drove through. Our car was hit on Mike's side."

Kate could feel Simon's body tighten, but his voice was soft as he said things that made her feel safe and hopeful. Kindness without pity.

"Thanks for listening," she said, after a moment of peaceful silence. "Has anyone ever told you that deep down you have a heart of gold?"

He laughed. "It would have to be deep, deep down. As in totally undiscovered territory."

She leaned her head on his shoulder again. "No. I discovered it. Telling you about Mike scared me, but I'm glad I did."

"Don't be afraid, Kate. I promise I'll never hurt you."

These words were also designed to comfort, but unlike the other things Simon had said that evening, something about them made her worry. Nothing scared Kate more than broken promises.

Chapter 19

Daisy

"We meet again, fair lady." The man who stood at the library window put a hand to his hip and offered a small bow. "This is the third time in a fortnight, I believe."

"Are you complaining?" Daisy asked with a smile.

"No. Merely making an observation."

"I can see if Mr. Darcy is available."

"Darcy, eh?" Sydney Carton from *A Tale of Two Cities* sat down across from Daisy. "Well, that explains why you prefer my company."

He wore a great deal of black: coat, vest, and breeches. His white linen shirt was plain, the cravat at his throat carelessly knotted. A thin silk ribbon tied back his dark hair.

Sydney watched her with equally dark eyes. "Heaven knows I am no pillar of virtue. Quite the opposite in fact." He crossed his legs and fiddled with the lace at his wrists. "Miss Austen's creation might be a better influence on a girl such as yourself."

"Nonsense," Daisy scoffed. "Dickens didn't know what he had when he wrote you. If I were Lucie Manette, I would have chosen Sidney Carton over Charles Darnay."

"But he is everything noble and good. While I am an intemperate barrister given to fits of self-pity and cynicism."

She laughed merrily. "Only on the surface. Underneath, you're capable of great things. You just need something to believe in."

He looked unmoved, bored even, so Daisy took several books from her pack. "Have you any idea how you've influenced writers today?"

"Must you enlighten me?" Sydney asked, grimacing.

She read off some of the titles. "Don't you see, you're the reluctant hero! The bad man with a good heart who redeems himself by sacrificing all for the one he loves. Yet, in my head, I always change your story."

"Oh, come now, it ends as it should, Daisy. And I must say, I do rather enjoy saving the others. Even that prig Darnay."

"I hate that you have to die to do it."

Sydney's face turned wise. "Ah. Now I understand. You have called me here because of your mother."

"No. Ma's sick—"

"And a drunk, if you'll pardon my indelicacy. We both are."

Daisy gripped the arms of her chair. "You made yourself stop because you loved Lucie. You didn't wish to see her suffer."

"Yes," he said, rising to his feet. "I loved Lucie enough to stop drinking."

She turned away from him. "I don't want Ma to sacrifice herself like you did. I don't want her to die for me. Just stay sober. And get rid of Alec."

"Are you still living at his home?"

"When I'm not here," Daisy replied dolefully. "Alec's not

like the others. He's smarter . . . meaner." She hugged herself and began to rock back and forth.

Sydney moved around the table and stopped at her side. "Is there someone you can turn to? A real person, instead of a character from a book."

"Yes," Daisy murmured. "My neighbor Lolly would help if I asked her, but I don't want to get Ma in trouble. The worse things become, the less I can talk about them with other people."

"This place cannot protect you forever." Sydney returned to the window and looked outside, frowning. "Eventually, someone will discover your subterfuge."

"I know. I'll figure something out."

"Of course, you will. You're a bright, resourceful girl."

Daisy felt better after their talk. Sydney always seemed to have that effect on her. He smiled and bowed. "If you need help, call on *me*. Not Darcy. Romantic figure that he is, he would be entirely out of his depth in this situation."

Sydney Carton disappeared into her imagination and Daisy was alone once more.

Chapter 20

Northwest Portland

Simon locked up his tools in a vacant classroom the next afternoon and headed toward the office. It was nearing five. He found Kate sitting at her desk, fiddling with an Abbot and Costello DVD. She muttered a few words, something about being completely done with a crappy day.

Her apartment had been broken into only an hour or so after she arrived at work that morning. A neighbor had called to report the break-in and Kate had gone home to meet with the police, insurance company, and landlord. The television was stolen, along with her violin, a few pieces of jewelry, and some cash that she stored in a Snoopy cookie jar. Mirrors and dishes were broken and glass scattered across the floor. The drywall had holes—like it had been punched repeatedly—and the thief had even left a burning cigarette on a table in the living room. Strangely, he did not touch the paintings. They still hung in the alcove.

When Kate later returned to work, she spent most of the afternoon with patients. During a quick break, Simon overheard fragments of an additional phone call to the cops. Kate told them about a man named Julian Quinton, apparently someone she suspected of holding a grudge against her. It sounded as if the man had a history of violence. Simon didn't know who this Julian was but he liked the idea of beating him to a pulp if he was the one who stole from Kate.

Simon knocked on the office door. "Hey, beautiful. What's with the DVD?"

"Oh," Kate said, slipping the movie into her purse. "I'm going to see my dad for a quick visit. He's been sick lately. I thought I'd take him his favorite flick. He thinks there's some obscure parallel between *Who's on First?* and Herodotus."

Simon thought about that and crossed his arms. "I can't picture it. You've stumped me."

Kate nodded in agreement. "I know. No sane person would ever make the connection. My father has his own unique vision of the world."

"What subject does he teach?"

"He's a Classics professor. Loves anything old." She pushed her chair back and stood up. "I'd invite you to come, but he isn't really good with people."

Kate looked like she needed support. Simon could tolerate her father for one evening. "I don't mind. I could hang out with your dad."

"I'm his daughter, and I don't even want to hang out with him."

He held up his keys. "I'll drive and after the movie we can get a new door for your apartment."

Relief seemed to flow through her body. "Thanks. That would be so great." Kate shot Simon a worried glance as they left the community center. "You're being so kind and helpful replacing the door at my apartment. I don't want my dad to offend you, but he'll probably try."

"I can handle it. Besides, I'm pretty sure my father is worse."

Simon understood challenging parent-child relationships, having tiptoed around Jack as a boy. His mother and sisters had been there to pick up the pieces and make him feel loved. Who did Kate turn to as a little girl when she needed sympathy and reassurance?

Simon didn't think it was the right time to ask as they drove to her father's house. They talked about architecture and Matthew's years teaching at Reed. Then Kate pointed ahead, at a narrow three-story home with tall fir trees on either side. The front lawn needed mowing and the shrubs had grown out of control.

"He doesn't like to work outside much," Kate explained. "Remember the absent-minded professor? That's him—except he's not really goofy or even especially loveable like the character in the movie. He has a universal philosophy of benign neglect toward anything non-academic."

Simon wondered if Matthew applied his philosophy of benign neglect to his daughter as well as the yard.

They walked past the overgrown lawn and rang the bell. It took a moment, but the door opened slowly. Matthew squinted out at them.

"Did you lose your glasses, Dad?" Kate asked, voice bright. "It's just us. This is my friend, Simon."

Simon immediately noticed the physical traits Kate shared with her father. Tall and slim. Fair hair, light, intelligent eyes. Matthew stepped back into his home as Simon tried to shake his hand.

"Come in, come in. I'm too tired to stand here in the doorway," Matthew grumbled. He waved them toward a faded sofa and sat down in his recliner. Kate put the DVD on top of the television.

"I'm sorry you've been having migraines again, Dad. Is there anything I can do?"

"No, Kat. I'll be all right. The medication helps when I take it in time." He picked up his glasses, wiped the lenses on the robe he wore, and placed them on his nose. "I was in the middle of reading an interesting thesis paper. I knew I should have stopped, but I didn't. Same old story."

Matthew looked over at Simon. Seconds ticked by in silence and Kate cleared her throat. "Simon has been doing some beautiful woodwork over at the clinic."

"Are you a carpenter?" Matthew asked. "You don't look like one."

"Actually, sir, I'm an attorney. I'm just working on a few projects for Robert."

Sweat began to form between Simon's shoulder blades. This was like a job interview. One wrong word and you'd be asked to leave the building.

Matthew turned to his daughter. "You seem tired, Kat. Is Robert still working you too much?"

"Oh, I feel fine, Dad. I have a busy schedule, but I wouldn't say it's too much for me."

He cleaned his glasses once again. "I wish you would take more time off."

"Don't worry," she reassured her father. "Everything's good."

As Kate talked, Simon realized she wasn't going to tell Matthew about the break-in at her apartment. In fact, she shared very few details regarding her personal life. Merely glossed over them and changed the subject. They watched Abbott and

Costello, Kate and Simon laughing at all the right parts, while Matthew only smiled on two occasions. When the movie was over, Kate took the DVD out of the machine and put it back in the case.

"I brought this copy for you to keep. That way you can watch it whenever you like." She straightened the cushions on the sofa. "I hope you feel better."

"Thank you for the movie, Kat." It looked like Matthew was reaching for a hug but he ended up patting her arm. "Tell Robert hello."

Kate smiled. "I will. Please call if you need anything."

Simon offered his hand, and again it was rejected. "It's been a pleasure to meet you, sir."

"I doubt that, young man."

With this farewell, Kate and Simon soon found themselves walking across the unkempt grass and getting into the Mercedes.

She could hardly look at him. "How was that for awkward?"

Simon started the car. "I like Matthew. Besides, now you'll have to cut me some slack when you see my father again."

"You're just trying to make me feel better."

Steering the Mercedes away from the curb, he said, "Jack is charming to clients and neighbors and saves his worst manners for his family. I've always had to prove that I'm worthy to be his son." Simon heard the bitterness in his own voice.

"He must be proud of you," Kate replied, touching his hand.

He caught her fingers and held them in his for the rest of the journey.

Kate told herself not to overthink this. *Don't go all soft and mushy just because he's holding your hand. It's only a matter of time before he finishes at the community center and leaves.*

His real life was back at the law firm. A year from now, she'd be someone he once knew, a woman who looked vaguely familiar if he saw her on the street. Maybe they'd even meet a sixth and seventh time in the future. It hurt to imagine them becoming strangers again.

Slipping her hand free, Kate said, "Don't worry about helping me get a door tonight. I'll do it tomorrow."

Simon looked at her and then turned his attention back to the road. "Where will you sleep? At Beth's? Your apartment isn't safe. A trip to the hardware store won't take long."

"I know, but I can do it myself."

The relaxed atmosphere slipped away. "What aren't you telling me, Kate? Did I do something wrong?"

"No."

They turned off of Everett and parked in front of the community center. Kate climbed out of the Mercedes. She hurried past Simon like her sneakers were on fire.

"Why are you taking off?" he asked, looking genuinely confused.

Simon caught up with Kate and put his hand on her arm. "Don't just leave. Talk to me."

Kate couldn't talk to him right then without falling apart. First there was the break-in. Then speaking with the police about Julian. Seeing her father. Feeling emotions for Simon. All of them together were more than Kate could handle. Her body felt so wired and anxious, she wondered if sleep would even be possible that night. How could she with this kind of stress going on? And now the six-foot-two lawyer had planted himself right in her way.

Questions that had bothered Kate for days rose to the surface. Why was Simon interested in her? Why did he seem to care so much? She put her hands in her pockets. "Okay. Let's talk. When you first came to the clinic, you were completely focused on getting back to your firm. I was a nobody. I drove you crazy. Why the big change where I'm concerned? You could find someone easier than me to spend time with in any restaurant, bar, or nightclub."

Simon's eyes kindled with a steady heat. "What makes you think I want easier? I was stupid. I didn't know you then. You sacrifice, put yourself last, and defend children in need. You were never a nobody."

She was tempted to sink into him. Forget questions about his motives and her own past. "Do you like me because I'm different? The kind of novelty you want for a while and then discard?"

Simon moved closer and lowered his voice. "My giving a damn about someone else is the novelty here, Kate. That doesn't say much about me as a person but I'm trying to change. You've had a shock. I want to be there when you go home and face your apartment tonight. No strings attached. No obligations. Just a friend helping out."

His eyes never wavered from hers. Kate suddenly felt less anxious. Simon liked her for herself. "I really am afraid to go home alone," she confessed. "I want you to be there."

"You've got me." Simon backed toward his Mercedes. "Ride your bike to the apartment, and I'll follow you. I'd like to look at that door."

"I need my helmet. It's inside the office."

After making a quick trip into the community center, Kate locked up again and hurried over to the Triumph. She stopped in her tracks. The back tire looked wrong. Flat. Simon pulled up in the Mercedes and rolled down his window.

"Ready?"

"No." Kate pointed at the tire. "It's a pancake."

He got out of his car. They knelt together beside the bike. "Look at that, Kate. That isn't the result of a nail or a rock. It's been sliced. See how long the gash is?"

Someone did this intentionally? Anger burned through her body. She stood up and called over to Larry and Earl. The two homeless men were reading in front of their tents, seated on foldout chairs.

"Hiya, Doc," Earl replied. "How you doing?"

"Did you see anyone near the Triumph today?"

Larry shook his head. "No. You didn't give us ten bucks to watch it."

Kate's anger blazed, so she took a deep breath. She couldn't snap at them. They were sensitive to criticism and offended easily.

Earl scratched behind his ear. "Wait, I did see a guy when I cooked beans for lunch over the gas stove. They turned out perfect, by the way. A little savory, a little sweet—"

"What did the guy look like?" Simon asked impatiently.

"Long brown hair. Tall. That's all I remember."

"I'll kill Julian," Kate said, kicking a broken cement pillar. "So help me, I will."

Simon interrupted her tantrum. "Who's Julian?"

"My mother's boyfriend." The words were out before she could sensor them. Might as well say it all. "He's stalked me for years."

She saw Simon suck in a breath. It hissed across his teeth and for a moment he looked as though he would like to murder Julian himself. "You think he broke into your apartment, too?"

Kate rubbed her face, tired to the bone. "Probably. He's done it before, when Mike and I lived over on Highland Road. I took out a restraining order, but it didn't help much."

He put his hand on her shoulder. The weight of it made her feel safe. "That's why you carry a gun. Because of him." His touch and tone were gentle, but she sensed his anger, cold and carefully focused on the man who made her fear for her life.

"I never know when he'll show up. He's a British citizen from a wealthy family. Like Sir Richard Branson wealthy. They're friends with the royals, own islands, and private jets."

Simon scanned the parking lot and the surrounding streets. "Do you have a spare for your bike here? Or at your apartment?"

She sighed. "It's flat too but there's a dealership nearby. I'll call them."

Ten minutes later, Kate ended the call and sat with Simon in his car, waiting for the mechanic to arrive. She shivered and he automatically turned on the heat.

Simon rubbed her back. As he massaged the tense muscles, he asked, "How long has Julian done things like this?"

"Since my mom died. He went to prison for a while, about the same time I came to America to live with my dad. But then he started up again when I was in college. I'd be waiting on a street corner for the light to change and I'd hear his voice behind me. Or he'd track me down at school, show up to parties I was invited to. Leave stuff outside my apartment. It scared me enough that I didn't want to go out, couldn't sleep or eat. I started training with a Krav Maga instructor so I could defend myself."

"That was smart," Simon replied. "When was the last time you saw him? Did you document it?"

Her body slumped forward, allowing his fingers more access to her back. "It was the day of Mike's funeral. In the middle of the graveside service, I looked up and saw Julian standing across the cemetery near some trees."

"What a bastard," Simon muttered. "He needs to be put away."

"He's served time for manslaughter, selling drugs, domestic abuse. Yet the sentencing is always light for the crime. A slap on the wrist because of his father's money." Kate pulled the sweater she was wearing tighter around her midsection. It didn't take away the chill inside. "That day in Old Town three years ago? When you saw that I was crying and got me a cab? It was a few hours after the funeral and Mike's sister served lunch for his cop friends and college buddies. I couldn't stay there as they laughed and ate and acted normal. I had to get out before I lost my mind."

"You went to Old Town?" Simon's hand still rested on her back.

Kate never wanted it to move. She could go on talking about that day if he touched her. "I left the house without any idea of where I was going. Walked and walked. A part of me wanted Julian to appear from an alley and end all my pain. But I kept going and eventually passed you on the sidewalk. You helped me get home."

Simon's hand flexed slightly. It didn't take a psychic to know he was seething inside. "You could find a lawyer, Kate. A ruthless one who's mean as hell. They'll track down the son of a bitch and sue his ass. Then go after the rich father in civil court, exposing his duplicity in every dirty deed Julian committed against you." Simon exhaled and rolled his shoulders. "We need someone familiar with the English legal system. I'll research and make a list of names."

Before Kate could respond, the motorcycle mechanic pulled into the parking lot. They got out of the Mercedes and Simon asked him a lot of questions while he worked, in case Kate ever needed to replace her own tire. Once the bike was good to go, she paid the mechanic and gave him a bonus for coming to the community center.

"You okay to ride?" Simon asked.

"Fine." Kate cinched her helmet and climbed on the bike.

"I'll be right behind you."

Traffic was moderate and they made it to Kate's home in fairly good time. She parked the Triumph in her space while Simon found a spot on the street for his car. The ride had cleared her head and stopped the shaking in her hands.

Kate waited for him at the top of the stairs. The door to her apartment was secured with several thick boards. The sight of it made her heart sink. This was her place, her retreat from the world, and it had been violated. In a matter of seconds, Simon took some measurements and they drove over to the hardware store in his car. Kate chose a steel door and a deadbolt lock set, while Simon got some patching supplies for the walls. The store manager said one of the clerks could deliver Kate's door that night. The kid lived near her and had just finished his shift.

The evening air was still warm as she and Simon walked toward his car. He smiled at her. "That went surprisingly well. Why don't we pick up dinner at a drive-through on the way back?"

They ordered a big box of fried chicken, biscuits, and mashed potatoes. When they got to her place, Simon took a hammer and crowbar from the trunk of his car and removed the boards from the old door. "I'll check the rooms," he said, going inside first. "And make sure they're safe."

Kate followed at a distance. Her shoes crunched over the broken glass. Simon backtracked a few minutes later.

"Looks okay. Where do you want me to start?"

She sighed wearily. "Can we eat first?"

"Sure. Let's do that."

As they entered the kitchen, there was a knocking sound outside. The kid had arrived with the steel security door. Kate gave him a twenty for making the delivery on his way home. He thanked her and left.

She took the Walther from its holster near her hip and set it on the kitchen counter before unpacking the food. Simon ate quickly, swinging his foot as he sat on a barstool. He nodded at the new steel door.

"What do you want to paint that thing? Red? Blue?"

Kate thought for a moment. "How about teal?"

"Cheerful. Bright. I like it." Simon threw his paper plate in the trash. "But you need more security. Have you considered a good wireless system to monitor things? Wouldn't take long to set up once it arrives."

"Okay," Kate agreed. "It's been at the top of my list. I meant to have one installed when I first moved in."

They talked casually while Simon worked on the door. The order and balance of her world gradually began to fall into place as she swept, straightened the couch cushions, and put her books back on the shelf. This renewed sense of calm lasted until Simon asked about her mother and Julian.

Waiting for Kate's reply, he opened and closed the steel door. It swung smoothly on the bright, new hinges.

"You sure you're not a shrink?"

"Absolutely sure," he replied with a smile.

Watching his efficient movements, Kate gave a brief accounting of when her father left for America. How she and her mother had stayed with various relatives, living with each of them for a while before moving on.

"By the time I was nine, we moved to London with Aunt Helen."

Simon sorted through some screws and asked, "How long did you live there?"

"Maybe three or four months. My aunt was old, and her flat was too small for the three of us. She didn't like my mother's drinking."

He slipped the new deadbolt into position. "Where did you go after you left your aunt?"

"To an attic in Kilburn," she replied, leaning her broom against the wall. "Tess thought it was romantic, like an artist's garret. She did office work for a while, to buy canvas and paint, and started meeting new people. Always men."

Kate gathered the pieces of a broken mirror together, setting them carefully in the trashcan. The ceiling of the hall was reflected within the shattered glass, like pieces of an enormous puzzle. Her life felt a little like the mirror.

"What kind of men?"

She knelt down to dust the baseboards. "When you're eleven it's a shock to come to the breakfast table and find a stranger there, reading the paper. They were harmless enough . . . and never stayed long. But as the drinking grew worse, the quality of her friends deteriorated."

Simon went still. "Did any of them hurt you?"

She got up and stretched her back. "As far as I was concerned, everything outside my bedroom was a potential threat, so I locked myself in and kept quiet."

"How did you get by?" he asked gently, checking that the lock was solid. "Who fed you?"

It wasn't as hard to talk about as Kate had feared. The memories sort of felt surreal, like they happened in another life, to another girl. "I learned to cook for myself, to write checks and forge my mother's signature to pay the bills. I stole money from her wallet and hid it, so we'd have enough for food."

"That's a lot of responsibility for a kid. Did she try to quit drinking?" Simon had a way of asking things that made a person want to talk. He could probably get answers from a boulder.

"Tess tried many times, but I always knew the exact moment she gave up. I'd scour the apartment looking for hidden bottles, trying to protect her from herself. I'd miss one and the cycle would begin again." Kate wrinkled her nose. "The smell of alcohol still makes me sick: panic attacks, nausea, cold sweats, the works. Funny, isn't it? My mother got those symptoms when she quit drinking, and I get them when people start."

Suddenly cold again, she walked over to the thermostat and turned on the furnace. "Would you like some hot chocolate or coffee?" Kate asked Simon.

"A Coke would be great. Thanks."

After delivering the Coke, she made herself a cup of herb tea. The honey and lemon were refreshing. Kate sipped from her cup while watching Simon work. His hands were interesting. Strong, clever fingers. Wide palms with a few calluses.

Simon stopped to have a drink. He clicked his Coke bottle to her cup and she smiled. It occurred to Kate that he was a rich man's son, like Julian. He'd grown up in a big house with lots of money, again like Julian. Both handsome, intelligent, privileged younger sons, but the similarities ended there. Kate had never been afraid of Simon, even in times of conflict. She'd known he wouldn't harm her physically.

He put down his Coke and brushed the hair from her eyes. "You look beat. Why don't you take a hot shower and go to bed? I'll be out here, working on some projects."

"Very tempting. I am beat."

The shower idea was a good one but she still wasn't sure she could sleep. Kate picked up the kitchen before retiring to her room. She put the Walther in her nightstand drawer. The Victorian's old water heater seemed to be working since steam filled the bathroom when Kate turned on the shower. The pounding water loosened up her muscles. It was bliss.

When the water turned cold, Kate got out and dressed in a soft pair of pajamas. She could hear a few quiet movements out in the living room. Simon trying not to disturb her. His presence right then was better than a hundred steel doors and deadbolts.

By the light of a small lamp, Kate curled up on her bed, just to rest her eyes for a moment. Relax briefly before checking on Simon. She didn't want him to feel obligated to stay. Her bed was unbelievably soft and comfortable. She was asleep in minutes.

———————— • ————————

Simon heard the water in the bathroom shut off. He worked quietly, filling holes in the drywall, and hoped that Kate could rest after such a hard day. Simon was tired too but his body wasn't ready to stop moving. It helped him deal with the thoughts spinning around in his brain.

When he was done filling the holes, Simon walked down the hall to the kitchen. He opened the refrigerator and looked inside for several minutes. What did he want? He had no idea. Perhaps standing there was just something to do as he thought over Kate's revelations about her childhood.

Simon left the kitchen and returned to the living room, pausing at the hidden alcove. His gaze rested on the portrait of the little girl with the mermaid eyes.

Conflicting emotions consumed him. Anger because he felt for the girl in the picture, regret that she had to endure so much, sorrow that no one saved her. Disgust with himself for having the same weakness Tess had, the very one that nearly destroyed Kate. If Simon wasn't an alcoholic, he'd come damn close, living on the cusp of the disease. The thought of taking another drink made him ill. Why had he ever liked being so out of control, so dependent, and self-destructive?

Filled with shame, Simon turned back to the living room, shut off the lights, and lay down on the couch. What would Kate think if she saw the worst side of him? His feelings for her were too strong to be ignored. They'd slipped around his defenses somehow. Hadn't he told Kate a few hours ago that she didn't need to worry about strings being attached to their relationship?

But he wanted them. Strings, obligations, everything.

Chapter 21

The ER at Good Samaritan was packed all afternoon. There was no time for a break, no quick cup of tea in the staff lounge. Not with a minivan/SUV pileup on Sunset Highway and a knife fight between two teenage boys on Salmon Street. Long past her scheduled quitting time, Kate left the hospital at seven and drove to the community center. Simon and Robert were putting the finishing touches on a chalkboard wall and she'd wanted to be there.

Walking into the patient waiting room, Kate saw that the wall was done. Wood trim framed the chalkboard and gave it a neat, polished look. Simon was stacking erasers on the ledge while Robert printed a quote by Gandhi in bubble letters.

Kate clapped and the two men turned around. "It looks good," she said.

Robert grinned. "Can you read my writing from there?"

She squinted to make out the words. "Is it in bubble Sanskrit?"

"No, babe. It's English."

"I'd have Beth take over, then."

Robert ignored Kate's suggestion and went back to writing. Simon joined her and they watched the quote unfold. He shrugged. "In two days, it's going to be covered with kid scribble anyway."

"Good point," she murmured. "Never mind, Robert. Don't change a thing."

Kate went into the office to check her upcoming schedule. She threw away the empty wrappers in her candy drawer and went through the mail. In all, it took about ten minutes. Kate locked her desk and returned to the patient waiting room. Robert declined rather quickly when she asked if he wanted to get some dinner. Simon, on the other hand, seemed preoccupied. What had happened between them during her ten minutes away?

"Is everything all right?" Kate asked.

"Everything's fine," Robert replied, slipping his messenger bag over his shoulder. "I'm going home to sleep for ten hours straight."

He pushed the door open with his hip and frowned at Simon before leaving. Kate felt as if she'd missed something. She turned back to Simon. "Is Robert okay?"

"For the most part. We had a talk. He really cares about you."

"I know he does. We've been friends for a long time. What kind of talk?"

Raising one eyebrow, Kate crossed her arms and waited for Simon to spill the beans. His face grew slightly flushed.

"After you went into the office, Robert said that Beth had told him we were spending time together. He asked me to explain my intentions toward you. I think his exact words were, 'If I find that you are using Kate or hurting her in any way, I will kick your ass.' Like he could."

An embarrassed gurgle rose in Kate's throat. "Oh no. I'm sorry. He thinks he's my big brother sometimes."

"It was like watching Mother Teresa put up her dukes and come out swinging."

The gurgle evolved into a laugh. "Now there's an image."

They locked the building, and Simon walked her to the Triumph. "How's the new door working?"

"I feel like I'm in a fortress. Totally secure and safe."

Simon looked pleased. "Is it okay if I come over and hang your new light fixture? Won't take long."

"You worked here all day," Kate replied as she put on her helmet. "You've got to be tired."

The helmet slid back a little and he helped her adjust the chin strap. "No big deal, Kate. Fifteen minutes and I'll be done."

Simon smelled of wood dust, coffee, and a nice spicy cologne. She smiled up at him. "Thanks. Can I fix you dinner afterward? Leftovers from last night?"

"Deal."

They met up at her apartment and Simon began working on the light. All the apartment needed now was paint to cover the drywall repairs. Once the burn on the coffee table was sanded down, things would look almost like they did before the break-in. Kate was relieved to have her home looking normal, even though it would take some time to get over the sense of being invaded.

The dark, frightened part of Kate's brain pictured Julian sitting on the couch smoking a cigarette, then leaving it on the coffee table for her to find. He wanted Kate to think of him and be scared. She rubbed her arms, forcing herself to focus on the present. Something so ordinary as preparing a salad helped her feel more in control.

After Kate had warmed up the leftover mashed potatoes

and fried chicken from the night before, she went to find Simon. He had finished installing the light fixture and the living room looked bright and inviting.

"Thank you," Kate said. "I'm really grateful, Simon."

"Easy job. You don't need to keep thanking me." He put his screwdriver and pliers in an old toolbox. "Those leftovers smell good."

"There's a kale salad to balance things out. I hope that's okay."

"Sounds perfect."

They sat in the dining room and had dinner. It was the most peace Kate had known in the last twenty-four hours. She felt happy as Simon talked about the community center. He had finished Charlene's office and built a simple coffee bar for Beth in the tiny, closet-like break room. It contained a miniature fridge, a sink, and a coffee maker. No one stayed there for long, choosing to drink their coffee in the office instead. The bar Simon had built would make the space more organized and attractive.

"She'll love that," Kate replied, putting down her fork. She was full and a little sleepy.

Simon polished off the last piece of chicken. They shared an orange for dessert. "You know, I won't rest easy until that security system is in, Kate."

The orange segment leaked juice through her fingers. "It's on the way, and I have the Walther to protect me until then."

"You're okay being here alone?" Simon watched her eat the last bit of orange. "Didn't Beth say you could stay with her for a few days if you needed to? I can always sleep on the couch. I'm serious. This situation worries me—"

"No to both options," Kate insisted. The thought of hiding

at her friend's place or making Simon stay felt cowardly. "This is my home. The only one that's ever really been mine. I won't let someone drive me away and after all you've done, I'm safe. I want to be here."

"Kate—"

"I'm not kidding, Simon. I appreciate your concern, but I'll be fine."

She gathered the dishes and took them to the kitchen. He loaded their water glasses into the dishwasher. They gazed at each other as the grandfather clock chimed in the living room.

Shaking his head, Simon finally conceded. "Okay, but I'll still worry."

Simon reached for Kate's hand and tension filled the little room. The good kind that reminded her how nice it was to be alive, looking at an attractive man.

He brushed her wrist with one finger. "My parents want me to bring a date to a gala at the art museum. Would you go with me?"

This was a real date? And his parents would be there? Kate's insides turned to jelly. She didn't want to throw up in front of Simon, so she smiled. It felt lackluster at best. "I'm just trying to get my mind around this. Me at a gala?"

"I can picture you there."

"Then you have not seen my pitiful closet."

Simon's hand moved up her arm, leaving a trail of warmth behind. "You'd look good in sackcloth and tin foil. Will you be my date?"

"Yes."

How had she lived so long without this? Flirting, touching, making eyes at a man. But she felt so out of practice. Simon seemed to sense this. Moving slowly, clearly giving her the opportunity to decline, he leaned in. Nothing in the world could have kept Kate from meeting him halfway.

"Can I kiss you good night?"

"Please do," Kate murmured.

Simon took his time. He seemed to study each feature of her face, drinking her in. Kate must have looked impatient because laughter rumbled up from his chest. "Don't rush me."

He kissed her cheek, the side of her jaw, her neck. Kate's mind shut down when Simon finally reached her mouth. She didn't know how long the kiss went on, but when they pulled apart, they were both breathing hard.

Did she look shattered by the experience? Could he see the tumult of emotions tearing her apart? Senses on fire, Kate twisted her wedding band and immediately felt regret when she saw Simon's face. The nervous habit was such an obvious tell. Guilt at having forgotten she was a widow. For allowing herself to feel like a woman.

The cool blue gaze shifted away but not before Kate saw the irritation in his eyes, like he was beginning to resent the hell out of the symbol of her marriage to Mike. The chemistry between them immediately fizzled.

Simon took a step back. "I've got an early morning. I'd better go."

Kate wanted to say she was sorry, to ask if they could just forget the last sixty seconds, but the words seemed stuck in her throat. She walked with Simon to the front door and locked the deadbolt after he left. The purr of the Mercedes started out on the street.

Cursing herself, Kate went into the kitchen and began cleaning. How long would he put up with her baggage? This whole stupid hot and cold thing she was doing? Kate thought over what had just happened. Replayed every detail in her head. At first, it had been electric. She'd smelled the traces of sandalwood in his cologne. Felt the solid lines of his shoulders and the strength in his hands. He had murmured her name, his voice a rough whisper.

And the man could kiss . . . Like it was the most consuming, important event of his life. The world had fallen away for Kate, until the guilt and remorse showed up. She had thought she was getting past it. At least, a little bit over the last month.

Kate put the salad in the refrigerator and wiped the counters. She opened a Coke, took a long drink, and set the bottle down, knowing at once what troubled her. Much as she loved Mike, much as they adored each other, Kate had never felt with him the way she did in Simon's arms. They had been good together but never electric, never enough to make the world disappear.

Her head grew light. That must make her a crappy person. Weak. Indulgent. If her dead husband wasn't the love of her life, how could she cope?

It wasn't something she could say to his memory, was it? That comforting voice she listened to each day. Oh, sorry, Mike, but one touch and this new guy ignites me. He's the best kisser, too. Do you still feel okay with me moving on?

Kate grabbed her phone, tempted to play Mike's last message, but it seemed disrespectful. Unworthy. She left the kitchen and entered the bathroom. The tile was cold under her bare feet. Flipping on the light, Kate gave her reflection in the mirror a passing glance. Then took a second look. There was something about the tousled hair. The pink swollen lips.

Leaning closer to the mirror, Kate realized that she didn't look so much like her father, after all. Instead, Kate saw Tess.

She'd always thought herself more disciplined, less hedonistic than her mother, but were they the same?

After washing her face, Kate put on a T-shirt and baggy flannel shorts. She stuck an earbud in one ear and pushed the forward button on her playlist until she reached an aria by Puccini. Kate went into her bedroom and did the next best thing to cleaning when she was upset. She made a list.

The Pros and Cons of Starting a Relationship with Simon Phillips.

On the pros side Kate wrote: smart, funny, kind, well read, punctual, really listens, strong, can build or fix things, smells nice, works hard, physically fit, considerate, looks good in a suit, looks good in jeans and a tool belt . . .

Kate read over the pros a few times and started on the cons. LAWYER was written in caps and underlined.

Followed by: better hair than me, freakishly blue eyes and long lashes, arrogant (sometimes), pitchy singer, too smart (cancels #1 on pros list), does hard-level Sudoku in pen, rough chin stubble, habit of tapping foot on floor (irritating!), too cheerful in the morning, bad breath after eating a hoagie, chick magnet without trying (Nina), grew up rich, materialistic (i.e. Mercedes), too handsome.

Kate compared the lists. Even she had to admit that the cons were weak. Who wouldn't jump on a guy like that? A stupid person, that's who.

She put the pad of paper on her nightstand, turned out the light, and lay down, hoping to find some escape from the drama of her life.

A noise near the front door made her sit upright. *What time is it? Ten thirty or so?* Kate grabbed the Walther and snuck down the dark hallway. A shadowy figure stood outside. Not a tall man with long hair but a petite woman.

Jenny, Leo's mom. The little boy clung to his mother. Kate motioned them inside. "Are you guys okay? What happened?"

The skin around Jenny's eye was swollen and bruised. Her voice sounded so tired. "Our usual babysitter is out of town. I called everybody I know. My mom has Flynn, but she can't watch both boys."

Kate put her arm around Jenny. "Hey, I love Leo. He can stay with me."

Jenny's face crumpled. "Thank you. I'm working graves at the nursing home, so if you could take him to school, I'll pick him up."

A drowsy Leo stumbled into the living room. Kate and Jenny watched him crawl up on the couch. He pulled a crocheted blanket over his legs. His breathing became soft and slow almost immediately. Poor kid.

"I'll take good care of him," Kate whispered. "You don't need to worry."

Jenny murmured her thanks and turned for the door. Kate stopped her near the kitchen. "What happened to your face? Was it Axel?"

A tear rolled down Jenny's cheek. "He's never hit me before, but Leo saw it happen. I feel like such a bad mother."

"No," Kate said, hugging the other woman. "I've seen a lot of bad moms and you're amazing."

"Thanks."

Kate grabbed a box of Kleenex from the bathroom and handed her a couple. "Where's Axel now?"

"I don't know. He didn't hit me hard, but I stumbled back. Fell against the counter with my face. The police came and took him downtown."

"I'm so sorry, Jenny."

"Me too."

Jenny left for the nursing home and Kate checked on Leo, who was snoring softly. She plugged a night light into the hall outlet, so he wouldn't wake up in the dark. After quietly making a cup of tea, Kate took it to her room but left the door open. The hot liquid burned her mouth as she wondered if a family could be put back together once it had fallen apart.

Chapter 22

Daisy

She arrived at the library at half past four, careful to walk in with a woman and her two children. Daisy smiled at the woman and offered to hold the door. The lady thanked her as she ushered the little ones inside. Daisy hoped that it looked as though she were the woman's helpful oldest daughter.

Just one big happy family, she thought silently, her face blank.

There was old Burt the security guard, keys hanging from his belt. He had worked at the library for years and never missed a day, according to his gossiping coworkers. Daisy tried to blend into the crowd. She had almost reached the stairs when she heard a deep voice directly behind her.

"Stop. You there! Stop this minute!"

Daisy looked back to see Burt reaching toward her, and she jerked convulsively out of range. Her hip bone struck the metal handrail, but overwhelming panic offset the pain rocketing down her leg. She stared at Burt, fearing the worst.

A little out of breath, he held her coin purse in his hand. "You dropped this, young lady. Wouldn't want you to lose it."

She took the purse from him. "Thank you."

Burt's lips formed a don't-be-afraid-I'm-your-friend smile. "I see you round here most every day, don't I?"

"Yes. I like books."

He tapped his head with his finger. "That's what I thought. What's your name?"

Her carefully prepared responses vanished and she blurted out the very thing she didn't want him to know. "K-Kate."

The guard nodded. "It suits you, it does. Well, you'd better toddle off now. Closing time will be here before you know it." He dipped his chin and turned back to his post by the door.

Daisy hurried to her reading room. The wooden chair felt solid and reassuring. She covered her face with her hands and tried to assess the damage.

How could I tell him my real name? How could I be that stupid? It's easier if people call me Daisy. All the bad stuff happens to her. She's the one who has the drunken mother with the terrible boyfriend, not Kate.

After a few minutes of thinking, Daisy calmed down. The guard might forget her. She was just another face among many. Even so, maybe she should avoid the library and take herself out of the picture for a while. Her heart ached at the thought.

Where would she go?

Christmas had been horrible with the library shut for winter break and her being stuck at home. Daisy had to think. She also had to do her studies. *Lessons first, thinking second*, she decided. After emptying her book bag, Daisy began her Advanced French homework. She read a section of Moliere's *Tartuffe ou L'Imposteur* and began translating lines into English.

As entertaining as this was, Daisy felt distracted after only a few moments by a strangely uncomfortable sensation. She looked up to find the older maid scowling at her as she locked the supply closet. Daisy lifted an eyebrow and smiled at the woman. The cleaning lady pushed her trolley down the hall and mumbled to herself.

She acts like I'm getting away with something. Which technically I am.

Daisy sniggered for a moment and then returned to Moliere. An hour later, she put the Frenchman away. A single worry was emerging from the usual pile of worries that plagued her. She had already accepted the fact that she couldn't hide out in the library all night since Old Maid was working.

Daisy identified her stress with a heavy heart. It was the growth spurt. She hated the growth spurt. It caused her ribs to hurt and her legs and arms to increase in length. The growth spurt was even wreaking havoc with Daisy's ability to fold herself up behind the boxes in the storage closet.

Of course, she still had the skills of 007. It just wasn't as easy.

No longer timid, Daisy had turned into a hiding professional. She slid into the closet and melted behind the boxes with James-Bond-like expertise, each movement precisely timed. In the library, she was confident and skilled . . . except for her encounter with Burt that day. It was a one-off, a blip, if you will, in her ten-month library-hiding career. Pragmatist that she was, Daisy knew her days of hiding were nearly at an end. She sighed.

Lolly would be willing to help.

Daisy thought of her adopted grandmother from Jamaica who lived on her block. Lolly had a grown son named Andre still at home. Maybe he could install a better lock on her bedroom door. The old one was broken. She removed a packet of Post-its from her bag, tore off the plastic cover, and lifted a yellow square to her nose, enjoying the fresh paper smell.

The Post-its were one of the few luxuries in her life. Daisy would save up loose change until she had enough to buy a packet. She used them sparingly, covering every inch and then folding them backward and bending them in half so she could take advantage of both sides.

New lock on door. Andre install?

Putting her books back in the bag, Daisy rolled her eyes when she came to the last one. It was required reading. Most books were automatically her friends, but not this one. She found *Tess of the d'Urbervilles* tiresome. Too many similarities to Daisy's own life.

Inevitably, her mother Tess would be cast as the tragic, flawed heroine. Matthew, Daisy's father, was Angel Clare—the man who claimed undying love for Tess yet never bothered to stay around and actually save her. And last, there was the devil, Alec d'Urberville. Julian could play him with his eyes closed. As a private joke, Daisy's mother had given her boyfriend the nickname of Alec, knowing he'd never read the book.

"Julian's wild, but he isn't bad," Ma had said. "What's the harm in playing a trick on him? It's all in fun, love."

Daisy didn't want to pollute the library with thoughts of Julian/Alec, so she stuffed the book into her bag and snapped the fasteners tight.

It was dark and cold as she walked home. Daisy pulled her duffle coat around her, hating that she looked like Paddington Bear when she wore it. Still, the big, blue coat was the best she could find when she went to Oxfam last fall. It was certainly better than nothing. A few snowflakes fell from the sky amid scattered raindrops. Daisy began a quick walk-trot and reached the top of her street without getting soaked. Using her key, she opened the door to Julian's house and relocked it behind her. Like a thorn that caught the skin, dread snagged Daisy's heart as she heard Tess softly weeping.

"Ma?"

The muffled noises behind the bedroom door ceased. "Is that you, love?" her mother asked, quavering.

"It's Daisy."

"Come in. Terrible, terrible news I have. They wouldn't listen to me. It wasn't his fault. The other one started the fight."

As usual, her mother's bedroom was a mess, bottles, newspapers, and take-out boxes stacked all over the sleek modern furniture. Had the occupants of the master suite not been so sick and addicted, their room would have looked like a showplace.

Julian's colossally rich family stowed him away at the house in Notting Hill, hoping against hope that he wouldn't cause another scandal. Evidently, they were getting tired of cleaning up after him. She had heard Julian's father say so during their last argument.

Tess was shaking, her pallor as much a result of needing a drink as it was a display of grief. "They have him in jail."

"Start at the beginning, Ma."

"We went to the club as usual. Had a few laughs, we did. I danced a bit with my friends, and this bloke kept asking for my name, my number. Wouldn't take no for an answer. Alec picked up a broken bottle. He wasn't going to hurt anyone. He was just defending me."

"Call him Julian. It's who he is." Daisy patted her mother's shoulder. "Have you contacted Sir Allan?"

Tess clutched her hand. "That's just it, love. His father

won't help this time. No more money until Julian gets treatment."

A glowing satisfaction stirred Daisy's heart. "Sir Allan said that?"

"He did." Her mother began to weep in earnest. "What am I to do?"

"I don't see as there's anything that can be done tonight, Ma. I'll take care of you, shall I? I'll bring you tea."

"I don't want it."

She wrapped a blanket around her mother's thin shoulders and held her. "Just a spot of tea and a slice of toast. To get your strength back, so you can figure a way to help Julian."

Soothed, Tess leaned against her daughter and closed her eyes. Daisy rubbed her mother's back until she knew Tess was dozing, and then she lowered her to the pillow. Leaving the bedroom for the kitchen, Daisy closed the door softly, a small, triumphant smile on her lips.

Chapter 23

Hayden-Grace Clinic

Simon stood at the waiting room door, watching Kate work with an obviously troubled woman. "I'd be happy to help, Rosa, but I don't specialize in adults. Although I could try talking to your cardiologist, to find out more about his diagnosis of your heart condition."

"*Gracias*," Rosa replied, beaming.

"Do you have his number?"

"In . . . *mi cartera?*"

"Purse," her son Tony said.

As Rosa sifted through her bag, Kate motioned to the boy. "T, get your sister, and let's go."

Simon, having heard Kate's directive, steered the wandering toddler toward her brother. As the Gomez family walked into an exam room, Kate dialed a number on her cell phone and put it to her ear.

"Dr. Swanson, please," she said. "This is Dr. Spencer calling on behalf of Rosa Gomez. Yes, thank you. I'll wait." Kate shut the door after Tony came in with the baby.

Samson, the new UPS guy, was in the office getting a signature. "Thanks, Beth. That'll do it."

Simon sat in the chair by Robert's desk as the deliveryman

headed out the door. Nina, Tanya, and Beth all sighed.

Nina said, "I love a man in uniform."

"Did you see his arms?" Beth asked with a grin. "And those *buns.*"

"Buns are cliché, y'all," Tanya said as she dropped a file into place. "Nice pecs, though." She wiggled her eyebrows and left the office to escort Robert's next patient to an exam room.

Simon looked at the other women in shock. Comments like that got you written up for harassment or sued at his firm. "You talk pecs and buns? At work?"

Robert entered the office during this comment. "Pecs and buns? What did I miss?"

"We were just discussing the UPS guy," Beth said. "By the way, the purchase order is on your desk."

Robert picked up the order. "I'm straight, and even I think Sam's an improvement over Butt-Chin Bill."

Beth groaned. "He did not have a butt chin, Robert. He had a nice cleft."

"It was a defect."

"You're just jealous."

"I don't think so, babe. But don't let me interrupt you ladies. I can see that you're hard at work analyzing men's body parts."

Beth leaned to the side in her chair, calling after Robert as he walked out the door. "Come back! We can analyze you next." Grinning, she looked at Simon. "Good to see our handyman this morning."

"Good to be seen." He slipped off his leather jacket and hung it over the back of Robert's chair.

Nina touched Simon's arm, ran one fingernail along his shoulder. "What are you up to?"

This really did feel like harassment. He moved his arm away. "I'm installing new blinds."

Kate entered the office and took a medical book from a shelf by the file cabinet. Nina leaned near his ear and said, "You know what they say about all work and no play?" Smirking, Nina left the room. Beth rolled her eyes and followed Nina out the door.

Simon turned to Kate, glad that they had a moment alone. "How are you today?"

She flipped through some pages without looking up. "It's been hectic. You?"

"Good. I'd like to talk sometime, about what happened last night. Want to get some lunch later?"

"I'll have to see how the morning goes," Kate said, closing the book. "We're slammed."

He could hear the people in the crowded waiting room. "Sounds like it."

She took a step toward him. "Simon, I'm sorry if I hurt your feelings. You're great. I'm just working through some stuff."

He shook his head. "I shouldn't have left the way I did."

A child began to wail in the distance. Kate bit her lip. "I've got to go. I'll look for you if I take a lunch."

"Okay."

She smiled and left the office. They hadn't parted the night before on the best of terms but it didn't seem to matter. They'd get past it. Simon felt an odd, unexplainable surge of satisfaction with life, though nothing had changed except his perception of it.

The two-inch faux wood blinds he'd ordered weeks ago had finally been delivered to the clinic. They were stacked in the west cloakroom, so he went to take a look. Simon opened several of the cardboard boxes and checked through their contents. The blinds would be easy to install. Simon figured that he could have them all done in a couple of days.

He decided to buy a cold drink from the vending machine before getting started, only to find that it hadn't been refilled that week. Tony's little sister was wandering toward him down the hall. Simon took her hand and turned her around the other way. "Okay, sweetie. Let's find your brother. You can't walk around here by yourself."

He kept talking in a soft, encouraging voice, their pace slow because the child took small, erratic steps, her legs stiff and new to walking. They reached the waiting room and Simon looked through the glass window in the door. Tony was sitting in a chair, reading a copy of *Sports Illustrated*.

Simon opened the door. "Tony? Come get your sister."

"Marisol!" Tony looked embarrassed as he hurried over to the little girl. "Sorry. I thought she was with my mom."

"I found her down by the counseling offices."

Simon glanced around the room. It was noisy and smelled of Cheerios and perspiration. Children were everywhere. He noticed Leo and Flynn in one corner. The toddler stooped a little bit, holding something heavy. Simon's brain barely processed what he saw, but his body shot forward. In seconds, he reached Flynn as he sat on the floor by his mother's purse, a 9mm Beretta in his hands.

———— • ————

Kate gave Rosa a list of handwritten instructions. "If you do these things, you'll feel better. Tony can explain them to you."

"*Gracias. Gracias.*"

"*De nada.*"

As Rosa took her leave, Kate noticed another woman walking toward her down the hall. "Hi, Jenny. How did the rest of your shift go?"

"Fine, thanks to you. Has Leo been okay?"

The bruises around Jenny's eye had turned an angry yellow and purple. Her uniform was stained and the odor of an unclean nursing home hung about her.

"Leo's been great. Slept well. Ate oatmeal and fruit for breakfast. I gave him some graham crackers and he's been coloring out in the waiting room."

"I know," Jenny replied, smiling. "I left Flynn with him so I could thank you."

Kate squeezed her shoulder. "Anytime. I love your family, you know that."

Talking about her kids, they walked back toward the office, turned the corner, and saw Beth, holding an armful of patient files. Her face went from happy to horrified in a split second.

"Is that a gun?" she asked, pushing open the door to the crowded waiting room.

Kate hustled past her. Simon was kneeling down in front of Flynn, softly whispering to the baby. He took the gun from the toddler's chubby fingers. Kate swallowed the scream in her throat and covered her mouth with her hands.

Time seemed to stop, like she was watching events happen in slow motion. Jenny scooped up Flynn and hugged him. She rocked the baby back and forth. Flynn began to cry and squirm, unhappy with being held so tight. As Kate looked around the room, she saw that most of the other parents were oblivious to the tragedy that might have occurred if the Beretta had been fired. They read books to their kids, texted or watched something on their phones, or stared into the distance as children played around them. No one seemed to notice anything outside their personal bubble. Reality returned as Flynn let out an earth-shattering squeal and the slow motion feeling vanished.

Jenny called for Leo. "Take your brother to the train set and keep him busy."

"I unzipped your purse to get a piece of gum, Mom," Leo said, eyes brimming with unshed tears.

"It's not your fault," Jenny assured him. Even though her voice was calm, her face was white as bone. "I never should have left my bag on the floor. Go on, Leo. Go play with Flynn."

With the boys gone, Jenny looked at Simon. "Thank you," she said. "Thank you for getting to him in time. I'm so glad the safety was on."

Simon checked the gun in his hand, sliding the safety into place. "It wasn't."

Tears slid down Jenny's face as she took the Beretta and put it away in her purse. "I'm not used to having it yet."

He patted her shoulder awkwardly. "It's okay. He's fine, and I doubt you'll forget again."

She nodded. "Not after this."

Simon walked to the door. His gaze rested on Kate for a moment before he turned and left. She followed him into the hall, feeling shaky and weak.

"Simon," Kate called. "Wait a minute."

His shirt was wrinkled at the hem. The work boots he wore were scuffed. To Kate, he had never looked better. Simon seemed to know what she wanted and opened his arms. She hugged him hard, until the urge to cry left her.

Their lunch date wasn't going to happen. Too many people needed Kate's help. Some of their problems fell within her job description, but others didn't. Like the grandfather of one of her patients who brought in his social security documents so she could help him fill them out. Or the teenager who was cutting herself. She couldn't talk to her mother about it, but she did with Kate for over an hour. And the newly divorced father bordering on a nervous breakdown. He cried in exam room A, pouring out the painful details of his broken life.

Between those emergencies, there was child after child. Sick babies, well babies, and all those in between. Kate was physically and mentally spent by the time seven rolled around that night. Evening classes were just starting, and people filtered into the community center. Kate locked the office door and went to look for Simon. She knew he was still around and thought he might be hungry too.

Kate found him in Nina's set of rooms. He had a pencil tucked behind his ear and frowned at the numbers on his note pad.

"Something wrong?" she asked.

He turned his head toward her. "Yeah, I ordered the wrong-sized blind for one of these windows."

Kate wandered in and leaned on the wall near the door. "Sorry. You want some food? I'm famished."

"Sure," Simon agreed. "I just need to finish a few things first."

"I'll wait. Mind if I collapse on the floor?"

"You can sit on my jacket. It's cleaner than the carpet."

He spread his jacket on the floor and Kate sat down. "Thanks." She closed her eyes. A depressed sigh escaped her lips. "Sometimes I wonder if it really matters. I do what I can, but bad stuff still happens. Like baby Flynn with the Beretta today."

Simon whistled softly. "Seeing that gun in his hand took years off my life."

She opened her eyes and watched him fit his drill with a bit. "At least Flynn's got a life. He wasn't shot because you reached him first. But it kills me that Jenny felt the need to get a gun."

"You have a Walther PPK, Kate," he pointed out. "A bigger PPQ, a Beretta, and a Colt."

"Yes, thank you, counselor. That's me, not her. Jenny's family was perfect a year ago."

"Axel gave her the bruises on her face?"

Kate straightened her posture, as if that would eliminate the sick feeling in her heart. "Leo saw it. He stayed with me last night because his usual sitter was unavailable."

Simon attached the blind to the brackets in the wall. He untied the cord, hooked the wand, and drew the blind closed. "This was after I left?"

"Yes. Jenny was beside herself. Seeing their family fall apart reminds me so much of my own. Being single seems like a cakewalk by comparison. I only have to worry about myself."

Simon made a disparaging sound. "Being single has its own set of issues."

"But less risk is involved. There's less potential for pain."

More drilling, another blind went up. "If you're alive, you're taking a risk, Kate."

She pointed at him. "Exactly. That's the problem. Maybe it's for the best that I'm not a mother. What if I became another Tess? We're more alike than I thought."

"Wow. You really have had a bad day." Simon put down his

tools and sat on the corner of Nina's desk. "I guarantee that you're not like your mother. You would never drink yourself to death just because your boyfriend dumped you."

It was strange to have someone else know about her life. She had kept the truth to herself for so long. "Julian didn't leave Tess. He killed her."

"Oh, Kate," Simon replied softly. "I'm sorry. I just assumed it was the drinking."

"Alcoholism was always a problem. Drugs are what actually killed her."

Simon brushed off his pant legs and stood. "Being around Jenny and Leo brought all this back?"

"Apparently so." Kate got up from the floor, overwhelmed with weariness. "I'm keeping you from finishing."

"No. I'm done for the day." He put his arm around her shoulders. "How about you come to my house and I cook?"

She leaned into him. "It's been years since a man said that to me."

"Let's get out of here, then."

Simon drove her to his house and after some deliberating in front of the Sub-Zero refrigerator, they decided on scrambled eggs, bacon, and toast. Kate sat at the oversized island and admired his gourmet kitchen. White marble floors and counters, round glass pendant lights, gray cabinets, all glossy and perfect. The whole house looked like a spread from *Architectural Digest*.

He cracked the eggs and whipped them with a fork. "I know I've said this before, but how did you make it through your childhood?"

Kate watched him put the bacon in a pan, almost hypnotized by the capable movements of his hands. "Books, I guess. A library. Some imagination."

"Which library?"

She grew wistful, wishing that Simon could see it for himself. "To me everything in that place was beautiful. I walked inside and it felt like the home I'd always wanted. So I stayed after the closing announcements."

He melted butter in another skillet. It smelled sweet, nutty. The eggs went in next. "What do you mean you stayed?"

"I hid until everyone left and spent the night there. I was desperate. I didn't have a plan. It just worked somehow." Kate listened to the hiss of bacon sizzling, savoring the domesticity of it. "I told Tess and Julian that I'd spent the night with a classmate. That was my usual excuse for staying away."

Simon flipped the bacon easily. His attention seemed to be focused on preparing the food. "What did you do in the library after hours?"

Kate remembered her fear that first night and shivered. "I wanted my mother, not the way she was, but as she had been before everything went wrong. I opened *Jane Eyre* and began reading. I loved Jane. I imagined her comforting me, giving me a little of her courage. She looked just like Tess. Gray eyes, dark hair."

Simon eased the crispy strips onto two plates. He added kosher salt and freshly cracked pepper to the eggs, then a bit of curry powder, some green onions, and herbs. The kitchen was a warm, delicious-smelling sanctuary, a little like her library but with food.

"Did your plan work?" Simon asked, looking up. "Did you get away with it?"

Kate poured each of them a glass of orange juice. "It went more or less as I had hoped. Tess didn't ask what happened while she slept, Julian didn't tell her he'd been violent, and I had a night out at the library. It took me a few months to get accustomed to hiding there, and I had some close calls when I was nearly caught at the beginning."

Simon cut a half dozen slices of challah bread from a braided loaf and toasted them in the oven. When the eggs were set, he divided the pan between the two plates. "How long did you keep this up?"

Kate took some utensils from a drawer and arranged them on the island, so they could sit side by side. She brought the glasses of juice over. "About ten months, a few times a week. Other nights I'd stay at a twenty-four-hour laundromat or my neighbor Lolly's. I don't think I could hide in a library today, what with alarm systems and everything, but back then it was easier. There weren't any valuable exhibits to protect, no fancy displays, just an old building full of books. I had to play it by ear, and it always depended on the cleaning staff."

Simon handed her a cloth napkin. "The cleaning staff?"

His quiet, matter of fact manner gave Kate the assurance she needed to continue. If he'd appeared too shocked or sympathetic, she would have stopped. "One of the maids was a little incompetent. The other was not. I stayed over when the incompetent girl worked because it was a lot easier to hide then. I learned the routine of the place, and it worked. When I was there, I didn't have to sleep with a chair against my door and one ear listening. At the library, I could pretend I was anything I wanted to be, and I made up my own friends."

He sat down beside Kate. Her stomach rumbled loudly in the space between them and Simon pushed her plate closer. "We should eat before it gets cold."

She blew on the steaming eggs and took a bite. The taste of

sweet butter and curry burst over her tongue. Then fresh basil, minced parsley, and the heat of Tabasco and cracked pepper. They ate in silence for a few minutes before Simon asked, "Who were they? Your made-up friends?"

Fear swept through her. Could he possibly understand? Could anyone? She hadn't told Robert this much or even Mike. Kate forked up another bite of eggs, hoping that Simon wouldn't think she was crazy. Perhaps she had been.

Kate's eyes stung and she wiped at them. Her heart was so full of gratitude, for writers long ago who had created friends that she would need one day to survive. "Jane Eyre . . . was a mother to me. Huck Finn and Eponine Thenardier were my brother and sister. Sydney Carton was my first crush. They all helped me hang on until I didn't need them anymore."

A hot tear rolled down her face and she laughed quietly, embarrassed and awkward. Simon watched her over his glass of orange juice. His hand shook a little when he put it down. "You're a miracle, baby. That's all I can say."

Kate was surprised that she liked him calling her baby. It made her feel cared for, rather than being stuck in her usual role of caretaker.

Simon touched her hand. "Don't stop, Kate. Tell me the rest."

But the rest of the story was so sad. It hurt to think about those days leading up to her mother's loss. "I remember praying at night. Talking to God like a friend, asking for help. I didn't need the imaginary characters so much when I started doing that. My circumstances didn't change, but my ability to deal with them did. I learned how to stand up to Julian."

Simon didn't look freaked out like before, when they hardly knew each other and Robert had mentioned that she believed in God. "What did you do?"

"I knew Julian was a bully and wanted to be in control. I'd seen the way he manipulated my mother. He liked feeling powerful. I didn't know how to defend myself against him until I said a prayer about it. Afterward, I remembered a book I had read about snakes."

"Snakes?"

She gave him a crooked smile. "I know. Weird, right? These snakes frightened off predators by pretending to be rattlers. You know, shaking their tails and making noises? I thought I could keep Julian off-balance by standing up to him and not acting afraid. It was all a huge bluff because I was terrified the entire time, but it worked. Things got better."

"He left you alone?" Simon sat back and waited for her to answer.

Kate realized that patience was one of his chief characteristics, even though she had left it off her pros and cons list. Perhaps that was why he was such a good lawyer. He wasn't afraid to wait and listen. To gather the important information from other data.

Kate felt a sudden affection for the man sitting next to her. Some guys would have been scared off by now, but not him. He stuck. Sometimes like a prickly burr on the skin, but mostly as a supportive presence. Never pushing. Or at least not pushing in a bad way.

She wiped her mouth and said, "Every day became a game of cat and mouse. Julian enjoyed my being afraid, but I tried to be like the snake in the book. I treated him with disdain. Talked back. It threw Julian enough to keep him away from me."

"What happened to your mother?"

The question sounded easy, as if they were old friends and

he was asking her to tell him about the family. Or it could have been the lead-up to the punchline of a joke. Kate wished either were true. "Tess had never used heroin before, and Julian gave her too much. I didn't do anything to stop it."

He took her hand, squeezing gently. "What could you have done? You were a kid."

Kate didn't want to ugly cry in his beautiful kitchen. She took a deep breath in and let it out. The smothered feeling in her lungs was another symptom of guilt. Survivor's remorse. "I should have told someone how things were at our house. I should have spent less time protecting myself and more time helping her." Kate turned on the stool and faced him. "I think we all have people that we're meant to save in this life. When it came down to it, I chose to save myself instead of Tess."

"Kate . . ." Simon stopped whatever he was going to say.

He gave her a hug and led her into the study. With one push of a button, pastel flames came to life in the fireplace. They sat on a leather couch. The quiet settled around them comfortably and Kate rested her head on Simon's shoulder. How long did they sit that way? She didn't know or care.

Simon finally said, "You were a child faced with problems that most people never have to deal with, and you were remarkable. You lived through it. That's what your mother would have wanted."

Watching the flames snap and pop, she almost believed him. It would be so nice not to blame herself anymore.

Kate traced the back of Simon's hand with her thumb. "I was looking through a box in my closet, and I found a note my mother wrote me the month before she died. It was short and jotted down on school paper. She said, 'Thanks for a happy Christmas.' I tried all day to remember what I did for her, and I couldn't. I couldn't remember anything good about that Christmas." The oppressive memory brought Kate to the edge of panic. Breathing deep again made it recede.

Simon pulled her into his side. "Was it a hard adjustment when you moved to America? You don't have even a trace of a British accent."

Snuggling into him, she said, "I've been here for sixteen years, since the week after Tess died. The accent wore off eventually."

"You went to junior high in Portland? Where?"

"Nope. Skipped all that. I tested three grades ahead of my age. Graduated high school early, got my bachelor's in two years. I always wanted to be a doctor. To help neglected kids and get their families the care they needed."

"Your patients love you."

"Ditto."

The corners of Kate's mouth turned up a fraction, and Simon touched her cheek. "I love you."

She froze like a deer caught by an oncoming car. She waited for the guilt to arrive. Waited for the familiar pain or a sense of unworthiness, but it didn't come. Why didn't it?

"I love you, too," Kate said in wonder.

Joy as she hadn't known in years, maybe ever, filled her heart. "It's been good to talk about my past. I didn't think it would be at first, but it is."

Simon wrapped a blanket around her shoulders. They went to the kitchen and made hot chocolate. Standing near enough to feel Simon's warmth, she held her mug tightly and sipped the semisweet mixture at intervals.

He must have noticed her eyeing the vase of flowers sitting nearby on the counter. "Don't you like daisies?

"They're not my favorite."

"Why?"

"My mother wanted to name me after Daisy Buchanan from *The Great Gatsby*, but my dad insisted on Katherine. After the divorce, Tess didn't call me Kate anymore, just Daisy. I was fine with it. I figured I'd be Daisy for as long as I lived with her, but when I grew up, I'd make a fresh start for myself. I'd leave Daisy behind and become Kate again. Then my life would be happy and good."

Simon leaned his head against hers. "You do have a good life now."

"I know I do. Daisy's long gone, but please, I beg of you, don't ever give me a copy of *The Great Gatsby*. I'm not kidding. I hate that book. No Thomas Hardy either."

Simon laughed and crossed his heart. "You have my word."

"Good." She held out her pinky finger and they shook.

Kate rinsed her mug in the sink and stifled a yawn.

"Do you want to stay over?" He looked innocent and held up his hands. "Best of intentions, really. You can use the guest room, if you'd prefer."

"Better not," she replied with a wink. Code for Nice Try.

He brushed his lips across hers, gentle though not hesitant in the least. The kiss went on and a rush of sensual heat made Kate breathless. Simon released her and they looked at each other, neither saying a word, yet each communicating all sorts of want and need and desire.

Stepping back, Simon took the keys to the Mercedes from the counter. "I'll drive you home."

She slipped her purse under her arm. "When I stepped into Nina's office a few hours ago and asked if you'd like to get food, I had no idea that I would share things I'd kept hidden from everyone else. Thank you. I'll never forget tonight."

Simon kissed Kate again at her apartment, leaving only after they'd checked that all was safe inside, and she'd bolted the door. He thought of her story during the drive back to his house. It played out like a movie in his mind. He parked the Mercedes in the far corner of the garage as rage coiled within him.

Civilized, that's how Simon would have described himself in the past, but he wasn't. Not when he felt this level of anger and helplessness. He'd been gentle with Kate as she told him about Julian, hoping that talking about him might release some of the pain she still carried. But here, alone with his dark thoughts, Simon wanted blood. Some had to be spilled for what she'd gone through.

He punched the wall over and over again until the skin across his knuckles tore open and turned the wall pink. After a few more blows the pink became a dark red. His hand hurt like hell when he went inside. Simon rinsed the blood away in the sink, then he searched in the freezer for a bag of peas and sat down in his study. The peas helped to numb his damaged hand.

The sadness he felt for Kate hurt worse than the throbbing in his knuckles. Much as he would like to, Simon couldn't change her childhood or bring her mother back. No amount of money could do that. All he had was the present and the future and he'd try his damnedest to make her happy.

Someone had once told him that falling in love was like having your heart taken from your body. He'd never believed it before but now he did. That ache in his chest was sweeter than anything he had known before.

Chapter 24

A vase of white lilacs sat on her desk. The arrangement was lush and abundant and Kate loved it. She stopped working to smell their sweet fragrance, a silly smile on her face. Simon had brought her a breakfast burrito that morning. The flowers were delivered two hours later. She'd noticed that the knuckles on his right hand were swollen and raw. When Kate questioned him about the injury, he'd said it was nothing.

Why had Simon closed up like that? What happened after he left her the night before? The white, lacy beauty of the lilacs drew her eye again. Robert walked through the door and leaned down to smell the flowers.

"Why did he do this, Kate?"

"I believe I am being courted."

Robert groaned in disgust. "How will you get any paperwork done? Your desk is a springtime meadow."

"Isn't it wonderful?"

"Not if you're allergic to romance like me. A gift card to a fast-food restaurant or Netflix would have been a lot more practical."

"Poor Beth." Kate made a sad face. "You really are allergic to romance."

Glaring at the huge arrangement, he muttered, "Dude must be compensating for something."

"Doubtful," Kate replied and patted Robert's arm. "But think that if it makes you feel better."

———— ● ————

At three that afternoon, Simon walked through the lobby and entered the office. The lilacs were sitting on Kate's desk like a snowy beacon. Were they too much? He'd gone to the flower shop himself and picked the lilacs from buckets in the cooler. The owner of the shop was a client. Simon always ordered flowers from him, but he usually had Linda call and charge them to his black Amex card. Most of his purchases—for family, clients, or girlfriends—were made that way. But not this time. Simon had wanted to do it.

Did Kate even like flowers? Or consider them a waste of money?

He noticed Beth standing by Spike. "Kate left these at my house last night," Simon murmured, handing her a ChapStick and a travel-size bottle of lotion. "Would you put them in her purse?"

"You can do it." Beth pointed at Kate's desk. "Top right drawer. She wouldn't mind."

Simon took a step back. "I don't like getting involved with women's handbags."

"Coward," Beth said, laughing. She took the lotion and ChapStick.

He checked his watch. Simon had to finish with the blinds today in order to begin sanding down some peeling paint in the auditorium. "Thanks, Beth. I had a scarring experience once with my sister. She's a prank artist."

"Post-purse-trauma? Oh, I've got to hear that story."

"Still can't talk about it."

Beth leaned against Spike. "Our girl looks happy this morning."

He smiled, pleased to hear Kate was having a good day. "Great. Is she with a patient?"

"Yes. Sit down a minute. I've been meaning to talk to you." Beth left the copy machine to sit at her desk and nodded at a nearby chair.

Meaning to talk to me? Now? Simon sat down with a sigh. He could feel himself falling behind on his schedule. "What's up?"

"Well, it's about Kate."

His eyebrow lifted a fraction of an inch. "Beth, if this conversation is going to be about what I think it is, I've already had it with Robert. My intentions are honorable. I'm not going to hurt her."

She looked up at the ceiling. "I don't think Robert covered what I want to talk about."

"Should I expect a visit from Charlene, Nina, and Tanya next?"

"Nina won't say anything. I can't vouch for Charlene or Tanya."

"Okay," he said, crossing his ankles. "Go ahead. I'm ready."

"I doubt that." Beth played with a pen, then put it down. "Let's see . . . My mother used euphemisms when she spoke with me about things like this. Here goes. You're going to have to buy the cow if you want the milk."

"What?"

"Ah . . . um. Let me try again. You won't get past first base unless you put a ring on it."

Understanding slammed into his brain like a rock. "Are you saying—?" he asked, sitting forward.

"That's what I'm saying, cowboy. Mike was a fifth-generation preacher's son. Very strict Baptist upbringing. He was the first guy she dated, and they abstained until their wedding night. Instead of alluding to driven snow, we could say she's *almost* as pure as those white lilacs you gave her." Beth looked him square in the eye. "If you want a disposable relationship, keep on looking. Kate's not built that way."

Simon dropped eye contact with Beth. He stood up and walked toward the door. He'd never really thought about Kate's marriage, other than a few jealous twinges and a dislike of that damn platinum band on her finger. Though he knew she was religious, Simon had always assumed even good churchgoing people ignored a commandment or two now and then.

Though their relationship was new, he'd sensed Kate had boundaries he couldn't pass. Simon just hadn't known how deeply they went.

"So," Beth called from her desk. "Is it a deal-breaker?"

Her intrusive tone was irritating. Simon reached the door and turned back to face Beth. "A deal-breaker? You expect me to answer that? It's none of your damn business."

Beth put her hands up in surrender. "Sorry if you think I'm getting too personal. All I can say is that I love her, and I think she loves you. I want you two to be happy. I'm on your side."

"Really? It sounded like you were prying. Kate and I can work things out ourselves."

"I didn't mean to meddle, Simon. I just want to help."

Robert brushed past him as he entered the office. "Dude, you look mad. Big-time. What's Beth trying to help you with?

Helping is like a sickness with her."

"It is not!" she replied hotly.

"Mama, you know it is. What's going on, Simon?"

He looked from Robert to Beth and shrugged. "She was just giving me advice about Kate."

The doctor pulled up a chair. "Oh, man. I have a good one. *Books.* Did you know she loves them?"

Everyone and their dog knew this about Kate but Simon acted surprised. "Is that right?"

"A book always patches things up with her. Give her one and just look at her. It's like when a guy sees his first muscle car."

"I'll keep that in mind." Simon slipped his hands into his pockets, planning his escape.

But Robert was on a roll. "She has a good vocabulary, too. Hang around another month and you'll find yourself using words like linchpin and hubris. I've worked hard to resist Kate's influence that way."

"Thanks for the heads up." Simon nodded at Beth and Robert. "I better move. Stuff to do."

"Anytime, dude."

Having fled the office, Simon got his tools and cranked out the last of the blinds in some classrooms on the east side of the building. The space felt quiet and remote and allowed him to empty his mind. To put off thinking about Beth's bombshell.

He stood in the east hall, before moving on to the next project. There was a roped-off section to the right, where more extensive work needed to be done. It was phase two of the rehab project, a total gut job that needed new floors, new ceilings, walls torn out for better function, improved plumbing . . . Simon wouldn't be here to work on it. Something inside him regretted that fact.

Heading back toward the west side, Simon took a mental inventory of what he'd need to clean away the peeling paint in the auditorium: ladder, mask, drop cloth, wire brush, scraper. Everything had been gathered earlier. Lucky for him, the paint had been tested and was lead-free.

Simon entered the auditorium and remembered touching Kate's hand that first time, when they were adversaries and had both reached for the door handle. It seemed so vivid. He could feel that electric awareness even now. Simon put down the drop cloth and used the wire brush to loosen the debris on the wall.

Now that time had passed, he felt ready to consider what Beth had told him about Kate. Abstaining was a pretty foreign concept. Archaic, really. A throw-back to provincial times. Paint flecked his shirt and jeans as he scraped the wall. While Simon worked, some of his irritation faded.

He loved Kate. That was the one absolutely true thing he knew in his life. And wasn't that truth worth some sacrifice? No one else had expected it of him in the past but that didn't matter. What Simon had found with her made him want to be a better man. The best version of himself.

An hour passed and he covered a quarter of the wall. His watch read half past five. Kate should be about ready to go home. Leaving the ladder and drop cloth in place for the next day, Simon went to the restroom and washed his hands. He met Kate at the office door.

"Thank you again for the lilacs."

A small, private smile appeared, just for him, and Simon knew he was lost. He'd give her the world if it was in his power.

Robert was sitting on the front porch the next day. His mouth was turned down and he was polishing his glasses. Simon had gone to the law firm to meet with Leonard and it had taken longer than expected. He'd picked up a snack on the way over to the community center. Simon got out of the Mercedes and reached back inside the car for two pink pastry boxes.

Seeing the boxes, the doctor cast a panicked look over his shoulder. "I can smell the baked goods from here. You're a dead man walking."

"Translate, Robert. I have no idea what you're talking about."

They entered the foyer together. Robert walked behind Simon, like he was using him as a human shield. "I was hiding outside because Beth is livid with me for ordering pizza. I've bought Mama Leone's every third Wednesday, at four in the afternoon, since the clinic opened. It's a freakin' tradition."

"Why'd she get upset?"

"Beth found out that her scale was stuck and she actually weighs seven pounds more than initially suspected."

"I don't understand." Simon tucked the pink boxes under his arm, hoping to avoid a scolding himself. "She looks fine."

"I keep telling her that, but Beth's convinced she'll blow up like one of her sisters. She's wearing an industrial-strength rubber band on her wrist. You know, to condition herself against thinking about unhealthy food. Beth's snapping it all the damn time now."

The office was empty. Simon put the pastries down on a little table near Spike, where they wouldn't be immediately noticeable. He had just taken the first bite of a raspberry tart when Charlene strolled through the office door.

"Hey, everybody. Talk about timing. Hello, doughnuts!"

Simon smiled at her. Charlene's ability to hear a doughnut calling from half a building away was legendary.

Robert opened a pizza box. "Dude, help yourself."

"Why do you insist on calling me 'dude'?" Charlene asked, grabbing a slice of cheese. "I don't like it. I'm too old."

"Never. You'll be dude to me when you're ninety."

"Ninety? Don't even joke about that." Charlene pinched his bearded cheek. "You should be married. I have a niece . . ."

He grew paler than usual. The topic of marriage always shut him up.

Balancing a plate on each hand, Charlene turned to leave with a grin. "Back to my roomy new office. See you later, boys."

Simon moved on from pastries to pizza. He was on his second piece of pepperoni and mushroom when Kate and Tanya arrived. He wiped his mouth with a crinkly napkin. "You must be hungry, sweetheart. Can I get you something?"

"Aw, Simon," Tanya replied, smirking. "You calling me sweetheart again?"

Kate reached past him for a Post-it square. "I need to write a note for Beth before I forget what I'm thinking." She waved her hand toward the delicacies in the pink boxes, still sitting near Spike, and raised her eyebrows. "Has she seen those? You might want to hide them. Her wrist is a brilliant pink from all the snapping."

Robert took another slice of supreme. "I tried to warn him, Power Pack, but he wouldn't listen."

"Uh-oh." Kate wrote the note and stuck it to a corkboard. She draped her arm around Simon's neck. "I'd hate for anything to happen to this pretty face."

"You think I'm pretty?" He pulled her closer.

"Please," Robert said, between bites of pizza. "You guys are too cute. But why work that hard? Lower your expectations. Beth gets starry-eyed if I don't belch after eating."

Footsteps stopped behind them and they all three turned around.

Robert didn't bat an eye when Beth sat down beside him. "Did I hear my name?"

He smiled. "Just saying I'm lucky to have you."

Beth rose and went to Spike. "Damn it, Simon." She took an éclair from the nearest pink box. "Fine. I'm giving up the whole diet thing. I hope you like round women, Robert."

Kate squeezed Simon's arm and then released him. Her lips were clamped shut, like she was trying very hard not to laugh. "I've got to go. Save me some food, okay?" She left for her next appointment, glancing back with a smile.

Robert seemed to be choosing his words carefully. Simon could almost hear the gears working in his brain. If he said that he liked round women, Beth would think he was calling her fat. Yet if he didn't like them, he was calling Beth fat while being unsupportive and judgmental. Dangerous dilemma.

"I like you any way you choose to be," Robert muttered.

Beth looked pleased, but then her smile faded. "I'm turning forty soon. Do I look that old?"

Robert shot out of the room before she could engage him in a conversation about aging. Beth turned to find Simon eating a cruller.

"I like round women," he said with a grin.

"Oh, shut up! You remind me of my little brother. I used to give him a quarter to leave me alone."

"I cost more than that. At least a buck."

"On second thought," Beth mused. "I think we need to keep

Quinn Coleridge

you around. Who else can I blame for the numbers on my scale?"

Simon looked pointedly at her and she punched him in the shoulder before opening a diet soda. After taking a drink, Beth asked, "When's the big event?"

He choked on the éclair, thinking that this was a segue leading to another discussion about abstinence.

"Geez, Simon," Beth said, hitting him on the back. "I just wanted to know when you're installing the new cabinets."

What a relief. The cabinets. "I'm bringing them here in a moving van on Saturday."

"Robert will be so happy. You've done so much for this place."

"It's been fun," Simon replied as he threw paper plates and napkins into a garbage bag.

Beth got up to leave. Kate nearly bumped into her at the door and stepped aside. "Sorry, Beth." She walked over to Simon. "My last appointment cancelled. You're smiling."

Simon sat back, relaxed and content. "I'm feeling good."

"You look like it."

"Oh, I am." He watched Kate take a bite of pizza. "I'd feel even better if you moved closer."

"I think I'll stay over here." She sat in Robert's chair, near enough that their knees were touching. "You're looking at me like I'm one of those éclairs."

He checked that they were alone. "Want to rent a movie and have a quiet night at my place? You could park the Triumph at your apartment, and I'll drive you back later."

"I'd like to help pick up but then I'm free."

Beth was organizing a huge pile of toys in the waiting room. Simon took an armful of stuffed animals and put them in the storage box. He picked up a colorful board book and flipped through the pages.

Beth glanced over to see what he was doing. Her expression turned nostalgic. "My boys used to ask for *Goodnight Moon* all the time. Those were the days."

Simon felt a little nostalgic too. Especially about the little old lady and the bowl full of mush. "I remember my mom reading this to me when I was little. Along with *The Runaway Bunny.*"

Kate came in to empty the trash. Simon put the board books up on a shelf. "We're discussing the oeuvre of Margaret Wise Brown."

She tied her trash bag and dropped it by the door. "One of my favorite children's book authors. She died at forty-two, during a book tour in France. It was a tragic story, actually, and lends a certain poignancy to her work."

Simon grinned at Beth. "She's on my team if we play Trivial Pursuit."

Beth jammed a Tonka truck into the toy box. "Don't tell me anything else, Kate! I don't want to know the deeper meaning behind those stories. Let me escape real life and enjoy them in ignorance."

After cleaning the exam rooms and locking up, Kate rode her bike to her apartment. Simon followed and picked her up. They made popcorn in his kitchen. Halfway through *The Proposal*, Kate laughed at something Ryan Reynolds said and turned to Simon. Her vitality and joy dazzled him. Happy just to hold her hand, he linked their fingers and saw that the damn wedding band was still in place.

Cursing in his head, Simon wondered at what point it would be acceptable for him to ask her to take it off. Then he understood why Kate had once said that she was afraid of being happy.

When things were this good, you had a lot to lose.

Chapter 25

Kate locked the door to her basement apartment, then jogged up the short set of brick steps. Humming softly, she carried her pack on one shoulder and walked down the path that led to the carport. The late afternoon sky was nearly cloudless and the blue seemed to go on forever as she gazed at it.

Thinking of her shift that night at the ER, Kate was barely aware of the Walther strapped to her hip. She was about to put on her motorcycle helmet when something metallic hit the pavement. The sound was so soft she'd barely heard it. Kate checked the area at her feet. Nothing.

She knelt down by the Triumph. The carport floor had that standard oil-and-gas smell but another odor caught her attention. Cigarettes. A few burned remnants lay near her front tire. Kate stood, turned in a circle, and searched the surrounding area. Her heart stalled as she thought of a man appearing from behind that parked car. Shadows moving out of those trees. A deep voice behind her.

The things women feared when they were vulnerable and alone.

No movements. The parking lot remained quiet and secretive. Kate looked back at the ash by her tire. First there were the butts in the garden shed, then the break-in at her apartment and the cigarette left smoldering on her coffee table, and now these ashes. Was it Julian? Was he here, watching?

From the corner of her eye, Kate caught a faint flash of gold. Crabgrass grew up through a crack in the cement and she knelt down again, pushing the grass away. A gold heart peeked out at her. Her mother's charm bracelet glittered in the fading sunlight.

How did it get down there?

She picked up the bracelet, ran her finger over the dented heart, and tried to fasten the chain around her wrist. It slid off and fell to the ground again.

A loose clasp, maybe? Kate snatched it up.

She looked around the carport once more but couldn't detect any obvious danger signs. Kate slipped the bracelet into her backpack, put on her helmet, and got on the bike. The street was bustling with cars. She couldn't be late to the hospital again. Her job there paid the rent and all her other bills.

Kate tried a shortcut but a new restaurant was having its grand opening, which congested the whole area. Traffic inched along. Muttering impatiently, she stopped at a four-way intersection and worried about whether the bracelet would be safe. What if it fell out of the backpack? Her makeup bag might be a better choice.

There was a break in the traffic as the light changed. Kate shot the gap and zoomed through the intersection. The next five blocks felt like an obstacle course as she pulled around a double-parked delivery truck and passed a swerving student driver who didn't seem aware of motorcyclists or the purpose of signaling. Kate took the last corner and rolled to a stop in the hospital employee parking area. There wasn't enough time to drop stuff off at her locker. She'd only brought a handful of things: a book, her makeup bag, hospital ID, wallet, etc. She slipped the lanyard with the ID over her head and put the wallet in her back pocket. With only three minutes to go, Kate locked her pack in the hard saddlebag on her bike and ran to the elevator.

Hours later, toward the end of her shift, she logged into a computer and typed up detailed instructions for a patient's care. Kate checked her watch: 4:07 a.m. A sudden onslaught of nerves made her tremble. This was the day she'd been dreading.

Simon's invitation to the gala at the museum had seemed like a good idea a week ago. She'd still felt confident then but now that the event was nigh, all confidence was non-existent. Meeting Jack and Cecily Phillips was scary. What would they think of her?

Simon had a photograph of his parents in his study, and Kate found it hard to reconcile the motherly person he described with the beautiful woman in the picture. She was dark and elegant, like Jacqueline Kennedy at her most stylish. But that wasn't all. Cecily had brains and did charity work too. She was a Vassar grad who'd attended the Sorbonne, a museum docent, and a member of the Junior League. Kate felt uncouth by comparison. A country bumpkin with a sordid past.

In the same photograph, Jack Phillips wore a flinty expression while holding his laughing grandson. Kate tried to keep panic from bubbling up to the surface as she imagined meeting him again. The first time in the community center lobby hadn't gone so hot. Exhaling slowly, Kate focused on not hyperventilating or throwing up.

Fortunately, she knew that if she passed out at the gala from anxiety, at least she'd go down looking good. A personal stylist at Nordstrom had seen to that. Kate tried not to think of how much she'd paid for her gown. Evidently the designer had been heavily influenced by Chanel when he created a column of ecru Chantilly lace that fell in beaded, shimmering tiers from just below her hips to the floor. A narrow black velvet sash tied at the waist and a black beaded shrug covered her bare shoulders.

The gown was classic. Tasteful. Tess would never have selected it for herself, not in a million years.

———————— • ————————

Installing the new cabinets at the clinic wasn't easy. The 'muscle' Robert had promised to help move the heavy pieces into the building never showed up. Simon, Robert, and a few teenagers who happened to be passing by, managed to get them inside. It had been a busy afternoon, but once the installation was complete, Robert was ecstatic. There was nothing shabby or neglected about the office now. The whole space was transfigured by the smooth, glowing wood. Robert couldn't say enough nice things, and with tears in his eyes, he hugged Simon roughly and slapped him on the back.

"Thanks, brother," Robert choked out. "Even if I end up selling this place, it's so much better than before."

Simon couldn't smile at this or feel good about Robert's praise. Over the last month and a half, his sense of right and wrong had grown more defined.

"Don't sell," he heard himself say. "People need you here. Let me help you find a way to keep it."

Robert's face turned pink, then red. A storm cloud at sunset. "What about all the figures you've given me? The plumbing, the entire second phase of the project? I can't pay for that!"

Simon's figures were absolutely correct, but they hadn't

been right. Or good. Or hopeful. He put a hand on Robert's arm. "Forget what I said. If a developer buys this, they'll tear it down."

"The roof," Robert started to argue. "The boiler—"

"I know all that." Simon's eyes felt gritty, like they had finally opened after a long sleep. "The place is a mess. A monstrosity. But it's amazing too. Work here for a while and it gets under your skin. If you sell, sell to me."

Simon shocked himself. He couldn't believe the outrageous words he'd just spoken. And he wasn't even drunk.

As Robert gasped at the offer, Beth entered the lobby. "Hey," she said. "We better head out if we're going to return the rental truck. Robert?"

The doctor's face was slack, mouth open, eyes wide. "I'll drive the truck," he replied, coming out of his stupor. "You follow me in your minivan."

Simon walked with them to the door. "Think about what I said, Robert."

As they drove out of the parking lot, Simon contemplated the insane thing he'd just set in motion. He'd lose the *Annus Mirabilis* to Carter Wright. Lose his standing as the most financially successful lawyer at the firm since his brother West left for Dubai.

Strangely, Simon didn't want to recant. He would help Robert keep the community center running, one way or another.

Tanya shut the door to the office. She and Beth had wiped out the cabinets, before filling them with supplies and files. "I'm going now. Why are you still hanging around? Isn't there a gala at the museum tonight?"

The gala. Simon had almost forgotten. Beth had asked him to lock up the community center. As he went through the steps of closing things down, it felt significant, like the end to a chapter of his life. This depressed Simon briefly. He'd liked who he was when he worked here. He'd left a piece of himself, a mark of his own behind.

Driving home, Simon made a call to Ed Moyer. Ed exploded when he told him that the property on Everett wasn't available since a third party had made an offer. Simon didn't mention that he was the third party.

"I should have listened to Carter Wright," Ed said, after calming down. "He gets things done."

"I'm sorry to disappoint you, Ed."

Moyer hung up and Simon called Carter Wright. "What do you want, Phillips? Have you called to gloat?"

Simon pulled into his driveway and parked. "What is there to gloat about?"

"The shareholders sided with the target company. I have nothing to show for my time in L.A. but a lousy tan."

After the failure in California, Carter would be hungry for another deal. He'd swoop down to snatch up Ed Moyer like a barracuda.

"I didn't call to gloat," Simon assured him. "I need you to take on Moyer Unlimited exclusively. Ed wants you on the real estate deal."

Carter was silent for a half second and then he laughed. "But I'll win. I'll get the trophy, the money, the bragging rights. All of it."

Winning now seemed like a relative term. It encompassed a lot more than those prizes. "Congratulations, Carter. You've earned it."

Simon entered his home and went to the living room. He stood in front of the huge gleaming trophy in the corner, twin of the Stanley Cup. Two names were engraved at the base: West Phillips and Simon Phillips. What had it cost them? Hours and hours of life. Nights without sleep. Untold stress.

"Good riddance," Simon told *Annus Mirabilis.*

While cleaning up for the gala, he felt free in a way that had eluded him since law school. Simon passed over the Armani tux hanging in his closet and instead chose a suit from a shop on London's Savile Row, to honor Kate's British heritage. The classic lines were dressy without being too formal. He selected a tailored white shirt and a black silk tie. Fastening his stainless-steel cufflinks, Simon examined his reflection. His mother would not make it through the night without telling him to get a haircut.

Ready at last, Simon got into the Mercedes and turned on the engine. Metallica blared from the speakers. He smiled. Kate had been in charge of music, and the volume button, last time they drove together. Simon pulled out of his driveway and headed downtown. He'd attended scores of parties and fundraisers—wasted hours of small talk spent with a drink in his hand. Tonight would be something else entirely. Time spent with Kate was never a waste.

Chapter 26

A flowery scent blew through the open window. Poet's jasmine grew all around the old Victorian house. The balmy evening air was tempting. It felt exotic and seemed to promise a lot more fun than being indoors. After working at the ER all night, Kate had spent most of the day sleeping. She was eager now to get outside and see the world. Kate closed the ground-level window, then slipped two twenties into her beaded bag, along with a lipstick and her house keys. No Walther on her hip tonight. There wasn't a place to hide it that wouldn't show under the gown. And an ankle holster didn't seem appropriate.

Kate wasn't really worried. She and Simon would be surrounded by crowds at the gala. He was driving her there and back. It felt safe to go unarmed.

The grandfather clock in the living room chimed six times. Simon had told her he'd be there at six o'clock. Kate locked the apartment door and went up to the garden to sit at the picnic table under the pergola. Massive rhododendrons and hydrangeas grew on all sides and the poet's jasmine smelled even more intense. She waited for a minute or two, rubbed her hands together, and stood. The garden usually felt peaceful. Was this unsettled feeling just nerves? Worry that she'd make a fool of herself at the gala?

Kate tried to analyze the strange sensation. The dress she wore was pretty, she was excited to see Simon, even her hair looked good. None of that distressed her. Still, Kate felt odd—tense—as if her every move was being watched. Which was stupid. People were around, why wouldn't they watch a woman in a fancy gown under the pergola? Martha, one of her neighbors, was watering some potted plants. Her granddaughters sat on the grass nearby playing with dolls.

Yet Kate's uneasiness remained. She lifted her gaze to the blank windows on the upper floors. The curtains were drawn, the shades neatly in place. *Listen to your instincts,* Mike had always said. *Go with your gut.*

Right then her gut didn't know what to do. Going back inside didn't seem right. She hated being imprisoned by fear but how could she protect herself if there was trouble?

Kate counted to ten and felt better. She looked over her shoulder toward the garden shed. It hadn't changed, just a rectangle with a pitched roof, painted blue and white. But the side door was open. Was someone there? Kate was about to go investigate when a female voice called her name.

"Going somewhere special?"

Hand on her pounding heart, Kate turned to see her neighbor turning off the hose. She was done watering her plants. "Martha?"

The older woman was one of Kate's favorite neighbors. Kind and always ready to share a story from a full, well-lived life.

"Hello, dear." Martha smiled, showing straight teeth slightly yellowed with age. Her granddaughters must have gone inside the apartment but their dolls were still strewn over the grass. "What a pretty dress."

A car door slammed out by the street and Kate wondered if Simon had arrived. She gave her lacy skirt a flounce. "We're attending a benefit at the art museum."

"The girls thought you looked like a princess." Martha opened the door to her apartment and switched on the security light. "Have a wonderful time. Let's do tea next week and you can tell me all about it."

"I'll try to remember all the details."

"Goodnight," Martha said before going inside.

"'Night."

Kate walked to the gate at the side of the Victorian, where she could see the street, and the fine hairs on the back of her neck rose. She turned toward the shadows beyond the shed. An evergreen branch swayed softly, like someone had brushed against it only moments before.

———————•———————

Simon parked at the curb, surprised to see Kate standing on the sidewalk. She stuck out her thumb to hitch a ride and coyly lifted the hem of her dress to show a flash of ankle.

"Going my way?" he asked, admiring the view.

"I was over at the gate and saw your car turn the corner." Kate's sudden smile was brilliant. Playful. "My date stood me up. Mind taking his place?"

Her dress glittered in the last shards of sunlight. "Honey," he said. "If your date showed up now, I'd have to hurt him."

Simon got out of the car and circled Kate without saying a word, surveying her from head to foot. "Wow. You clean up good." He leaned in for a kiss.

When Simon released her, Kate appeared too mesmerized

to move, eyes half-closed, hands wrinkling the sides of his dress shirt. He gave her a little smile, nodding toward the car. "Ladies first."

"Thank you." Kate noticed that Simon stayed a few steps behind. "What are you doing?"

"Just watching you walk."

She put a hand on her hip, the gentle sway of her movements a shade more pronounced. A few more steps, and Simon was jogging after her. He opened the door on her side of the car.

"A personal shopper got you this dress?" he asked, taking a piece of the lace between his fingers. "Worth every penny."

The parking attendant took Simon's keys as black, white, and silver limousines waited at the curb to drop off their passengers. Simon led Kate toward the museum entrance along a blue-carpeted pathway. She was glad to have his hand in hers, surrounded as they were by wealthy partygoers.

So many of them looked bored. It made no sense to Kate. At what point did being beautiful and well-dressed grow tiresome? Make such fortunate people appear so blasé?

As Simon introduced her to family friends, Kate's lungs stopped working. They felt small and inadequate for a panicking person's breathing needs. *Inhale, exhale. Inhale, exhale. No fainting allowed.*

Still holding her hand, he whispered in her ear, "Thanks for doing this with me. I love you."

Those last three words were like a tonic. Her lungs expanded properly and she could breathe. Even smile at the man talking to her about his yacht. Then Kate recognized Simon's mother as she waved to them from the courtyard, her diamond rings catching the light. Kate was dazzled by the sheer magnitude of carats Cecily wore and resisted the gentle tug of Simon's hand. Her newfound courage faltered. Would Cecily recognize Kate as the girl who scrubbed her bathrooms that one summer?

No, of course not. She had grown up since then. Her body was thinner now and her hair was better, cut at a salon regularly instead of at home. Life experience had given Kate a confidence that she'd lacked as a girl.

All that aside, Cecily wouldn't know her because maids were invisible creatures to the rich. "Go visit your family," Kate whispered. "I'll meet you later."

He pulled her forward. "Not without you. It'll be fine. Trust me."

After being introduced to both of Simon's parents, Kate thought that they were only slightly less terrifying than she had imagined. Cecily did not show any signs of recognizing Kate but she was friendly and gracious. She chatted with Simon about Leonard, apparently one of the partners at his firm. Jack shook Kate's hand, like they had never met at the clinic, and asked about her medical practice. While she responded to his question, he signaled a waiter for a fresh gin and tonic. The alcohol smell made her stomach turn.

"A nonprofit you say?" Jack asked after taking a sip. "You're not a banner-waving hippie, are you?"

I've waved a few banners in my time, Kate thought to herself. *And my best friend would like to be a hippie.*

Jack's condescending tone made her stand up straighter. She wasn't intimidated anymore. "All the people I work with are highly skilled professionals."

"No leftist liberals?"

Kate smiled inside. Robert was a definite liberal but he didn't sacrifice so much because of a specific party. "Politics aren't a motivating factor. People are, though. We hope to ease the suffering that can be remedied with proper medical care, regardless of the patient's ability to pay."

Jack gave a cynical nod. "Then it's safe to assume you're not a gold digger?"

"Yes, I'd say it is." Kate kept her voice even. She saw that Simon was now talking to a man standing behind Cecily, leaning far enough away that he couldn't hear their conversation.

Kate turned her attention back to Jack. "Do you often ask new acquaintances that question?"

"Not often . . . but a rich man always worries that he's being stolen from, Doctor. It's one of the drawbacks of being wealthy."

Keeping her temper in check, Kate said, "We're always grateful for donations at the clinic, Mr. Phillips, but I'm sure we'd stop short of larceny to get them."

The corners of his mouth moved fractionally toward his cheeks, giving the faintest impression of a smile. "Oh, please call me Jack, since we're talking about something as personal as money."

———————————— • ————————————

Dinner chimes rang. The four of them walked into the gala together and sat down in their designated seats. Tables identical to theirs filled the room, each one with an arrangement of lilies in the center. Chamber music echoed softly in the background as projected images of famous impressionist artwork covered the walls. The paintings changed at timed intervals with the music.

Cecily touched Kate's arm. Simon was right. As beautiful as the woman was, she did have a maternal quality about her. Cecily nodded at the centerpieces. "They represent Monet's *Water Lilies*."

Kate smiled back. "They're beautiful. I love the work Monet did at Giverny. Lucky for us he didn't become a grocer as his father intended."

"What a loss that would have been!" Cecily replied. Her face turned wistful. "I had a crush on him when I studied art history. He was so dashing."

"To crushes." Jack saluted her with his gin and tonic.

Cecily patted his cheek and the diamond flashed again, nearly blinding Kate. "Never mind, darling. I prefer retired lawyers now."

Smiling faintly, Jack signaled a waiter. "What will it be, son? Scotch, vodka? How about you, Kate? Shall we order wine?"

"No, thank you," Kate replied. "I don't drink."

Simon had been quiet since joining Jack and Cecily. He didn't seem unhappy, listening as his parents talked, but now he glared at his father. Why was Simon so tense? Did he not want her to know that he drank? Kate remembered seeing the old society page article and the photo of Simon surrounded by women, a bottle of champagne in one hand. Was he holding back now because he knew she didn't like alcohol? Kate had not considered their compatibility in that regard. They'd gone out to eat several times and he had never even ordered a beer.

Simon shook his head at Jack. "I'm going to pass, Dad."

"It's just so unprecedented—"

Cecily interrupted her husband. "Simon's an adult. He can choose for himself."

The tension grew less pronounced as Jack turned his scrutiny away from Simon and moved on to the appetizers. Kate examined the rectangular plate before her. It held a warm purplish-green fig stuffed with goat cheese, a miniature ramekin of white truffle risotto, and a lobster salad served over a bed of peppery watercress. She marveled silently, watching the others to see which fork she should use. A waiter brought a chilled bottle of chardonnay to their table. When he reached Kate, Simon indicated that they would both have water to drink for the evening. His father laughed quietly across the table. It didn't sound kind.

A cold, spicy cucumber soup arrived next. It had a smooth, light texture perfect for summer. The main course followed, consisting of tiny servings of tender medallions of rare Kobe beef, white asparagus spears, and a seared filet of salmon with a citrus and berry reduction. What people in Kate's world would call a fancy surf and turf. The flavors were sweet, salty, earthy, and rich. Their dessert course concluded the meal with a meringue cloud sitting in the center of a pool of raspberry puree.

Simon winked at her when the last dish was cleared away. This wink said he was ready for a nap.

She winked back in total agreement. "I've never been this full in my life. But it was amazing."

The auction turned out to be a lively, competitive event. All of the artwork was done by local artists, many of them students, and Jack bought a still life of water lilies for Cecily. It took a large amount of money for him to secure the painting since his competitors were as determined as he was to win.

"There you are, my love," Jack said, reaching for his

wallet. "If you can't have Monet himself, you can at least have some flowers to remember him by."

Kate watched the Phillips family interact. Cecily kept the conversation going, guiding it along with appropriate comments. She occasionally stopped to brush the hair from her son's eyes. Jack and Simon did not exchange more than a few sentences. Even those had a contentious undertone. It seemed sad, that such intelligent, beautiful people, who had a long history together, couldn't relax at the same table for a couple of hours.

At the end of the evening, Simon's parents said goodbye as a valet brought their car to a halt at the curb. Jack shook Kate's hand, sounding rather perfunctory as he murmured that it had been a pleasure. Cecily hugged her and then Simon.

"Bring Kate with you tomorrow. We're having pot roast for dinner." She touched his overgrown hair. "And cut your mane."

Simon smiled at her. "I knew you were going to say that."

Watching his parents drive away, he put his arm loosely around Kate's shoulders. His easy, warm manner had returned. "Well, what did you think?"

Kate was ready for this question. She knew Simon would want to know her impressions of Cecily or whether she'd been offended by Jack. "Your mother is just like you said—kind, smart, beautiful."

"Absolutely," Simon agreed. "And my dad?"

"Jack's different. He's—"

"Like being stabbed in the eye with a hot poker?" This was suggested in such a matter-of-fact way.

"Yuck! No. I wasn't going to say that." Simon must have been a mischievous child. It was easy to imagine him as an unholy terror, running off nannies and housekeepers.

Laughing, Kate put her hands on each side of his face. "No. Jack—"

"Makes you want to go base jumping without a parachute?"

"I'm afraid of heights. And stop interrupting." Kate was tempted to kiss Simon right there in front of all the rich, stuffy people waiting for their cars. "My impression is that your dad is comfortable with himself. He says what he thinks and makes no apologies. He'll keep me on my toes."

Simon acted like he hadn't heard right. "Was that a compliment? For my father? You have a softer heart than I do." He pulled her closer and whispered near her ear. "Along with soft skin, soft lips, soft hair, soft . . ."

"I get the idea."

He sent her a glittering look. "I'm really glad your date stood you up."

Once they were inside Simon's car, he drove to Kate's near-empty street and pulled over. He turned toward her. "I have news I need to share with you."

"News?"

"My leave from the law firm is over."

"Oh, that's great, Simon." She kept her tone light, tried to sound supportive. "It's what you wanted, right?"

"It is and it isn't." He exhaled slowly, shaking his head. "I have to be honest with you, Kate."

Her heart tripped in her chest. Nothing good ever came from someone claiming they needed to be honest. "Are you married? Do you have kids?"

He rolled his eyes. "Not funny. Will you let me say this?"

"All right."

Silence filled the Mercedes. Kate dreaded what was coming next. *Sorry. I won't have time for you anymore.* Or *It's been nice, but I think it's best if we take a break . . . My career is my focus right now . . .*

In lieu of those things, he said, "I've invested so many years at the firm—my dad's firm, my brother's firm—but I don't know if I want to continue on there for the rest of my career. I thought I did once, but I don't know if that's true now. I need to find out."

She ruffled the hair at his collar. "You could always stay with us and be the most overqualified handyman ever."

A brief smile. "Thanks, but no."

Kate could hear the strain in his voice. Simon must feel incredible pressure with his family so invested in the firm. "You should go back and give it your best shot."

"I plan to. I'll be working long days, sometimes nights."

The shaky hope that had pushed her fear away took a hit. Was a relationship between them really possible with such busy lives? "I understand. I have similar hours."

"That's why I want us to make a pact."

What did he mean? A pact? Kate cocked her head. "Like the Kellogg-Briand Pact of 1928?"

He tugged on his tie and laughed. "No, you weirdo. Who knows things like that? I want us to agree to talk every day."

She helped him with the tie, loosening the knot. The hope in her heart returned. "Talk each day? Yes. I will agree to that. Are we going to make a blood oath too?"

He breathed a longsuffering sigh. "Maybe later. In addition to daily conversation, I propose that we don't go more than seventy-two hours without seeing each other."

"Hmm." Kate was feeling better and better about the whole discussion. "Okay."

He held out his hand. "We've got a pact then?"

They shook on it. "Now what about the blood oath?"

"I'd prefer a kiss to seal the deal." Simon motioned toward the gearshift. "This is my side. That's your side. Don't get too handsy."

"Handsy?" She could tell it was a joke, sort of.

"I think we should, you know, establish some rules of courtship. Rules that involve keeping you and that dress over there."

Simon looked pretty irresistible when he was trying to be prudish. "Rules, huh? As in the Courtship and Kissing Goodnight Rules of 1827?"

He snorted in response. "You're the worst, Kate. Can't we act like grownups for one—"

"Oops!" She moved her arm slightly past the gearshift. "Look what I did."

Watching her, a new light entered his eyes. "I appreciate how seriously you're taking this."

"It's a totally serious situation." Kate marched her fingers up his arm. "Is this too handsy?"

Simon caught her by the wrist. "I should warn you, Spencer. You're playing with fire."

"Oooh. I'm scared."

He silenced her with a kiss. It began with a little laughter on both sides and evolved into something more meaningful and tender. When the kiss came to an end, Kate managed to find her voice. She traced the strong lines of Simon's cheekbone and jaw. "I love you something massive. Do you know that?"

"I think I do."

"Great," she replied. "Now what about that goodnight kiss?"

"I thought we'd already done that." He brushed a curl from her cheek.

Kate shook her head and smiled. "That was to seal the pact. The next one is for goodnight."

———————• • ———————

After several more—final, very last—goodnight kisses, they got out of the Mercedes and walked toward Kate's apartment. The evening had an enchanted feeling with just enough warmth to the wind and a milky-colored moon hanging in the sky. Her dress glowed in the lamplight. Simon held the gate and looked over toward the carport as Kate entered the yard. The Triumph was laying on its side in her parking space. Simon hoped that whatever happened had been accidental, but he knew it wasn't.

"Oh no," she whispered, covering her mouth with one hand. "My bike. . ."

Simon went ahead of Kate, glass crunching under his shoes as he drew near the Triumph. All of its lights had been smashed, the seat cut several times, and the hard saddlebags on the sides broken. Probably with a baseball bat.

"Don't touch anything," he said. "Let's call the police."

It was so difficult to sound logical when he wanted to put the bat to better use and find whoever ruined her bike. But Simon didn't want to scare Kate.

She looked so strong and brave. Hadn't shed one tear or cursed. A black-and-white patrol car arrived just as Kate was leaving a message for her insurance agent. The officers interviewed them, took photographs of her bike, got an estimate of its value, and checked for security camera footage. They discussed the restraining order for Julian Quinton, the break-in at her apartment, and the tire that had been slashed recently. That done, the cops went off to speak with some of her neighbors to see if anyone had heard or seen anything suspicious.

One of the policemen asked if there was anything of value in the saddlebags.

"I keep a few dollars in there for emergencies . . ." Then through the flashing red and blue lights, Kate's face grew pale.

She knelt by the bike and looked into a saddlebag. Simon checked the other one. "Careful, Kate. There's still some glass. Don't cut yourself."

Both saddlebags were empty and the expression on her face broke his heart. He helped her up. She swayed a little on her feet. "What were you looking for?"

Kate's shoulders dropped. The bravery and strength from before were gone. Simon couldn't be sure, but it seemed like grief had taken their place.

Stepping away from the bike, Kate said, "I bought a few groceries on the way home today. Some canned goods, bread, and pasta. I carried them into my apartment, but I left my pack behind. I was so tired and the saddlebags were locked, so I thought it would be okay."

"Was your wallet in there?"

"No. Just a copy of *The Old Man and the Sea*, sunglasses, lip balm, and a makeup bag."

He felt relief. Her ID and credit cards were safe. "So, nothing really valuable?"

Kate lowered her chin, visibly trembling. "Yes, there was. The clasp on my mother's charm bracelet broke. I zipped it in the makeup bag and planned to go to the repair shop on my next day off. It was valuable to me."

An officer took down a description of the bracelet and added it to the report. After the police left, Simon walked with Kate to her apartment. She offered him the key and he opened the door. Kate made it to the kitchen table, sat down, and covered her face, taking deep breaths while obviously trying not to cry.

Simon kissed the top of her head and squatted down beside her. "We'll find it, Kate. If I have to scour every pawnshop and jewelry store in the city, I promise you I'll get it back."

A minute passed, her breathing grew easier, and Simon got up. He removed two china cups and saucers from the cabinet.

"How could I be so stupid?" Kate asked. "That bracelet was all I had left of her. Who would even want it? All banged up and scratched like that?"

Simon filled a kettle and put it on the burner. "I don't know, baby. But it isn't all you have of Tess. There are the paintings. They're amazing. And your love of music and art. The way you charm everyone that crosses your path. The best of her is still around."

One of the tears Kate had been trying so hard to hold back rolled down her cheek. "Thanks."

When the tea had finished steeping, Simon poured out two cups of chamomile. "Is it okay if the teapot doesn't match the cup, or would that violate some age-old British custom?"

A soft gasp escaped her lips. Then a ghost of a smile. "I expect it will taste the same either way."

He sat down at the small table and added a packet of sweetener to his tea. "Don't give up. We'll work out a recovery plan for the bracelet tomorrow."

"It's just a thing, right?" Looking up at him, she wiped her face. "It's just a thing. It's not Tess. I didn't lose her again. Nothing's really changed."

"Nothing's changed," Simon agreed. "You're the same smart, beautiful woman I took to the gala and walked with in the moonlight. The same dedicated doctor with a heart of gold. An actual heart, not the banged-up charm on your mother's bracelet."

Eyes glistening, Kate picked up her cup. Simon took a large sip of his tea and tried not to spray it everywhere. He grimaced and swallowed. "Oh, that's terrible! How can you drink it? It's like warm ditchwater."

She bent over, laughing silently. "I guess chamomile is an acquired taste. Maybe it needs more sweetening."

He fetched the honey bear from the pantry and squeezed some of the amber syrup into his cup. Simon was cautious about the second sip. "Okay. Honey ditchwater is a *little* better."

"There's enough for you to have seconds."

He pulled a face, making Kate laugh again. "I was afraid you were going to say that."

Chapter 27

Kate looked at the clock on the wall and snuck out of the chapel just before the Sunday service ended. The church building was just a few blocks north of her home. She hurried back as quickly as she could, but Simon was already there, wearing dark sunglasses and leaning against the Mercedes at the curb.

"I'm sorry, I'm sorry," she said, kissing him as she flew by on the way to her side of the car.

"It's okay. My parents won't mind if we're ten minutes late."

"What if the roast burns? I don't want to ruin your mom's plans. She said five."

Simon grabbed her hand. "My mom's a messy cook, and everything is approximated. Especially the serving time. You look nice. I like eyelet. It's the peekaboo fabric."

"Is the dress too much?"

"Yes. If there were less of it, I'd like it better." Simon kissed her again and opened the car door.

She climbed in, checking to see if her skirt revealed more than it should. "You can't really see anything through this, can you?"

"Unfortunately, no."

They cruised to his parents' home with the windows open. Warm pine needles and freshly trimmed lawns scented the air, but Kate felt her stomach flip with nerves as they pulled into the long driveway. Trees of all kinds grew in profusion, shielding the house from the road until they came to its final curve. An enormous stone mansion rose from the shelter of an old pine grove, surrounded by well-tended, manicured gardens. Stunned, Kate coughed, feeling as though she had been punched in the throat. Putting on her sunglasses, she tried to appear calm. They drove to the back of the house and parked.

When she had come here to clean that summer, Kate was but one of many maids in a twelve-passenger van. They had already cleaned two other mansions that day and she had fallen asleep during the ride over. Her impressions of the Phillips' home back then were white walls, white marble, glass chandeliers, and high ceilings. Everything was spotless and clean. Kate didn't see a spec of dirt in the bathroom but she did her job anyway. Besides her chance encounter with Simon and his girlfriend that one time, she didn't remember much else. Just cleaning an already clean house and riding in the van.

Kate undid her seatbelt and got out of the car before Simon arrived to help. If she hadn't noticed much on her first visit, she did now. Details seemed to jump out at her from all directions.

To the right, there was a large oval swimming pool surrounded by Adirondack lounge chairs. Beyond that stood a cottage with a slate roof. The walls were draped with wisteria, roses, and ivy, like a scene from the Cotswolds in England. To the left, a tennis court with pristine white lines. She saw a stable in the distance. The cupola on the stable featured a running horse weathervane. Kate turned in a circle. It was crazy. Flower gardens didn't seem to end in any direction. Is this how the second Mrs. de Winter felt in *Rebecca*, when she saw Manderley?

Simon put his arm around her. "Let's go inside."

Those words made Kate feel as if her feet could move again. Her stunned brain began to work. "Yes," she mumbled. "Sorry."

They walked across a massive stone porch and Simon opened the door. He took her hand, drawing her inside. Kate made the mistake of looking up at the chandelier above. Hundreds of crystals cast refracted light against the walls, and she froze like a dazzled raccoon.

Simon rubbed her hands. "You can do this. Breathe, Breathe . . ."

She tore her gaze away from the chandelier and nodded at him, repeating, "I can do this. I can do this ..." But it came out as a question. Could she? People like her didn't know people who actually lived in houses like this. "Maybe I can't, Simon. I feel a little sick."

He smiled and towed her toward the hall. "I've got an idea. You'll like it, I promise."

Keeping her hands in his, Simon backed down the hallway and she followed. Kate didn't look away from him, but she had the vague impression of passing a music room and a wood-paneled office.

"Keep going," Simon murmured. "Almost there."

Then he swung her into a two-story room with a big fireplace. Tall shelves of books lined the walls on both floors, some with sliding ladders. Kate felt like she was in heaven. Her feet wanted to take her everywhere, to explore all of the library at once.

"Well?" Simon asked. "What do you think?"

"It's glorious. Amazing."

She gravitated to a section of books kept under lock and key. Kate turned to Simon, pointing at a first-edition copy of Joyce's *Ulysses*.

"Do you know how rare this is? You could buy a new car for what it's worth. Look at the Melville, it's absolutely beautiful . . . and I've never even *heard* of that Steinbeck. I think it still has the original dust jacket!"

Kate continued to examine the collection. "How could you ever leave, with all this?" She sucked in her breath. "Matthew Arnold."

Simon put his arm around her shoulders. "The dreamy look on your face is making me uncomfortable. I'm here. Matthew Arnold isn't."

"If you had read 'Dover Beach,' you'd be dreamy too. 'Ah, love, let us be true to one another!'"

He turned to leave. "I'll give you and the library a moment alone."

She caught up with Simon, hugging him from behind. "Sorry. I can get carried away." Her voice was muffled against his jacket. "Thank you for taking me there. I feel more myself."

Cecily stepped out of a doorway up ahead. "I thought I heard voices. Where's Kate?"

Simon stepped aside. "She's right here."

Cecily wore gray linen trousers with a white silk blouse. She smelled faintly of Joy perfume when she hugged Kate.

"Do you like to cook?" Cecily asked.

"If it's a simple recipe."

Cecily motioned them forward. "When Simon was young, I left the cooking to someone else. Now I have to beg him to come home and let me fix him dinner."

They passed an art gallery on their way to the kitchen. Kate recognized the whimsical talent of Maxfield Parrish and a bleak, almost disturbing landscape by Wyeth. Other paintings hung on the walls but she couldn't identify them. The part of her that had shared her mother's passion for art wanted to go back and examine each one.

When they finally entered the kitchen, Jack stood at the faucet with his finger under the running tap. His wife sighed and placed a first-aid kit on the counter. "Next time, let the roast cool a bit before you taste it."

Cecily encouraged Kate, Simon, and Jack to sit on the couch and watch something on television while she finished fixing supper. When Kate offered to help, Cecily told her that she had things under control.

"Go relax. I'll call you in about ten minutes."

Dinner was delicious, the meat perfectly cooked and the scalloped potatoes creamy. As they ate, Cecily shared anecdotes from Simon's childhood. Although he kept trying to change the subject, she ignored him and continued talking.

"Have I told you about the time he dislocated his finger in the mixer and then fainted on a hot stove?"

"*Mom.*"

"It was so sad. I felt terrible for him."

"It does sound terrible," Kate agreed, patting Simon's hand.

"Please, don't encourage her." He put his napkin on the table. "And to set the record straight, I did not *faint.* I passed out. I was trying to steal some of the cookie dough my sister Liza was making, and she didn't see that my hand was in the bowl. She turned on the mixer, and the whisk attachment caught my pinkie. When I looked at my finger, I passed out near a stove."

Cecily smiled at Kate. "Here Simon was, this big six-foot-plus teenager who played soccer and basketball, unconscious on the kitchen floor."

Jack pointed his fork at his son. "You shouldn't have had your hand in the bowl in the first place. Those cookies were for everyone, not just you."

"Right, Dad," Simon replied with a shrewd look. "But enough about me. How was your golf game this week?"

"Profitable," his father immediately answered. "Nick Harper owes me."

"Jackson Hawthorne Phillips!" Cecily said. "Have you been gambling again?"

Jack frowned at Simon after incriminating himself. "Nothing significant, my dear. Just a little bet to make things interesting. Why don't you tell Kate about the time Annie slammed Simon's foot in the car door when he was a baby?"

Cecily beamed at her son, and Jack's lips quivered slightly at the look of dread on Simon's face.

"Poor little thing. His sisters and I took him to an infant beauty contest, and Annie accidentally shut the door on his foot. Simon frowned in every single picture they took of him. I should go and get one."

Kate bit her lip in an effort not to laugh. Simon stood up. "Dinner was wonderful, Mom, but we'd like to be excused now."

"Oh." Cecily looked surprised. "Well, of course."

Rising to her feet, Kate said, "Thank you. Everything was delicious. Can I clear the table before we go?"

"There isn't much to do. You two go on."

Simon propelled Kate toward the doorway. "We'll be back

in a while. Thanks, Mom."

They wandered across the lawn until they reached the largest yew tree Kate had ever seen. The thick trunk stretched gnarled and twisted branches toward the sky like giant-sized arthritic fingers. At first Kate didn't notice the stone bench since it blended so well into the shadows, but Simon took a seat, patting the spot next to him. She sat down, and his arm slid around her. He lowered his head to her shoulder, his face near her neck.

"We finally escaped. No more stories."

"Your mom loves you." Kate stroked his cheek softly. "I liked the stories."

Simon groaned.

"Your dad was pretty nice this time."

"It was scary, wasn't it? He's been that way since I told Leonard I was coming back to work."

Although distant, the sunroom was still visible from the bench, and Kate saw Cecily peeking through a window. Simon gave his mother a thumbs up.

"She'd love to know what we're saying." He looked at Kate, his eyes laughing. "You want to give her something to think about?"

"I'm not sure I could do that with an audience."

Now both of his parents were watching. Jack went away after a few seconds, but Cecily lasted a minute or two longer.

"And there she goes . . ." Simon looked rueful as he moved closer to Kate. "Another opportunity to shock them wasted."

Teasing him, she held back, her breath on his lips. "But what about your Courtship and Kissing Rules? How do they work without the gearshift?"

"Would you just shut up and kiss me?"

After a lengthy interlude, Simon kept his arm around Kate's shoulders. "My mom would read books to me on this bench when I was little. I'd put my head on her knee and listen. The best moments of my childhood were spent right here."

Simon offered her his hand and she took it. He stooped beneath one of the yew trees enormous branches, holding it high for Kate once he was on the other side. She crossed under the limb and found that she could stand up to her full height inside the tree. Looking upward, she saw a complex network of branches, almost like a nature-made jungle gym.

"This must have been a child's paradise," Kate said, touching the cracked bark with her fingers.

"It was my secret fort."

"A European yew, isn't it? I saw these in churchyards sometimes in England. Did you know that the Celtic druids believed they represented immortality?"

Simon touched her cheek with the back of his knuckles. "No, Kate, I didn't."

He lifted the heavy branch, and they climbed out of the hidden tree room. She looked up at the sky, past sunset yet not completely dark. A few stars had started to twinkle.

Kate pointed at the brightest one. The North Star. "My mother once told me that stars link the past, present, and future."

"How does that work?" Simon asked, coming to stand beside her.

"According to Tess, past light shines through time and space until it reaches us in the present. And years from now, after we're gone, people in the future will see the same star and make a wish."

Simon tilted his head back. "I've never thought of it that way."

Kate reached higher until it looked as though she had caught the moon. "Books do the same thing for me. Link the past, present, and future." She dropped her hand and looked at Simon. "Like when I go to a library and find a poem written two hundred years ago. The writer's thoughts reach out through time to me, and so on to future generations. Starlight in the darkness."

"You thought that up yourself?"

"Partly," she replied with a laugh. "In *On Writing*, Stephen King said it's a meeting of the minds, and James Elroy Flecker wrote 'To a Poet a Thousand Years Hence.' Both philosophies are similar."

"Will your encyclopedic nature always amaze me?" Simon asked as they walked hand in hand toward the house, the windows of his old home bright. "Or will you someday run out of facts I've never heard before?"

Heart filled with love for him, Kate smiled. "Useless trivia *is* my specialty."

"Never useless, honey. Surprising maybe, but never useless."

After taking Kate back to her apartment, Simon returned home and listened to the messages on his cell.

"This is Leonard calling. We'll be expecting to see you at eight thirty tomorrow for the Monday morning conference. Looking forward to your return, son."

"Carter Wright here. I have a question to ask you."

"Hello, it's Linda. What would you like me to order for your lunch tomorrow? Call me when you can."

All the messages sounded fairly routine, but there was one

surprise.

"Hey, buddy. This is Greg. Heard through the grapevine that you're back at the firm. Give me a ring. I have something I'd like you to seriously consider. The wife and kids send their love. Talk with you soon."

Simon had a good idea of what Greg wanted. It was certainly something to think about, but could they mix business and friendship? He shut off the kitchen lights, went to the master bedroom, and set his alarm. If he woke early enough, he'd have time in the morning for his usual run before reporting to work.

Two hours later, Simon gave up the pretense of sleeping. His mind wouldn't shut off. It kept mulling over Greg's message. Thinking about the future. He reached for the remote and turned on the television, surfing from one channel to the next. Sleep finally overtook him at the end of a *Matlock* episode.

Chapter 28

Simon went over his schedule as he ran the next morning, preparing himself for the day ahead. He set a faster pace than usual, and when the run was finished, he was breathing heavy, bent over at the end of his driveway.

The steam shower relieved Simon's sore muscles but did little for his anxiety. He chose a lightweight gray suit and hurried through breakfast, glancing at the newspaper without any real interest. After following his typical route to work, Simon drove the Mercedes into the underground parking structure. He pulled alongside the plexiglass security booth. Gaining access beyond this point had never been an easy thing.

Laverne, the parking lot agent, knew exactly who he was. Yet she examined his employee identification card as if he were an extremist radical bent on storming the law offices. This was something she had done every single day without fail, every year he had worked for Phillips, Cronin and Goddard. Sometimes, when Laverne seemed especially contrary, she would call Leonard just to make sure the firm was okay with Simon entering the building. He knew he must have offended her in the past, but for the life of him, he couldn't remember what he had done.

Simon tried to make nice. "Long time, no see."

She slapped him down with a cold stare and lifted the security gate. "Thank you," Simon called before driving past.

Frank and Mario, the two guards at the desk by the elevators, smiled broadly as Simon approached. "I knew you'd be back," Mario said.

Frank, the older guard, lowered his voice. "Good thing, too. We need a friendly face around here."

"Thanks, gentlemen."

Simon took the elevator to his floor and recognized the familiar hum of the well-organized legal machine that was P, C and G. Linda gave him a hug and began rattling off the latest office gossip. Apparently, Melanie from Human Resources had moved on and no longer asked for his personal number. Simon tolerated fifteen minutes of workplace hearsay and then sent Linda back to the reception area outside his door.

Everything had stayed the same. Switch a few of the names and faces and even the gossip sounded identical to what it had been two months before.

"Well, well. At long last." Leonard stood in the doorway, Carter Wright at his side.

Simon extended his hand. "Hello, Leonard. Carter."

They shook and the old man gave him the once-over. "Would you care to explain your hair length?"

"I plan to slip out today and have it trimmed."

"A wise decision on your part. There's no time for that now, however. We need you in the conference room." Leonard's eyes were nearly lost in wrinkles when he smiled. "You remember where it is, don't you?"

The meeting proved to be uneventful, and Simon worked through the rest of the morning, reading contracts and catching up. By midafternoon, a young group of lawyers converged in his office. Mac, a senior associate from family law, suggested a "Return of the Delinquent" party at a sports bar later that night. Tax-law Bernie wanted to get some barbeque and catch up. Ricardo, a fellow corporate, brought Simon an extra-large bottle of antacids as a welcome back gift.

In reality, the visit was a token gesture and lasted about as long as a brief coffee break would allow. Bernie passed Simon on his way out, bouncing on his toes and shadow boxing. "Kill it today, man. Slaughter the competition."

"Thanks, Bernie."

Simon ground his teeth. He wouldn't be going anywhere with those guys. They'd shunned him at the beginning of his leave. At that point, Simon had been a persona non grata. Some law firms, his included, were very political arenas, and scandals were viewed with the same consternation as the Black Plague.

His so-called friends didn't care about him as a person. Simon was only valuable to them if he had something they needed to get ahead.

Kate immediately looked up from the book she was reading on her lunch break when she heard someone calling her name, the voice familiar yet unexpected. Cecily Phillips stood just beyond the office doorway. Her dark hair and warm smile reminded Kate of Simon.

"What a nice surprise, Cecily!"

"Glad to hear it." She crossed the room and placed a white box on Kate's desk. "I brought a chicken salad for your lunch. One of my best recipes, if I say so myself."

How did Cecily know chicken salad was her favorite? She opened the box and peeked inside. "Thank you. It looks beautiful. Do I smell lemon and dill in there?"

"Maybe. You'll just have to try it and see."

Kate felt awkward sitting down, so she got to her feet. "Thank you again, for going to all this trouble."

"Well," Cecily said, surreptitiously inspecting the office. "I know my son wishes he could be here to deliver it himself."

Cecily insisted on taking a tour of the building. Kate was happy to show her Simon's projects and brag on him a little bit. She made sure to point out the extra effort he'd put into everything he did. They also walked through the unused side of the community center, and Cecily listened to the plans they had to expand in the future.

A low, raspy voice interrupted them. "Let me guess. You're Simon's mother." Robert shook Cecily's hand, a grin on his face.

"How did you know?"

"He has to get his good looks from someone. I'm Robert."

Cecily touched his arm. "Simon mentioned you. He said that you're responsible for this wonderful place."

The doctor blushed red, making his strawberry-blond hair appear even brighter. "We're in much better shape because of his help. He went above and beyond."

"That's nice to hear."

Kate smiled to herself as she listened to their conversation. Robert didn't call Cecily "dude" once. After the tour was over, she escorted Simon's mother out to her Range Rover.

Cecily glanced back at the community center. "I'd like to buy new furniture and toys for the waiting room, if I may. The folding chairs work fine, but I want to see those babies sitting on something soft and comfortable. There's nothing I like better than buying presents. Just ask my grandchildren."

"Wow." Kate was completely caught off guard. "Thank you."

"It's an honor for me to do it," Cecily replied. She put on her black Jackie-O sunglasses. "I don't mean to overstep my bounds, but I can see why Simon loves you."

This casual comment floored Kate. Her eyes stung but she kept her composure. Feeling like part of a couple again, like part of a family, was still so new. If she concentrated too long on those feelings of belonging to others, of being wanted, she'd lose it on the spot. But Cecily left quickly, late for a meeting with the Junior League.

Kate went back inside and ate the delicious chicken salad while taking a virtual vacation to the Florida Keys on her computer. She went diving and explored a shipwreck in the clear, warm water. At the end of her break, Kate jotted down a reminder to write a thank-you note to Cecily, with a request for her chicken salad recipe.

At six that night, Kate and Robert closed the clinic and talked about the new waiting-room furniture. They decided to pitch in and buy some fresh art for the walls. In spite of the other improvements that particular spot had been neglected.

Kate wrote another note to herself. "We really should paint too. Marcus and Tony could help. They're going to need school clothes in another month."

"Good idea, babe." Robert was giving her a ride home, since the Triumph was in the shop, and they walked to his Subaru. "I'm leaning toward a happy yellow. What do you think?"

"Happy yellow is perfect."

They stopped by the grocery store on the way to Kate's apartment. She wasn't buying much, just a few special things. As Robert shopped for himself, Kate splurged on two T-bone steaks, fresh Dungeness crab, and artichokes. Simon might enjoy a nice dinner later in the week.

Robert ended up getting a month's worth of groceries, and he was in a rush to get home, so his ice cream and frozen dinners wouldn't melt. He dropped Kate off in front of her home and honked before driving away. She walked across the lawn, then stepped up onto the creaky porch.

The old Victorian's mailroom was empty. Kate could hear music playing in one of the apartments upstairs, a Louis Armstrong standard. She hummed along and opened her cubby with a small key. It was stuffed with junk mail and a few bills. Kate shoved it all into one of her shopping bags. She flipped the switch for the outside light before exiting through the side door. Though it wasn't too dark yet, the area around her apartment felt murky. The motion-sensitive flood should have flashed on, but it didn't.

Kate hurried to unlock her door. Once she was inside, she quickly flipped the deadbolt into place. Kate put the steak and crab in the fridge, a little anxious even with the new door and lock. She'd received an email that morning from the company who sold her a home security system online. Their product was on backorder and wouldn't arrive for at least another two weeks. After learning that, Kate had made some calls to local businesses about putting in a system, but they were all busy. Booked up at least as long as the online business.

Kate took off her gun and holster, placing them on the counter. Her hip was a little sore from the hard edge of the leather. She rubbed the spot while searching her freezer for a frozen pizza.

As it cooked in the microwave, Kate sorted her mail. Good coupons went to the right. Shreddable stuff to the left. A light blue envelope peeked out from under her electric bill. The letter had a large smudge next to Kate's name, as though it had fallen in the dirt and been hastily wiped clean.

Kate's stomach felt queasy when she saw the British stamp in the right corner. According to its postmark, the letter had left London months before. She turned the envelope over, her heart pumping hard as she read the identity of the sender.

Quinton.

Julian's last name. Kate dropped the blue envelope as if it were a hissing serpent. He had written many times when she was younger, describing her mother's last moments on earth. Kate had torn the letters to pieces and never mentioned their existence to her father.

Steeling herself, Kate picked up the envelope and ripped it open. But the letter didn't come from Julian. His stepmother had sent it. She started by saying that he was making strides: getting therapy, living at home, eating well. Then Mrs. Quinton asked if Kate would consider talking to him on the phone. Both of them surely needed closure. He had carried the burden of Tess's death long enough, hadn't he? Her overdose was a tragic accident that had ruined three lives.

Couldn't they meet and make amends?

Kate sat down on a bar stool, shaking with rage. "No way in hell, lady."

Make amends with her mother's killer? Were all of the Quintons delusional? Did Julian's stepmother not get the fact that he was an evil psychopath?

Labels on the envelope showed that it had been redirected

to several different addresses, most likely causing the delay. In her note, Mrs. Quinton said that Julian was living in London. Was she telling the truth? Or was the whole thing a deceit? He had told Kate that he hated his parents. Why would he be living with them?

Her whole body shivered while she considered the possibility that Julian had come to America since his stepmother posted the letter. She didn't tear it up this time, choosing to put it away in a bedroom drawer instead. The stuff Mrs. Quinton wrote might make Julian appear less of a suspect to the police. *He's trying. Making progress. What a load of crap.*

She went back into the kitchen and scrubbed her hands with blue dishwashing liquid. Her wedding ring glistened under the water. Kate knew she should take it off now that Simon was in her life. Her heart didn't hurt quite as much at the thought of removing the band, but it was so familiar and comforting. Like Mike. She would take it off. Just not tonight. Kate needed all the comfort she could get.

The microwave beeped that the pizza was ready. She burned her hand where the sauce had bubbled over onto the black plastic plate. The pepperoni and sausage looked good but Kate was no longer hungry. Despite the steel door, the new deadbolt, the guns, her cozy little home felt unsafe once more.

———————— ● ————————

Simon spent all of Tuesday in the conference room. He liked to think of the space as especially his. It was the exact location where his fellow partners had decided that he needed to take a break. However, instead of standing on the table and giving an intoxicated discourse to a roomful of powerful attorneys, this time he was using the highly polished piece of furniture to support piles of statements and documents. A couple of paralegals and an associate had worked with him for hours. They had ordered Indian food at eight thirty, and it had long since been consumed, the take-out boxes disposed of by the nighttime cleaning crew. Simon checked his Omega. Twelve fifteen.

He had no idea where the time had gone, and even after going home, his mind couldn't stop whirring along at top speed.

Wednesday was as busy as the day before, but it started poorly with Simon sleeping through his alarm. He didn't have time to run, so he threw himself together and hurried to the office. His partners called another meeting to track the progress on a new tech merger, and Simon pored over more contracts. Hours of phone tag later, he finally reached Kate when he pushed the redial button on his cell phone and unexpectedly heard her voice. His heart tripped like a jackhammer as he listened to her talk, and when Simon unlocked the door to his house late that night, he was still thinking over their conversation.

Kate had found her charm bracelet. She was reading Joseph Conrad's *Heart of Darkness* at lunch, turned a page, and the little gold chain fell out.

"Robert saw me put the book on my desk that morning. It sat there for hours before lunch. Nobody came into the office— at least that's what Beth and Tanya said. When I called the detective working my case, he asked if I couldn't have just mislaid the bracelet. Or worse yet, if I might be attention-seeking."

Simon had covered his phone and cursed. "They know you have a stalker with a restraining order. I was there when you told them. The break-in and the damage to your bike—none of that is attention-seeking."

Kate's voice had sounded so tired. "Not one of my neighbors remember seeing anyone of Julian's description around my place. There were no fingerprints on the bike or in the apartment, except my own. And now the bracelet is back."

"What about looking for prints on the bracelet?"

"Robert picked it up to examine the clasp and Beth tried to polish the heart. I touched it, too. I'm sorry. I feel so dumb but it was such a shock."

"Don't blame yourself for anything, Kate. We'll find a way to catch him."

Simon had wanted to drive over to the community center right then, but she'd insisted he stay at the firm. They were both booked for the rest of the day.

Keeping their pact of not letting more than three days pass without getting together, Simon and Kate made plans for the next evening. He staged a coup at his office by leaving at seven thirty. As soon as Kate opened her door, she launched herself into his arms. He held her tight against his chest, so her bare feet dangled a few inches off the ground. She looked so good. Simon felt as if he'd been starved for the sight of her.

Kate ran her fingers through his hair. "It's short but I like it."

"I can't be scruffy anymore."

"You never looked that way to me."

Simon carried her into the apartment as they kissed hello again and reluctantly put her down.

"Dinner's ready," Kate said. She took his hand, leading him toward the kitchen. "You like steak, right?"

He felt the tension ease from his body as he entered the little room. "Love it. But anything will do."

The sound and smell of sizzling meat made his mouth water. All the takeout in the world didn't satisfy like a meal cooked at home.

Simon hung his jacket on a doorknob. Kate wouldn't let him help her with the food. She placed steamed artichokes on a serving dish, beside two small bowls of melted butter. The Dungeness crab was chilling in the fridge on a bed of lettuce. Simon found himself lightly touching Kate's hair, watching her turn the steaks and talk about the children at the clinic.

They ate in the living room and then looked through Kate's vinyl records. She chose one by Billie Holiday. The volume was low enough so they could still talk while dancing slowly side to side. The songs played one after another until the record needle brushed against the inside of the turntable.

The evening was perfect except for one thing. It had been weighing on him for weeks. Simon hated himself for what he had to confess. He'd put off telling Kate the truth about himself many times, but he didn't want to lose her. What would she say when Simon revealed why he was sent on the leave of absence? She had shared so much about her childhood and the trauma she'd endured. What had he done? Hidden all the details of his own drinking problem. Would that feel like a betrayal to her?

The more Simon's love for Kate grew, the harder his issues were to conceal. He'd given up alcohol, but she had a right to know that it had been a problem. Simon couldn't stand hiding things from her anymore.

* * *

As they danced, Simon fell out of sync with the music and stopped moving. Kate held his shoulders to keep him steady. He looked tired. And sort of sad.

Was it the Billie Holiday music? Work? His family? "Sit down on the sofa," she said. "I'll make hot chocolate."

The milk took a few minutes to heat in the saucepan, but it was worth the extra effort when Kate added the semisweet chocolate. Her kitchen smelled like a candy shop. She returned to the living room and found that Simon had fallen asleep. Kate put the mugs on the table and snuggled against him. He pulled her closer, sinking them both further into the overstuffed cushions. His face had fine lines around the eyes and mouth that she hadn't noticed before. Those beautifully shaped lips were soft, his breathing deep and slow.

Simon mumbled, jerked in his sleep, and woke up. "Sorry, baby. I didn't mean to doze off."

"Don't be sorry. I liked it." Kate sat up and reached for the hot chocolate. She handed him a mug. The sadness she had noticed before was still there. "What is it, Simon? You don't want cocoa?"

"I do. It smells great."

But Simon put the mug back on the table. He lowered his head, cursed softly, and looked up at her. "I used to drink, Kate. A lot. I don't anymore. I never want to be that way again." His voice grew quieter. "I thought you should know."

Kate absorbed his words. She had assumed he drank alcohol. Mike did all through their marriage. He met his cop buddies sometimes for a beer. He'd drink with his dad and brothers when they went hunting or fishing. But Mike kept it separate from Kate. He enjoyed alcohol in moderation and that was his choice. She respected him, just as he respected her.

What did drinking 'a lot' mean to Simon? Was he addicted? She thought of the unhealthy pallor of his skin when she first met him, of how thin he had been. Comparing him to her mother, Kate saw some similarities.

There were differences too. Tess had mental health issues that Kate didn't sense in Simon. He was far more disciplined in his life. Stronger. Simon didn't wallow in neediness like Tess did.

How could Kate know for sure, though? She began to feel sick, thinking about that question. Perhaps he was just better at hiding his symptoms than her mother had been. His issues might be light compared to hers, or they could be worse. And the hard thing about loving someone who had a drinking problem was knowing they could revert to their old habits at any time.

When work became too hard, when Simon felt depressed or lonely. If the stress of living was too great. If the sky was too blue . . .

Kate could break her heart trying to help him, as she had with Tess, but it wouldn't matter. The choice to stay sober was his alone.

Watching Kate's face, Simon pulled away. "If this changes how you feel about me, I understand."

Kate looked into those blue eyes, wishing she could see into his soul. "It doesn't change the fact that I love you. I'm just . . . surprised. Concerned. Worried about the future. Take your pick, I've got all of those feelings right now."

He nodded. "You're justified."

"Did you tell your other girlfriends?"

"No," Simon replied instantly. "I didn't care about them, Kate. I didn't care about much, actually. Not about my health or whether I was happy. All that mattered was surpassing my brother. And proving to my father that he was wrong about me."

"And now you care?"

Peace seemed to settle over him. "A whole new perspective has opened up to me while being sober. I don't need to compete with my brother to be successful, and I can't force my dad to show support or unconditional love. I've finally accepted that and it's a relief. Everything is better without the booze."

His answer made Kate want to cry. She didn't have peace—she still couldn't accept what had happened to her mother. If Simon had come to terms with his demons, he was one step ahead. Tess had made so many promises and broken each one. Kate wondered if she could survive Simon doing the same. Was she willing to put her faith in him?

Then it dawned on Kate that Tess was right about one thing, love equaled pain. Opened your heart wide for it. Everyone risked being hurt when they loved another person. It was a leap into the unknown, a matter of trust and faith. Maybe they would fail, maybe the future would be everything she feared, but Simon was worth taking a chance. He deserved one.

Kate reached for him and Simon expelled a breath of air. As if he'd been holding it, hoping she wouldn't reject him. They clung to each other for a long time.

When the grandfather clock chimed eleven, Kate pulled away and straightened his collar. "You've got an early start tomorrow. Go home and sleep for as long as you can."

"Yeah, I'd better get going."

Simon stretched his shoulders, stood up, and put on his suit jacket. He leaned down and kissed her. She walked with him to the front door.

"What happened to the floodlight?" Simon asked, nodding toward the fixture mounted over the stairs. "It should have turned on."

"I'll put new bulbs in tomorrow."

"I could do it now."

"No," she said. "Go home. You're exhausted."

Worry lines creased his forehead. "Let's go down and talk to that detective. Put a little pressure on them to step up the investigation." Simon moved back from the doorway. "I'll leave after you lock up. Talk to you tomorrow? Around lunchtime?"

"It's a date."

Kate shut and locked the door. Simon's revelation about giving up alcohol had made her momentarily forget all that had happened before his arrival. She had intended to tell him about the letter from Mrs. Quinton, but it wasn't the right time. His life was complicated enough.

Anger turned her heart cold, rather than hot. She was sick of being afraid.

Chapter 29

Daisy

It had been the best two weeks of her life.

Actually, it was only the best four days because her mother took a week and a half to feel human again after giving up alcohol. That was when Tess had risen from her bed and cooked oatmeal on the stove. The cereal was gummy and tasteless, but Daisy didn't complain. She couldn't remember the last time her mother had made anything for her to eat, and in all honesty, Daisy was truly the better cook. The food itself wasn't important.

What made her happy was the simple fact that by making the cereal her mother had acted like a mother. Since that day, they had done the most wonderful things together.

Tess had kept Daisy home from school one afternoon, and they had gone to the Victoria and Albert Museum. Because Daisy had never been. They visited Harrods Food Hall another time. She had never been there either. It was the most fantastic place! Tess had given her money for sweets, and Daisy bought a small bag of bridge mix. They shared it on the tube, eating a piece of chocolate at each stop.

She and Tess had gone to Oxfam, and for once, Daisy didn't

care that the clothes were secondhand. Tess bought her a broom handle skirt and another jumper, since she was always cold. Her heart was so happy she was afraid it might rupture. Even then, Daisy had known it wouldn't last. Tess would get sad and give up, or Julian would get out of jail and Daisy would be afraid again. But for a moment, she could pretend her life was easy, like any other girl her age.

This morning, her mum had asked her to pick up the ingredients for a farmer's stew. After school, Daisy went to the Portobello Market. It was crowded and the produce was picked over, but the lad who sold the best potatoes said he had a delivery coming, so she waited. When the new potatoes finally arrived, she bought some and hurried home.

Daisy unlocked the door and rushed into the house. "It's me, Ma," she called. "I had to wait an age at the market."

Pushing open the kitchen door, she saw Julian sitting at the table next to her mother. Daisy couldn't say anything, her mouth suddenly too dry to speak.

Tess pushed a liquor bottle away from her arm—as if its proximity to her body was what made her guilty.

"I'm glad you're home, Daisy love. Where's your welcome for Julian?"

Daisy hated when his eyes were like that, cold and reptilian. She swallowed and forced the words out. "W-welcome home."

"Now there's a lovely greeting." He poured himself a drink, slopping a little of the gin over the edge of his glass. "Doesn't mean much, though, does it? When your mum has to tell you to say it to me."

A gust of stale air passed over Daisy. It smelled like gin and Julian. Her stomach curdled. She would forever associate alcohol and this terrible man. Tess put her hand on his, giving the appearance of solidarity. "We've been talking just now, Julian and I. It's not that we think you're lying, Daisy, but lately you've been rather secretive. Rarely home, staying away at night. Julian was wondering—*we* were wondering—if you've been meeting a boy."

Daisy drew herself up to her full height. "I haven't done anything like that, and you know it."

Tess flinched under her daughter's gaze. "Oh, of course, love. Of course. We only had to ask though, didn't we, caring about you as we do?"

"I've looked after her better than her own father ever did." Julian grunted and took another drink. "He can't be bothered with the bloody git."

Daisy summoned the kind of dignity children possess when the adults around them are course and deficient, and without a word, she placed the shopping on the counter and left the kitchen. She heard Julian's chair scrape back from the table, heard him shout her real name. It was painful to hear the identity she'd tried to keep clean, her true self, come from his dirty mouth.

"You don't walk out on me, Kate."

"Never say that name again," she shouted back. "I'm Daisy to you."

Daisy ran to her bedroom and bolted the door, so thankful that she had asked Lolly's son to install the new lock. She sat on her bed and took the Holy Bible from under her pillow, clutching it to her chest. In the kitchen, her mother laughed. Daisy could hear the clank of glass on glass and music playing on the radio.

Lying down, she pulled her knees up and opened the Bible.

Daisy had seen churches. You couldn't live in London without bumping into a few. But she had never thought much about them until entering the religion section of the library one night. A King James edition had fallen to the floor and opened to John 3:16.

The words had sunk inside Daisy, and she thought about them often when times were hard. If God loved the world enough to give His Son for it, then maybe, maybe . . . He could love her a little, too.

There was a sudden crash in the bedroom next to hers, and Daisy covered her ears with her hands. Julian was throwing things around and breaking them. It wasn't the first time. He wanted Daisy to feel the violence and hatred inside him, to imagine him doing those things to her.

When she closed her eyes, it seemed to make the sounds louder and closer, so she kept them open, praying under her breath. Wood splintered, glass shattered, as it hit the floor. Daisy wanted Jane Eyre.

"Please, Jane. I need you. Help me."

She tried to imagine the governess seated at the end of the bed, but it didn't work. Daisy couldn't imagine anything good in this house. Not Huck Finn or Eponine or Sydney . . .

Outside her bedroom, Julian began to curse as if he had cut himself. She heard Tess begging him to stop, to come with her so she could tend to his hand. It was quiet for a while after that, until her mother began laughing again.

Why were they still here? They should be at the pub by now.

It was too late for Daisy to go to the library, but maybe she could run to Lolly's and stay with her. There was the sound of glasses clinking again downstairs. Had they opened a new bottle? Julian never opened one without finishing it. Daisy inhaled the tangy leather smell of the Bible and felt the cool softness of the cover. Eventually she slept.

Her bladder woke her up hours later. Daisy didn't want to wet the bed, and there wasn't a cup or bowl that she could use. She waited for a long time, listening in the darkness. The whole house was quiet except for the sounds from the street. Checking the watch pinned to her blouse, Daisy saw that it was after midnight.

Did they leave when she was sleeping?

She took off her shoes and silently crossed the room. Easing the bolt back, she opened the door without a sound. The hallway beyond her bedroom was empty and dark, so she walked slowly toward the bath. Daisy kept her hand over her mouth in the hope that Julian wouldn't hear the shallow breaths coming from her throat. Inside the loo, she turned the knob and shut the door softly.

Daisy knew she wasn't safe yet, but as she used the toilet, she exhaled with relief. She would have liked to wash her hands, but she didn't dare turn the water on. Biting her lip, Daisy reached for the doorknob and turned it.

The door crashed inward and her body flew back into the sink. Pain. Shock. Her protesting muscles stiffened and her brain grew slow. The bathroom light flashed to life, and Julian's delicately handsome face twisted with fury. Shoving Daisy against the wall, his hand went to her throat, fingers on each side of her windpipe.

"Stupid, worthless brat." His voice struck her ear as if he were chopping each word with a cleaver. "Mummy's asleep now and there's no one here but us."

He squeezed his fingers and her eyes watered. Suddenly,

Daisy didn't care what he did. She didn't care if he killed her or beat her unconscious. She wasn't going to give in to him.

It felt as though fire burned from her eyes. "I'm not stupid or worthless. But we both know what you are, don't we?"

Julian pulled back like he had been singed. He lifted his hand, the gauze covering it stained with blood, and slid it down her cheek. The smell of him and the gin made her gag.

His smile reminded her of a wolf. "You've heard about Nabokov. I could claim the *Lolita* defense in court. I'd get away with it, too."

Fast and hard, she dug her fingernails into his face so he could feel the sharp points. "I'll leave marks on you if you try it, and you'll have to kill me besides. Where's your defense then, Julian, with me dead and your face scratched to pieces? People will know you're a monster."

Daisy saw the fear in his eyes. He shoved her away and she fell to the floor. "Get out of my sight."

She scrambled to her feet and sped down the hall to her room. Her hands shook as she locked the door. Sleep was impossible for most of the night, but Daisy nodded off shortly before dawn, waking only when sunlight streamed through a gap in her curtains.

Her watch said that school began in ten minutes. She picked up her bag and went to the door without putting on a fresh uniform, without combing the tangles from her hair. The house was quiet and Daisy stepped out into the hall. She could see into the master suite. Tess and Julian were lying on the bed, tangled up in the sheets. A wave of revulsion overwhelmed Daisy, and she turned her back on them, putting one foot in front of the other until she reached the front door.

Daisy closed it behind her, and with a deep breath, walked

out into the world.

——————● ●——————

She went directly to the library after school. The children in her class had wrinkled their noses every time she drew near, telling her as rudely as possible that she smelled bad.

To make matters worse, Daisy overheard the girl at the lending desk say that the young maid had become redundant. This news was almost more than she could bear, and the horrible rumor appeared to be true since Old Maid was working an extra shift. After the closing announcement, Daisy sighed heavily and left with the rest of the patrons. She formulated a plan while walking home and decided to go to Auntie Helen's after picking up a clean set of clothes.

Turning onto her street, Daisy nodded to Lolly's son Andre. A strange look crossed his face as he recognized her, a combination of pity and alarm. He went into his house and came out quickly with Lolly right behind him. The big woman wore a flowered housedress, all orange and yellow. It billowed about her as she reached toward Daisy, even though twenty meters still separated them. The expression in Lolly's eyes made Daisy stop in the middle of the sidewalk.

Daisy opened her mouth, but she couldn't speak. In her head, she screamed. *No, no, no . . .*

The wrinkles in Lolly's skin were shiny, her tears caught in the grooves. "Come here. Come to Granny."

Daisy moved forward like a sleepwalker, and Lolly's arms enfolded her. "I'm so sorry. Your mum's passed. She's gone."

"Shame," Andre murmured. "Shame."

Lolly rocked Daisy. With her gentle Jamaican voice, she said, "That bad man gave her a drug, and her heart couldn't take it. Beat too fast, then just stopped. The police took him away."

Daisy's legs gave out and she slid down to the steps. Lolly hugged her tight, stroking the hair away from her forehead. Daisy barely noticed. The only person she had loved in the whole world, and the only person who had loved her, was gone.

Julian had found a way to break Daisy for good. He'd won.

Chapter 30

Northwest Portland

Simon parked the Mercedes next to the little white church. He squinted at the heavens, in the event there were any electrical storms brewing, before opening the door and stepping inside. A clergyman stood at the pulpit, and the congregation seemed to be intrigued by what he was saying.

Simon scanned the pews. The person he was looking for sat in the very back. He joined her on the bench as the organ music began.

"Oh!" Kate said, far too loud for the inside of a church. "Is something wrong?"

The lady in the next row turned around and shushed her.

Simon sat by Kate. "Don't look so worried." The woman turned around again and he smiled at her. "I'm the one who's going to get struck by lightning. We need to talk."

Kate pulled a paper program for the service out of her purse and wrote on it, handing the paper to Simon when she was done. He didn't bother to write back after reading it. "No, we don't have to leave. This is important to you. We'll talk after."

Kate grabbed the paper and began furiously writing again. She shoved it into Simon's hands. He squinted this time, having trouble with her cursive.

"No. Everyone's fine in my family. There's no emergency. Listen to the old guy with the microphone. You may miss something."

Simon leaned back against the hard pew. If the meeting was boring, he could always take a nap. Thirty minutes passed, and Simon remained awake. It wasn't so bad. Nothing earth-shattering or controversial: just a group of Methodists, an organist who needed to practice more, and an enthusiastic speaker.

Once the service was over, Simon took Kate out to his car. He kissed her perplexed face and told her about the decisions he had made concerning his job.

*   *   *

Leonard stopped by Simon's office the next day. Their discussion lasted almost an hour, but at its conclusion Leonard shook his hand.

"Take care of yourself, son. I'll miss you."

When he exited the parking garage that night, Simon noticed Laverne in her see-through cubicle. He stopped and tapped on her window. She spoke through the mounted speaker. "*What?* Move through. I've already pushed the button."

"I need to say something."

She rolled her eyes. "Yes?" The poor woman could hardly stop him from talking, or walk out during her shift, or even turn her chair around in such a tight space.

"I owe you an apology."

Laverne couldn't have looked more shocked had Simon handed her a basket of candy and proclaimed himself the Easter Rabbit.

"I don't remember what I said or how many times I've been

rude in the past, but I'm certain that I haven't treated you with the respect you deserve. I'm sorry for that." He looked at her name tag. "Ms. Hopkins."

Laverne Hopkins paused for a moment and then nodded at Simon. "Move on through." But then she added, "Have a good night."

"Thanks. I wish you the same."

Simon drove out onto the street, and all too soon he was parking in his usual place behind his parents' home. Cecily's car wasn't in the garage.

It was probably better this way.

He let himself into the house and called for his dad. Jack answered from the second floor, where he and Cecily shared a private wing. They had their own kitchen, living room, study, and bedroom.

Simon found his father sitting on a large leather couch, watching television. "Quiet," Jack said, pointing at the screen. "Golf highlights."

Sitting down in a club chair, Simon knew it was wiser not to interrupt. Golf was life to his father. It had helped him evolve into someone new, a person who didn't come from a little town on the Oregon coast, where hard work and poverty went hand in hand. No, golfers went to ivy league schools without needing a scholarship. They wore expensive clothes, drove nice cars, and spent a lot of time at country clubs. Jack had used golf to change everything.

He turned toward Simon once a commercial came on. "Did your mother tell you she's taking me to play at St. Andrews in Scotland? That's where it all started, you know. I haven't been this excited in years." Jack frowned briefly. "Of course, she made me agree to visit London afterward."

It wasn't that his father disliked London, he just hated sightseeing and doing touristy things. Simon couldn't help rubbing it in a little. "Knowing Mom, she'll probably drag you from museum to museum. Then to a musical in the West End."

The commercials ended and a montage of baseball clips came on. Jack lost interest immediately. He took a sip of the protein shake for active seniors that Cecily made him drink. "Last time we were in London, I sat through *Cats*. That's what it was about . . . cats! Over two hours of singing, dancing felines." Jack put his drink down and looked at Simon. "You seem happy. What's going on? Did you beat Carter Wright? Is he as good as I've heard?"

"He's like a megalodon with a drop of blood in the water."

His father smiled. "So he's like you."

Like I used to be. "No. Carter's got sharper teeth."

"Well, hell. Get off your ass and go to work."

This comment actually helped Simon feel better about dropping a grenade on Jack's peaceful golfing interlude. He pulled out the figurative pin and said, "You may remember my clients, Ed Moyer and Jim Mayes. They sold their software company to Greg Jacobsen."

"I remember." Jack got up from the couch and rooted around in his refrigerator for a snack. He settled on some string cheese. "It happened the day you went barhopping and had your breakdown at the firm, I believe."

Simon chose to ignore his father's attack. Even so, Jack would expect some sort of reaction from him. He didn't think highly of anyone who showed weakness or acted hurt. "There was no barhopping, Dad. I went to one. If you remember Jim and Ed, you know Greg Jacobsen. He purchased MSquared."

"I'm retired. I'm not dead. Everybody knows Greg

Jacobsen. It was quite a boon for Lake Oswego when he chose it as the new location for his computer company. Family matters, right?"

"Lisa's parents live in Portland. She wanted to be closer to them, so they moved from Seattle."

Jack wrinkled his brow. "A rather sentimental reason to uproot your company."

"I'm sure Greg knew what he was doing."

Finished with the cheese stick, his father chose a banana from a fruit bowl and returned to the couch. "With a net worth of two point five billion, Greg can do whatever he likes."

Holding Jack's gaze, Simon released the grenade. "He's offered me a job. I've decided to accept."

The banana dropped out of Jack's hand. "Damn thing." He bent down and picked it up. "For a moment there, I thought you said you were accepting a job with Greg Jacobsen. Which is ludicrous. His lawyers never quit. Once they're in, they stay."

"Actually, the lawyer in question didn't quit—he died. Greg wants me to replace him as his chief legal adviser. I'm going to do it."

"The hell you are, Simon!" Jack looked down at his sticky hand. He had squeezed the banana so hard that the peel burst.

Simon watched his father try to maneuver his way off the couch. Jack flailed among the sunken cushions, holding the pulverized banana aloft. Simon offered to help him.

"No, damn it." Jack slapped his son's hand away. When he finally pulled himself out of the couch, his face was red and sweaty. Washing his hands at the sink, Jack glared at Simon. "I didn't build my law firm up from nothing just so you could turn your back on it!"

"I spoke with Leonard this afternoon," he replied calmly.

"It's all arranged."

"Then you'll have to un-arrange it. Call Leonard right now and tell him you've changed your mind."

One . . . two . . . three . . . Simon counted in an effort to control his temper. "No, I won't. I begin working at Jacobsen Technologies tomorrow."

Jack walked over to the window. He pushed the curtain aside as if the sight of it was offensive. "Would you like to explain the logic behind this brilliant move of yours? Because, I have to say, it escapes me. Think of the money, of the power you'd have at the firm. You just need to pay—"

"The *price*. I know, Dad, but I'm not willing to do it anymore."

Simon didn't want to fight with Jack. Dropping the grenade hadn't been so great after all. The result was just a wider chasm between them. Jack would never understand him. He wouldn't even attempt it.

West, on the other hand, had remained the golden boy when he went off to Dubai. No arguing or demanding that he change his mind. No, Jack had encouraged West and been happy for him. While Simon had stayed and bled to keep the family firm as successful as it had always been.

His message had been delivered, so Simon took a few steps toward the door, but he couldn't leave without saying one more thing. "I admire you for building a business from the ground up. It's thriving and important, and I've learned so much working there. Thank you for that, Dad. All of my old clients stay at the firm. They're in love with Carter anyway. He's more than filled my shoes."

Jack began pacing: window to couch, couch back to window. "But you have a share in the profits."

"I also share in the losses and the enormous pressure of keeping a titanic law firm afloat. Greg has offered me a job with fewer hours and an excellent salary. I'll work hard while I'm at work, and then I'll go home and forget about it until the next day."

"Will Jacobsen pay you more than you're already making?"

"Not quite, but I have savings and investments. My retirement is put away. I'll still be a wealthy man with what Greg is offering."

His father sat in a chair, muttering words like "stupid" and "shortsighted." "What if JT fails after you move there?"

Simon leaned against the wall across from Jack. "Jacobsen Tech might not be the largest software company, but it's been wildly successful. It has a great reputation, and if I were anyone else, you would tell me I'd be lucky to work there."

Jack pinched his lips together, like he did when Simon was young and scared. Young Simon called it the Look. The one that came out when Jack was especially disappointed. It worked back then but didn't now.

"What exactly is your life lacking, Simon? Don't you live in a nice house and drive a Mercedes? That would be enough for most people."

"I thought so. For a while. But I'm thirty-three, Dad, and I'd like to get married someday and have a family. I want to see my kids at breakfast and tuck them in after dinner. It's not too much to ask for a few hours each day outside the office to spend with the people I love."

The Look again. "Are you saying I neglected you because I had a demanding career? You lived a good life because of my job." Jack rubbed his face with his hands. "West never caused me grief. He was always so easy."

Simon refrained from calling BS on this statement. His brother West was many things, but easy wasn't one of them. Aggressive, bold, and self-centered were more accurate descriptions. He was a steamroller in a three-piece suit who crushed whatever lay in his path.

"West isn't here, Dad. He left years ago."

Jack's face paled. "Your brother couldn't turn down the job in Dubai. He's a legal adviser to the grandson of a sultan, for heaven's sake. It isn't as though he's forgotten about us. We're still important to him."

"Right," Simon replied. He felt like a robot as he turned toward the door. "If I don't see you before you leave, I hope the trip to Scotland goes well. Enjoy St. Andrews."

Jack didn't respond. He turned up the volume on the television and switched the channel to another game of golf.

———————— • ————————

Simon spent Monday evening with Kate. They cooked pork chops and green beans for dinner in her little kitchen. She washed the dishes, he dried. While waiting for the next dish, Simon imagined losing his wealth, his career, the Mercedes, and the fancy house. Being disbarred, friendless. A soap bubble floated through the air above Kate's head. She handed him a gleaming plate and smiled.

It devastated him. Everything could go but her. She was the one thing he couldn't do without.

After dinner, they watched *Abbott and Costello Meet Frankenstein.* Kate laughed aloud, saying, "The werewolf part gets me every time. Poor Costello."

She took the almost empty bowl of popcorn to the kitchen

when the flick ended. Simon looked through the books on her coffee table. "Who's your favorite author?"

She returned to the living room, looking thoughtful. "I don't know. I couldn't pick a favorite."

"What are you reading now?"

Kate picked up Jack London's *The Call of the Wild* and opened it to where her bookmark was pressed between the pages. Simon stretched out on the couch, laying his head on her knee. The first few words carried through the room, and soon he was gripped by Buck's adventure in the Yukon. Watching Kate's face as she read to him soothed and healed like a cooling rain. Simon closed his eyes, at peace because he knew his life was finally right.

———— • ————

Robert's boombox vibrated as it played Otis Redding. Kate turned it down a few decibels, until it was merely loud rather than deafening. This made her feel like a disapproving granny who told kids to get off her lawn. Simon's influence was obviously subduing her lead-finger ways.

Marcus and Tony watched as Robert picked up a brush and a tray of the happy yellow semi-gloss. He approached the wall with an angry squint and listened to it like it was talking smack.

"Say what? You don't like this color?" Robert swished a big stripe of paint over the wall. "Too bad, dude. You're yellow."

Marcus pushed his roller up and down. "Yeah, wall. What do you *mean* I missed a spot?"

"Does your mama know you talk like that?" Tony joined in. "Look at me when I'm paintin' you."

Kate grinned. "Dumb, ungrateful wall. You're fired."

In the end, the result of their labors was a success. The waiting room had that freshly-painted smell and looked bright and clean. Before leaving, Tony and Marcus collected thirty dollars each from Robert while Kate slipped them another twenty apiece on the side.

Coat missing, tie loose, Simon came in just as the two boys reached the door. "I can see you've been working hard," he said, nodding at their messy clothes. "Robert, on the other hand, is neat as a pin."

"He got you there, Doc," Marcus called over his shoulder, following Tony outside.

"I don't waste paint, dude." Robert grinned. "That's why there isn't a drop on me."

Kate rinsed out the paint brushes in the women's bathroom. Simon watched her while leaning on the next sink.

"How was your first day working for Greg?" she asked. Kate wanted him to have liked it. She'd been a bundle of nerves all day.

Simon rolled up his sleeves and motioned toward the clean brush. Kate handed it to him, and he dried it with a paper towel. She waited for him to answer her question. Not one word came out of the man's mouth.

Simon seemed to grow nostalgic as he looked around. "You know, my whole life began to change when I woke up in a bathroom, wearing my Tom Ford suit." He appeared to rethink his choice of words. "It wasn't exclusively a women's room. All the executives used it."

What was he talking about? "Where are you going with this?" Kate asked. "How does it apply to your new job?"

"Oh, it doesn't. I was just pointing out that I've come full circle." He smiled at her.

"Full circle?" Kate stood there, confused.

Simon took the last paint brush from her hand. "We make a good team. You wash . . . I dry. I dry . . . you wash."

She stared at him. Did he not see how anxious she was? "I'm dying, Simon. I've been worried about you since I woke up this morning. How did it go?"

He bumped her shoulder with his. "You are so easy to tease."

Kate lifted her eyebrow and remained silent.

"Okay, sorry," Simon said, laughing. "Let's start with my office. It's decorated in soothing tones and has a pretty view of a serenity garden. All the people I met were nice. Smart and capable, but so mellow I had to remind myself they were lawyers. Everyone kept saying that they wanted me to feel at home. At noon, Greg dropped by and took me to lunch."

Relief spread through Kate's chest. Simon had taken a risk, leaving his dad's firm. She didn't want him to regret it. "Great. I'm so happy for you."

"It was weird, though."

"Why?" Had it not been a good day? Was he having second thoughts?

Simon leaned against the sink again. "After the intensity of the last decade, everything seemed too relaxed. No drama at all."

Kate kissed his shoulder. "Do you really miss office drama?"

"Hell, no," he replied, with a smirk. "Got you again. You really are easy to tease. I had the best first day ever. I loved it."

"You treat me bad." Kate threw a wadded-up paper towel at him. "I'm sorry I asked."

"Let me make it up to you. How about ice cream? A sundae

with sprinkles?"

"Damn it. My kryptonite."

Simon kissed the side of her neck and Kate laughed. He stacked the painting supplies in a storage closet while she got her purse out of the glossy walnut cabinet in the office. Kate called down the hall to Robert. "See you tomorrow."

"Night, babe," he answered from some distant corner of the community center.

They walked out into the balmy evening. "The Triumph's still in the shop, right?" Simon asked.

"Right." Kate linked her arm with his as they walked toward his car. "What's the best part of your new gig?"

Simon opened the passenger door. "All of it. I'm expected to be at the office four days a week, but I can work from home on Friday, with the occasional Saturday as needed. And get this, according to my new schedule, nine-hour days are typical. Not twelve or fourteen. Not all night."

"No way."

He laughed. "Way."

Kate felt giddy. "I think I want to work for Greg Jacobsen."

"We talked a lot at lunch and bonded over a shared love of running. He said that he knew I would represent him well, that he could trust me to protect his interests." Simon stood back so she could get in the car. "I'm so lucky."

"No one deserves it more." Kate meant it with her whole heart.

"Thanks. Let's just hope this job isn't too good to be true."

———————— • ————————

The new furniture was scheduled to arrive at the clinic that afternoon. Cecily had taken Kate shopping for couches, tables, rugs, and lamps. They even found a child-sized set of four blue-and-white-striped club chairs with a hickory coffee table to match. The toys Cecily had brought by earlier were a huge hit.

Kate had thanked her in person but she wanted to send a letter of appreciation. Have the older kids write a few words and the little ones draw pictures. It wouldn't arrive before Cecily and Jack left for Scotland, since they flew out early the next morning, but it could be waiting for her when she returned.

Kate just needed to get the address from Simon. After texting him, she noticed that her cell phone battery was low and plugged it in before going to meet her next patient.

The delivery truck arrived at five and Kate and Robert went out to meet it while the rest of the clinic staff took turns coming to the door to ooh and ahh. Thirty minutes later, the waiting room was almost impossible to recognize. Some of the parents helped set up furniture. They talked happily, tearing off the plastic wrap and arranging the pieces into groups. Jenny tried out the red mid-century modern sofa. Flynn sat on her lap and Leo stroked the suede-like microfiber with short, grubby fingers.

"Be careful," his mother warned. "Don't smudge it."

The bruises on Jenny's face had faded. She looked better physically but had grown more withdrawn since the day Flynn had picked up her gun. Kate put her hand on Jenny's arm. "The slipcovers are washable. Nothing to worry about."

Kate squatted down by Leo. "What do you think, buddy? Does the new room meet with your approval?"

He looked around with big eyes and nodded.

"Oh, yeah?" Kate asked. "What's your favorite part?"

Giggling, Leo took her hand and led her toward the toys. He showed Kate the ones he and Flynn liked best. It was a relief to see him acting like a happy little boy again.

Chapter 31

On Thursday of the following week, Simon stood by his desk looking out at the serenity garden, thinking of where he wanted to eat lunch. A hoagie sounded good. He checked out with his secretary and left the building. Simon reached the Mercedes a moment before his private cell phone rang. Assuming it was Kate, he answered the phone without looking at the number.

"Hey, Gorgeous."

Soft, muffled weeping carried over the line. His stomach dropped. "Kate? Are you all right?"

The crying stopped abruptly. "It's Liza, Simon. Sorry to fall apart like this."

Liza? His sister? "What's wrong?"

"Mom called from London about thirty minutes ago," Liza said with a sniffle. "She and Dad left their hotel to go for a walk, and he collapsed on the street. They're at Charing Cross Hospital. The doctors said it was a heart attack."

Simon felt like the air had been sucked out of his lungs. "Is he alive?"

"Yes. They got him to the hospital quickly. Mom wanted me to call you. I talked with Annie already, and she's a mess, too."

"Tell me exactly what Mom said."

"They were walking down the street and Dad complained that his chest hurt. He just fell, mid-sentence."

The phone rattled, as though his sister had shifted it to her shoulder. "They did some tests at the hospital, and Dad's going to need an angioplasty."

"When?"

"He's having the procedure right now." Liza heaved a weary sigh. "Mom sounded so upset. She needs someone to go over and be with her, Simon. I've been stuck with sick kids all week and now I have the flu as well. And Bart's out of town, so Annie can't leave. Weston is stuck in Dubai."

Simon started up the Mercedes and backed out of his parking space in one fluid motion. "I'll go, don't worry. I'll take the next flight."

Liza started to cry again.

"You've done everything you can, sis. Try to take care of yourself, and I'll call you when I get there."

She blew her nose. "Thanks, little brother."

Simon might be his father's least favorite child, and Jack would probably prefer West or Annie instead, but he was going anyway.

After disconnecting with Liza, Simon phoned an airline and booked passage on a flight. It was scheduled to leave PDX in three hours. He called Greg Jacobsen to explain his situation, and Greg immediately told him to go help his family. Simon left a message on Kate's cell, threw a change of clothes into his carry-on bag, and drove to the airport.

The trip to Portland International was fast due to a midday lull in traffic. But his luck didn't hold once he landed in Newark. The plane scheduled to fly him to England was delayed several hours. Simon ate a tasty pretzel, drank a soda, and then wandered around the airport. Nothing against Newark, but he had places to be.

Finally in the air once more, Simon looked through the small airplane window into nothing but darkness. Would his presence be welcome at the hospital? What if he caused Jack greater stress?

As the hours passed, Simon couldn't sleep. The darkness grew less substantial, until the first hint of daybreak illuminated the vast Atlantic. A flight attendant arrived with a steaming washcloth, and Simon cleaned the travel fatigue, more a feeling than a substance, from his face. Farther east, the sun flashed across the horizon. He closed his eyes and slept for the remainder of the flight, waking as the pilot announced their descent to Gatwick.

Kate's first patient at the ER was a colicky infant. The problem could have been dealt with at home, but the baby's parents were completely rattled after walking the floor with the screaming child for hours. Kate had given him a complete exam. Everything looked normal. Then she got a couple of heated blankets from the warmer near the nurse's station. She swaddled the baby snugly in the blankets and rubbed his back. His pitiful cries grew softer and less insistent.

"You said you're breastfeeding?" Kate asked the mother.

"Yes."

"And he's getting enough to eat?"

The father spoke up. "We get plenty of wet diapers."

Mom became agitated. "Maybe it's the Brussels sprouts I had for lunch. Would that make him sick like this?"

"Could be," Kate replied. "I'd avoid the sprouts next time, but colic is just a normal part of being a baby. He should grow out of it in a month or so."

The baby began to snore on Kate's shoulder and she handed him to his father.

After that, things got busy. She treated a seven-year-old girl who had a case of strep that was just ahead of the usual return-to-school-and-catch-it-from-your-friends season. In addition to needing antibiotics, the child was dehydrated enough to require an IV. A teenager was wheeled into the hospital, screaming at the top of his lungs because of the nail embedded in his foot. After being sedated, he promised Kate never to go skateboarding without shoes again.

She later dislodged a piece of foam from a child's nose and diagnosed a type-I diabetic. Yet the grand finale for Kate was when Beth's ex-husband Stan brought their son Josh to the ER with a broken arm. The boy had been trying to climb out of a top bunk to make a trip to the bathroom. Being half-asleep, Josh had missed the ladder, falling straight to the floor on top of his arm. It was a traumatic way to wake up and ended in a transverse fracture. Josh had X-rays and a temporary splint. Kate stayed with him and Stan until an orthopedic specialist arrived, followed by a stressed-out Beth.

Checking her messages, Kate went into the doctors' lounge to get some juice. The small room was a linoleum paradise complete with home-like amenities and industrial-grade furniture. It smelled as though someone had brewed coffee for a hundred years straight, until it became a foul, tar-like substance that absorbed light and air. No other room in the whole hospital smelled like it. Some of the nurses claimed it was haunted by odors.

Smiling at the thought of ghost coffee, Kate stretched out on the hard couch, tilting her head back and holding the cell phone in place with her shoulder.

"Kat?" Her father's distinctive voice reverberated. "Would you have time to come over for lunch next Saturday? Call me and let me know if it's possible."

Neill, her neighbor who leased the second-floor corner apartment, was next. "Some guy's been hanging around the house, asking about your schedule. Just because I work at home doesn't mean that I have time to take messages for you. Will you speak with your friend? Thanks."

Some guy was hanging around? The only "guys" she spent time with were Robert or Simon, and they knew her schedule better than she did. Kate made a mental note to call Neill later to get a description of her visitor.

The next message came from Simon. It was short and she had to listen twice to get the details. He must have called the day before, early in the afternoon when she was sleeping.

"Hello, Kate? It's me. Dad had a heart attack. I'm flying to London tonight." Simon talked through some static, his voice rough. "He's at Charing Cross Hospital, and my parents have a room at the Draycott. I'll probably be staying there as well. I love you."

Her heart went out to Simon and his family. He and Cecily had to be under a lot of stress. Kate hoped that they had a good medical team working with Jack. She felt useless, a continent and an ocean away. If Kate were with Simon, she could at least hold his hand.

Her final message didn't have any words. Just the sound of someone on the line. They hung up after a few seconds and she checked the identity of the caller.

The name was Quinton.

Muscles growing tense, Kate sat up. *Julian? How did he get my number for hell's sake?*

But with all the money at a Quinton's disposal, it probably wasn't that difficult to acquire.

When Kate left the hospital at five, she took an Uber home. The Triumph was supposed to be ready that morning, but of course it wasn't. Hence the Uber. The entire trip was a blur. Her mind was focused on two things: what was transpiring with Simon's family thousands of miles away in London and whether Julian or his stepmother had called her cell.

Her brain was so filled with thoughts, Kate was amazed she hadn't spoken aloud, just to let some of them out of her head. When she opened her front door, it was nice to see that her apartment was empty. No stalkers. No weird cigarette butts.

Once Kate took a shower and washed her hair, she swept and mopped the floors in her apartment. Although she was physically exhausted, sleep was impossible with the queasy, nervous ache in her stomach. Work was her magic bullet, and Kate wiped out her oven and microwave until they looked almost new. The automated message on Simon's cell phone said that it was not in service when she tried to call him again.

She washed a small load of delicates in her sink and hung them in the bathroom to dry. Despite the pounding in her head, Kate dusted the living room before finally admitting that she was too tired to continue. She lay down under her comforter, her phone and the Walther on her nightstand, and fitfully fell asleep.

———————— • ————————

Irritable tourists occupied every inch of the sidewalk. They all wanted to get into the city, and empty cabs were as easy to come by as iridium. The car rental agencies weren't any help either since they were completely out of vehicles. Simon walked toward the airport rail station and purchased a Cherry Coke and an A-Z street atlas on the way.

He boarded the Gatwick Express bound for Victoria tube station and closed his eyes. The hum of the railway car was almost hypnotic in his fatigued state. Forty minutes later, Simon disembarked and switched over to the Underground line heading toward Ealing. He gave his seat at the back of the car to an expectant mother who was carrying her shopping and looked tired. Simon stood and held the handrail, trying not to hit anyone with his bag. He switched to another line, walked a bit, and eventually found himself on Fulham Palace Road, with Charing Cross Hospital directly ahead.

During his trip from the airport, he had quietly listened to people. Languages from around the world were being spoken at any given time. Simon had vacationed in London before, though not recently, and he had forgotten the city's great ethnic diversity.

He entered the hospital, where a friendly, middle-aged nurse showed him into his father's recovery room. Cecily sat next to Jack's bed, a blanket wrapped around her body and a Styrofoam cup in her hand. Simon could see the surprise in her eyes as they widened and filled with tears. Cecily put the cup down, covered her face with her hands, and wept.

"It's all right, Mom." He went to her and rubbed her back gently. "I'm sorry it took me so long to get here."

"Thank you for coming." She nodded, trying to regain control. "Thank you."

As Jack slept, Simon studied his father's haggard face. His

graying hair looked oily and disheveled. He had never seen Jack that way. Simon listened to the heart monitor beeping steadily in the background and sat next to his mother. Maybe it was bone-deep fatigue, or just profound relief that Jack was still alive, but he felt like crying too. Simon exhaled slowly and tried to keep his emotions in check.

"Your father is doing really well," Cecily whispered. "He needs to rest, but I couldn't leave him here alone."

The mantle of sophistication and style that his mother wore so naturally was gone. Deep lines circled her mouth, and her eyes looked red and bloodshot. She was just an exhausted wife and mother in her early sixties who had been through a crisis and was still reeling from the ordeal.

"Why don't you go back to the hotel to sleep? I'll take care of Dad." Simon held Cecily's hand, giving it a reassuring squeeze.

His mother grasped his hand tightly. Instead of leaving, she talked, recounting their traumatic experience in detail. Her narrative flowed from her, as though she needed to release the fear and uncertainty she had borne over the last two days.

"Our cardiologist is Scottish. His name is Dr. Wilkins. Everyone's been wonderful. Really efficient and kind."

"I'm glad you've been treated so well."

"Your dad's recovering right on schedule. Dr. Wilkins said that he's a classic example of everything going right. A real success story so far."

"Has the doctor given you a possible release date?"

Cecily shook her head. "He wants to keep Jack a bit longer than usual, just to ensure that he's stable. If things continue going the way they are, it looks like Wednesday."

"What about air travel? Did he say anything about that?"

"Dr. Wilkins didn't recommend flying for several weeks. When your dad leaves the hospital, I think we'll just hang around the Draycott and enjoy some quiet time together."

Simon's body felt like it could sink to the floor. He hadn't noticed how tense he'd been. "It all sounds good."

"Jack's just happy to be alive. He didn't even grumble when he was told that cigars, alcohol, and rich foods would have to go. Not one complaint. He's been an angel."

"Really? My father?"

Cecily had her version of Jack's Look. It always conveyed to her children what she expected of them. This time the Look prohibited any criticism of Jack while he was ill. "When you have an experience like this, it's scary and humbling. He's willing to make changes in order to live."

"I imagine that's true."

"I spoke with Liza and Annie an hour ago, but I couldn't get in touch with West. His phone sends me straight to voice mail. Will you keep calling him while I get some sleep at the hotel?"

Simon didn't relish speaking with his brother at the moment. He wasn't sure that he could conceal years of anger and resentment if they did make contact.

Cecily covered her mouth, trying to stifle a yawn. Simon called the concierge at the Draycott and arranged for a driver to pick her up at the hospital. She hugged Simon tightly before she left, thanking him again and again for dropping everything and flying to London.

Jack slept for the next hour. A nurse came in to check his vitals and Simon stepped into the hall to call West. When he was sent to voice mail, Simon instantly adopted his pissed-off lawyer persona.

"Call Mom or I'm coming to Dubai. You really don't want that, West. I'm the bad son, remember? The one who causes drunken scenes and gets thrown out of law firms? I'll raise such unmitigated hell in your office that the sultan's grandson will curse the day he hired you . . ."

Then Simon hung up and tried Kate, who sounded a little breathless and disoriented when she answered. It was eight hours earlier in Portland, and he'd only thought of how much he missed her, not whether it was the best time to call.

"I'm so sorry I woke you." He imagined her face rosy and flushed from sleep. "Everything's okay here. I'll talk to you later."

Kate protested before Simon could hang up. "Please don't go. I tried to stay awake in case you called. Is your dad all right?"

He relayed the information his mother had given him.

"I'm so glad for your family. How are you—"

Simon held the phone closer, trying to hear as a group of footballers went by, cheering their injured mate. "How are you holding up?" Kate asked again.

"I didn't sleep much on the plane, so I'm tired. But I feel fine. Relieved."

"Is there anything I can do for you back here?"

He smiled like she was standing beside him. "Just hearing your voice makes me forget the jet lag and the fact that I haven't eaten in what feels like forever."

"Go find something. Chips. Sausage rolls. Hobnobs."

"What are Hobnobs?"

Kate laughed. "Only the best chocolate-dipped oatmeal biscuits in history."

"Sold. I'll get those." Simon watched the nurse leave his

father's room. She motioned to him and he said, "Be right there."

"Something wrong?" Kate asked.

"The nurse wants to talk. I'll call you tomorrow, sweetheart."

"Okay. Miss you."

Her voice faded away. Simon hung up the phone and felt every one of the miles that separated them.

———————●●———————

As it happened, the nurse didn't have anything crucial to report about Jack, just that his vitals were good and he no longer needed his catheter. She warned Simon that he might have to help Jack to the bathroom, where he would pee in a special sleeve in the toilet. Simon smirked at this, knowing how much Jack would hate it.

"He went back to sleep, though I expect he'll be up and around soon," the nurse said. "If you need to go to the bank or get tea, now's the time to do it."

Simon slipped out of the hospital to quickly exchange U.S. dollars for British pounds. He stopped at a little shop on the way back and bought three sausage rolls, crisps, and candy with odd-sounding names like Curly Wurly and Flake. To this he added Kate's Hobnobs and a package of custard creams.

Simon returned to the hospital and saw that the nurse who had removed Jack's catheter was now sitting at her station. He smiled and asked her name. She told him it was Eve.

He opened his shopping bag. "Would you care for some chocolate Buttons?"

"Thanks, but no." She looked critically at his food stash. "That's not a proper meal for a big fellow like you. You need something better."

Eve wrote down directions to "the best place in London for English fare" and handed the paper to Simon. She nodded toward the candy and cookies. "You'll need something to drink with that lot. Will bottled water do?"

"Thanks. I'd appreciate it." Simon turned down the hallway and heard Eve call after a young male orderly.

"Oy, Reg! Get us some water, will you?"

Jack was snoring when Simon entered his room. He pulled a chair closer to his father's bed and sat down. After eating the sausage rolls, Simon tried the crisps. He was halfway through his package of Hobnobs when Eve came in, followed by two younger women in scrubs. Eve handed Simon several bottles of water.

"This is Nicollette and Sybil. They're mad for Americans. Can't get enough of the way you talk."

Simon wasn't sure what to say to that. "Umm . . . thank you for the water, ladies. Would you like a cookie?"

Laughing, the women each took a custard cream. Eve ushered her coworkers out the door. "You'll have to pardon them, Simon, but they think you're a movie star from the States." She pulled the curtain around his father's side of the bed. "I'll try and keep the girls out, love."

Jack muttered and opened his eyes. "Would you and your fan club keep it down? People are sleeping."

Simon leaned his forearms against the railing of the bed. "It's good to hear you telling me what to do again. You had us all worried for a while. Want some water?"

He held the straw steady in the green plastic cup as Jack drank. The simple gesture seemed to trigger his father's emotions. Jack struggled to wipe his eyes with a pulse monitor attached to his finger, so Simon took a tissue and dried the places he missed. His father grabbed the wilted tissue and waved him away with it.

Giving Jack time to compose himself, Simon sat back in his chair and waited. For five long minutes. Jack would begin a sentence, then his eyes would fill again and he'd stop.

After regaining control, he blew his nose and said, "The last time we talked, I said some things I'm not proud of."

"Forget it. It's not important now."

Jack waved his tissue in a way that reminded Simon of Queen Elizabeth acknowledging her subjects. "When I thought I was going to die, I didn't want my life to end with this breach between us. It's always been there, and I don't know how to stop."

"There's no need to go into this now, Dad."

Jack slumped down against the mattress. "I remember what you were like when you were young and needed a father."

"I still need you. I always will." Simon rested his hand on his father's shoulder. It had been so long since he'd touched him, beyond the occasional businesslike handshake. Maybe since he was a boy.

Tears filled Jack's eyes again. "You've always reminded me so much of my father."

Simon thought of Joseph and felt a lump form in his throat. He still missed him every day. "Grandpa was a good man."

Jack gazed past Simon. "Dad was different by the time you were born. Easier. Kinder. I grew up with nothing. Or next to nothing. It was a struggle to survive. We never said the words, never talked about loving each other." He caught a bead of water as it raced down his cup and stared at the moisture on his finger. "Our beach town was great for the tourists during the summer, but hard to scrape out a decent living in as a native. I did well in school because I knew I could become something with an education."

Simon remembered his grandfather's house. A tiny cabin a few steps from the windswept beach, with no furnace or television. It had two bedrooms, a fireplace, and a small kitchen off the screened-in porch out back. The driveway led past the house to the workshop, where a plaque hung over the door emblazoned with *Phillips and Son.*

A long time ago, Jack had mentioned in passing that it had been a lonely place to grow up. From family stories and personal experience, Simon knew Joseph Phillips was a perfectionist. If you weren't enthusiastic about a job, he'd work you until you changed your mind. It appeared that Joseph's method of teaching hadn't been successful with Jack. He wasn't cut out for the kind of life his father lived.

The wrinkles around Jack's eyes lifted as he smiled. "I was the first member of our family to go to college. To Harvard on scholarship, no less. When I met your mother, I saw all the things I could never be wrapped up together. She was beautiful, sweet, and kind. Marrying that woman was the smartest thing I ever did."

"Mom's the best. I'm glad she let you catch her."

Jack thought for a moment and then grew restless, shifting his legs under the blanket. "Yesterday, as they loaded me into that ambulance? I had a moment when I realized that I couldn't negotiate my way out of this. Money wouldn't reverse my condition or keep me from dying if it was my time."

"You're not dying. You have years yet to keep us all in line."

Jack turned toward the monitor near his bed, the one

showing his heartbeat. "But I thought it might be the end, Simon, and I knew what mattered most. I didn't give a damn about my possessions or my career, I just wanted to see my family."

As a kid, Simon had always wanted Jack to open up to him, hoping they would get to know one another and have a real relationship. He never expected that it would happen here, in a cramped hospital room, thousands of miles from home. Happiness grew inside him by slow degrees.

Simon's phone started to play the theme to *The Good, the Bad and the Ugly*. His threat to come to Dubai must have worked on West. He hit answer and handed the phone to his father.

Jack put it to his ear and smiled. An actual honest-to-goodness smile. No bitterness or anger. "Weston? Is it you?"

His brother's voice was a soft murmur, but Simon heard a few sentence fragments clearly. *I'm so sorry . . . Tied up in meetings . . . How's that heart?*

Jack continued to beam as he listened. After rising to his feet, Simon decided to leave and give them time to chat without interruption. He pulled the door open and was about to step into the hall when his father called him back.

"Don't go," Jack said, hand covering the cell phone. "Stay with me, son."

* * *

His father was discharged from the hospital the next evening. Jack's positive attitude regarding healthy lifestyle changes died in a blaze of glory at the Draycott. Voice rising in volume, he argued with his rent-a-nurse, Miss Bell, over portion size.

"Steamed vegetables with a sliver of chicken? You can't be

serious."

"Oh, I assure you, I am rarely anything but," Miss Bell said, prying the bill of fare from his hands. "You may also have a nonfat yogurt if you'd like."

"*Yogurt?* This is ridiculous! Stop treating me like I'm a child."

"Then stop acting like one, Mr. Phillips . . ."

Jack's color and energy level improved over the next three days. His increased strength did much to alleviate Cecily's stress, and she was able to sleep through the night. She even had her hair and nails done. Simon observed these developments and knew that his presence was no longer needed. Both parents were on the mend.

His mother watched him make his flight reservation online and frowned. "You could stay. Have a vacation. See the sights."

"I've got to get back to work. Greg's been very understanding."

Cecily agreed and helped Simon pack his small suitcase. They sat down for lunch in his parents' suite and Jack began arguing with Miss Bell again.

When the meal was over, Simon stepped out into the hall. He had been closed up in the hotel for days, listening to his father and the nurse quarrel every time they spoke to each other. Simon had played cards, watched football matches, and read newspapers to block them out, but the bright spot of his stay had been calling West for his parents. They would take the phone and talk for twenty minutes without blinking an eye. And Simon just smiled, imagining the havoc this caused his brother's busy schedule.

He strolled down to the concierge and checked out of the Draycott. The departure time of his flight wasn't until later that afternoon. It gave him a few hours to see a little of London. An idea popped into his head. As the concierge arranged his transportation, Simon went back upstairs and said goodbye to his family. His parents and Miss Bell were all distracted by a British television program, so the farewell was short and sweet.

Simon got his bag, left the Draycott, and climbed into a black cab. The cabdriver looked over his shoulder. "Where can I take you today, sir?"

"I'd like to go to a library."

"Of course, sir. If I could make a suggestion, there's the British Library on Euston Road."

"No," Simon replied. "I want the one in Notting Hill."

Chapter 32

He examined the sturdy white building and handed the cabdriver twenty quid. "Keep the change."

"Thanks, mate. You sure this is the spot?"

"I think so."

"Right." The cabby nodded. "Bye then."

People passed Simon as he walked along the sidewalk. He took his time and savored the moment by studying the row houses. Looking over the pub nearby, the old tree-lined street. Kate's library sat on the corner of an intersection, a well-maintained example of Georgian architecture. Excitement rushed through him. He had found her childhood sanctuary.

The door was locked, but Simon could see through the glass panels. Movement within the library caught his attention. A white-haired man was standing inside buttoning his jacket. He wore a tag that said he was a security guard. The old man hooked an umbrella over his arm before pushing the door open.

"We're shut, sir. Sorry if you made the trip for nothing."

Simon smiled. "It wasn't for nothing. I heard about this library from a friend, and I wanted to see it."

"Not the biggest of tourist attractions, if you'll pardon me saying."

Simon didn't agree. He had never wanted to see the inside

of a building more. "I'm still glad I came."

"There's nothing in the world like a library." The guard looked at the sky, like he was assessing the weather. "Been known to pop into one or two myself."

"I imagine that's true," Simon replied, feeling a few raindrops fall on his shoulders, the side of his face. "How long have you worked here?"

"Since I was about your age, I suppose. I'm starting my pension next week."

Simon felt a tingling awareness, as though Fate stood at his shoulder. He held out his hand. "I'd like to introduce myself. My name is Simon, and you're Burt, if I'm not mistaken."

A vertical line formed between the unruly eyebrows. "Heard of me in America, have you?"

"From my friend. I don't know if you'd remember, but her name is Kate."

"Kate, is it?" Burt paused, searching his memory. "I've known my share of girls with that name."

"She was young then, early teens. Spent most of her time in a reading room."

The old man thought on this. "Lots of wild blonde hair? Greenish eyes?" Burt asked softly. "I do remember. Couldn't forget that one. Something special about her, there was."

The feeling of Fate intensified. "Yes, she is."

"And you say you know her? Kate?"

"I do."

Burt tilted his head like a curious owl. "She's all right?"

The rain fell a little harder and Simon hitched the collar of his jacket up. "Better than all right."

"Good," Burt said. He seemed genuinely happy and relieved. "Only talked with her a few times, but I sometimes worried things were hard at home."

"They were. I know the library's closed, but is there any way I could come in, just for a moment, to look around?"

Burt winced like the idea pained him. "I'd lose my job if it was found out."

"It's lucky then, that you'll be a pensioner as of next week." Simon watched Burt as he deliberated.

A sudden mischievous expression made his face look younger. "Right you are, Simon. They can't fire me if I'm retired." Burt glanced around the sidewalk. "You've got yourself five minutes."

Simon slipped through the doorway, heading straight for the staircase. The walls of the shadowy building tossed the sound of his footsteps back and forth. It smelled faintly of old paper and mildew. At the top of the landing, he turned down the hall. There it was, the janitor's closet right next to the ladies' lavatory. And across the hall, the reading room.

Kate had described the place so clearly that he had seen it in his mind. With a strong sense of déjá vu, Simon entered a room he had never been in before and yet knew it well. He went to the window. A small bookcase and two chairs stood in front of it now, no leather-like sofa. Simon looked outside. It was mid-afternoon but he thought of how the view would appear in the dark, the way it had when Kate stayed in the library. The streetlamp was dormant but it would snap on at dusk. Its light, shining through the window, had helped Kate to read her books.

Simon understood why she loved this library. It felt removed from the world. Safe. Peaceful. He walked through the aisles, random titles catching his eye.

Burt coughed apologetically from the doorway. "It's getting on, lad."

"I know. Thank you, Burt. You've been very kind."

Simon stepped around a metal trolley piled high with hardbacks. His arm brushed the nearest stack, toppling it to the floor. "Oh, sorry. I'll pick them up." He knelt down and began to gather the books.

"You needn't bother about them," Burt said. "They're going to the charity shop tomorrow."

"That's a shame."

"It's not really. They were read often and served their purpose."

Simon noticed a book sticking out from under the cart and reached for it. The grayish-blue face looked dull and nearly all the gold writing had been rubbed off the spine. The top letters were NE, followed by an RE below. Again, Simon felt a fateful awareness like a chill passing over him.

Opening the book, he could see that some pages were missing, the binding having given way. Simon held the papers in place and was beginning to close the back cover when he saw something familiar.

It can't be.

Chapter 33

K ate felt strange when she woke up, as though she had stumbled into the middle of a tricky situation just by opening her eyes. After sliding her feet into a pair of slippers, she pulled on a chenille robe to cover the white T-shirt she had slept in. Yawning loudly, Kate walked to the kitchen, rolling her shoulders and stretching.

She reached for an orange and took a paring knife from its wooden storage block. The sharp metallic edge of the blade bit into the fruit, and juice dripped over her fingers. Kate inhaled the sweet fresh scent and heard a faint brushing sound, like a hand rubbing against fabric. She held her breath. A sofa spring creaked in the living room.

Kate's blood raced through her veins. Who was in the apartment? The front door had been locked last night. She remembered the way the deadbolt clicked into place. And the windows were always secure . . .

Certainty fled like a mist before the sun. Kat had opened the one in the bathroom because the walls were wet with steam after her shower. She'd closed the damn thing, hadn't she? Sweat formed on her skin and froze.

No. Kate knew she had not.

Holding the knife against her chest, she edged quietly back toward her bedroom door and the Walther on her nightstand. Kate slid the knife into the pocket of her robe and picked up the pistol. Her hands shook badly, but the magazine was loaded, the safety switched off. All her life, Kate had feared being attacked. She knew it would happen eventually. It felt inevitable. Was this the day?

Terror made the things around her seem unreal and distant. Like she was watching the situation play out through thick glass. Kate crept down the hall, stepping only on the boards that wouldn't squeak and give her away. She peeked round the corner of the living room door. Kate could barely distinguish the features of the person on the couch. It was a man, his frame backlit by the radiant window. He had long dark hair and watched her with a disturbing intensity. His voice cracked as he spoke, like a hard, raspy shot in the silence.

"It took you long enough to wake up."

The voice sounded like the one she sometimes heard in those nightmares that came when she was unusually tired and vulnerable. When she tried to save Tess, over and over, only to watch her die.

"I guess you weren't expecting me." The man gave a humorless laugh. "I don't remember you being the quiet type. Cat got your tongue?"

Julian.

He stood, and his tall body was all shadow and darkness as he took a step toward her.

"What's wrong, Kate? You look like you've seen a ghost."

She lifted the Walther, put her finger on the sensitive trigger. Julian yelled and tackled her before she could fire off a shot. Pain ricocheted from her wrist to her shoulder as he knocked the Walther across the floor. Their bodies hit the coffee table, sending books in every direction.

"No," Kate screamed. "Get away."

He shook her hard. "Shut up. I don't want any cops—"

But she kicked and thrashed against the heavy weight on top of her and they rolled from the table. Kate remembered the knife and pulled it out of her pocket. Huge hands clamped onto her wrist, yanking it back and making her drop the blade. Kate screamed, and one of the big hands covered her mouth. Biting into the soft underside of his finger, she tasted salty, unwashed skin.

"You're hurting me. Knock it off."

It took a moment for Kate to really listen to that voice. There was no upper-crust British accent, no cultured tones like Julian's.

Not him. It's not him . . .

As the fear began to melt away, Kate stopped fighting the arms that circled her. Rolling over, she shoved at the man with all her strength. He fell back against the tile by the fireplace.

"Damn you, Axel!" Kate shouted. "What the hell are you doing in my house?" She struggled to her feet and cursed again. "I almost shot you."

"I'm sorry, Kate." Axel raised his hands like a flag of truce as she stooped and picked up the knife and the Walther. "I'm sorry . . . I'm sorry. I didn't know where else to go."

She shoved him again. "I could think of a million other places. Hospitals, rehab, shelters. Take your pick."

His eyes were sunken. The skin stretched across his cheekbones looked yellow. "Stop yelling," he said and began to cough. "I don't feel good."

Kate wasn't about to stop. "Of all the stupid, idiotic,

brainless . . . I should call the cops and turn you in." She ended her tirade abruptly as the doctor in her kicked into gear. "You look terrible."

Axel grabbed his stomach. "I need to use your can. I think I'm gonna puke."

"Around the corner and to your left."

As he hurried past her to the bathroom, Kate caught the strong odor of stale nicotine and unwashed body. She followed to see that he didn't pocket anything. Axel heaved a few times, so Kate closed the bathroom door, put the knife away, and sat down in the living room. Her body trembled after the sudden spike of adrenaline. The coppery taste of blood filled her mouth from when she bit her lip in the struggle with Axel. She pushed the safety lever on the Walther, and set it on a side table.

Several minutes later water rattled through the pipes under the old floor and Kate knew Axel had finished. He crossed the living room on unsteady legs, and she got her first good look at him. The long, black coat Axel wore concealed his emaciated state, adding a misleading bulk to his frame. He sat down and leaned his forearms on his legs, hands dangling between his knobby knees.

Tears rolled down Axel's cheeks, and he wiped them with the tail of his flannel shirt. "I didn't know how hard it would be. I can't do this by myself."

"Getting clean?"

"Yeah. Either that or I've died and gone to hell's ghetto." Axel's shoulders shook with laughter, and then he covered his face and sobbed like a child. Without saying a word, Kate watched him, and when Axel had finally worn himself out, he lifted his watery eyes to hers.

"News takes a while to reach the shelter, but I heard about

what happened at the clinic—I heard about my baby picking up that gun. Jenny wouldn't have bought it if not for me."

Axel took a pack of cigarettes and a lighter from his pocket. A tremor went through his body as he lit up. Kate glared at him and cracked open a window. "You've been sleeping in the shed out back. I saw the stubs you left behind on the floor."

He didn't deny it. "Only a few times. It was small but safe and out of the wind."

Kate felt weak with relief. It had been Axel the whole time. "You had a smoke by my bike as well."

He looked away. Nodded. Kate leaned forward, tempted to slap his face or shoot him. "Did you vandalize it, slash the tires? Break into my apartment?"

He took a long drag and started crying again. "I came to you for help that night in the parking lot. All you gave me was a number to another rehab place. I was pissed, Kate. And crazy, trying any drug I could get my hands on."

"So you took it out on me, Axel? Your friend?"

His eyes took on a canny expression. "Get real, Doc. Junkies don't have friends. We're just looking for a way to score."

"You broke into my place looking for money?"

He nodded again. "But you didn't have any. Just a whole lotta books and crap."

Picking up the Walther, Kate went to the kitchen. She brought back a hot, wet washcloth and a glass of water. "Wipe your face, Axel. Have a drink. You're dehydrated."

He followed her instructions humbly. While Axel cleaned himself up, Kate thought of Tess. How many times had she seen her act just this contrite? So sorry, so apologetic. Decades of anguish crashed over her but Kate reminded herself that she was not a child anymore. A spark of hope burned through those years of bitterness. What if Tess had been given another chance? If she'd lived a little longer and tried again. Maybe it would have worked. Maybe she'd still be alive. Kate took the washcloth from Axel and wiped a smudge of dirt from his forehead, the side of one brow. His eyes reminded her so much of Leo's. Her heart softened a little more.

She might not have been able to save her mother, but perhaps she could be there for Axel.

Taking the empty glass from his fingers, Kate said gently, "Your family needs you. Jenny, Leo, and Flynn didn't ask for any of this."

"I'm so sorry—"

"Being sorry won't save your kids." She took his hand in hers.

"Help me," Axel begged, clutching her fingers. "I can't live like this anymore."

<hr />

Gatwick Airport

Simon had bad travel karma on this trip. His flight over was delayed and the one back to America had been as well. His plane sat on the tarmac for an hour and when it finally took off, some of the other passengers cheered.

Things improved once they were in the air. It was a direct flight, so no connection in Newark this time. He ate a sandwich, skipped the movie, and read the *New York Times* cover to cover. Then he slept the rest of the flight. After a smooth landing at Portland International, Simon tossed his bag into the back of his car, thankful the Mercedes was still where he'd left it in long-term parking.

He drove home, dumped his bag on the kitchen table, and took a long, steaming shower. It felt so good to be in his own house again. His California king mattress and soft white comforter looked inviting, but Simon had slept enough on the plane. As his stomach rumbled with hunger, he threw on a washed-out T-shirt and an old pair of jeans. They smelled like the dryer sheets Mrs. Lee used. Simon picked up some bagels at a bakery and drove to Kate's house.

She opened her door with a tired scowl and then yelped when she realized it was him. Simon dropped the paper bag he carried and roughly hauled her up against him, their kiss frantic and breathless. The welcome went on and on, until Kate pulled away, laughing.

"We'll scandalize my neighbors."

Simon grinned. "I'm willing if you are."

She picked up the white bag and looked inside. "You brought bagels?"

"Hot, fresh ones." Simon towed her into the living room and plonked her down on the sofa beside him. "Thanks for taking time off from the hospital."

He had called from Gatwick, asking if she could skip a day and spend it with him. "It's probably for the best," Kate admitted. "You scramble my brainwaves."

"Honey, flattery will get you anywhere you want to go."

"Hmmm. I'll have to think about that."

Simon turned so he could see her eyes clearly. "I need to tell you what I found in England."

"British health care at its finest?"

"Something even better." He put his arm around her. "I saw your library."

Kate pulled back. "What? You went to Notting Hill?"

"I had time before my flight. It was just like you described."

Disbelief faded, replaced by a smile. Simon enjoyed the way happiness turned Kate's skin a soft rosy color. Almost like a warm light had been turned on inside.

"Wow. When you surprise somebody, you don't mess around."

"I met Burt."

"*My* Burt?" Kate's voice rose half an octave. "Security-guard Burt? He must be ancient by now."

Simon shrugged. "He has a few wrinkles, but he seemed fit. He remembered you."

"Really?" Kate sank back against him. "After all these years?"

"He did. He asked if you were doing well. I told him you were."

"I'm just stunned." She was quiet for a while and then nestled into his body.

Simon rested his head next to hers. He turned his face into the hair curling around her neck. It smelled like warm honey. His mind hurtled along at warp speed.

"How many kids do you want? I want a houseful of little Kates."

The words had slipped from Simon's mouth without any consideration of whether Kate was ready to hear them. As soon as they were out, he knew he'd made a mistake.

Kate could see the future in his eyes. He wanted to be her friend and her lover. He wanted her to have his children, to share his life. With a look, he had said it all.

A flush crested his cheekbones. "Lawyers are supposed to think first and speak second, but I have no filter at all when I'm with you."

She couldn't think of a thing to say that didn't sound stupid. "You'll be a great dad. Someday."

Simon didn't respond. He just watched her.

But Kate didn't want to talk about kids, their relationship, or the future. She kissed Simon, ending all conversation for a while, and then they made coffee and ate the bagels.

Apparently, Kate lacked a filter with Simon as well, because she told him about Axel's appearance in her house the morning before. She had wanted to wait until later, after thinking of a way to do it that wouldn't make him mad at her drug-addicted friend.

His eyes turned electric blue. "Axel really did that? Snuck in through the bathroom window?"

"Don't be angry. He's in rehab now."

Simon worked his jaw, his expression hard. "Where? I'd like to go see him."

Knowing that would be a big mistake, Kate put her hands on his chest. "I think Axel would be safer if I kept his location a secret. Believe me, he's already suffering."

"Not enough." Simon began to count on his fingers. "Slashed your tires, broke into your home, smashed the bike, terrorized you—"

Kate cut him off. "Stop counting! I've got the Triumph back, and Axel is in treatment. Everything's okay now."

Simon took out his keys. "There are only so many rehab centers in Portland. It's just a matter of time until I find the right one." He looked down at Kate. "Axel took your charm bracelet, didn't he?"

Kate had hoped Simon wouldn't remember how upset she'd been when the bracelet went missing. How bewildered she'd felt when it suddenly appeared again at the clinic within the pages of her book. "After smashing the bike. He felt guilty and couldn't bring himself to trade it with his dealer."

Simon's body stilled. "In other words, the bracelet was too banged up for the dealer to accept."

"Maybe, but I'd like to think Axel's developing a conscience. When Robert and I carried lunch over to Larry and Earl, he slipped into the clinic and tucked the bracelet into my book."

Simon rubbed the center of his chest as if it hurt. "I sat here, totally helpless, and watched you fight back tears when you thought it was gone. That really sucked. Not to mention the fact that Axel broke the law. I never thought I'd say this, but I wish I were a district attorney. It makes me crazy to think of him coming in here."

Kate's heart hurt too. Because Simon loved her and he was so damned cute standing there, blue eyes blazing and wanting to kick Axel's poor scrawny butt.

"I understand, and I feel kind of violated, but I'm not ready to give up on Axel yet. He and his family need another chance." Kate put her arms around his neck. "Can I ask a favor?"

His face grew incredulous. "You want me to forgive him? No. It's not happening. I have a long memory."

Kate's smile was so big her face hurt. "Spend today with me and forget everything else."

He held his ground for about two minutes and then caved. "Forget what?"

To catch up on some of the work he had missed while in England, Simon went into the office over the weekend. Kate's schedule was equally full, and they talked briefly as she drove to the hospital. By Sunday night, he'd accomplished all the goals he set for himself.

During his run the next morning, Simon realized that the seasons had started to change. Fall had settled, all reddish-yellow, into the Pacific Northwest. Exhilarated, he breathed deep, lifting his face to the mild warmth of the sun.

His new secretary was not a motherly sort like Linda, but she was nice. Simon surprised her with a cup of coffee and sat down at his desk. He was occupied with meetings until early afternoon. At half past one, Simon had lunch with Greg again, but they didn't talk business. They covered more important topics like climbing documentaries, flyfishing, and Greg's kids.

He took calls in his office after lunch and worked until six. The legal floor was empty by the time Simon emerged. He was the last to leave but it was still light outside. There was none of the fatigue he usually felt, just the satisfaction of doing good work with people he enjoyed.

Pulling out his private cell, Simon realized that he'd forgotten to charge it. He swung by Kate's home and saw Neill, the cranky writer who lived upstairs, standing on the front porch. Simon waved as he opened the gate, set to follow the path to Kate's apartment.

"She isn't home," Neill said. "She left town."

Simon stopped abruptly. "Kate? You're sure?"

"I don't have all the details. I just know she's gone."

Where did she go? Kate hadn't told him anything about

leaving town. Simon looked at his watch and decided to stop by the community center to see if Robert had more information about her whereabouts. He entered the building, calling Robert's name as he approached the office.

The doctor turned from his desk, his face pinched and red. "What did you do? I told you not to hurt her."

Why did he look so mad? Before Simon could say a word, Robert lunged at him. Something rubbery connected with Simon's nose at the same time a finger jabbed his eye.

"What the *hell*, Robert?"

"You did something. She wouldn't leave like this."

Simon wiped blood from his nose. "What are you talking about? Kate and I are fine."

"Then why isn't she here?" Robert asked, even more red than before. "Kate never takes personal days."

"Maybe she needed one. What was her excuse?"

Robert's hand twitched, like it was getting ready to swing again.

Simon pointed at him. "Don't even think about it."

"Nina was the one who talked to her. Kate sounded like she was in tears."

In tears? But she had been happy when they spoke earlier in the day. Simon had called Kate after his run and they had shared breakfast over the phone. "Did she tell Nina where she was going?"

"No. None of us have any idea." He looked apologetic. "Sorry I hammered you."

The doctor couldn't hammer Simon on his best day. "Your watchband clipped me. If you're going to hit somebody, do it right. That was embarrassing."

Robert lifted his chin. "Come again?"

"Don't slap your opponent. Use your fists."

"I don't know how to punch."

Simon positioned Robert's arm, moving his hand into place. "Throw your shoulder into it, rotate your arm, and add a little knuckle." Robert punched Simon's open palm. "There you go. Better."

"You've been in fights before this? Dude, that's awesome."

The fact that Robert thought they had been in a real fight made Simon want to smile but he didn't. "No fighting since law school." He lifted his palm again, allowing Robert another punch. "The idea is to knock someone down, not blind them for life."

"Ouch." The doctor squinted at the fingernail indentation he had left near Simon's eye. "That looks like it hurts."

"You think?"

"Oh man. I'm sorry. I just thought . . ."

Simon pushed Robert's hand away when he fake-punched again. He had never been disappointed with him before. Or angry. They were friends, weren't they? He'd expected better.

"I know what you thought, Robert. You don't give me much credit, do you?"

"Well, in the beginning you were a little slick—"

"But when did I do anything wrong? Was it while I was tiling bathrooms? Installing the windows? Painting?"

Robert backed up a step. "Chill. I'm sorry I assumed the worst. I just worry about her. It's like she has no one."

"She has me."

Simon left the community center, wishing he had never gone there to look for Kate. Driving home, he berated himself for not charging his personal phone. Simon plugged it into the car's outlet and listened to his voice mail. There was a call from

Kate's number, but static made the message unintelligible.

"Dial Kate," he said, and his phone automatically rang her cell. No answer.

Thinking over their last day together, Simon understood her need for a break. He had blurted out his desire to settle down with her and have a family. Kate had looked panicked in that brief moment before she shuttered her eyes and made herself unreadable.

Then they spent hours together: watching movies, reading books, listening to records. It had felt like they were already married. Simon wondered if that had frightened Kate enough to make her leave.

Chapter 34

Another call from her number came through just as Simon sat down at his desk in the study. He answered his cell and heard Kate's voice loud and clear, the connection excellent this time.

"Hi," he said. "Where are you?"

"Hood River," she answered, sounding like her usual self. "Didn't you get my message?"

"I couldn't understand it. There was static. Are you all right?"

"I'm great. The Columbia is so blue, Simon. It's smooth as glass today."

He sat back in his chair. Relieved. Happy to hear her voice. "Sounds beautiful. I'm glad you're enjoying some R&R. Robert was kind of worried though. We both were actually."

There was a pause. She made a humming noise. "I asked Nina to tell Robert that I needed to visit my in-laws. Mike's parents live in Hood River."

Kate went to see Mike's family? What did that mean? Simon accidentally knocked the paperweight off his desk. It broke into pieces on the floor, and he bit back a swear word.

"That wasn't the message Robert received. I'm thinking he was the victim of Nina's wild sense of humor."

"It doesn't seem very funny."

Simon got up from his desk to look for a broom. "Nope. Robert was beside himself when you didn't show up for work."

"I can imagine. He relies on me."

That was an understatement. Kate was Robert's right arm. "Why didn't you text?"

She made an irritated noise. "Because my phone is a piece of crap. Sometimes my texts take hours to arrive. I told Nina about that too."

Simon had forgotten about Kate's phone issues. This made him feel stupid since they had recently talked about getting her a better one. "Sorry. I'm afraid she kept all that to herself."

"Weird," Kate replied slowly. "She acted so nice. She even recommended a good sunblock and told me to have fun."

He didn't doubt that Nina would sabotage Kate any way she could. "Never mind. I'll pass the word along to Robert. Don't worry about it. Is your visit going well?"

"Yes, they've been asking me to come over for months." Her voice was happy. Relaxed. "Ginny called after I spoke with you this morning. I figured today was a good time to go."

"Sure. Makes sense."

And it did, but Simon couldn't help feeling worried about why this was a good time for Kate to visit her husband's family. Was it grief? Was she wishing she could go back instead of forward? Had he pushed her too fast?

———————— • ————————

Kate enjoyed her visit with Ginny and Martin. They ate lunch at a nice restaurant and shared memories of Mike. She was a connection to their son, a link to a happier time. Kate could spare a day and drive a couple of hours if it brought them comfort.

But lunch had ended quite a while ago and now she was sitting on a smooth green plot of grass in Hood River, surrounded by headstones carved with the names of people who had once lived and loved and died. Mike's parents had wanted him close, so they could visit often. How could Kate say no to their request? The Mike she knew wasn't there in that casket. He was with her all the time, not in a cemetery. Regardless, Kate had come today to sit and talk. Maybe, somehow, he would hear.

She put her hand on the gravestone. It was hard to find the words.

Tracing the carved letters of her husband's name, Kate said, "I wouldn't be here without you, Mikey." Her eyes misted over. "Remember how scared I used to be? Jumping at my own shadow?"

It took some time before she could speak again. "But you taught me to hope. To feel worthy of love and happiness." A warm breeze touched her cheek and the sun shone brighter overhead. "You'd like Simon. He's a good man. I think we can build a future together."

It took a little effort, but Kate twisted the platinum band from her finger and kissed the cool metal. "I'll always love you. Forever, just like I promised."

Warmth and peace surrounded her—like a farewell hug—as Kate slid the wedding ring into place next to Mike's on the chain with the Saint Christopher medal.

———— ● ● ————

Later that evening, Simon heard a soft knock on the front door. He knew who it was. At least he hoped he did.

It was dark outside, and moths batted against the glass

sections of the lanterns lighting his porch. All Simon saw was the woman smiling up at him and stepping into his arms for a kiss. As he hugged her, he felt a cold chill in the vicinity of his heart. Literally. She was holding a quart of vanilla ice cream and a bag of sundae toppings.

"Come on in," he said with a smile. As though he hadn't worried over her and watched the clock.

"Thanks."

Kate followed Simon into the kitchen and took off her coat. They ate the ice cream and talked about Hood River, the Columbia River Gorge, and the pictures she had taken of both. In the middle of a sentence, he looked down at Kate's left hand and noticed the pale white line on her finger.

No wedding band.

A profound feeling entered his heart and mind. The sudden realization that this was a moment he would look back on when he was old. A milestone.

Simon lifted her hand and kissed it. Neither of them spoke. Her eyes looked a little puffy, like maybe she'd cried earlier that evening, but they were bright and steady now. Trusting.

He didn't choose that moment to ask if Kate knew how grateful he was to have her in his life. He didn't plead his devotion or pledge to make her happy. Instead, Simon winked.

She didn't pour out her heart. Or explain why she had taken the ring off that particular day. Kate winked too.

And then they just smiled at one another.

Simon ran his thumb under the chain at her wrist. The gold heart swung back and forth.

"You had the clasp fixed."

"Yeah, I used your mom's jeweler." She touched the charm and brought the swinging to a stop. "This was my father's first anniversary gift to my mother."

"Nice."

Kate snapped the charm open. "See? He had a message inscribed on one side and put a little picture of them on the other."

Simon squinted down at the inscription. "What does it say?"

"Love is the only gold. It's a quote by Tennyson." Kate looked at the small photo inside the heart. "I like picturing my parents loving each other that way. Even if it was for a short time."

"How did the bracelet come to you?"

"Tess gave it to me when I turned eight." She clicked the charm shut and touched one of the scratches on top. "I think of these marks as a metaphor."

"Metaphor?" he asked, smiling. "You're such a reader."

Simon knew he would never tire of this woman. Never tire of those mermaid eyes, the wild curling hair, or the way her mind worked.

"Me, my parents, everyone," Kate explained. "We're all like this heart."

He thought for a second. "We're . . . dented?"

"Or damaged by something. But that isn't who we really are. Not on the inside."

"It isn't?" Simon was doubtful. He knew quite a few people who were bad to the core.

"Of course not." Her eyes darkened with emotion as she slipped the bracelet under the sleeve of her shirt. "There's twenty-four karat gold beneath those scars. Rare. Valuable. I try to see my parents that way. And not to sound preachy, but I think that's how God sees each of us."

A little choked up, Simon pulled her into his arms. "That's one hell of a metaphor, Kate."

She looked at him, joy in her eyes, and Simon knew that if he hadn't already fallen for her, he would have done so in that moment.

———— • ————

Jack pushed the dish of fruit away. "It's not that I have anything against strawberries, my dear. I just prefer them dipped in chocolate."

Cecily nudged the dish back toward her husband. "I know. Just like you have nothing against broccoli when it's covered in melted cheddar."

He looked toward the refrigerator, longingly. "It doesn't have to be cheddar. It could be any kind of cheese. Brie, Jarlsberg, Stilton. Damn those doctors for restricting dairy."

Cecily added some whipped cream to Simon's strawberries. "Your father's personality has returned."

"I feel for you, Mom."

Kate did, too. Even when Jack was in a good mood, he was a lot of work.

"Don't pity your mother, son. She can have all the cheese and chocolate she wants." Jack pointed at Simon and Kate. "Why do they get cream and sugar?"

"Because we didn't just have a heart attack, that's why." Simon held out the bowl of whipped cream. "Have some if you want. Kate, you can resuscitate him, right?"

She nodded. "My paddles are all charged up."

Jack shot her a mutinous look. "They've turned you against me already."

Kate felt a little guilty for teasing him. "No, they haven't. I feel your pain. I love dairy, too."

"An ally at last."

Smiling at Jack, she praised the progress he'd made so far with his diet. "You can still reward yourself with chocolate-covered strawberries on special occasions. When's your birthday?"

"Six months from now," he groaned. "*Six months.*"

Looking away from Simon's father, Kate saw Cecily watching her with moist eyes and a trembling smile. She'd caught her doing this throughout the meal. "Cecily, thank you for a wonderful dinner."

"Oh, it was my pleasure."

"May I clean up?"

"No," Cecily said, beaming. "No, I want you and Simon to go outside and look at the leaves. Autumn is my favorite season."

Kate checked the time. "It must be dark outside."

Simon picked up his water glass and drank the entire thing, rattling the table as he set it down. "Is it *hot* in here? I feel hot." He pulled the collar of his T-shirt away from his neck.

Kate turned toward Jack to see if he noticed his family's strange behavior, but he was muttering to himself as he took a pill out of his daily medication container.

This was the first Sunday dinner at Jack and Cecily's home since their return from England two weeks earlier, and it felt off somehow.

"Outside," Simon murmured, tugging Kate by the hand. "The leaves . . ."

In the mudroom, he swung a heavy wool coat over her shoulders. When she slipped it on, Kate knew the coat belonged to Jack. It smelled like the cigars he used to smoke. The hem hung to her ankles and the sleeves went at least two inches past her fingertips. As they stepped outside, Kate gasped softly. The back garden shimmered with clear miniature lights. They hung high in the treetops, twinkling. The entire world seemed to glow.

She turned to Simon. "It must have taken hours to do all this. Are your parents having a party?"

Without a word, he led her toward the yew tree. They sat down on the stone bench where his mother had read to him. The place with the happiest memories he had known as a child.

Cecily and Jack were watching from the kitchen window, and when Kate waved at them, they immediately went to work. Jack wiped the windowpane, and Cecily began to read an upside-down cookbook.

Simon took her hand. "I saw your father yesterday, Kate. He sends his love."

"Oh, did you run into him at the store?"

"No. I had to ask him a question."

Simon took a quick breath, like a diver just before the jump. His voice shook when he said:

> "'Had I the heavens' embroidered cloths,
>
> Enwrought with golden and silver light,
>
> The blue and the dim and the dark cloths
>
> Of night and light and the half light,
>
> I would spread the cloths under your

feet . . .'"

He stopped, wiping his eyes, and Kate could hardly breathe. Yeats? Simon didn't even like poetry. She wrapped her arms around him and whispered the next lines.

"'But I, being poor, have only my
dreams;
I have spread my dreams under your
feet—'"

Kate hadn't imagined that love could look tender and fierce at the same time, but it was there in his face. He leaned his forehead against hers.

"'Tread softly because you tread on
my dreams.'"

A moment passed between them, silent except for the gentle sound of the wind. "Thank you," Kate finally said. "And I thought you didn't like poetry."

"I don't," Simon murmured, and they laughed.

As the heavens glowed above, and the trees shone below, he knelt, taking her hand. "You're my starlight in the darkness, Kate. Past, present, and future. They all lead me to you. Will you marry me?"

His words struck her right in the heart. Simon quoting Yeats. Starlight everywhere. Was this a dream? Excitement made her dizzy. Could people get drunk on love?

"Uh . . . Kate?"

"Yes?" It was like falling into blue when she met his solemn gaze.

"Is that your answer or . . ."

Laughing and crying simultaneously, Kate grabbed Simon around the neck and kissed him hard, completely forgetting about his parents.

He drew away, a little breathless. "Just to be clear. You agreed to marry me?"

"Nothing would make me happier than being your wife." Kate memorized the details of Simon's face, the way the cool air felt against her warm skin, the joy bouncing around inside her chest.

He reached into the side pocket of the coat Kate was wearing and pulled out a distinctive robins-egg-blue box with a white ribbon tied around it.

Tiffany's?

Simon pulled the ribbon off, dropping it to the ground. The box opened with a click, and he held it up for her to see. Kate swallowed and her throat felt tight. What had he done? Was the man mad?

Under the twinkling lights, the brilliant-cut solitaire blazed against a velvet backdrop. Channel-set diamond eternity bands were stacked on each side. Kate inhaled sharply, transfixed by the fire of the stones.

Simon slid an eternity band onto her finger. "You'll probably only want to wear one, but I figure this way we can have three daughters and each of them can inherit a ring."

Overcoming the diamonds' spell, Kate lifted an eyebrow. "And what if we have *four* daughters?"

"Then I make another trip to Tiffany's." He pulled her up from the bench and into his arms.

Chapter 35

The official date on the wedding invitations was December 4.

The ceremony was being held in a chapel with large stained-glass windows and dark wooden benches. The historic building could accommodate two hundred, and that was a good thing since guest response indicated it would be filled to capacity.

The personal stylist from Nordstrom found the Dress on a trip to New York in late October. The lace bodice and silk taffeta skirt reminded Kate a little of the gown Grace Kelly wore when she married the prince of Monaco.

Cecily went wild choosing the bouquet. Since the wedding was in December, it was a mixture of deep scarlet, frosty white, and dark green. Kate didn't know the names of all the flowers but they were beautiful.

The week before Thanksgiving, Matthew came to her apartment unexpectedly one night. He stood at the door, wearing an old fedora, a scarf, and a tweed overcoat.

"May I give you away?" Mathew asked, as if the matter were in question.

It made her sad that he looked worried she might say no. Kate hugged him. His cheek felt frozen against hers. "Of course. I need you there with me."

She brought Matthew inside and put him in the chair by the fireplace. They drank hot chocolate as wind buffeted the trees outside, and it felt like a real family moment, where people understood and loved each other. Just what Kate had longed for her whole life. The only thing missing was Tess.

Kate refilled his mug. "I haven't made a decision yet on the aisle-walking music. Do you have any suggestions?"

His head lifted as he considered her request, thought for a time. The corner of his mouth quirked up. "I've always favored Beethoven's 'Ode to Joy.'"

"Perfect! Why didn't I think of that?"

Matthew smiled at her, as hopeful and engaged as she had ever seen him. Would he retreat into his shell again? Or could this be the start of a new level of closeness between them? It startled her, how deeply she wanted this Matthew to stay.

———————— • ————————

Thanksgiving arrived, cold and frosty. Cecily's kitchen smelled of roasting turkey, fresh cranberry sauce, and rolls rising on the countertop.

"Put me to work," Kate said, pushing up the sleeves of her sweater. "What can I do?"

Cecily helped tie her apron strings. "How do you feel about making pies?"

"Total novice, I'm afraid, but I'm sure I'll love it."

They stayed in the warm, steamy kitchen for hours, and by early afternoon Kate knew the best way to make pate brisee, chestnut stuffing, and fluffy, buttery mashed potatoes. Matthew joined them for dinner, meeting Jack and Cecily for the first time. He was more awkward than usual and his cheeks turned pink whenever Cecily spoke to him. The meal went off without a hitch, and Jack, finally allowed to have what he wanted for one meal, was in heaven.

"Thank you for having me," Matthew said. "It was very kind of you."

"Not at all," Cecily replied. "We're family now."

Too full for dessert, Matthew didn't linger to socialize but she insisted that he take a pumpkin pie for later. Jack, Kate, and Simon fell asleep on the enormous sectional in the theater room while watching the movie *Spartacus*.

Near dusk, Kate kissed Cecily and Jack goodbye and Simon drove her home. They sat side by side on her living room floor, packing books into cardboard moving boxes.

Simon whistled a bouncy tune. "Doing stuff like this with you makes me happy."

She paused and looked at him. "Packing books?"

"Yep. In one week, these books and I will be sharing the same address."

Kate smiled, feeling warm and tingly, and handed him a trio of antique encyclopedias. "There's a wedding advent calendar at the clinic."

"No, really?"

She turned on her cell and scrolled through the messages. "Tanya and Beth put it up in the waiting area, and every day I check off another number to the sound of applause from a roomful of children."

"One down," Simon announced, taping his box shut. "Seventy-five more to go."

He used a Sharpie to write on the cardboard. "This pen's almost out of ink. Where can I find another one?"

Kate worried that she had packed them with her office

supplies. "Try the desk in my bedroom."

She scrolled some more. Stopped. The smile on her face disappeared.

Simon came back with a handful of pens and a crumpled piece of paper. The Pros and Cons list Kate had written about him months ago. He read it aloud. "Pros: smart, funny, looks good in a suit. Cons: better hair than me, does hard-level Sudoku in pen, bad breath after eating a hoagie . . ." Simon refolded the paper and slid it into his back pocket. "I am so keeping this list."

He looked happy, and Kate wanted to laugh with him, but she couldn't. She smiled but Simon seemed to sense that her mind was somewhere else. "Something wrong?"

Feeling sick, she held up her cell phone. "I've had it off all day and just checked my calls. There were three from London this afternoon. No messages. The name says Quinton, but I'm not sure if it's him. It could be his stepmother. She's contacted me before. This has been such a wonderful day. I'm sorry to mess it up."

Simon put the pens down on the nearest box. "You didn't mess up a damn thing. It's not your fault. It's his."

When Kate remained silent, he knelt by her and said, "Baby, as good as today has been, it's just the beginning. You're not alone anymore. You have a big group of people who love you." He tapped her phone. "I say notify the police that he's trying to contact you, change your number, and tell the bastard to go to hell in court. But it's not my decision, it's yours."

Simon returned to the pile of books and began filling a new box. Kate put the phone aside and went back to wiping off vinyl record covers. Her cell rang, the sound chiming across the room. Kate dropped her cloth and the old, stupid fear returned.

Would she ever not react that way? Simon got up and checked the number before Kate could reach the phone.

He nodded. "Quinton. You want me to talk to him? I'd love to, believe me."

Kate pushed the answer button and hit speaker, her eyes never leaving Simon's. Their connection felt like a lifeline.

"You have ten seconds," she said to the caller. "What do you want?"

"Hello? Am I speaking with Kate Spencer?" The male voice sounded very *Downton Abbey*. So proper and upper-crust. And also surprised, as if he didn't really expect Kate to answer. She recognized the voice immediately.

"This is Dr. Spencer. You have seven seconds now."

The man cleared his throat. "Yes. Of course. I'm sorry, but I feel rather nervous. Please don't hang up."

Simon mouthed the words, Is it him? Kate shook her head.

It was Sir Alan, the British industrialist, and Julian's father. Kate could picture his patrician profile, white hair, and blue eyes. Even if he wasn't in magazines or on television, his likeness was branded in her memories.

"Did your wife ask you to call? She sent a letter requesting that I speak with your son. The answer is still no."

The dignified voice grew soft. Sad. "There's no chance of that, I assure you. Julian died last night."

The room spun and Kate saw black at the corners of her vision. *The monster? He's dead?*

She couldn't breathe. Her body shook. It didn't seem real. Was it a joke? A lie to put her off her guard? Simon knelt down beside Kate and almost spoke aloud, but she shook her head. He rubbed her back, encouragingly, and a rush of air entered her lungs.

Taking the phone off speaker, Kate put it to her ear. "You're a hard man to reach, Sir Alan." Her voice sounded cold and hard. "I know because I tried for years to get in touch with you, to get help, but I was always put off."

"Yes," the clipped voice replied. Guilt was as much a part of his accent right then as his Eton education. "I am sorry. More than I can say. Julian really is dead. You don't have to worry about him anymore."

Kate clutched the phone until her fingers hurt. "I'm not sure that I can accept your word on that. I've *worried* about your son since I was twelve. What proof can you give?"

Sir Alan sighed raggedly. "You have every right to be skeptical. It's been many years since I last saw you, but you've never been far from my thoughts."

"My, my," Kate murmured. "Like father, like son."

"We were never alike, Dr. Spencer. Not even remotely. But I remember the girl you were when you and your mother lived with my son in London. I was always impressed by your good manners and the way you spoke and presented yourself, though I didn't acknowledge it back then."

Furious, Kate made a fist and punched the floor. She didn't know what to do with the anger inside her. "You didn't acknowledge anything. Not his behavior, or the drinking, or the abuse. You enabled him to continue doing it."

"Yes . . . yes, that's true. If I could go back, I assure you I would do many things differently."

These words wounded. Kate had wished a million times to change the past. "Take it from me. You can't go back."

"No, you're right. I can't." Sir Alan coughed for a long time. When he finally stopped, his breath rattled in his throat. How old was he? Early seventies, perhaps?

"Pardon," Sir Alan said at last. "The years have not been kind, and my doctors say the time left to me is short. That's why I'm contacting you. As I've said, you've been on my mind. Or perhaps, more accurately, my conscience."

Kate didn't allow herself to soften. "You have one of those?"

"Please let me explain, Dr. Spencer. I want you to understand about me and Julian."

"I'll give you five minutes," Kate said, looking at the clock. "And then this is over. Finished. Don't call again."

"Yes. All right." Sir Alan took a shallow breath. "Let me begin by saying that I loved him. He was a sweet little boy. My first wife fought cancer for several years and died when Julian was six. He was inconsolable. His stepmother and I tried to raise him well, to see to his education, and offer whatever help he needed. My daughters have productive, happy lives, and I cannot say what made the difference there or why he turned out as he did."

Kate flinched. She didn't want to think of Julian as a child. One who had, like her, felt the pain of losing a well-loved mother. Her whole purpose in life was protecting children from monsters like him. "Get to the point."

The old man coughed. "The point is that I was blind where Julian was concerned. I always saw that sweet little boy instead of the man he became. I sent him to the finest clinics, to mental health specialists, rehabilitation centers. But I couldn't abandon him. Can you understand that at all?"

Even as she fought to stay angry, the hardness inside Kate began to yield. She knew what it was like to try to help a doomed soul. Her mother. Axel. A tear ran down her cheek. "Yes, but you didn't stop him."

Sir Alan was silent and Kate wondered if he was going to hang up. But he didn't, though his voice sounded faint. "That will always haunt me. I can't change the past or make up for what Julian did. I can, however, express my deepest sympathies over the passing of your mother. I know how much you loved her, and I did not properly share my condolences with you at the time. I am very sorry, for it was a great loss, to be sure." Sir Alan began to weep. "I'm feeling rather heartsick myself at the moment. My boy died alone on a filthy floor, in prison. Knifed in the back by another inmate."

Over the years, Kate had imagined killing Julian. Shooting him with her Walther and watching his bright blood spill. She found no peace now, no resolution in hearing of his brutal death.

Sir Alan got himself under control. "I thought you should know what happened. When I learned that Julian had attended your husband's funeral, I was appalled." He paused and struggled to breathe.

The five minutes had passed, but Kate didn't interrupt the old man when he began to speak again. "I failed to protect you when you were young but I tried to these last few years. I had Julian followed. He flew to Oregon on several occasions with the intention of harassing you, but my employees forced him to return home. My wife was not objective where he was concerned. She wanted the two of you to work things out together, but I knew that was impossible."

Sir Alan seemed to fade quickly after making his confession. "Goodbye, Dr. Spencer. Please accept the apology of a dying man. Don't let the past ruin the life you've built for yourself."

The line went dead. Kate sat quietly, cradling the phone in her hand. Her mind seemed numb, like it couldn't really comprehend a world without monsters or fear. Simon had scooted closer, until they were hip to hip, sitting alongside each other amid the boxes. He watched her, concern in every line of his body, sensing somehow that Kate didn't want to be touched or coddled.

The dark place inside became a crushing weight. She wanted to shut herself away from everyone and everything until her heart didn't hurt anymore. How could she move forward? Kate felt stuck, hiding in that bedroom in Julian's house, hoping the lock on the door would hold. It didn't matter if he was dead, a part of her was still there.

No one could open that door but Kate herself.

Simon had said that she wasn't alone. He said a big group of people loved her. As she thought this, the darkness grew less oppressive. It was like rising from the bottom of a fathomless black pool toward air and light.

While Kate might have to open the door to that room herself, she had help this time. Robert, Beth, Simon . . .

A dry sob escaped Kate's throat and her body sagged with relief. She felt free. From guilt, violence, and survivor's remorse. As though the door had blown off its hinges. Her body could have floated off the floor.

Kate smiled up at Simon and wiped her face. How had they been lucky enough to find each other in a world where billions of people lived? He smiled back.

Maybe luck had nothing to do with it.

After a few seconds, Simon touched the side of her face. "Are you okay?"

Kate nodded, still stunned by the burden that had been lifted from her soul. She might have flashbacks or bad days in the future, when she would have to remind herself of this breakthrough, but it would never be so hard again. Warmth spread through her muscles and bones. Healing was a tangible thing.

Kate leaned into his touch. "I'm okay. I'm going to be okay." She made an odd sound. Not quite a laugh, but more than a sigh. "I don't have to carry the Walther anymore."

Simon hugged her. "No, baby. Not unless you want to."

She got up from the floor and went straight to her purse. The lines of the gun were as sleek and deadly as before. It didn't seem imperative to her very survival now. Or a weapon of vengeance to shed a sick man's blood. Kate's legs threatened to give out and she braced herself against the table, marveling. What would it be like to go a day without wearing the uncomfortable holster and carrying the gun? To just practice with it at the range now and then, rather than feel its weight on her life . . .

Kate pushed away from the table and padded to her room. She locked the Walther in the safe with the other firearms. *See you when I see you.*

When Kate returned to the living room, Simon was sitting on the floor writing on another box. Her heart felt so full. Humble and blessed. "Hey you," she said softly. "Guy with the ink stains on his fingers. You're going to make some girl an amazing husband."

He stopped writing and looked up. "Thanks. I'll be sure to tell my fiancée."

"Well, if she backs out, let me know." Kate nodded toward the boxes. "Toss me one of those cardboard things. I've got books to pack."

The night before the wedding, Simon and Kate carried her paintings out to the car, stowing them carefully in the trunk. Then she went back to lock up her empty apartment. It seemed so remote, as if it already belonged to the future tenant. Had her life really changed so much in just a few months? Walking into the living room, Kate remembered Tanya's birthday party. That was the real start of their relationship, when she had put aside some of her prejudices against Simon. How they had talked over a plate of Pete's brownies and he'd asked about her charm bracelet.

He entered the apartment, whistling. "Did we forget anything?"

She took one last look around. "No. Let's go home."

Simon grinned. "I like the sound of that."

They drove to his house and hung the artwork in the study. "Big improvement," he said, taking Kate's arm.

With all her furniture relocated to Simon's basement, she had stayed with Cecily and Jack the last few nights. All that remained to be brought in from the car was one box of cleaning supplies and a mop and broom. The trip out to the Mercedes took less than a minute. She walked back into his garage, dreamy-eyed. Tomorrow they'd be man and wife, living in this house together.

Simon looked sideways at her. "I think we should practice carrying you over the threshold."

Before she could protest, he dropped the box and swooped her up like a sack of potatoes. The mop and broom fell to the floor. Scrubbing powder flew everywhere, a white cloud that smelled of bleach. Kate coughed and waved her hand in the air.

"Sorry," Simon said, laughing. "That wasn't part of the plan."

After he deposited Kate in the kitchen, she clocked him on the shoulder. "Maybe you should think ahead."

"Noted." Simon ducked out of the way of another playful punch. He feinted left and trapped her against the wall. "I have a special gift for you."

"Your *gift* can wait, mister."

He rolled his eyes. "Get your mind out of the gutter. Come on, I want to show you something."

"What?"

Simon took Kate's hand and led her from the kitchen to the study. He picked up a roll of papers that looked like an architectural blueprint. "Unroll it. I've been waiting a month for this."

Frowning, Kate didn't move. How could she have forgotten to get him a wedding gift? "But I don't have anything for you."

"Believe me, you do. Open it."

She slid the rubber band off and spread the papers out. It was a room, with tall windows and a fireplace, built-in bookcases and wood floors. A library.

What had he done? It was beyond anything she'd dreamed of. "Oh, Simon." Kate shook her head, lips trembling. "It's too much."

"No, baby, it isn't. All those books gotta go somewhere. Look at it." Simon ran his finger along the blueprints. "We'll build on the back of the house across from the trees. That way you'll always have something pretty to look at."

"It's beautiful."

He reached into a plastic bag and brought out a small package. "This needs to be first on the shelf."

Kate ripped the wrapping paper. "I bet I know what this is

. . ."

"Oh, I think it'll be a surprise."

As she turned the volume right side up, she saw the missing letters. The tattered grayish-blue book felt lighter in her hand than she remembered, as if it had somehow contracted over the years. Kate read the cover page.

Jane Eyre
by Charlotte Bronte

She took a deep breath and turned to the back. There it was, in loopy cursive.

Dear Reader,
If you love books as I do,
we shall be great friends.
Daisy XOXO

Kate went directly into Simon's arms and he held her tight. Eyes closed, she listened to the sound of his heart. A perfect match for her own.

Chapter 36

December 4

A stylist attached the veil of delicate English net to Kate's hair, fixing it in place with Cecily's combs. His name was Timothy, and within ten minutes of their meeting she thought of him as a best friend. Perhaps it was the excitement of the day, but she seemed to love everyone in the world. He pinned the tiny white rosebuds and ivy leaves in place and stepped back to survey Kate's hair.

"Just right," Timothy whispered. Cecily and Simon's sisters, Annie and Liza, stood next to him.

"I hope our little brother doesn't go into cardiac arrest," Annie commented to the room at large.

Liza grinned. "I wouldn't blame him if he did."

Jack waited at the bottom of the formal staircase as Kate descended. Offering his arm, he gave her the first real smile she had ever received from him. "We need to hurry to the church, Cecily, before this girl changes her mind."

Jack led the bride and his wife to the white 1956 Bentley limousine he had rented. The conversation on the way to the church was engineered to give Kate something to think about other than her wedding. She didn't want to spoil her eye makeup before the vows were even said. When they arrived at the little church, Kate was amazed that the parking lot was already filled to capacity, with overflow parking extending down the street.

Minister Witherspoon met them in the chapel foyer. "Simon is waiting in one of the classrooms. He keeps asking everyone that goes by if you've arrived yet." Witherspoon motioned toward Jack. "Please tell your son his bride is here, and that he needs to take his place for the ceremony."

Matthew gave Kate a kiss on the cheek and tucked her hand into the crook of his arm. "Let's not make your young man suffer any longer, shall we?"

She looked in through the chapel doors. Many of the people she loved were there—Robert, Beth, Tanya and Charlene, patients and their families, even Larry and Earl, dressed in clothes Robert had loaned them.

People who had given her a place in their lives.

Garlands of fresh flowers hung on each side of the aisle, and up ahead Simon stood waiting. Kate smiled at her dad. "You're right. Let's not wait."

───── • ─────

Roses and pine boughs perfumed the chapel as row after row of smiling faces watched Simon. His family took their seats and waved, but he was focused on the back of the room.

As the string quartet began the intricate, glorious strains of Beethoven's "Ode to Joy," the congregation rose, and there she was, his heart, stepping into the church and moving toward him. Sunlight filtered through the stained-glass windows, casting its colors over the floor.

Simon knew he would forever remember this image of Kate looking so young and happy, her dress sparkling with vivid splashes of gold, blue, and red refracted light. He nodded to

Matthew when they met him at the front of the chapel and lifted the veil from Kate's face.

"Dearly beloved, we are gathered here today to join this man and this woman in holy matrimony . . ." While the traditional vows carried across the church, the world became very small to Simon. It consisted of Kate and him and the words that would unite them for life. He knew her every expression and mannerism by now. How would they change in the years to come?

Watching Kate as the minister spoke of commitment through sickness and health, Simon had never considered that enduring hardship or growing old with another person could be something desirable. But he wanted every year ahead of them, easy or not. To love and to cherish.

Caught up as he was, Simon almost missed his cue. The silence as Minister Witherspoon waited for his answer jolted Simon back to reality. "I do," he said. "I really, really do."

From his seat, Jack called, "That's my boy," and the listening crowd burst into laughter.

Then it was Kate's turn. She gazed at Simon, radiant and calm as the vows were repeated. When the minister said 'til death do you part,' he gave Kate an expectant look, checking to see if she was paying attention. She nodded that she was, and then said, "I do. A lot."

The congregation laughed again. But the best moment came when Minister Witherspoon concluded with, "I now pronounce you man and wife."

The kiss that followed was pretty spectacular too.

◆ ●

Holding Kate's hand in his, Simon moved her wedding ring

with his thumb, just to assure himself they were really, finally married. The Bentley carried the bride and groom, and his parents, to the country club in style. Cecily and Jack talked about the friends they saw at the church, Kate's stunning bridal photographs, and the entertainment planned for the upcoming reception. Simon lifted Kate's hand as his parents chatted and kissed it softly, looking at her as though they were the only people in the car.

Liza, Annie, and Matthew arrived at the club minutes behind them in a limo of their own. The reception center looked like an enchanted forest filled with twinkling lights and glowing Christmas trees. Tables were placed here and there throughout the wonderland, and waiters wearing white tuxedos served the guests dinner. Matthew and Jack gave very different, but equally lovely, toasts and eventually it was time for the couple to share their first dance as husband and wife.

Simon held Kate in his arms as their favorite Norah Jones song played. He swayed with her, thinking that nothing could be better. Nothing but more dances, more time. Years of sleeping together and waking up side by side. Hearing her laugh. Having kids that were part Kate. Birthdays. Holidays. A life they would make together.

There was a commotion by the doors, and Simon turned his head to see his brother Weston entering the ballroom. *Well, would you look at that? Big brother made it.*

Cecily grabbed West in a hug. Jack was obviously choked up and just stood there shaking his head. Disbelief that his son had finally come home after years away? Gratitude? Simon thought it was a combination of both.

"Who's that?" Kate asked.

"That's your brother-in-law, West."

She gasped softly. "Really? I didn't think anyone could get in contact with him."

Simon had sent an invitation and left several messages on West's phone. He may have implied that he wouldn't take no for an answer. Not unless West wanted visitors in Dubai . . .

When the dance ended, Simon led Kate off the dance floor. He studied his brother as they walked toward him. Bespoke suit, perfectly styled gold hair, Patek Philippe watch on his wrist. Hard, hungry eyes and a body restless and unable to slow down. West was a lot like Simon had been, but with an even higher level of money and pressure involved. It made him sad. His brother would be paying the price for the rest of his days.

West sent Simon a measuring look. "You'd really have come to Dubai if I hadn't shown up?" His expression said that he'd talk with him later about being coerced.

Simon stepped forward and hugged West. "Damn straight. I've got frequent flyer miles and I'm not afraid to use them."

"You would, too. That's the scary part." They slapped each other's backs in manly fashion. "Congratulations, brother. A married man, huh? Never thought I'd see the day." And then he looked at Kate.

"Welcome to the clan. I hear you're a doctor? Nonprofit?"

"That's me," she replied, giving him a quick peck on the cheek. "I can't believe it. Until this moment I thought you were a family myth. But you're real. Thanks for coming all this way."

West nodded at Simon. "Had to."

They talked for a while, catching up on their lives, and then Robert tapped Kate on the shoulder. "Hey, babe. Is this our dance?"

She smiled at Simon and West. "Excuse me, gentlemen. The Electric Slide is calling."

Simon whistled encouragement as she and Robert walked onto the floor. West leaned toward him. "She's great. Not what I expected for you, though."

"I married above myself."

"You did," West agreed. "Any way I could talk her into flying back with me to Dubai and leaving you behind?"

"Not a chance."

Simon put his hand on his brother's shoulder. He had missed West. Memories filled his mind, clear and vivid. All the good times when they were kids, how they defended each other, stayed up late talking, plotted against their sisters. Wouldn't it be something if they got in touch more often? Sent photos. Had a real relationship . . . Simon decided he'd have to make that happen, even if West did resist a little at first.

He smiled at his brother. "Thank you. For being here today, even if you did miss the ceremony—"

West had his phone in hand and was checking his messages. "I was on a conference call in the parking lot."

"I know," Simon replied. "It means a lot to Mom and Dad to have you home."

West smirked. "What's a little extortion between brothers? Besides, it's good to see the folks. Still winning my old trophy? The *Annus Mirabilis*?"

"Sorry. Carter Wright has it."

Eyes wide, West stepped back. Like Jack and Cecily, he had his own Look but with a skeptical, older brother spin. "I forgot that you moved firms. I need a drink."

Simon gestured toward the open bar. "Help yourself. There's lemonade, sparkling water. A bunch of virgin concoctions."

West did a double take. "Virgin what?"

"No alcohol," Simon said, laughing. "I don't drink anymore."

An expletive left West's mouth before he could shut it. "You're an alien imposter. Where's my real brother?" He spotted Cecily waving him over to the table she shared with Jack. "I better go talk to them."

He left Simon and sat down with their parents. Leonard Cronin strolled over, extending his hand. They shook. "Carter Wright sends his best."

Surprised, Simon asked, "Does he? That's nice to hear."

"Yes. I just spoke to him on the way to the party." Leonard's eyes twinkled. "He's still at the office."

"Give Carter my regards."

"And your sympathies?"

Simon nodded. "Those, too."

By eight thirty that evening, he and Kate had finished their final dance at the reception. Rose petals and bubbles stuck to their clothes and hair as they ran the gauntlet and jumped into the Bentley.

The official honeymoon started tomorrow morning with a flight to Kauai and a condo on the beach, but they were spending their wedding night at home. Anticipating this, he loosened his tie and undid the top two buttons of his shirt.

His facial expression must have made Kate curious, because she asked, "What are you thinking?"

He told her precisely what was on his mind and laughed at the look on her face. "I gave you an honest answer . . ."

As Kate blushed, they turned onto Simon's street, drove a few blocks, and pulled into the driveway. He held her veil and helped with the yards of silk taffeta as she climbed out of the limo. The driver congratulated them before leaving.

Kate took Simon's arm and they stood for a moment, gazing up at the stars. One seemed brighter than the rest. "I had a dream about my mother just after I met you. She said it was time for me to be happy."

"Did she?" Looking down at his wife, Simon felt like Tess had somehow played a part in bringing them together. "Well, you don't argue with an Irish angel."

Kate's mermaid eyes smiled up at him. "No, you don't."

Epilogue

Eighteen months later
Northwest Portland

L ife was good for Simon Phillips. Present tense.

Eyes closed, he leaned against the hood of his car, enjoying the afternoon sun on his face. For some reason he couldn't immediately identify, Simon knew something important was about to happen. He opened his eyes to see a woman leaving the community center. There she was . . . everything he worked for and dreamed of, walking right toward him.

Kate Spencer was now Kate Phillips and had been for a year and a half. They had traveled to the Seychelles on their first anniversary, bringing back more than the palm tree charm he had bought her as a souvenir. As was evident by her rounded belly. Six months and counting.

The Phillips family would increase by two in a few more months. Joseph Matthew Jackson and Jane Cecily Tess were expected at the end of August. They were already showing an excess of personality. The near-constant fatigue and nausea of the first sixteen weeks of Kate's pregnancy had been hard on her, but now, at the end of the second trimester, she felt great.

Tilting down his sunglasses, Simon watched Kate stride

toward him, tall and energetic. He had heard that pregnant women were beautiful but never realized how true it was. Simon didn't know how or why, but Kate tempted him like some lush fruit ripe on the vine. He couldn't look at or touch her enough.

She no longer worked at the hospital and spent her days here at the community center. His employer, Greg Jacobsen, had donated enough to Robert's nonprofit to cover a complete restoration of the entire building and maintenance for years to come.

When the babies were born, Kate was taking some time off, but she wanted to work a few days a week at the clinic once the twins had adjusted to a routine. His mother was ecstatic at the thought of having little ones in her house again. Cecily was ready and waiting to babysit.

"You'll never guess what happened," Kate said when she joined Simon. "I was surprised, and I work with them every day."

"Robert and Beth are getting married?"

Her shoulders fell. "How did you know?"

"He asked me to be his best man." Simon placed his hand on her stomach. "Are they behaving themselves, or do I need to talk to them?"

"They got a little excited when I had an Oreo, but they're quiet now."

He kissed Kate, right there in front of the old community center. A warm breeze caught the branches of the trees, making them dance. Simon watched nature's show for a moment. The world was alive with fragrance, color, and growing things. Then he did something he found himself doing more and more often.

Simon counted his blessings: his wife's smile, healthy

babies, good friends, a sunny day. The kind of wealth that didn't cost a thing.

Acknowledgements

I worked on this book for many years and appreciate everyone who helped and supported me along the way. Especially my critique group: Ruth Craddock, Adrienne Monson, Jennifer Greyson, Rebecca Rode, Angela Brimhall, Karen Pellett, and Karyn Holmgren. Thank you for your patience, encouragement, and wonderful advice. You're the best!

Kira Rubenthaler of Bookfly Design helped me fix this story. I am always floored by the mistakes she finds that I missed. No one can replace you in my editing process, Kira. Thank you so much.

And I'm grateful to James Egan of Bookfly Design for this beautiful cover. It begins telling the story without turning a page.

Thank you to Bob Houston of Bob Houston eBook Formatting. He always makes my books look great. He's also kind, patient, and helpful during the process. Thanks, Bob.

Above all, thank you to my family. I love you forever.

About the Author

Quinn Coleridge grew up in the Pacific Northwest, where she learned to love rain, green growing things, and reading books by a crackling fire. As a young adult, Quinn traveled to England, another green rainy place. While there, she met a man with the prettiest eyes, and they later got married and had a lot of kids. (She blames the eyes.)

Then their family moved to a place with little rain or greenery. They have a cat that the man with the pretty eyes never even remotely wanted, although he's a good sport about it. Crackling fires are a rarity at Quinn's house these days, but it's seldom boring. And she still loves books.

Reader Friends, if you are so inclined, please leave a review of Heart of Gold at Amazon or Goodreads.

Cheers!

Made in the USA
Middletown, DE
09 March 2022

62298561R10234